A charity-working, dust-ignoring bookworm the beautiful and histo husband, one daughter dog-loathing cats and a g dreaming is her very favourite hobby and she loves a good happy-ever-after Jessica can't believe she's lucky enough to write romance for a living. Say hi on Twitter at @yrosered or visit sprigmuslin.blogspot.com

Karin Baine lives in Northern Ireland with her husband, two sons, and her out-of-control notebook collection. Her Mother and Grandmother's vast collection of books inspired her love of reading and her dream of becoming a Mills & Boon author. Now she can tell people she has a proper job! You can follow Karin on Twitter, @karinbaine1 or visit her website for the latest news karinbaine.com

Annie O'Neil spent most of her childhood with a leg draped over the family rocking chair and a book in her hand. Novels, baking and writing too much teenage angst poetry ate up most of her youth. Now, Annie splits her time between corralling her husband into helping her with their cows, listening to audio books whilst weeding and spending some very happy hours at her computer writing.

About the Authors

... dog-walking, child-wrangling, ... Jessica Gilmore lives in ... northern British city of York with one patient husband, one very fluffy dog, two ... a goldfish called Bob. As day ...

Meet Me Under the Mistletoe

JESSICA GILMORE

KARIN BAINE

ANNIE O'NEIL

MILLS & BOON

First Published in Great Britain 2022
By Mills & Boon, an imprint of HarperCollins*Publishers*
1 London Bridge Street, London, SE1 9GF

www.harpercollins.co.uk

HarperCollins*Publishers*
1st Floor, Watermarque Building,
Ringsend Road, Dublin 4, Ireland

MEET ME UNDER THE MISTLETOE © 2022
Harlequin Enterprises ULC

Reawakened by His Christmas Kiss © 2019 Jessica Gilmore
Their One-Night Christmas Gift © 2019 Karin Baine
The Army Doc's Christmas Angel © 2018 Harlequin Enterprises ULC.

Special thanks and acknowledgement are given to Annie O'Neil for her contribution to the *Hope Children's Hospital* series.

ISBN: 978-0-263-31781-7

REAWAKENED BY
HIS CHRISTMAS KISS

JESSICA GILMORE

For Rose, Rich, Ol and Jake.
Thank you for everything.

PROLOGUE

FINN HAWKIN ACCEPTED a glass of champagne from a passing waiter and surveyed the scene before him, his lips curving into an appreciative smile. Fairy lights and gossamer white drapes, elaborate costumes and a vast ballroom might be wasted on him, but his small nieces would want to hear about every single detail of the night. The Armarian Midsummer Ball was like every one of their favourite fairy-tales brought to life.

A masked and cloaked figure paused beside him. 'Having fun?'

'Laurent!' Finn turned to greet his old friend with genuine delight. His presence here might be more business than personal, but it was good to see his host. 'Thanks for the invite.'

'You are more than welcome. I'm glad you could come.'

A hint of sympathy tinged the other man's voice; Finn didn't confide in many people, but Laurent knew how difficult the last year had been, the hard choices Finn had been faced with.

'How are your nieces?'

'Tired out after a week of enjoying your glorious beaches. Not that they'll admit it. Tonight they are most put out at not coming with me to a real-life royal ball. I've promised to smuggle cake back to the villa. Hopefully that will mollify them.'

'Bring them to the palace,' Laurent offered. 'It'll still be chaotic tomorrow, but maybe the day after? We have puppies in the stables they can meet, and I'll take them to the highest turret and tell them grisly stories about how my ancestors repelled would-be invaders.'

'They'll like that. Thanks, Laurent.'

'And we can catch up properly. It'll be easier when I'm not hosting several hundred people.'

'Perils of being a prince.'

But Finn couldn't help noticing that Laurent seemed more at ease than usual. He was usually so reserved, so rigid when in public, but this evening he was like a different man, his smile genuine and easy, his whole being infused with a lightness and joy that Finn couldn't imagine feeling.

'Who's the girl?'

'What girl?' Laurent's grin only widened, his eyes softening as they rested on a slim figure in yellow and silver, standing to the side of the ballroom, directing a group of waitresses.

'The girl you haven't been able to take your eyes off all night. When you haven't been disappearing outside with her, that is.'

It was unlike Laurent to be openly seen with a woman—and, although his costume gave him a degree of anonymity, it wasn't enough of a disguise to ensure complete privacy. No, if Laurent was dancing, flirting and holding intense, smouldering conversations so publicly, then his intentions must be pretty serious, and that was unexpected from a man who had seemed reconciled to a sensible marriage of convenience.

'That's Emilia. She's the party planner. She put this whole ball together in less than a month.' Laurent might have been aiming for offhand, but the pride in his voice was a dead giveaway; he was in deep.

'She's done a great job. The whole evening is magical.'

'Says the man standing on the side alone. I didn't expect you to use your plus one, Finn, but there are plenty of beautiful women here who I'm sure would love to dance with you. Would you like me to introduce you to anyone? How about the Contessa, over there?' Laurent indicated a haughty blonde waving a fan as she ignored an eager crowd of young men.

Finn laughed. 'She looks a little above my pay grade.'

'Modesty doesn't become you, Finn. You're young, active, and you still have all your own hair and teeth. That puts you above half the men in this room, and that's before we take into account your very successful company and the small fact that you've just bought your own castle. Even the Contessa would think that makes you very suitable for one dance at least.'

'Blakeley hardly compares with a royal palace,' Finn protested, but pride swelled through him at the thought of the ancient old building, currently being restored to make a home for his nieces and a base for his rapidly expanding business.

He hadn't inherited the castle, he'd bought it with money he'd earned the hard way. Although he'd grown up on the Blakeley estate, nothing had been handed to him. His success was down to pure hard work and some lucky—and canny—decisions.

'I'm happy for you,' Laurent said softly. 'You've achieved your goal. How many men can say that?'

Finn sipped his drink. Laurent was right. He was barely thirty and he'd hit every one of the goals he'd set when they were students in Paris: to found his own business, make a fortune, and live on an estate like the one he'd grown up on. Only this time he'd be the one in the big house, not the gardener's boy, doffing his cap to his so-called betters.

'We never stop setting goals, Laurent, we just change the goalposts. Now my nieces come first. Giving them the kind of happiness and security they need…that's my priority.'

'If anyone can, you can.'

They stood there in silence for a moment, watching the opulently adorned dancers waltz around the dance floor until Laurent's gaze strayed once again to the girl in the yellow dress. Finn followed his gaze. She had moved away from the waitresses and was talking animatedly to a tall, elegant woman dressed in a demure black dress, her light brown hair elegantly coiled into a chignon.

Recognition punched him. It couldn't be…

Or could it? Was this the girl he'd searched for in vain through the years, right here in a ballroom hundreds of miles away from the place where they'd grown up?

Last time he had seen her, her hair had been bleached platinum blonde and cut into a choppy bob which had instantly spawned a thousand imitations. She'd been a decade younger, coltish and angular, with cheekbones sharp enough to cut through butter and a knowing, slanting gaze that had pouted down from billboards and magazine covers across the globe—before she had disappeared from public view and from his life, as if she had never been.

'Lola?' he half whispered. And, as if she'd heard him, the woman looked up, alert, scenting danger.

He must be imagining things. Lola Beaumont was gone, disappeared into the ether. He knew that. He'd looked for her for long enough. He blinked and refocussed. He must be mistaken. The woman was clearly working at the event, and Lola was always the guest of honour, not the help. It was a passing resemblance, that was all.

He'd thought he'd cured himself of seeing Lola at every corner years ago. But Finn couldn't stop himself from turning to Laurent. 'Who is that? Talking to Emilia?'

'Who? Oh, that's Alex—Alexandra Davenport. She co-owns a party planning agency with Emilia and two other women. She arrived yesterday, I think, to oversee things tonight so Emilia could attend the ball. Why?' Laurent's smile turned sly. 'Would you like an introduction to her?'

'No, thanks. Just curious.'

But Finn's mind was working furiously. Alexandra was Lola's middle name, wasn't it? Surely it was a co-incidence—a similarity of features, a shared name, that was all. But as he gazed across at the woman he couldn't help feeling that there were no such things as coincidences and now, just as his life was exactly where he wanted it to be, Lola Beaumont had returned to disrupt it all over again.

The question was, what was he going to do about it?

CHAPTER ONE

WITH A HERCULEAN effort, Alexandra Davenport managed to wait until she had passed through Passport Control before she turned on her phone. Pulling her small case behind her, she headed towards Customs and the exit, impatient as her phone whirred through its settings and began to process all communications from the last eight hours.

All around her people staggered past, eyes red, clothes wrinkled from the overnight flight. Alex, on the other hand, felt surprisingly well-rested. Thank goodness she'd packed a washcloth and a clean top in her overnight bag, and had freshened up just before the fasten seat belts sign came on. She was refreshed, she had slept, and she was ready for anything.

She glanced at her phone, not surprised to see every notification symbol jostling for space at the top. There was always a crisis somewhere. Which for her was a good thing; promotional PR paid the bills, but it was managing the unexpected and spinning disaster into gold where she excelled.

She dialled up voicemail and waited for the first message to come through.

'Alex? It's me.'

Alex smiled as she heard the voice of Amber, her colleague and, more importantly, her friend. With just three words she was home. Home. A place she had stopped believing existed. After all, hadn't she trained herself not to rely on people or places?

'Hope you get this in time. What am I saying? Of course you will. There's no way you don't have a fully charged phone ready to switch on the second you land! So, we've had a last-minute booking. It's a residential stay and the client is very much demanding that you get there asap. So you need to head straight there. I've arranged for a car to pick you up and take you. Give me a call when you're on the way and I can go through everything with you. Don't worry, I packed up some clothes for you and they've been collected. Well done again on New York. You rocked it. Can't believe we're properly international! Talk soon!'

The voicemail ended and Alex frowned as she saved it. She hadn't been expecting to head straight out again—after a week away she was more than ready to return to the Chelsea townhouse she had inherited the year before and turned into both a home and the business premises for her three closest—and only—friends. Together they had set up the Happy Ever After Agency, offering regular, one-off and consultancy support in everything from admin to events, PR to bespoke jobs.

Only eight months after opening they already had a strong reputation, backed up by glowing testimonials from previous clients. Glowing testimonials thanks to their ability to react quickly. Exactly as she needed to do right now, she reminded herself. Her feelings didn't matter. The client always came first.

Of course it didn't hurt their reputation that one of

their previous clients, Prince Laurent, Archduke of Armaria, was currently courting Emilia, their events specialist, whilst tech billionaire Deangelo Santos was engaged to Harriet, his former PA and their head of admin.

Alex suppressed a sigh. They'd been open less than a year and already it was all change. Next year Harriet would marry Deangelo and officially move out of the townhouse, and they all knew Laurent would propose to Emilia any day now.

Harriet intended to carry on working once she was married but, although Emilia would remain a business partner, there was no way she would be able to take on any jobs once she became Archduchess. Alex was absolutely delighted for her friends, but she couldn't help wishing they'd had more time together first. Time to really build the agency.

She swallowed, not wanting to admit even to herself that the ache she felt deep inside wasn't just down to the changes in the business. She'd been so happy these last few months, living and working with her friends. She'd trained herself to enjoy her own company, but the house felt alive with the four of them in it. It was welcoming. Would it seem empty when there were just two?

Pushing the dark thoughts away, Alex walked swiftly through Customs, checking her emails as she did so and flicking through her clients' social media feeds to make sure there was nothing requiring immediate attention.

She was just aware enough of her surroundings to make sure she didn't crash into anyone, otherwise she zoned out the noise and hubbub as she exited into the Arrivals Hall. She stopped for a moment, scanning the waiting crowds for a sign with her name on it, but before she could spot it her attention was snagged by a teenage girl running past her to launch herself into the arms of a middle-aged couple, whose wide smiles and bright eyes showed how very glad they were to see her.

No one had ever waited for Alex unless they'd been paid to be there, like the driver today. She watched as the couple enfolded the girl in their arms, unable to help noticing other reunions, some loud, some tearful, and one so passionate she felt like a voyeur.

She straightened. Enough of this nonsense. She had just had a very successful few days, turning the agency into an international proposition, and she was heading straight into another job. Success, security, everything she was working towards was within reach. That was where she needed to focus.

With a jolt of relief, she spotted the sign with her name on it and headed towards it. The sooner she was out of the airport the better.

Ten minutes later Alex found herself ensconced in the back of a comfortable saloon car, her laptop purring to life beside her, a notebook on the folded-out tray table, a chilled bottle of water and a pot of fruit beside it. She read through her emails again quickly, but there was nothing from Amber to indicate where she was going and what she would be doing once she was there.

The driver had volunteered the information that the journey would take around an hour and a half, depending on traffic, but hadn't mentioned the destination. No matter. Amber would fill her in.

Despite the earliness of the hour the roads were busy and the car crawled along. Looking out of the darkened windows into the pre-dawn winter gloom, Alex noted how low and heavy the skies were. The temperature had dropped as well, now closer to the New York chill she'd just left than the autumnal mildness she'd flown away from just a week ago.

It was easy to believe that Christmas was less than three weeks away and winter was well and truly settling in.

A sign caught her eye and she winced at the realisation that they were heading out to the M40. Hopefully they'd turn off soon. She normally avoided the area around the Chilterns. It was far too full of memories.

She checked her phone and decided that it was late enough to call Amber. Barely had she pressed the call button when her friend answered, sounding, as always, far too chipper for first thing in the morning.

'Hi, Alex! You got my message?'

'I did. Which is why I am in the back of a car heading *out* of London and not into it. Who's the client and what's so urgent that I'm needed on site straight away? A threatened exposé? PR disaster?' Her mind whirled. The thornier the problem the more she loved it.

'Nothing so exciting. I'm sorry. But hopefully you'll still enjoy the brief. Have you heard of Hawk?'

Alex thought for a moment, the name niggling at her. 'It sounds familiar.'

'It's an outdoor lifestyle brand, all rugged clothing, popular with those people who like to leave their city pad in their four-by-four to go for a ten-minute walk on the beach, but the clothes are the real deal as well, you know? They're worn by loads of serious climbers and explorer types. They have that cute hawk symbol on all their clothes. Like my winter coat?'

'Yes. I know who you mean.' She didn't own any of their clothing personally, but she was aware of the company's stellar reputation. 'What's happened? Why do they need me?'

'A broken leg.'

Alex blinked. Maybe she wasn't as refreshed as she thought. 'A broken leg?'

'Their PR manager has managed to break her leg in several places. She's confined to bed with her leg in a cage.'

That made more sense. 'I see.'

'They've just moved their headquarters to some kind of stately home out towards Swindon, I think. That's where you're headed.'

Alex let out a breath she hadn't quite realised she was holding. Swindon was past the danger area. 'Okay…'

'The owner is opening up the whole estate as an outdoor activity and nature destination. You know the kind of thing: adventure playgrounds and forest trails, all in line with the whole Hawk brand. They're running the business out of converted barns, or stables, or something suitably rustic. They're officially opening at the end of the week, with a ton of Christmas-themed events. Apparently the house and grounds were all neglected and it's the kind of area where jobs are sparse, house prices sky-high and lots of incomers are buying second homes, so there's a whole rejuvenating-the-village and local-jobs-for-local-people thing going on as well.'

'Very worthy,' Alex said drily. 'But any Communications and PR plan for all that will have been agreed months ago. What do they need me for?'

'To look after things while the PR manager is on bed-rest.'

Alex shifted, staring out of the window at the pinkening sky. 'Amber, that's not a difficult job. Any of our temps could take a plan and implement it. They don't need me for anything so simple. It's not like I'm cheap.'

'They were adamant they wanted you. It's a big deal, Alex. Opening up the house after all this time is a huge undertaking, and it's very different to anything they've done before. They see the estate as the embodiment of their brand. They're really big on sustainability and corporate responsibility, which fits in with the job creation and community stuff. They need a safe pair of hands to make sure it's properly publicised. Besides, they hinted that there might be bigger work coming our way if they were happy. Maybe this is some kind of test.'

'Maybe…' But Alex had entered PR for a reason. She knew when someone was spinning a story and this situation just didn't ring true. 'Send me the brief, will you?'

'I don't have it. They wanted to talk you through it all in person. But, honestly, they are opening with a whole Christmassy bang. You'll be kept suitably busy, I promise.'

All Alex's senses tingled. As soon as she finished the call she planned to find out every last bit of knowledge she could about Hawk and its owner. If it was in the public domain—or semi-public—then she would find it. Maybe she was wrong, and this situation was all absolutely legitimate, but she needed to be prepared for any and every eventuality.

'Alex, before you go… Dalstone sent over their press release for you to work your magic on and they want it back before nine this morning. Can you take a look now?'

'Of course. I'll send it right back. Is everything else okay?'

'All's good. Harriet's working from home today.

Deangelo just got back from an oversea trip so she wants to see him. Emilia's event went really well, but she didn't get in until after two so I think she'll be sleeping in.'

Amber sounded wistful. She thrived on the company of others and was happiest when they were all together. It didn't help that Christmas was so close. For the last few years the four of them had spent Christmas together, but this year Deangelo was taking Harriet back to his native Rio De Janeiro for the holiday, and Emilia would be spending two weeks in Armaria. All three of them expected their friend to come back sporting an engagement ring.

'I was thinking,' Alex said with an impulsiveness that surprised her. 'You and I should do something this Christmas. Skiing, maybe? Or we could have a city break somewhere wintry, like Vienna?'

'Really?'

'Absolutely. Why don't you look into it? After all the hard work we've had over the last few months we deserve a short break.'

'It will have to be short,' Amber reminded her. 'Your contract with Hawk lasts until Christmas Eve, and we have the Van Daemon New Year's Eve charity ball, but we could do three days in between without any problems.'

'Three days sounds perfect. Okay, I'll get the press release straight back. Speak later.'

'Give me a call when you're fully briefed and settled in. I'm sorry you had to head out on another job without coming home first.'

'It's fine. It's what we're here to do. It's a good sign, Amber. A sign we're where we want to be.'

Alex finished the call and opened her laptop, connecting it to her phone's data so she could access the press release Amber had mentioned. And then, she reminded herself, it would be time to investigate her new employers and check just why her every hackle was up and sensing danger.

But the press release needed far more work than she had anticipated, and between the pull of her work and the lull induced by the car's steady process she soon got lost in it, any thought of research flying out of her head.

She didn't notice the car turn off the motorway long before Swindon, and nor was she aware as they drove through a succession of idyllic villages, more like a film set than real places, with a succession of village greens, quirky pubs and thatched cottages.

It wasn't until the car slowed and turned in at a pair of elaborate gates that she realised she'd arrived at her destination.

'Already?' she muttered, glancing at the time on her laptop.

Only an hour had passed. There was no way they had made it to Swindon in that time. Which meant they were somewhere else entirely; somewhere an hour west of London. Inhaling slowly, Alex looked up. There was no need to worry. She was in control; she was always in control.

Repeating the mantra, she looked straight ahead at the gates, taking in every detail of the ornate gilt-covered iron, the curlicues and symbols, time stilling as she noted every familiar detail. Her breath caught painfully in her throat, and her mouth was dry as the old, unwelcome panic, banished for a decade, thundered through her.

She hadn't just arrived. She'd returned. She was at Blakeley. Ten years after swearing never to set foot here again. Ten years after renouncing her way of life and starting anew.

Calm deserted her. She couldn't do this. Wouldn't. The car would have to turn around and take her straight back to London.

Hands shaking, she began to bundle her phone back into her bag, snapping her laptop shut. But she couldn't find the words to tell the driver to stop. Her chest was too tight, her throat swollen with fear and long-buried memories.

And still the car purred inexorably on. Every curve of the drive, every tree and view was familiar. More. It was part of her soul. Alex sat transfixed, fear giving way to nostalgic wonder, and for a moment she saw the ghost of a fearless long-limbed girl flitting through the trees.

But that girl was long gone. Lady Lola Beaumont had disappeared the day the Beaumonts' fortunes had crashed and in her place Alexandra Davenport had appeared. Any resemblance was purely superficial.

Besides, who would recognise flamboyant Lola in demure Alex? Alexandra didn't party or flirt, she didn't dance through life expecting favours to be bestowed upon her, and she didn't try to shock or crave publicity. She worked hard; she lived a quiet existence. Her clothes were fashionable and stylish, yes, but on the sensible side. Her hair was coiled neatly, her jewellery discreet. And it was Alexandra Davenport who had been employed to do a job. The fact that the job was at her old family home must be one awful coincidence.

It *had* to be. After all, no one knew who she once had been. Not even her best friends.

Alex sat frozen, still undecided. Turning tail and running wasn't her style, but she had stayed clear of this entire region for a reason. She might not feel like Lola any longer, might not act like her, but what if someone recognised her?

Her hands folded into fists. She managed the story; she was no longer the story herself. She'd left her tabloid headline existence in the past, where it belonged, but she knew her reappearance at her childhood home would create nothing but speculation and the kind of publicity she'd spent a decade avoiding.

If she turned around now she wouldn't be running away, she'd be making a prudent retreat. She could claim a double booking and send one of her many capable temps in her stead, with a discreet discount and an apology. It was the right—the only—thing to do.

Only at that moment the car swept round the last bend and there it was, gleaming gold in the winter morning sun. Blakeley Castle. Alex could only stare transfixed at the long, grand façade, at the famous turrets, the formal gardens, now autumnal in browns and oranges and red, the trees bare of leaves, their spindly branches reaching high to the grey-blue sky. Her breath quickened and she leaned forward as if in a trance.

Blakeley Castle was beautiful. There was nowhere like it. Nowhere as steeped in myth and legend and history. Kings had fallen in love within its walls; queens had fallen from favour. Dukes had lost their hearts, and sometimes their heads, and the Beaumonts had gambled their fortunes, their titles, their freedom, their looks and their marriages on games of chance, of love, of treason.

Until one had gambled too much and lost it all. His freedom, his family, his home.

And now his daughter, the last Beaumont, was returning to Blakeley. But as an anonymous employee, no longer the spoiled darling of the house.

Alex took a deep breath, straightening her shoulders. She might have changed her name and changed her destiny but the old ancestral cry of 'Semper porsum', always forward, ran through her veins. This was just a job. And Blakeley was just a house—well, a castle. But it was still bricks and mortar. There were no ghosts here apart from the few that still haunted her dreams. And she made sure they vanished in the cold light of day.

She wasn't Lola Beaumont. She was Alexandra Davenport. She was calm and capable and she always saw her commitments through. Her life was sensible and measured and it was ridiculous to think of upsetting any aspect of it because of an old link to a mere place. A link that had been severed ten years ago. Nobody here knew her. She would do her job to the best of her ability and leave without looking back once. No regrets. She'd had too many of them.

Mind made up, Alex sat back as the car swept into the parking area at the side of the house, checking herself in her mirror. Her lipstick was in place, her hair neat, her expression coolly inscrutable. All was as it should be. The panic had gone. It was back in the past where it belonged. Nothing fazed her, nothing touched her, and her walls were firmly back in place.

She couldn't help noticing the changes in the familiar. Everything looked better cared for, and the flag flying from the highest turret bore a bird of prey, not the Beaumont crest. The car park was freshly laid, not a pothole to be seen, shielded from the castle by a tall hedge. She glimpsed the grand front entrance as the car turned. Doors stood open, the old faded steps were now gleaming, and the rug half covering them sported the same golden bird as that flying overhead on the flag.

Alexandra Davenport had never been to Blakeley Castle before. She would wait for the driver to open the door and then look around her in curiosity as she exited the car, asking if she should go in through the back door or report somewhere else. All would be unfamiliar, all new. She would be focussed on the task ahead. The beauty of the old house and grounds were of secondary importance, and her curiosity about the new owners confined to a moment's idle speculation before work took over, as it always did.

One deep breath and any dangerous traces of Lola disappeared as Alexandra stepped out of the car, her expression bland, her smile practised, and turned to face the person who had appeared to greet her.

The smile only wavered for one infinitesimal second as she took in the tall, broad-shouldered man, his dark jacket and jeans showcasing lean, powerful muscles, his hair swept back off his face, dark eyes as cold as the December air.

'Hello.' Her voice stayed calm and in control as she held out a hand. 'Alexandra Davenport.'

The man's gaze only grew more sardonic as he took her hand in his. His clasp was strong, almost too strong, as if he had something to prove.

'Finn Hawkin. But you knew that. Didn't you, Lola?'

CHAPTER TWO

FINN LOOSENED HIS grip and Alex withdrew her hand from his in a smooth gesture.

'I go by Alexandra now.'

'I know. Alexandra Davenport, I believe? Of course Alexandra *is* your middle name.'

He noted her slight blink of acknowledgement with satisfaction. Maybe she wasn't quite as calm as she seemed. 'Where's the Davenport from?'

'My grandmother's maiden name.' She stepped back and looked around before her cool gaze rested on him once again, understanding in her grey eyes. 'Hawkin… hawk. Of course. I see. You always did say you'd earn enough to own somewhere like Blakeley some day. I didn't think you actually meant Blakeley itself, but that wasn't the first time I underestimated you. Congratulations, Finn, you've obviously done very well.'

Finn had been rehearsing this meeting for the last few hours. Ever since he'd heard about his Head of PR, Penelope, having an accident. No, longer than that. Since the summer, when he had glimpsed Lola across the ballroom floor and done some digging into the agency which had organised the Armarian Midsummer Ball and its four founders. From the moment he'd realised that Alexandra Davenport was exactly who he thought she was.

Lola Beaumont was unfinished business. Business he needed to resolve in order to move on once and for all—especially now that he was master of Blakeley and all that entailed. He had to focus on the future, on his nieces, and let go all the regrets that still haunted him. And he could only do that by confronting the past—and the woman who dominated it.

And then the fates had aligned, for good or for ill, and he had taken advantage of them. Penelope's accident was more than unfortunate, coming at such a very crucial time. The castle would be opening to the public for the first time in its history this weekend, and he needed an experienced pair of hands to manage all the resulting publicity. Who better than the woman who had grown up here? Who now worked as a PR consultant?

The Lola he'd known would have reacted to her homecoming in some dramatic fashion, with tears or laughter equally likely, but this new version radiated a disconcerting cool calmness. A calmness he hadn't anticipated, hadn't prepared for. Nor had he missed her slight emphasis on the words 'underestimated'.

His mouth tightened. He didn't reply, not at first, taking a moment to observe the woman who had been his oldest friend—and his first love.

'You didn't know I founded Hawk?'

He didn't hide his polite disbelief. Maybe she'd walked away and never so much as typed his name into a search engine or on a social media site, but his business was a global brand, and as founder and CEO he had been extensively profiled.

Alex was a PR professional. It didn't seem possible

that she had no idea of who he had become and what he'd achieved.

But her smile was apologetic. 'Sorry. Outdoor pursuits aren't my speciality and nor is clothing. I'm aware of Hawk, of course, but you've never been a rival of any of my clients, so I haven't ever needed to investigate further. That was why I was so surprised when Amber said you had requested me specifically. I have to say I am even more surprised now I'm here. Finn, obviously it's flattering that you would like me to cover your PR. But, given everything, I don't think that our working together is in any way a good idea.'

'Everything?' He kept his voice icily smooth, but she still didn't react, her expression unruffled.

'Our shared history.'

He raised an eyebrow. 'Shared history? That's one way of putting it, I suppose.'

He stopped himself from saying anything else, from letting the bitter words he'd been holding back for ten years come spilling out. He was no longer a young man with no idea how to handle his emotions, how to cope with accusations and betrayal and heartbreak.

'However, that's exactly why you're perfect for this job. After all, you know the castle better than anyone else.'

Again, just a blink as her reaction. Finn folded his arms and waited for her to respond, refusing to allow her calmness to throw him. After all, whether she called herself Alexandra Davenport or Lola Beaumont, there was one thing he knew for sure: she didn't just know Blakeley Castle, she loved it with every fibre of her fiery being.

But, he conceded as he studied her, this woman

wasn't fiery. Gone was the platinum blonde hair and dramatic eyeliner, the cutting-edge fashion and almost fey wildness. Instead Alexandra's hair was her natural light brown, neatly pinned up, her make-up discreet, her clothes professional. There was nothing wild in the way she stood, nor in her eyes. Instead Finn noted her absolute air of control. Was there any trace of Lola trapped inside this stranger?

'The castle, yes. Your brand, no.'

'But you specialise in short-term jobs, in getting up to speed quickly,' he pointed out silkily. 'I have a whole team who can manage Hawk's PR work. What I need is someone to help me launch Blakeley Castle as a destination. Your expertise and knowledge make you the logical choice. Your colleague, Amber, didn't think there would be any problem.'

'Amber doesn't know that I have any personal connection to Blakeley—or to you,' she added in a low voice. 'So of course she wouldn't foresee any conflict of interest. But there are conflicts, and it's my professional opinion that you would be better off with one of our excellent consultants instead of me. I can think of at least three who would be perfect. I propose I go back to London now and send you their profiles. I can make sure your preferred candidate is with you by the end of the day. I'm sorry you have wasted your time. It's unfortunate that I was out of contact when you called.'

She picked up her bag and took a decisive step back.

'I'm glad to see you've done so well, Finn. I look forward to our companies working together. I'm sure it will be a successful partnership.'

Not so fast. He hadn't got her back just to watch her drive off into the sunset with nothing resolved.

'You've signed a contract.'

Her eyes flickered. 'And we'll honour that contract...'

'The contract specifies you, Alex. That *you* will work here at Blakeley Castle until Christmas Eve. Not one of your consultants, however excellent they may be.'

'Yes, but—'

'It's you I have employed, your expertise I want, and your exorbitant rates I have agreed to.'

'We can, of course, offer a discount to offset any inconvenience.'

'I don't need a discount. Either you fulfil the terms of your contract or I sue you for breaking them. Your choice. I'm sure you'll be happy to stand up in court and tell everyone why you didn't feel able to work for me.'

Her silence and stillness were absolute. 'I see. I'm sorry that you hate me this much, Finn...'

'I don't hate you, Lola. I have absolutely no feelings at all towards you. This isn't personal. This is business. So what will it be?'

He held her gaze, conscious of the lie. Of course it was personal, but his business reasons were more than valid. And he didn't hate her. He never had.

She sighed. 'If you're absolutely adamant that I stay then of course I will, but I'd like to make it clear that I think you would be better letting me assign someone else to this job. Are you sure this is what you want?'

'I'm sure. Come along and I'll show you to your desk. Not that you need me to show you anywhere. I'm sure you remember your way around.'

Her eyes dipped briefly and she laid a hand on his arm, her touch light. Even her touch had lost its fire.

Or maybe he was immune, their past having inoculated him against any spells she might cast.

'Finn, I need to get one thing straight. If you really want me to work for you then please forget you ever knew me. Forget I ever lived here. Lola Beaumont is gone. I left her behind a long time ago.'

'Shame. There was a lot of good in Lola behind it all.'

'That's neither here nor there. Do I have your word that you will respect my anonymity? The reputation I have built up? I don't know how you tracked me down, Finn, but if you really have brought me here to do my best for your business and not to create a whole other kind of publicity then you'll forget about Lola.'

She fixed her disconcerting gaze on him. Still no trace of visible emotion in their grey depths. No longer could a lovestruck boy compare them to stormy seas or windswept skies. Instead they were more like a glossy pebble, smooth and unreadable.

'Unless, of course, it's other publicity that you are after? Not my expertise but my past?'

Finn stared at her, incredulous as her meaning took shape. 'You think I brought you here to expose you?'

She shrugged. 'It would be excellent PR. The last Beaumont back at Blakeley… The papers would love it. They'll rake up the old scandal anyway, you know that—you must be counting on it. Everyone loves the idea of an old, proud family brought down, and now they can stand on the spot where it happened. I am quite happy to facilitate that, Finn, but I am no longer personally part of that story.'

His hands curled once more into fists as he fought to match her calmness. 'I don't expect you to be the story. Blakeley is mine now. I prefer to concentrate on the future and on building prosperity for everyone who works here.'

'Thank you. I'm glad we understand each other.'

Even with the toned-down make-up and hair, the professional clothes, he could still see traces of the vibrant girl he had known in the tilt of Alexandra's pointed chin, the curve of her cheekbones, her elegant posture. But any resemblance was purely skin-deep.

Lola was gone, and with her all that fire and passion. It might have got her—and all who knew her—into trouble sometimes, but she had at least known how to live. He got the impression that the woman in front of him didn't really live a single day of her ordered life. Rather she sleepwalked through it, merely existing. Of all the tragedies that had hit the Beaumonts, this seemed like the biggest tragedy of all.

But whether she called herself Alexandra or Lola one thing was clear—she still thought he would use her, expose her for his own personal gain, just as she had believed ten years ago. No matter what he had achieved, to the woman opposite he was still the boy she thought had betrayed her. Well, his word might not have been good enough then, but she would have to believe in it now.

His future awaited him, and once Christmas was over Lola/Alexandra would be out of his life and his memories for good.

Control had been at the centre of Alex's life for many years now, but she had never had to fight so hard for it as she did right now. Standing beside her old home, with its turrets reaching up into the skies, standing opposite the man she had once given her whole heart and trust to, only for him to rip them—and her—to pieces, had whipped up feelings and emotions she had long thought buried and gone. Nausea swirled through her and her hands shook, but she fought to keep her voice even and her expression bland.

Finn could never know the effect he had on her. She would never give him—or anyone—that kind of power again.

'I think I'd better get started. Where shall I set up? I would usually arrive fully prepared, but I was told I'd be briefed when I got here.'

She allowed the merest hint of accusation to hang in the air. Finn had deliberately allowed her to turn up un-prepared and wrong-footed. Although, she allowed, if she hadn't been too absorbed in her work to do the back-ground check she'd promised herself, then she wouldn't have been quite so unprepared. She couldn't blame Finn for everything. Not this time.

'I'll take you to meet your team and brief you on the way. Leave your bags. One of the staff will take them to your rooms. The Hawk offices are in the sta-bles. This way.'

Finn indicated the freshly laid woodchip path which wound away from the car park into the small copse which separated the newly refurbished offices from the castle. Alexandra hefted her leather laptop bag onto her shoulder and followed him—as if she didn't know the way to the stables just as well as he did.

'Amber said you're planning to open the castle up to the public and the launch is this week—is that right?' She barely waited for his nod before continuing. 'So, will you open all year round or just for Christmas? Sea-sonally? Weekends? What about the gardens? Will they have different opening hours and prices? Obviously I should have researched this before I started, but I only got off my flight a couple of hours ago.'

Every question was direct and to the point. Information-gathering for her job, no more. She had to treat this like any other job, Finn like any other client. It was the only way she was going to get through this.

'My apartments are in the top two floors of the west wing, and private, but the rest of the castle, including the grounds, will be open every day. Houses like this should be for everyone, not just for the privileged few.'

Alex swallowed, tightening her hold on her bag. Finn was living in her home, her beloved castle. Once she had daydreamed of such a situation, only in her dreams she had been living there alongside him. Was there a woman living with him? He wasn't wearing a wedding ring but that didn't mean anything. Not that she cared. She just hoped he'd learnt loyalty in the last decade. How to love, not how to use.

Although, judging by the way he was using her right now, she wouldn't bet on it.

'I assume all the paintings and furniture are still here? I know the castle was bought complete.'

She fought to suppress a dangerously revealing wobble in her voice. This was a job, not personal. Blakeley and all its treasures meant nothing to her. She couldn't think about the old oak furniture that dated back to Tudor times, or the famous collection of Pre-Raphaelite paintings. She couldn't remember the old dolls' house or Strawberry, her beloved pony.

Finn nodded. 'Luckily for me the castle was bought by an oligarch who never actually visited the place. Rumour in the village is that he wanted a hunting lodge and didn't realise the estate wasn't suitable for the kind of stag-hunting he'd planned. I don't think he even set foot in the place. Blakeley hadn't been touched since the day you left.'

Alex allowed herself one dangerous moment of memory. One flashback to the desperate girl with tears streaming down her face, the police tape still flickering around the lake, the hardness on Finn's face, the paparazzi pressed up against the gates. And the last look back before she had slipped out of the secret door in the wall and out of her life, leaving Lola in the headlines and her heart in Blakeley's keeping.

And then she pushed that memory firmly back down and picked up the pace. 'So, Finn,' she said as brightly as she could. 'Tell me more about your plans and what you need me to do.'

Work was the answer. Work had always been the answer. And for the next few weeks she suspected it was going to be her salvation.

CHAPTER THREE

ALEXANDRA DREW IN a deep breath and stared fixedly at her laptop screen, refusing to let the letters in front of her blur or her mind wander. She was focussed and busy, just the way she liked it, with all messy emotions kept at bay.

All around was a low hum of activity: the sound of a contented, productive office. Sitting here, it was hard to imagine that this building had once been ramshackle stables. There wasn't a whiff of straw or old leather to be found. When she'd first walked in she'd passed the place where her old mare, Strawberry, had been stabled, and for one terrifying moment had been catapulted back in time. Luckily, the receptionist had spoken to her and pulled her back to the present.

She didn't want to go back. She couldn't…

No, better to focus on the present. And if she concentrated hard she could do exactly that.

It helped that the once familiar room was now so unfamiliar. The architect had done an amazing job of transforming the dark old buildings into a light, airy and modern space. On the ground floor was a spacious reception area, meeting rooms, and what Finn had described as 'creative space', filled with sofas, board games and a kitchen area.

The executive offices were also housed on the bottom floor, but she hadn't been shown them. Instead Finn had taken her upstairs to the general offices, making it very clear what her position was.

Upstairs was one big office area, with pale wood desks blending in with old oiled beams, the walls matt white, the floor gleaming parquet, and wide windows showcasing breathtaking views of the parkland and estate gardens.

Alexandra had barely given them a glance. There was a reason she'd moved to London. Not only did she prefer the anonymity of the city, she also liked the way the noise and hubbub gave her so little space to think. London was overwhelming, and that was exactly how she liked it. There was no space to be an individual. The city assimilated you and you just had to be swept away.

Finn had introduced her to the team and his marketing director before leaving her with a curt nod. For a moment, watching him stride away, she had almost felt lost. She'd swiftly shaken that absurdity from her mind, but now, as she read through her handover notes and began to get to grips with her workload, it began to dawn on Alex just what Finn had achieved. Her childhood playmate, her first crush, the boy she had naively thought she might love, had achieved his dream.

She tapped a pencil absentmindedly on the desk as she looked around at the comfortable space filled with people hard at work. He had always proclaimed that one day he would travel around the world, that he'd own his own company and make a fortune, and live in a place like Blakeley, not just work there. And she'd believed him, that fierce determined, skinny boy with his messy dark brown hair and chocolate eyes. Even though he'd never even travelled as far as Oxford, and his father and grandfather and every generation before them had been born, had worked and died within the castle grounds.

But for a while it had looked as if his dreams had stagnated—a pregnant sister, an alcoholic father demanding all his time and attention. The boy who had dreamt of the world had found himself bound to one place, and meanwhile her burgeoning modelling career had taken her around the globe. How he must have resented it. Resented her.

The pencil stilled and the old questions once more flooded her mind. Was that why he had done it? Betrayed her when she had already been as down as a girl could be? The money from those photos must have freed him. And look what he had achieved with that freedom. Did he ever consider that he'd purchased it with her innocence and happiness? Or did he think that it was a fair trade for the generations of Hawkins who had been trampled on by generations of Beaumonts?

Another inhale. Another exhale. Push it all away. All those inconvenient feelings. Concentrate on the job in front of you.

She'd been Alex for so long there were times when she forgot that Lola had even existed. She needed that blissful ignorance now. She had to treat this as any other job, forget she knew Finn, not allow herself to speculate on how he'd found her and why he had gone to such trouble to bring her here. Forget everything but the task at hand.

She put the pencil down firmly, pulling her laptop

closer, and as she did so a pretty dark-haired girl approached her desk.

'Hi, is it Alex or Alexandra?'

'I answer to both.' She smiled in welcome as she desperately searched her mind for the girl's name. Katy? Kitty?

'I'm Kaitlin.' The girl smiled shyly back. 'I doubt you'll remember anyone after that quick introduction. I've never known Finn to be in such a hurry. I thought you might want to get settled in today, but I'll make sure you get properly introduced to everyone tomorrow, so you know what they actually do. I'm the PR Assistant, so technically I report to you. I suggest you ask me anything you need to know and I'll do my best to point you in the right direction.'

Kaitlin's friendliness was disarming—and a relief after the frosty civility Finn had shown. 'That's good to know. Nice to meet you properly, Kaitlin.'

'Penelope asked me to talk you through her strategy and plans so you can go to her with any questions before things get too manic. Is now good?'

'Now's great, thanks.'

Alex looked at her neat notes, perfectly aligned, finding the long to-do list its usual balm. At first she had been at a loss as to why she was so urgently required. Penelope, Hawk's laid-up Head of PR was organised and had clearly taught her junior staff well. Looking through her notes, strategies and task lists, Alex saw that it appeared that there was little left for Alex to actually do, apart from follow instructions. A job anyone with half a brain could manage. It didn't seem worth her substantial fee, and her lurking suspicion that Finn had tracked her down and employed her simply to gloat about their reversal of fortune had deepened.

But as she read on it became clear that the plan Penelope had put together would need careful tweaks and adjustments as the castle was finally opened to the public, and the potential press interest needed to be handled by someone with experience. It was a job she was confident any of the temps on her books could handle, but she could see that Finn genuinely needed outside help, and as it was unlikely he'd manufactured Penelope's accident her presence here was in some way coincidental, even if her concern as to how he had tracked her down remained.

After all, if he could then so could any of those journalists who still ran occasional stories on the fall of the Beaumonts.

Kaitlin pulled a chair up to the desk. 'So, the first thing is the media launch party. May I...?'

Alex nodded permission and the younger woman manipulated the mouse on the PC Alex had been allocated and brought up the appropriate file.

'Here are the notes and the event plan. It's on Thursday night, and the party is for journalists, local dignitaries and VIPs. The castle will then have a soft opening for two weeks and will officially celebrate with a second, bigger party on the twenty-fourth of December. That party will include locals, colleagues, suppliers, partners...everyone, really.'

Alex inhaled as she read the timeline.

The official opening of the castle and grounds will be marked with a traditional Christmas Eve party.

'Christmas Eve?' Somehow she kept her voice calm.

'Apparently it's a real tradition at Blakeley. I hear the parties here used to be wild. Full of every kind of celebrity from pop stars to princes.'

'Right. Then we need to make sure we publicise that angle.'

Her heart began to thump; her hands felt damp. Christmas Eve. Her birthday. More than that, the day Blakeley had always celebrated Christmas.

For generations, friends and lovers, enemies and rivals had descended on Blakeley on Christmas Eve to feast and dance, intrigue and plot.

As a child Alex would spend the afternoon hosting a sumptuously over-the-top party for her friends—and then spend the evening darting through the dancing, flirting adults, sipping champagne from discarded glasses and sneaking canapés. No one had ever told her to go to bed. Instead she had been the spoilt princess of the house, petted and indulged, falling asleep on a chair or a sofa, where she would wake on Christmas morning to find herself covered with some discarded jacket.

In her mid-teens the two parties had been combined, with lithe, knowing teenagers far too at home amidst the glamour and heady atmosphere of the adult affair. At least they'd pretended they were at home. Alex had been very good at pretending. Until the night of her eighteenth birthday, that was, when her world had become real for the first time—for a few blissful hours, until the moment when it had stilled and stopped for ever.

She tried to inhale again, to take those sweet, calming breaths that kept her pulse even, her heart still, her head clear. But her breath caught in her throat.

I can't do this, she thought, panic threatening to flood through the walls she had built so carefully, so painstakingly, solid walls, covered in ivy and thorns, ready to repel all invaders. *I can't*.

But she could. She had no choice. Stay and deal with it or leave and run the risk of exposure.

She was stronger than this. Nothing and no one could hurt her now. Blakeley was just a place, Christmas Eve was just a date, her birthday would go unremarked. She would show Finn that he hadn't won. Not then, not now. And she would do so by making sure his planned launch ran absolutely perfectly.

Gradually her pulse returned to normal, her emotions stilled, and she calmly made another note.

Check the invite list for the Christmas party.

'Okay,' she said, her voice as steady as ever. 'What's next?'

The conversation with Kaitlin was illuminating in several ways, taking up the rest of the morning and lunch. It had been a long time since her airline breakfast, and Alex had had no chance to get anything to eat, but Kaitlin ordered a working lunch, which the two ate at the desk as they finished going through the notes. Alex's to-do list was getting satisfactorily ever longer.

At some point in the afternoon the younger woman finally returned to her own desk and Alex sank thankfully into work. There she could forget that Christmas Eve had once meant something, meant everything, deep in the absorption that working out how to craft and manipulate a story gave her.

As always, she lost track of time, and when she finally stretched and looked up she realised it was now dark outside, the office lights bright against the gloom. The room was almost deserted. Just a few people were left at their desks and they seemed to be packing up. Alex leaned back and stretched again, glad that the weeks ahead looked interesting but achievable.

She would give Finn no reason, no excuse to find fault with a single thing she did. He had the power and the influence now. With one word he could tell everyone who she was—who she'd used to be—and trash her fledgling agency's reputation. She wouldn't have thought him capable once. She knew better now.

'Alex?' Kaitlin hovered by her desk, her bag already on her shoulder. 'I'm off now. Is there anything you need before I leave?'

'No, I'm fine. Thank you. You've been so helpful.'

'I hope so.' The younger woman looked pleased, brushing her thick dark hair away from her face as her cheeks turned a little pink.

Alex looked around at the gleaming new office. 'I guess you haven't been based here very long?'

'No, Finn's been here since the summer, but the rest of us moved in October. There's still a London office, but the plan is to scale it right back. For now some people are splitting their time between there and here. It's easier for those of us without families, I guess. Finn has converted an old mill into flats and a few rent there. One or two rent in the village and quite a lot of us are in Reading—we're not ready for a totally rural life just yet!'

'It's impressive that so many of you were ready to uproot yourselves.'

'Finn's so inspiring…his whole ethos. I wouldn't want to be anywhere else.'

'That's reassuring to hear. I hope I'll feel the same way.'

'I hope so too.'

The deep masculine tones made both Alex and Kaitlin jump, the latter's cheeks going even redder as Finn sauntered towards them.

'Loyalty is very important here at Hawk.'

But it wasn't Finn's unexpected appearance that made Alex's pulse speed up, and nor was it the sardonic gleam in his eye as he looked at her. It was the two small girls holding on to his hands. Finn had *children*? He had security, money, her old home and a family? Everything she had lost. Everything she would never have.

The oldest girl looked, to Alex's inexperienced eye, to be about nine, the other around five. They were both in school uniform, their dark hair so like Finn's own in messy plaits, and the same dark, dark eyes fixed on Alex.

'It's the Sleeping Princess,' the younger one said, pointing at Alex. 'Look, Saffy, it's the Princess from the painting.'

Finn suppressed a grin as Alexandra's startled gaze flew to his. Turned out the lady could show surprise after all.

'Alex…' The name felt clumsy on his tongue. 'I'd like you to meet my nieces. Saffron, Scarlett, this is Alex. She's working here for a little while.'

'No, Uncle Finn.' Scarlett tugged at his hand. 'She's a princess in disguise.'

Wasn't that the truth?

'Nice to meet you.' Alex smiled uncertainly at the

girls. 'But I'm afraid it's a case of mistaken identity. I'm not a princess, although it's lovely to be thought one.'

'You *are*,' Scarlett insisted.

Kaitlin nodded. 'I see what you mean, Scarlett. You're thinking of that painting, aren't you? The one of Blakeley Castle and the Sleeping Beauty? She does look a little like Alex.'

Alex's cheeks reddened, just slightly. Finn was certain she knew exactly which painting Scarlett was referring to; it was a Rossetti, part of the castle's famed Pre-Raphaelite collection. Alex's great-great-grandmother was the model: a woman who in her youth had been as scandalous as her granddaughter several times removed.

What would the Pre-Raphaelite muse and late-Victorian It Girl think of her descendant? Would she recognise this poised, apparently emotion-free woman sitting in an office chair as if she were made for it, the very model of efficiency? Finn barely recognised her himself. It was all too easy to think her who she claimed to be.

'If you say so, but I can't see it myself,' he said, taking pity on Alex, even though her resemblance to the woman in the painting had been notable when she was younger and was still remarkable, despite her decidedly un-Pre-Raphaelite appearance. 'I'll take it from here, Kaitlin.' He nodded at the dark-haired girl. 'You get off now or you'll miss the last bus.'

'Bus?' Alex watched Kaitlin leave before swivelling back to face him. 'Since when was there a bus?'

'If I want my employees to come and bury themselves in the depths of the Chilterns then I have to make it manageable for them,' Finn pointed out. 'Some live on the estate in the Old Corn Mill, but that didn't suit everyone, so a mini-bus goes between here and Reading several times a day. It picks up at the train station too. Not everyone is ready to leave London just yet. And when the employees don't use it, the villagers do.'

'How very Sir Galahad of you…riding to the rescue with your jobs and renovations and buses.'

Alex's voice and face were bland, but Finn felt the barb, hidden as it was. The situation was getting to her more than she was letting on, and he had to admit he was relieved. It didn't seem normal for anyone to be so serene when confronted with their past in the way she had been.

'The village must be very grateful.'

He shrugged. 'Relieved more than grateful. Goodness knows it needed a Sir Galahad to swoop in after the Beaumonts' reign of benign neglect, followed by a decade of an indifferent and absent landlord.'

His barb wasn't hidden at all, and he saw her flinch with some satisfaction. The Beaumonts had adored being the Lord and Lady of the Manor but they hadn't been so interested in the people who lived and worked on the estate.

Blakeley might be situated in a wealthy commuter county, but the village itself was very rural, its twisty roads and the Chiltern Hills making even a short journey as the crow flew lengthy. Plus, it was a place where more than half the houses were owned by the castle, but where the jobs that had used to come with the houses had disappeared over the years.

Picturesque as Blakeley village was, not everyone wanted to rent a home where the colour of their front door and guttering was prescribed by the estate, public transport was non-existent and the nearest town a long, windy ten miles away.

'The locals are just happy to see new life breathed into the place, and enough staff are renting to make the local businesses and the school viable. My village is breathing again.'

'*Your* village? You wear Lord of the Manor pretty well.'

Another barb. Interesting.

Finn didn't react, simply nodded towards the door. 'Are you done here? The girls are ready for their dinner and I need to show you where you're staying.'

'There's a lot to do, but I can work in my room.' Alex folded her laptop closed and slipped it into its case. 'Look, if there's a bus to the train station I might as well go back to London. The train's only half an hour or so, right? Save you the problem of putting me up.'

'It's no problem. Besides, it's not just the train. You need to factor in the half-hour journey to Reading—and that's assuming you haven't missed the bus, which you have. Then say another fifteen minutes through traffic to get to the train station. Half an hour to Paddington and then your journey at the other end. You'd rather endure a four-hour return journey than stay here?'

Her gaze flickered away. 'I don't want to put anyone out.'

She didn't want to spend the night surrounded by her past, no doubt.

'You're needed evenings and weekends until Christmas. The contract says we expect you to be on site and that's exactly where you'll be. Unless you still want to walk away.'

He allowed the hint of a threat to linger in his voice,

hiding the doubt he'd spent the afternoon trying to dispel. Would it be better, after all, to take her advice and let her choose a consultant to come and work here? She could still advise from London. He'd wanted her here to resolve the past, but this woman wasn't Lola. She was a stranger.

Finn hardened his heart. He needed to give his nieces a place where they belonged, the security they hadn't had until now. He'd earnt a fortune, but a lot of his profits were ploughed back into the company and the foundation he'd set up. For the reopening of Blakeley he needed the best. And everyone agreed that Alexandra Davenport *was* the best. Her expertise and inside knowledge of the castle and estate meant she was exactly what he needed—whether she liked it or not.

Alex stood up decisively. 'I never walk away from a job, Finn, not until the client is happy. I'm fine staying here if that's what you want. Whatever's easiest. You're the client.'

Finn rubbed his chin, feeling the rasp of stubble under his fingertips, suddenly weary. 'Come on, then,' he said brusquely. 'I'll show you where you're staying.'

He rounded up the girls and made his way down the stairs, all too aware of Alex following behind, the tapping of her heels on the wooden treads. He'd called the last of the Beaumonts home to Blakeley. It was up to him to control the situation. He was the boss now, and the sooner Alex accepted that, the better.

CHAPTER FOUR

NEITHER SPOKE AS Finn led Alexandra out of the stable and onto the dimly lit path. The castle reared up, lit up against the winter dark sky, and he noticed Alex turn away from it. So she wasn't as impervious to coming home as she seemed. The girls skipped ahead, oblivious to the chilly atmosphere, which was colder than the rapidly lowering evening temperature.

'Do you think it might snow?' Alex said, looking up at the clouds overhead.

'It's early yet.'

'But it has snowed this early. Remember that year—' She broke off, sentence unfinished.

But he did remember. Snowball fights and sledging, hot chocolate in the kitchen and the skiing lesson she'd given him. They'd been children, no older than Saffy, still mesmerised by the wonder of snow.

A minute went by before Alex made another attempt to break the increasingly charged silence. 'Kaitlin mentioned that you'd converted the old Corn Mill into apartments. Is that where I'm staying? Or does the village pub still have rooms?'

'Yes, no and yes.'

Now it came to it, Finn felt profoundly uncomfortable. His decision on where to house her had seemed purely pragmatic at the time. Now he wasn't so sure that his thinking had been as rational as he'd told himself, with every step provoking memories.

'The Corn Mill doesn't have any space, but it isn't the only building we've renovated. For instance, we've turned the barns at the bottom of the estate into bunkhouses. Places where inner city school kids can come so they can get a chance at the outdoor life. Hiking in the Chilterns, orienteering around the estate, building shelters, that kind of thing.'

Her mouth quirked into a half-smile. A real half-smile, like the girl he'd used to know had had, and his pulse jumped at the sight.

'You're putting me in a bunkhouse?'

'No, that's just an example. We've also renovated some of the old estate cottages for holiday lets. As you know, we'll be running outdoor activities throughout most of the year, so it made sense to give people the chance to stay here.'

'Estate cottages? Not the ones in the village? The ones in the grounds? The Lodge, I suppose, and the Dower House, and...' Her voice trailed off.

'And the Gardener's Cottage. Yes.'

'I'm sleeping in the Gardener's Cottage.' It wasn't a question.

'It's the smallest so it made sense. Four of us lived there for years, Alex. I'm sure you won't find it too much of a squeeze. And don't worry. It's been done up since you last saw it. You won't have to endure my mother's taste in wallpaper or the sofa my father used to pass out on.'

'That's not what I...' She paused and then, voice

bright, said, 'It sounds very charming. I can maybe do some short videos for all the social media accounts about staying there. One weekend I'll do a full day's story—fresh eggs for breakfast in the café, a walk in the woods, that kind of thing. You're right; it makes complete sense for me to stay in a holiday cottage and I'd rattle around in the Dower House. Are the others booked yet?'

'The others?'

'The Dower House and the Lodge? I guess the Foreman's Cottage and the Blacksmith's Cottage are also holiday lets? Because if they're not let out yet then it might be worth offering them to journalists the night of the press party. And then to some influencers in the run-up to Christmas, maybe over Christmas Eve, with invitations for the party. I know the perfect people.'

For a moment, when she had said the words 'Christmas Eve' he could have sworn her voice wobbled. Just a little.

'They are all free; letting starts in the New Year. Invite whoever you'd like. Kaitlin can put you in touch with the letting team. Girls! It's getting dark. Stay close.'

Alex shot him a quick glance and he suspected she was curious about the girls' presence. But before she had a chance to ask any questions his nieces ran back, chattering on about a rabbit Scarlett was sure she'd seen in the wood, and they hadn't exhausted the topic by the time they reached the gate to the cottage.

As they neared the gate a security light was triggered, and Alex stopped just outside the fence and stared. 'It's exactly the same,' she said softly.

Finn inhaled. From the outside nothing much had

changed. His father had always kept it immaculate, even at his worst—on the surface respectable, behind the perfectly painted front door a secret drinker and despot.

'Not quite the same, I hope.'

The first sight of the house still gave Finn a sucker punch to the chest every time he walked through the gate. He'd thought buying Blakeley Castle and turning it into the place he had dreamed it could be would put some of his ghosts to rest, but sometimes they haunted him even more.

'I've put in new windows and fencing and the garden needed a lot of work.' He shot a quick look at the girls, but they were playing hopscotch on the path. 'In the end Dad stopped pretending to function—I suppose there was no one here to judge. Things were in a sorry state when I took over.'

'When did your father die?'

Alex had lowered her voice. She must have noticed he didn't want the girls to overhear. Finn couldn't help remembering just how empathic she had been, especially where his family were concerned. She was the only person living who knew the whole truth. There was a strange freedom in their conversation, in not having to watch what he said, how much he revealed.

'Two years ago. He refused to leave the cottage, refused to let me pay for anyone to help him. Sacked the cleaners I sent, left the groceries I ordered outside to rot in the rain. He died as he lived. On his own terms and with difficulty.' He snapped his mouth closed. He'd never said those words aloud before, not to anyone.

'I'm sorry,' Alex said softly. 'How about your sister? Where is she now? The girls are hers, I suppose?'

But Finn had already said too much, shown too

much—and his sister and her actions was a topic he wasn't ready to share. Not yet. Although he'd need to talk about both with Alex at some point.

'Here's a key,' he said instead. 'Your bag should be inside.'

Alex took the hint, made her voice efficient again. The moment of shared memory was gone and with it an intimacy he'd not realised he'd missed.

'Right. Is there anything I need to know about the boiler or hot water?'

'It should all be working. If not, then there's an information book in the kitchen.'

'Great. Just one more thing: is there any milk or bread in? Because I came straight from the airport and I'm not as prepared as I usually like to be.'

She looked slightly embarrassed, as if she would usually turn up at a work assignment with a week's worth of groceries on her, just in case. And maybe she would.

Finn winced. The Gardener's Cottage was the first to be completely ready. All the linen and towels were there but, because they hadn't started letting, welcome hampers were yet to be organised—and they'd only known for sure that Alex was coming late the night before. The fridge and cupboards were emptier than Mother Hubbard's.

He had meant to ask Kaitlin to sort out the basics, but once he'd seen Alex to the office he had headed out onto the estate and spent the day rebuilding a wall, not questioning why he'd felt the need for hard physical exercise. The mental note to email Kaitlin had uncharacteristically slipped right out of his mind.

'Once we're up and running we'll be leaving welcome hampers, of course, but we haven't started yet. Sorry.'

'Okay,' she pulled her phone out of her pocket. 'Look into sourcing hampers,' she said clearly, before smiling at him—a brisk, businesslike smile that reminded him just what a stranger she was now. 'Believe me, if I'm going to be inviting journalists and influencers we need highly photogenic hampers. Don't worry, I'll get on to it.'

'Right. Of course.' This efficiency was why he had employed her.

She took the key and pocketed it. 'You'd better get the girls back and fed. I'll head down to the village shop.'

Ah… 'It closes at six.'

'Or the pub…'

She bit her lip on the last word and he understood her hesitation. If she was going to be recognised anywhere it would be the pub, with its loyal clientele of locals who had known her since she was a baby. But not tonight.

'They don't serve food on a Monday night.'

'Oh.' Her smile got even brighter, but there was no warmth, no light in it. 'In that case a takeaway it is.'

Finn didn't have the heart to tell her that the only takeaways available to the village were at the weekend, when a fish and chips and pizza van set up on the green for a couple of hours.

'Look, this is my fault, so I had better fix it. Come over to the castle and I'll make you some food.'

As soon as the words were said he wanted to recall them. It was too much, too soon. There were things to say, but not tonight, not when he was still trying to work out just who Alex was.

And she clearly felt the same way, stepping back, away from him, away from his invitation. 'You don't have to do that.'

'I do,' he said drily. 'Your only alternative is water. There's not even any tea bags in the cottage as far as I know.'

'But you cooking is too much,' she protested. 'Honestly, it's been a long day, and I have a lot to be getting on with. I can just grab some eggs and beans or something and bring them back here. I don't want to be any trouble.'

'Once,' he said, in a voice so low he didn't know if she could hear him, or if he wanted her to hear him. 'Once you said trouble was your middle name.'

She looked up at him then, eyes bright. 'I was wrong. Trouble was the family curse. That's why I avoid it whenever I can.'

Finn stared back at her. At a face at once as familiar as his dreams but also that of a stranger. The same almond-shaped grey eyes, the same high cheekbones and full mouth. The same pointed chin and high forehead and look of determination. But the spark that had made Lola so irresistible was gone, and he couldn't tell if it was extinguished entirely or just slumbering, waiting for someone to rekindle it. For one soul-aching moment he wanted to find out, to take this beautiful yet lifeless woman and kiss life back into her.

'Uncle Finn! I'm hungry!'

Now it was his turn to take a step back in denial, and the cold early winter evening breeze was a welcome wake-up call. Finn couldn't believe what had just nearly happened. Kissing Lola Beaumont or kissing Alexandra Davenport—no matter which woman she was, any personal contact was a terrible idea. After all, look what had happened last time.

Even worse, he wasn't alone. The girls were right here. Weren't they damaged enough? He had promised them, promised himself, that they would only ever have love and stability in their lives, had vowed to himself that there would be no women flitting in and out. They'd only meet a girlfriend if he was pretty damn sure she'd be permanent.

'Sorry, Scarlett.' He threw her an apologetic smile and noted with a pang the pinched look on Saffy's face. 'I was just trying to persuade Alex to eat with us, I forgot to put food in her house.'

'Yes, then you can look at the picture,' Scarlett said with a beaming grin.

But Saffron's scowl just tightened further and Finn's heart ached for the small girl. With a jolt of surprise, he noticed a look of understanding cross Alex's face as she looked at his eldest niece, her expression relaxing with compassion.

'It's been a long day, so if it's okay I will just grab some bread and milk, maybe some cheese, and bring it back here,' she said, smiling at Scarlett. 'I'll see the picture some other time, though.'

'Promise?' Scarlett asked.

Alex nodded. 'Promise.'

As he turned to walk back to the castle Alex fell behind. Finn was preoccupied with Scarlett's chatter, and it wasn't until they reached the lights surrounding the castle that, looking back, he realised Alex was making determined conversation with Saffron. The girl wasn't answering—she was always slow to warm to strangers—

but her posture was less defensive and for one moment he thought he saw a slight smile on her face.

So Alex still had the old charm, when she wanted to use it, and he was absurdly grateful she was using it on his prickly niece.

And then he saw it, in the lowering of her gaze, the slight hunch in her posture—the reason Saffron's wariness had always seemed so familiar. It *was* familiar. It was the same wariness he had seen in Alex throughout her childhood—on the rare occasions when she hadn't been performing, being the bright, glittering Beaumont girl everyone had expected her to be.

He'd have done anything to protect his nieces, no matter what, but was the reason he had stepped in so very firmly, before things could go from difficult to toxic, because he had recognised the warning signs in Saffy's eyes?

He hadn't been able to protect Lola. Not from the consequences of her parents' selfishness and not from his own family's part in her downfall, and he'd been too full of his own bitterness to reassure and help her when she'd come back demanding answers at the time. No wonder he was making damned sure that Saffy was as protected as she could be. He knew the consequences.

He'd searched for Lola for years, dreading that he'd find her struggling and alone, and equally dreading that he'd find she'd moved on in true insouciant Beaumont style, not caring about the havoc she left behind her. But now he realised with blinding clarity that all he had wanted to do was put things right. And now she was finally here he had no idea if it was possible. She had her life, and he had the girls.

Maybe it was better to leave the past where it belonged. Lola was gone and Alex was a stranger. He could finally move on.

'So, if he proposes—and he will—Emilia will be a real-live princess. Well, an archduchess, but she'll be called Princess Emilia.'

Saffron's dark eyes widened. 'And she didn't know who he was when they met? It's just like a fairy-tale.'

Alex looked up and caught Finn watching them, the rather cold expression he'd been wearing much softer. Her breath caught. He really cared about his niece. Of course he did. He had always been someone who cared deeply. Which was why she had never understood why he had done what he did—to her, of all people. How he could have exposed her so publicly, sold her for thirty pieces of silver.

The old sense of betrayal caught at her heart and she swallowed back the bitterness. She couldn't indulge. Not here, not now, not ever.

But as she looked at the warmth in his eyes she couldn't help but wonder why he'd betrayed her so comprehensively. Money, she'd assumed then—and goodness knows he'd needed it—but it still felt wrong, just as it had back then.

She'd headed straight to him at the time, desperate for answers, for a way out of the dark labyrinth she'd found herself trapped in. But there had been no comfort, just cold anger. He'd been the last person to turn on her—and he would stay the last person. She'd vowed it then, and she needed to remember it now.

But she couldn't punish the girls for their uncle's transgressions.

Alex forced a smile as she nodded at the eagerly listening child. 'It is. And then she'll live in a castle too. Just like you.'

Not that living in a castle was any indicator of happiness. She knew that better than anyone. But maybe the curse had disappeared with the Beaumonts. She hoped so for the girls' sake, if not Finn's.

'But I'm not a princess,' Saffron said sadly. 'Princesses are beautiful and clever.'

'Some are. But a real princess, a true princess, has a big heart and she fights for what's right.'

'She does?'

'Absolutely.'

Alex managed to stop herself rushing in to tell Saffron that she was beautiful. It wouldn't be a lie—the little girl was very pretty, with her tangle of dark hair and darker eyes—but, having been brought up knowing that her appeal lay in her looks and her precociousness, Alex had no intention of laying that burden on another Blakeley child.

Smiling reassuringly at Saffron, Alex looked up at the castle looming overhead and stifled the panic rearing inside her. This wasn't a good idea. She wasn't prepared. How could she be prepared?

But it didn't matter whether she was prepared or not because she was here. Here with the man who had administered the final kick ten years ago, making sure she was both down and out.

She had to remember that no matter how disarming his smile, how familiar the warmth in his dark, dark eyes, how protective he was of his nieces, it was all deceptive. All she could do was protect herself the way she always did. Concentrate on the job at hand and block out all other emotions.

And right now her job was getting some food and getting out of the castle as quickly as she could.

But, try as she might to stay cool and collected, she felt her heart start to beat a frantic and painful rhythm as they neared the side door leading into the boot room. From there, the well-trodden path led to the old scullery and then into the kitchen. The heart of the castle. Not a place either of her parents had ever ventured, unless her father had reverted to his school days and crept in to steal a still-warm cake from the huge walk-in pantry.

Ruled over by Mrs Atkinson, the kitchen had been a refuge, a stage and a home. Once ensconced at the kitchen table, Alex had known that she would be ordered to do her homework and sent off to bed at a reasonable time. It had been oddly satisfying.

'Is Mrs Atkinson still here?' she asked as she and Saffron joined Finn and Scarlett at the side door, after checking that the girls weren't listening. She didn't want them suspecting that she and Finn had a prior friendship, or that she wasn't the stranger to Blakeley she pretended to be.

'No, none of the castle staff stayed on afterwards.'

The word hung there. *Afterwards.* Just three syllables to sum up the dissolution of her entire life.

'I tried to persuade her to come back to run the café, but she wasn't tempted. Too many ghosts, apparently.'

'That's a shame.'

Alex was split between relief that someone who would most definitely recognise her wasn't there to blow her cover and a surprisingly deep disappointment that she wouldn't be seeing one of the few people who had seemed to care about her when she was being just a normal child, not a precocious ingénue or a reckless daredevil.

She forced a smile. 'Her shortbread was legendary, and she'd never tell anyone the recipe. Your café would be a guaranteed success with her in the kitchen.'

She didn't usually chat so much, but talking helped mask the nerves tumbling through her body as Finn typed in a code on the back door and pushed it open, ushering her inside after the racing girls.

Alex blinked, recognition tingling in every nerve. Nothing had really changed. The same pegs on the walls, the same deep butler's sinks. The walls were a fresh white, the flagstones on the floor clean and oiled, and there were no dog bowls lining up against the far wall, but otherwise she could have been stepping back in time.

She swallowed as she followed Finn through the scullery, now a smart-looking utility room, and into the kitchen.

'The oligarch really didn't remodel,' she managed to say through the ever-increasing lump in her throat.

Again, the kitchen was almost untouched. Buffed and painted and fresh, but with the same wooden cabinets and vast stove chucking out welcome heat. The same huge table dominated the centre. The table she had eaten at, drawn at, cried at more times than she could remember.

'No, he never came here. Everything was left as it was.'

'Until you came along to make it a new and improved model.'

She didn't want or mean to sound bitter. It was bet-

ter that the castle was looked after. Of course it was.
But why did it have to be Finn doing the looking after?
And why did she have to be here, witnessing his success? Here on his payroll, her professional reputation
in his hands, dependent on him for her evening meal.

None of it matters, she told herself, as she had so
many times in the past. *None of it affects you.*

But the mantra didn't work. Not while she stood with
the past all around her. The past in front of her. Finn
had shed his winter coat and stood there in jeans and a
close-fitting cashmere long-sleeved T-shirt. He'd filled
out in the last few years. The snake-hipped passionate
boy was now a lean but muscled man, eyes as dark and
intent as ever, hair still falling over his brow.

For one treacherous moment something stirred inside
her. Maybe her heart, maybe long-dormant desire. But
she stood firm and pushed the feeling away. After all,
hadn't this man hurt her the most? She couldn't, mustn't
forget that. Ever. She'd worked too hard to move on.

She'd do her job to the best of her ability and leave,
reputation and secret intact. No more cosy walks with
Finn through the woods, no more trips down memory
lane, and no recognising kindred spirits in small girls.
It wasn't safe. The only time she would set foot in the
castle after this evening would be to work.

Stick to the rules and she'd survive this. She had before and she'd do it again. She just needed to remember
exactly who Finn Hawkin was.

CHAPTER FIVE

FINN LOOKED AROUND the crowded room, satisfaction running through him. All these people were here because of him. Journalists, influencers, local dignitaries, a scattering of celebrities. All drawn to Blakeley Castle once again.

Oh, he knew that many of them had only a passing interest in Hawk, in adventure trails, reinvigorating rural economies and bringing inner city kids into the countryside. They just wanted to set foot in the Blakeley Castle's legendary ballroom. To imagine they were one of the fabled generations of Bright Young Things who had danced, flirted, betrayed and seduced on this very floor.

Sometimes, at night, Finn would come in here and just for a moment catch a glimpse of a wisp of silk, a hint of taffeta, a flash of brocade. Every generation had its scandalous youth—whether they were Cavaliers, Regency beaux or jazz kids—and whatever the generation, whatever the scandal, they could all be found here at Blakeley.

But no more. His reign might be duller and more benign, but it would usher in a new tradition. One that was more inclusive. One with less misery in its wake.

Talking of which…

'Finn, here you are.'

Alex was playing the role of professional pen-pusher hard tonight. Finn knew that she hadn't lost her eye for fashion, or her taste, but there was no evidence of that eye or that taste tonight in the simple knee-length grey dress and matching jacket she wore. Her hair was tightly pulled back into a severe bun, a pair of black-rimmed glasses perched on her nose. She looked like a stock photo of a librarian rather than an attendee at a sought-after social event.

But Finn knew that her sartorial dullness was absolutely deliberate. After all, if her real identity was to be discovered then this was the time and place: back in her ancestral home surrounded by journalists. Not for the first time Finn wondered if he had done the right thing in bringing her back. Only this time it wasn't his peace of mind he was worried about. It was her anonymity. After all, hadn't he recognised her straight away?

But, then again, hadn't he known her better than anyone?

Alex ushered forward a petite woman. 'Can I introduce Isma Syed? Isma is the travel editor for the *Daily Courant* and she has a great blog as well—really inspiring and always ahead of the crowd. She's one of Blakeley's first guests too. She's spending the night in the Dower House.'

'Pleased to meet you.' Finn smiled at Isma, whose dark eyes were bright with interest. 'I hope you've enjoyed the day so far—and that the accommodation is up to your expectations?'

'It's very comfortable, thank you. And, yes! I wasn't sure that a treetop trail was really my thing, but I enjoyed it far more than I expected. So, Finn, how does it feel to come home? You grew up here, didn't you?'

It was no secret. 'My family have lived here for generations,' Finn agreed.

'But not in the castle itself? Do you know how the Beaumonts feel about the gardener becoming the Lord of the Manor?'

Finn sensed rather than saw Alex stiffen beside him. 'I haven't had an opportunity to discuss it with them, but I hope they would be pleased to know that the castle is being looked after by someone who loves it as much as they did…someone who has an ancestral affinity for the place.'

'Of course.' Isma leaned forward, her voice lowered confidentially. 'Lord Beaumont is dead and there were no male heirs. That's why the castle was for sale in the first place. But what about Lady Beaumont and her daughter? Do you have any idea where Lola Beaumont is right now?'

Lying didn't come easily to Finn, but he hadn't brought Alex here to embarrass her or, worse, to expose her to the media, no matter what he had said earlier that week when persuading her to stay.

'As far as I know Lady Beaumont is still in California. As for Lola, I haven't heard from her for many years. So, how does the Dower House compare with other holiday cottages you've seen? Any suggestions on how we can improve things?'

'Ah, you'll have to wait for my review. I hear you're also reviving the famous Christmas Eve party?'

Finn nodded. 'It is a Blakeley tradition.'

'But do you think it's wise? After all, the last party ended with the drowning of Lord Beaumont's mistress and that started it all…' She raised her eyebrows in query.

Finn was very careful not to look at Alex as he answered, focusing all his charm on the journalist. 'This is a new era at Blakeley and the party will reflect that. We are planning more of a community affair, including carols sung by the local primary school choir and a village nativity. Have you had a chance to look around the castle yet? Nearly all of it is publicly accessible now, from the servants' quarters to the room where Elizabeth I is reputed to have had a secret liaison, and it's all exactly as it has been for the last four hundred-odd years.'

Isma stepped forward, her phone in her hand, no doubt ready to record, her expression avid. 'Of course Blakeley is famous for its liaisons. When you lived here before did people know about what went on at the parties the Beaumonts held? The wife-swapping, the orgies, the drugs? The mountain of debt their lifestyle was built on? I mean, you were right here. You must have seen things? Heard things? What about Lola? You were around the same age. Did she ever pull a Lady Chatterley with the staff?'

Finn tensed. *Great.* The travel reporter was hot on the scent and Finn couldn't blame her. The drowning of a pop star's model wife at one of the most famous events in the social calendar had been the scandal of the year ten years ago.

The Blakely Christmas Eve party had always been filled with an eclectic mix of aristocracy, minor royalty, actors and musicians, a mecca for the rich, beautiful and cool. When it had been revealed that the dead woman was Lord Beaumont's lover—and that his own wife had been having an affair with the much younger pop star—the scandal had blown sky-high. Stories of years of excess had circulated, and at some point Lord Beaumont's debts had surfaced. Facing ruin, he had shot himself, and his wife had fled to LA with her lover, leaving her daughter alone to deal with the debts, with the press, with the scandal.

At that point Lola might have turned things round. She had been young, beautiful, and making a name for herself as a model, an It Girl. If she'd wanted to she could have ridden out the storm and kept her influential friends, her endorsements and her contracts. But then the photos had surfaced. Photos of her at that very same Christmas Eve party on her eighteenth birthday. Photos not meant for the public to see.

Photos for Finn's eyes only.

It was strange how she had been able to pose in a barely-there bikini, her almost nude body up on a billboard, and nobody had blinked. That was *fashion*. But private photos, in which she exposed more or less the same amount of skin, were salacious just because of their private nature.

And they'd been everywhere. Front pages, comedy panel shows, opinion pieces. The sins of her parents had been put squarely on her shoulders. She had become a symbol of everything that was wrong in a world that at the time had been facing a recession. The Beaumonts' excessive consumption had been held up as an example of a world that needed fixing.

Still she might have stayed and fought. If it hadn't been for the fact that only one person had had access to those photos.

Finn.

He glanced across at Alex, standing by the journalist's side, her face absolutely impervious, as if none of the things the journalist had said affected her at all. As if she really was someone completely different not just in name but in every way. Someone so closed down there was no knowing what, if anything, she was thinking. It was as if she was sleepwalking through life.

'I'm sorry, I didn't really take much notice of anything that happened in the castle. Too busy focusing on my future.'

His smile was tight as Alex turned to the journalist, as ever the consummate professional. Did none of this affect her at all? But then she hadn't asked to be put into this position. He had put her there. How could he judge her for the way she handled it?

'Isma, can I introduce you to Desiree?' Alex was saying. 'She's got over two hundred and fifty thousand Instagram followers and is thinking about writing a book about her love of travel. I said that you were absolutely the person to speak to. Your book about your year travelling solo was my favourite read last year… it was so inspirational. Thank you, Finn.'

And with a polite but firm smile Alex steered Isma away.

Finn took a glass of Prosecco from the table next to him and drank it down in one long gulp, closing his eyes briefly. He hadn't had a chance to talk to Alex about the photos, to make the explanation he should have forced her to listen to back then. At the time he'd been so angry and hurt that she'd believed him capable of such betrayal he hadn't been able to see how devastated she was, unable to see the wood for the trees as her world collapsed around her. Everyone and everything she had known was a lie. No wonder she'd thought him a lie as well.

It was too late to repair the damage. But it wasn't too late to tell her the truth.

Finn watched Alex as she introduced Isma to a striking young woman dressed in an eye-catching jumpsuit. The two women immediately fell into animated conversation and Alex stepped back, her clear gaze sweeping the room, making sure everyone was having a good time, talking to the right people, looking for anything that might need to be explained or contained.

Her disguise was completely effective. No one spared her a second glance.

It wasn't the glasses. They couldn't hide her long lashes or her large grey eyes with their provocative tilt, as if she was smiling at a joke only she could see. The severe bun couldn't disguise the glossiness of her hair, and her tall, lean curves weren't diminished by the unflattering cut and colour of her suit.

No, her beauty was as stunning as it had ever been, and no amount of stereotyped frumpy clothes could change that. It was inside. She was switched off. There was no vibrancy lighting her, no animation, and that was why she could slip through the crowds unseen.

But Finn saw her. He always had.

Alex inhaled as she looked around. Everything was in order. The ballroom was festively decorated, with fairy lights strung around the panelling, and a large Christmas tree dominated the far corner, tastefully blazing with white and silver lights, wrapped presents clustered at the bottom. So the presents were empty boxes? It didn't matter. This evening, like all this kind of occasion, was an illusion. The journalists, influencers and assembled celebrities were there to be charmed and to spread the word: Blakeley Castle was open once again.

Of course conversation turned again and again to the last owners. Who were Elizabeth I or Charles II or Beau Brummel compared to the disgraced Viscount and his family? But no one gossiping about the events of ten years ago really thought about the cost—about the two people who had died, about the families torn apart. The Blakeley scandal was like something out of a novel, not real life.

Only she knew all too well just how real it had been. No one else could ever know or understand what it had been like in the centre of that hurricane, with her life whirling more and more out of control, everyone wanting a piece of her.

Alex shivered, aware that she was being watched, Looking up, she saw Finn's dark gaze fixed unwaveringly on her. As if he saw *her*, not the woman she had worked so hard to be but the girl she had left behind her. That needy creature who had thought beauty and praise worth having, who hadn't understood how fleeting and insubstantial they were.

How dared he look at her that way? He had lost the right to see her the day he had betrayed her. What game was he playing anyway? How had he tracked her down? And how could she trust him not to betray her again?

The room was too hot, too busy. She needed to regroup. Slipping out of a side door, she let her feet lead her unerringly through the maze of corridors, up the stairs, until she reached the long picture gallery, still hung with portraits of her ancestors.

Alex stood in the cool, dim light and looked around.

Thank goodness that oligarch had bought the castle complete with all its contents—she would have hated for the pictures to have been sold off and separated, to hang in museums and private collections, even though the money raised would have been enough to pay off her father's debts and give her a nest egg to rebuild her life.

The gallery had been included in the tour of the house laid on for the party guests, and she had stood here in this room several times already today, but she hadn't allowed herself to look up, to be distracted, to remember how she'd used to come here and chat to her favourite pictures. Now, alone, she walked slowly from picture to picture. There was the Gainsborough, the Reynolds, the Holbein... Every ancestor had the same smile, the same sleepy cat eyes she herself had inherited, the same pointed chin.

'Hi,' she whispered softly to the spaniel hiding in one lady's skirts. 'Sorry I haven't been to visit for a while. Hello, handsome.' She reached a hand up to a grey horse, not quite touching it. As a child these painted animals had been her confidants and playmates. These animals—and Finn.

She wandered slowly up the long panelled gallery, reuniting with old friends, stopping to say hello to her favourites until she reached the end, where she stilled, barely breathing, her heart squeezing in on itself until her whole chest ached.

The huge painting of a nude with long red hair and a slanting smile dominated the room. Some had called her the most beautiful woman in the world. She could have married royalty or wealth, a Hollywood star or a business king, but she had chosen a boy with a minor

title and a castle, and she had reigned over that castle
with whimsical tyranny.

Alex stared up at the painting, at the creamy skin, the
curve of perfect pert breasts, the come-hither glance in
green, green eyes. 'Hi, Mum,' she said.

The portrait stared impassively back. No different
from its sitter. Alex could count on one hand the conversations she had had with her mother since that last
tragic Christmas Eve.

After breaking up with her pop star lover, the former
Lady Beaumont had married an actor some years her
senior. They now lived on a ranch with their two children, where her mother ran an online health and well-
being empire. A disgraced daughter who was a living
reminder of a past much better left behind didn't fit with
the brand she'd so painstakingly built up.

Occasionally, very occasionally, Alex would scroll
through her social media feed, full of nutritious home-
made food and yoga poses, outdoor living and glowing,
laughing children, and search for clues. Were her un-
known half-siblings really happy, or did they too spend
their lives waiting for a nod or a smile, desperately trying to please their capricious beautiful mother? Trying
to be the perfect child and always, always falling short?

She didn't really want an answer. She would hate for
them to be raised the way she had been, but on the other
hand, if her mother genuinely loved her new family, did
that mean there was something wrong with Alex? That
she was fundamentally unlovable?

History tended to bear that assumption out.

Swallowing, she turned her back on her mother,
smothering a gasp as she saw two white figures at the
far end of the gallery. 'Saffron! Scarlett, you startled

me,' she said, half laughing with nerves. 'Aren't you supposed to be in bed? You must be freezing,' she added as she took in their bare feet and thin white pyjamas.

'Not as cold as that lady.' Scarlett giggled as she pointed at the portrait of Alex's mother.

'True. At least you're wearing *some* clothes.' Alex managed to keep a straight face.

'Who is she? Is she a princess? And why isn't she wearing any clothes?'

'Not a princess, but she used to be married to someone who lived here. It's considered artistic to paint people without clothes, for some reason, and she was a very famous beauty.'

'I think she looks mean,' Saffron said suddenly. 'Like a wicked witch or a bad godmother who casts an evil spell.'

Alex swivelled to look back at the portrait, at the sensuous look in the famously hooded eyes, the knowing expression. 'Yes,' she said slowly. 'I suppose she does.'

'Alex, Alex, come and look at your picture!'

Before Alex could make her excuses and head back to the ballroom, Scarlett had run up to slip one small, cold hand in hers and begun to tug her towards the small antechamber where the castle's prized collection of Pre-Raphaelite paintings hung.

'Quickly,' she agreed. 'But then straight back to bed. It's far too cold—and late—for you two to be running around the castle.'

Hypocrite, she told herself. As if *she* hadn't spent many nights roaming the castle when other children her age had been fast asleep. But she would have loved someone to scoop her up and order her back to bed. Freedom palled when it was mixed with indifference.

'Will you read us a story?' Scarlett asked.

Alex looked down at the small heart-shaped face and the pleading expression in her dark eyes. She didn't know any children, and rarely needed to interact with them. Amber loved nothing more than organising a child's party or entertaining their younger clients, but Alex never knew what to say to them...how to be.

'I really need to get back and do my job,' she said.

'Don't be silly, Scarlett. Alex is far too busy to bother with us.'

There was a resigned loneliness in Saffron's sneer, one Alex recognised all too well.

'Let me check for messages,' she said. 'If no one has tried to contact me then one story. Okay?'

For once her phone showed no urgent messages or red-flagged emails.

'One short story,' she warned them. 'Before I'm missed.'

'Picture first,' Scarlett said.

Alex allowed herself to be towed into the dimly lit room where the Beaumont collection of Pre-Raphaelite paintings was displayed. She couldn't help but gasp in recognition as she looked at the jewel-like colours on the six perfectly displayed paintings. They weren't the best known, or the most critically well regarded, but it didn't matter because they were all set here at Blakeley.

The nymph in the lake eying up a young Narcissus was standing in Blakeley water. The goddess hiding from Actaeon's gaze stood in the woods Alex had walked through today on her way to the office. And the sleeping maiden, her hair falling to the floor, her nightgown dipping below one perfect white breast, a rose in her hand, slumbered in Alex's old bedchamber, on the Victorian bedstead where she had once slept.

'See, she looks like you,' Scarlett said triumphantly.

Saffron nodded. 'She does. If you weren't wearing glasses and if you grew your hair really long.'

'And I wore a see-through nightie and forgot to do it up properly? Sorry, girls. I'm a more of a scrunched-up ponytail and yoga pants kind of nightwear person.'

To her surprise both girls laughed at her weak attempt at humour, and the bell-like sound echoed off the panelled walls, warming the frigid air.

'Come on,' she said, taking Scarlett's hand and touching Saffron's shoulder. 'If you want me to read a story before I have to go back to the party—and before you both turn into blocks of ice—then we need to get you back to bed.'

But before she went she allowed herself one last lingering glance at the slumbering girl. At the stained glass in the window behind her and the way the light played across her supine figure. At the little dog curled up at his mistress's side. At the anticipation on the sleeper's face, the way her lips were parted ready. At the shadow at the window, the glimpse of thorns and the determined man ready to slash through them.

Some people thought the story insipid—a heroine who merely fell asleep and waited to be rescued—but Alex had always thought it the ultimate romance that no matter how lost you were, someone would find you. That you could be hidden behind one hundred years' worth of trees and thorns and someone would still see you, know you and fight for you.

She no longer felt like that. Now she knew better. Now she knew the only person to fight for you was you. And that sometimes the only way to do that, the only way to save yourself, was to retreat and keep all the things that could hurt you at bay. No hope, no love, no dreams.

But for one moment, as she walked through corridors she knew better than she knew her heart, listening to the chatter of two over-excited girls, she allowed herself to wish, just briefly, that she still believed in fairy-tales.

CHAPTER SIX

'ALEX!'

Alex turned at the sound of the high-pitched voice and saw a small child speeding towards her. It had turned even colder over the last few days and the trees glistened with morning frost, the grass crunchy white underfoot.

'Good morning, Scarlett.' She caught the small girl before she barrelled into her, suppressing a smile at the layers of clothing, the thick padded jacket, hat and gloves and the bright orange wellies on her small feet. 'Living the Hawk brand, I see.'

'Of course.'

Finn caught up with them and her breath caught in her throat. It was most unfair that he had turned out even more attractive than the boy she had loved, especially with his chin coated with overnight stubble, his hair tousled and his expression relaxed.

'Thanks for the other night,' he added. 'The press party seemed to go very well.'

'I'm never satisfied until I see all the reviews but I'm cautiously optimistic,' Alex agreed. 'Thank goodness the weather held for the afternoon. I'm not sure treetop treks and biking woodland trails would have been so much fun in the rain. It's just a shame the nature walk looks so bare at this time of year, but the interpretation was really good, so they got the gist of what you want to achieve.'

'The tweaks you made really enhanced the whole experience, especially housing some of the journalists here—even the ones in the Bunkhouse seemed to have fun, judging from the comments I heard at breakfast yesterday. Thank you.'

'Just doing my job.'

'It wasn't your job to return these two scamps to their bed, though.' Finn glared mock sternly at his nieces, and they shrieked and rushed along the path ahead. 'Thank you for keeping them out of trouble. That was above and beyond.'

'It was no problem. They're nice girls.' She paused, not wanting to prolong the conversation or bring up any more shared memories, but her curiosity overran her good sense. 'They must miss their mum. Where is Nicky? She was pregnant when I...'

Dammit, this was where curiosity took her. Right back to that night. And there were so many reasons not to go back to that night. Self-preservation for one.

Self-preservation took many routes. It meant not thinking about watching her father stagger out of the lake with a lifeless body in his arms. It meant not remembering the media storm, the reporters at every gate. It meant not reliving her rigid fear, sitting in the back of a police car as she was taken in for questioning, camera flashes blinding her.

And self-preservation meant not thinking about the photos or the moment she saw them all over the front pages. It meant remembering that this man couldn't be trusted, no matter how warm his gaze as it fell on his nieces, how attractive his crinkled smile.

A smile that was currently playing around his mouth as he watched Scarlett gravely hopscotching along the path leading through the woodland.

'Nicky finally signed over custody to me this summer.' As he spoke the smile disappeared and Finn's jaw set firm, his mouth a grim line, his eyes unreadable.

'Custody? You mean she isn't around at all?'

'She's flitted in and out of their lives for years. Every time she swears she's made a change. So I set her up in a house, make sure there's enough money for the girls, and then she meets another loser. Next thing I know he's moved in or she's moved out, and six months later the girls are returned to me for another "holiday" while she sorts herself out. It might be two weeks, it might be a month, or longer. I've had enough of enabling her. They need stability. Especially Saffy.'

'Yes. I see. She does seem fragile.'

They walked a little further in silence before Finn spoke again, his words tense and clipped. 'I should have done something sooner, said something sooner, but I didn't want to alienate Nicky. They were her daughters… what if she banned me from seeing them? And, despite everything, I wanted to believe that her heart was in the right place. She protected me, you know, from the worst of my dad's drinking. Even when she did something wrong her motives were good. I had to keep giving her the benefit of the doubt. But then Saffy…' He stopped and rubbed his hand against his jaw.

'Then Saffy what?'

Finn sighed, and she could see the indecision in his eyes as he weighed up whether or not to answer.

'She reminded me of you,' he said at last.

Alex's breath caught at his words, chills numbing her every nerve.

'That look you had when your parents would go away and you'd be waiting for them to come back, or when your mum barely knew you were there. That hopeful look. It used to break my heart then, but seeing it replicated on Saffy...' He shook his head, lost in some memory. 'I was no longer a boy. I have money, and a home, and I can give her the stability she needs. I thought Nicky would fight me for them, and I was prepared to involve the courts if I had to. Even though I know she loves them. But she just gave in.'

'Maybe she gave in *because* she loves them. Because she knows it's for the best.'

But Alex's heart was hammering so loudly she could hardly hear herself speak. She'd always thought she'd hidden her fear of rejection from everyone, including Finn. She'd worked so hard to be the smiling, impetuous, devil-may-care child her parents had wanted. Never cried, never sulked, never followed the rules. Charming, wild and beautiful. A Beaumont through and through.

Beaumonts didn't need or ask for approval and they felt stifled by rules and stability. Alex had done her very best to feel stifled too. But if Finn had seen it was all a pretence had others seen it too? Her parents?

'Maybe,' said Finn. 'I'd already bought Blakeley and I started to invest in turning it into the kind of outdoor centre I wanted it to be, decided to stop travelling so much. Moving my life here properly made perfect sense. The girls can go to the local schools. Stop chopping and changing, stay in one place.'

'And Nicky doesn't see them at all?'

'She's in India right now, but she can see them whenever she wants for as long as she wants when she's in the UK. So long as it's here. She has a bedroom here that's hers alone—not that she's even seen it. But the girls stay with me until they are out of formal education. That's the agreement.'

'Wow. That's a big commitment.'

'I didn't have a choice. I couldn't let them down. I've done enough of that. Letting people I care about down.'

His words hung in the air until Alex could hardly breathe. Did he mean his father, belligerent and difficult, refusing all offers of help? Or his sister, searching for an elusive happiness even her children couldn't provide? Or was he talking about back then? When he'd promised to be her knight but ended up her betrayer?

'No, you had a choice and you chose them. Even with money and a home that's an unselfish choice to make. Being a single parent is hard even when children have always known love and stability.'

'Which is why they come first. Their happiness is paramount.'

'Of course.'

Despite everything that hung between them, all that lay unsaid, all the secrets and lies and betrayals, she couldn't help but admire Finn for his dedication—and she allowed herself one tiny wish: that someone had put her first when she'd still needed somebody to care.

Once again Finn found Alex almost impossible to read. She had been curious about the girls, understandably, and she had sounded sympathetic whilst asking questions, but there was still an otherworldly air around her, as if she were miles away from here, in a different existence entirely.

That was probably what made her so good at her job. That sense she was somehow remote, untouched, that nothing really affected her. He'd seen her at work during the press party. Always watching, introducing, stepping in with a cool smile and a light but steely touch, making sure every message stayed on brand, that the assembled journalists experienced what she wanted them to experience. So unlike the girl he'd known, who had felt everything so very deeply a harsh word could cut her.

But only he had known that. She had been so adept at hiding her true nature. Did she still hide now? It was impossible to tell. But for a moment he badly wanted to find out.

'Uncle Finn, can Alex help us choose our tree?'

Scarlett appeared at his side, her cheeks the same colour as her name, her hair once again a tangled mess.

He passed a rueful hand over the curls. 'I need an uncle school to teach me how to do plaits,' he said.

'I told you. Emily's dad watched online videos and he can wind ribbons through her hair. You just have to try harder,' Scarlett told him.

He tugged one messy plait. 'Message understood.'

'So can she?' She turned eagerly to Alex. 'We get to choose our very own tree from our very own woods and then we take it back and decorate it. And Uncle Finn has all these amazing Christmas tree ornaments; he collects them everywhere he goes.'

Alex stilled, her cheeks paling. 'I used to collect Christmas tree ornaments,' she said softly.

'Do you still have them?'

'No. Not any more. I had to leave them behind when I left home. And some I gave away.'

Finn curled his hand into a loose fist as she steadfastly avoided looking at him, but he knew they were thinking of the same time. Of her first modelling job in New York, when she was barely fifteen and barely chaperoned by her mother. She'd brought him back an ornament from a world-famous department store: a perfect glass apple. Far too delicate for his Christmas tree, and far too beautiful for a seventeen-year-old boy whose focus had been on school and getting out. But he had thanked her, and from then on, on every trip to every place, she had brought home two Christmas tree ornaments: one for him and one for her to keep.

He still had every one.

'So, can she?' Scarlett asked.

Finn searched for an excuse, a reason to let Alex off the hook, but before he could speak Saffy mooched up to them, her thin shoulders hunched under her anorak.

'Are we going to choose this tree or not?'

'I was just explaining to Alex what we are doing,' Scarlett said with extraordinary dignity. 'And inviting her along to be one of the party.'

Finn looked at Alex, startled into a shout of laughter, and saw answering laughter soften her grey eyes, her mouth grow full and sweet with the natural curve of her smile. His breath caught in his throat. She had been a beautiful girl, but she had grown into a glorious woman. When she allowed herself to be natural. When her smile had meaning.

His pulse began to thud as he stared, unable to look away, drinking in the sight. He didn't care what she called herself, this was the only woman who had ever made his blood thrill; the only woman to make his heart thump so loud he was convinced it could be heard back at the castle; the only woman his hands ached to touch so badly the pain was physical. He knew how she tasted. Sweet and fresh and lush, like nectar. How she felt. Warm silk and soft velvet. And she knew him as well. For all she denied it.

'Uncle Finn!' Scarlett's insistent voice brought him out of his reverie and he stared at her and blinked. 'Ask Alex to join us.'

And Finn realised that he wanted nothing more. Not just because of that shared conspiratorial moment of amusement, or because of the sudden visceral memories that had blindsided him, but because he suspected that Alexandra Davenport was even lonelier than Lola Beaumont had been.

'Of course,' he said easily, taking Saffron's hand. 'If you have nothing better to do.'

'I...'

'You might as well,' Saffy said, staring down at the ground, and Finn saw Alex's expression soften with recognition.

'Only if you're sure I'm not intruding.'

'Yay!' Scarlett started dancing around, hair flying. 'Come on, Alex. After we choose the tree we're going to decorate it and have hot chocolate with cream and it's going to be the best day ever.'

She flew off down the path, tugging a startled-looking Alex with her, and Finn followed on more sedately, still holding Saffron's mittened hand.

'Do you mind, Saffy?' he said gently. 'I know today is meant to be a family day...'

A life filled with 'uncles' and 'new daddies' had left

Saffron wary of outsiders, especially ones who tried to step into her inner circle. But to his surprise Saffy shook her head.

'Alex is nice. She's really good at reading stories too. She did all the voices. Even though it was a babyish story of Scarlett's she made it seem really funny.'

'That's good. As long as you're okay, Saffy.'

His niece rolled her eyes in the pre-teen way she had perfected recently. 'I'm fine. Come on, Uncle Finn, bet I can beat you.'

And she was off, too-long skinny legs pumping furiously as she sped down the path, ponytail flying out behind her.

With a mock roar of rage Finn took off after her, but underneath a beat of anxiety pounded insistently. The girls had been hurt enough. It was good that they liked Alex, but she would be leaving at Christmas. He had to make sure they didn't get too attached.

And it wasn't just them he needed to watch. Having Alex back at Blakeley felt too right, too easy, especially when he saw glimpses of the girl he'd used to know. But they were both different people now, with very different lives, and far too old to believe in happy-ever-afters.

It was surprisingly easy to find and agree on the right tree, and before an hour had passed they were all back in the castle for the promised hot chocolate, the tree cut and delivered by one of the estate hands.

Alex paused as they left the kitchen, uncertainty on her face as the girls rushed into the sitting room. 'Are you sure it's okay for me to be here?'

'More than sure. I need someone to help carry these mugs.' Finn nodded at the large mugs filled with hot chocolate he'd just made, topped with cream and sprinkles, and slipped a packet of shortbread into his pocket before picking up two of them.

'Biscuits not served on plates? Mrs Atkinson would be horrified,' Alex said. 'Shop bought as well.'

'If you want to make some from scratch you're very welcome to try.'

Finn grinned as she shook her head.

'Amber's the baker in our house. She bakes to relax, which means there is always fresh bread and cakes and biscuits all over the kitchen. I'm dreading Emilia and Harriet moving out, leaving me to face temptation all alone.'

'Send her to me. Feeding two growing girls is exhausting. I feel like a mother bird, constantly pushing worms into open mouths.'

'What a lovely analogy.'

She picked up the remaining two mugs and slipped through the door he held open with his foot and into the sitting room, pausing uncertainly as she reached the threshold of what he knew was a room once familiar to her.

In her day this had been the family room, a space used only by Alex, Finn and Mrs Atkinson. Her parents had rarely set foot in the domestic quarters. They had used the entire castle with careless entitlement, sitting on sixteenth-century chairs and sleeping in beds older than entire family trees. They had thought nothing of dancing on priceless carpets or leaving glasses on Chippendale tables.

But the rooms and their contents had all been painstakingly cleaned and restored, and now the whole castle was open to the public. All except the west wing, which he'd turned into a spacious, comfortable home.

'This looks amazing.' Alex halted as she stepped into the sitting room. 'I can't believe the difference. Look how beautiful the floor is!'

Finn had opened the room up into the old dining room beyond to create a large, welcoming space, with grouped sofas and chairs, a huge fireplace, and filled bookshelves in every alcove. Cushion-covered window seats ran the length of the room, and the pale grey of the walls showcased the bright, modern paintings he'd chosen.

All the furniture in their living space had been bought especially, and every room was newly painted, every floor stripped and polished. He'd wanted a blank canvas, a new start, with no hint of the old aristocratic family imposing on his.

The only part of the west wing that hadn't been renovated was the long picture gallery which ran the entire second floor of the wing. That he *hadn't* opened up to public view, despite the fame of some of the portraits.

He hadn't allowed himself to wonder why. But seeing Alex here, back in her home, he knew why. He hadn't wanted to rake up the old scandal again with every visitor. He hadn't wanted them to look at the cat-shaped eyes and pointed chins of her ancestors and remember her, gossip about her. Without knowing it he'd protected her, as he had failed to do so long ago.

He set the mugs on a small table and looked over at the huge tree set in a corner of the room. 'Okay,' he said, trying to push the past back where it belonged. 'Who wants to decorate the tree?'

'Me! Me!'

The girls nearly upset their hot chocolate in their bid to get to the box of ornaments first.

'Thank goodness John put the lights on when he brought the tree in,' said Alex, her eyes narrowed in amusement as she watched the girls delve into the large box Finn had brought down from the box room earlier. 'They might have combusted if they'd had to wait any longer.'

She wrapped her hands around the large mug, lowering her nose to the fragrant chocolate and inhaling deeply.

'Thank you, Finn.'

'For what? The hot chocolate? I was making it anyway.'

But she didn't respond to his teasing smile. 'For not telling anyone who I am.'

'Alex…' Her name felt natural now. It suited this new incarnation. It was a name as anonymous as she seemed to be, yet with so many different layers and interpretations. 'It is completely within my interests to keep your secret. I want people to talk about Blakeley—of course I do. But I want them to talk about the local produce in the farm shop and the scones in the café, the treetop trail and the treasure hunt in the house, not to be sidetracked by old gossip. I'd much prefer that no one has the faintest idea who you are.'

'Then why hire me? And how did you even track me down?'

Finn inhaled, the scent of chocolate mixing with the pine tree and permeating the room. So, they were going to have this conversation. Well, maybe it was time. Maybe it was time he finally told her the truth. Maybe it was time to set the past free.

'Finn? I think I deserve some answers.'

'Yes,' he agreed. 'You do.'

CHAPTER SEVEN

'How DID YOU find me?' Alex repeated. She fixed her gaze on him firmly and waited.

Finn slanted a look towards Saffron and Scarlett, but they were intent on the tree, deliberating over where a Christmas angel Alex recognised as one she'd picked up in Prague should go. She'd never expected that he would still have the ornaments she'd bought him. Never expected to see them hung on a tree in Blakeley Castle. It shook all that she'd thought she knew. About him, about them.

She swallowed and waited some more. He set his hot chocolate down on a side table and leaned against the sofa arm, looking out of the window at the white mist swirling along the frost-covered lawn.

'Returning to Blakeley brought back old memories,' he said abruptly. 'But I had my own personal reasons to return. Reasons that have nothing to do with you. My ancestors are as much a part of this castle as yours, even if no one really cares about the people who spent their lives in the kitchens and the gardens, no matter how many generations they dedicated to serving the castle.'

'I care. And I don't dispute your claim on Blakeley.

If I can't be here to look after the castle, then there's no one I'd rather it should be than you.'

'Really?'

His eyebrows rose in disbelief, but she nodded, re-inforcing her statement.

'Finn, how can anyone *own* history? We're only ever custodians of a place like Blakeley. Now the castle has a custodian who loves her and knows her, respects her. That's a wonderful thing.'

She meant every word, but her chest ached with loss and regret as she spoke. She hoped he didn't sense her wistfulness, saw only her sincerity.

'Thank you. That means a lot.'

'So?' she prompted. 'You're back here and you need a temporary PR person and what? It's a huge coincidence that you chose me.'

'No. Not a coincidence. I've known where you are for six months.'

She froze. 'That long? How? Why? Were you looking for me?'

Damn it, was that hope she was feeling? Hope that he had been searching for her? That she hadn't been lost after all?

'Not straight away.' He stopped abruptly, jaw tightening. 'I should have,' he said, his voice resonant with regret. 'I should have come straight after you at the time…shouldn't have allowed you to walk away without an explanation. But for the first few days afterwards I was too hurt, too angry to speak to you. You were so sure I was guilty. After all we had been to each other, after all we'd said, you thought I'd sell photos of you to the press. *Those* photos.'

The utter disbelief in his expression floored her. Hurt

and anger were still evident in that disbelief. Had she got it so wrong? But who else could it have been? She'd sent the photos to him, not to anyone else…

'I'd have given anything for it not to be you. The papers were full of people who I'd trusted, who I'd thought cared about me, spilling every last sordid detail about my family. You needed money. You said so yourself. To help Nicky, to get to university…'

'And so I sold you for thirty pieces of silver? Did you really believe that? Do you still?'

'I…'

Of course she had. It had been the last revelation. The one that had tipped her from holding on to falling, falling into a dark, dark place. But now? Seeing all he had achieved, and more importantly what he was doing with that success—opening up the estate, working with inner city schools, raising his nieces… These were the actions of a decent man, not a man who would betray someone who'd loved him.

And, truthfully, nothing he had done back then had shown him to be capable of such an act. He'd been her one constant after all.

'Finn…' But she couldn't speak, and the silence thickened, broken only by the chatter of the girls, their words washing over Alex.

'I waited too long,' he said after a while. 'I waited for you to come back and apologise. And by the time I could see more clearly, by the time I understood, you had disappeared.'

'What did you understand?' she whispered; throat thick with fear. She wasn't sure she could cope with his answer.

'I understood that you needed to blame someone for

the way things fell apart. How could you blame your dad when he was no longer around to blame? And you always made every excuse for your mother. You had to blame me. I had to be the scapegoat. I knew that it was up to me, that I had to go to you. But, even though it had been just a few days since I'd seen you last, I couldn't find you anywhere. Not in any of the usual places, not with any of the usual people. In the end I told myself that you would show up eventually. I hoped to see you back in the gossip columns and on billboards within months, riding out the scandal. But months went by and you didn't appear in any headlines or adverts. It was as if you had been airbrushed out of existence and I knew I had lost you in every way possible. It didn't stop me hoping that one day you would turn up, that I would see you again, but finally I had to accept that you didn't want me to find you, that you didn't want anyone. I had to do my best to move on, to build my business and my life.'

Alex stood stock-still, her mind digesting every word he'd said, turning each phrase over and over and trying to make sense of it all. 'You *had* to have sold them,' she said. 'I only sent them to you. You needed money and you had them. There was no one else.'

He folded his arms and said nothing, but she saw his eyes flicker towards the still absorbed girls and clarity almost blinded her.

'It was Nicky.'

'Yes.'

'Nicky…'

Of course. She would have been able to access Finn's phone—goodness knew he'd always been mislaying it. She'd needed money and she'd always disliked Alex.

How had she not realised at the time? Maybe Finn was right. She had had to blame someone and he'd been right there, her one constant. She'd lashed out and driven him away just when she needed him most.

All this time she'd thought he had betrayed her, but *she* had betrayed him. The ache in her chest intensified, constricting her and making it hard to breathe. 'Finn, I—'

But he held up a hand to cut her off. 'Don't. Like I said, you needed a scapegoat. I was there. It's fine. It was long ago. I moved on and moved out, after realising my presence here wasn't going to save my father or change Nicky. I needed to start working for the future I'd always promised myself. To concentrate on university and a life of my own.'

'You've achieved that, all right.' Alex looked around at the original pieces of art on the walls, at the two happy girls, giggling over a bauble. 'Achieved so much. You should be so proud.'

'But I never stopped thinking about you. I've always known I could have done more, should have done more when you needed me. I hoped you were with your mother in the States, happy and fulfilled, but I always knew that was a long shot.' He sighed. 'I just wanted closure, I suppose. This last year, worrying about Saffy, buying the castle, just made me realise I hadn't really moved on, that maybe I never completely would.'

'Did you hire a detective?'

Alex sat on the window seat, her back to the wall, needing as much physical support as she could get. Because if Finn could track her down, then who else could? With the renewed interest in Blakeley it was surely a matter of time before another *Where is Lola?*

piece ran. What if a journalist really wanted answers? Look at Isma, just a couple of days ago, not even suspecting that the woman she wanted was standing right there.

'No. I considered it, several times, especially at the beginning. But back then I couldn't afford it, and later it didn't seem right…not when you had gone to such lengths to disappear. I tried to resign myself to living with the guilt, with never knowing, but I couldn't stop myself looking for you wherever I went, ridiculous as I knew that was. And then I was invited to a ball…'

'A ball?' She couldn't hide her surprise. It so wasn't the answer she'd been expecting.

Alex quickly ran through a mental list of all the charity balls she had helped organise over the last few months.

'A Midsummer Ball. The invite came from a guy I studied with briefly at the Sorbonne—a guy who just happens to be an archduke.'

Alex nodded slowly. All the pieces were coming together. 'Laurent?'

'Laurent,' he confirmed. 'At one point I was talking to him and he was so busy staring at a woman—your friend—he was barely focussing on what I was saying. When I looked over too, she was talking to a tall woman dressed in black. A woman I knew instantly. Although she had a different name, I knew that Alexandra Davenport and Lola Beaumont were the same person.'

'Why didn't you come and see me? Pick up the phone? Why make me come here after everything?'

'Because in just the brief glimpse I had of you it seemed that you had changed fundamentally, Alex. Not just your name, but you. It was as if the fire that used to fuel you had gone out. It got me wondering if I wasn't the only one who needed closure. I spent the next six months wondering what the right move would be—and of course I had the girls to settle into their new schools, the move of the business to manage, the opening up of the castle. Part of me wondered if you would hear about what was happening at Blakeley and contact me. Then Penelope was injured, and it just seemed the time was right. When I phoned that evening I thought I'd speak to you, so when Amber picked up it threw me somewhat. That was why I said I'd brief you when you got here. I wondered if you would simply refuse to come, but it didn't cross my mind that you had no idea I'd hired you.'

As he finished, he picked up their cups and headed back to the kitchen. Alex watched the door swing shut. She shivered. Sitting there in her old family room, with the past excavated, was almost more than she could bear—and yet for reasons she couldn't articulate to herself she was reluctant to leave, although she knew she should.

'Alex, we can't reach any higher.'

Saffron's voice drew her attention back to her surroundings and, shaking off her thoughts, Alex slid to her feet. It was Christmas and she was home again. It might be temporary, but Finn was right. She did need closure—and she also needed to remember the good times. Like the many evenings spent in this room with Mrs Atkinson and Finn. Preparing for Christmas with the scent of spice in the air as she and Finn decorated their own tree.

'Okay. But if I am going to help with a Christmas tree then you know what we need?'

Both girls stared at her wide-eyed and Alex brandished her phone. 'Christmas music, that's what.'

She searched through her library until she found the playlist Amber had shared with them all on the morning of the first of December. A playlist she had barely glanced at, let alone played. She hit the button.

As Mariah began to tell them what she wanted for Christmas, Alex stepped over to the tree and held out her hand for an ornament. 'This is your tree, girls, so you tell me where you want things to go. Okay?'

'Okay!' Scarlett handed her a delicate silver pinecone and stared solemnly at the tree. 'I want that to go there.'

She pointed at a spot near Alex's ear, and equally solemnly, with ceremonial care, Alex hooked the shining ornament onto the branch.

''You've done a great job so far.'

Alex stood back and surveyed her handiwork before scanning the opulently decorated tree, laden with delicate baubles and ornaments in every colour and style imaginable. A crystal reindeer hung next to a jolly carved wooden snowman, and a pottery Father Christmas beamed at a gold angel. It was as far from the stylised, professionally decorated tree in the ballroom as possible. It was perfect.

She held out her hand. 'You guys have quite the collection. Next.'

'They're all Uncle Finn's. He always brings us new ones, wherever he goes. Oh, my favourite!' Saffy said, clapping her hands together before reverentially picking up a small wooden box and opening it.

Nestled inside was a perfect red glass apple. Alex caught her breath. Finn still had it all these years later.

'Oh…' Scarlett's lip wobbled as she scanned the bottom of the box. 'Look, Saffy, we're almost done and there's still the whole top of the tree to do. We haven't got enough.'

Alex palmed the small red apple, feeling the cool glass against her skin and cringing for her fifteen-year-old self—of all the things to buy the seventeen-year-old boy you had a crush on. She'd almost died of embarrassment when she handed it over and saw the hastily hidden surprise on his face. She should have bought him a T-shirt or a Yankees hat—but, no, she'd bought him an ornament. Yet he still had it. And all the others she'd picked up over the next two years. Had them and had added to them.

'Don't worry, Scarlett, a place like Blakeley Castle has lots of hidden treasure. Wait here. I bet we can finish this tree off perfectly.'

Finn pushed the door open with his shoulder, balancing the tray carefully. Mrs Atkinson would approve; the crisps and nuts were in glass bowls. He set the tray down and picked up a glass of wine before realising that Alex was nowhere to be seen. Had she slipped away? Had he pushed too hard?

'Has Alex gone?' He made the question as light as possible, as if the answer barely concerned him. The last thing he wanted was for the girls to realise there was anything wrong. 'Is that music yours? I didn't know you two liked The Pogues.' It was great that they had such good taste, but he didn't think this song was entirely suitable.

'What's a Pogue?' Scarlett asked, wandering over to lean on his leg, one small hand straying towards the bowl of crisps.

Saffron looked up from the ornament she was examining. 'Alex has gone to look for treasure.'

'For treasure?'

'For the tree. We ran out of ornaments.'

'We did go for the biggest tree we could find. I suppose it was always a possibility.'

Finn suppressed a smile as he walked over to admire the tree. The bottom two-thirds was so full of decorations there was barely a patch of green to be found, but the top third was all bare branches, with just one silver cone and a solitary red apple. He reached one finger out and sent the apple spinning.

'Okay, who wants to excavate some treasure?'

Alex backed into the room, her arms full with a large, dusty cardboard box, and Finn hastily stepped over to her, relieving her of the box.

'Thanks. It's not heavy, but it is large.'

'Where did you find that?' Saffron asked.

Alex smiled. 'I followed the clues to the attic. Now, shall we see what's inside?'

Carefully the girls lifted the lid and peered inside.

'Ornaments!' Scarlett yelled. 'Look!'

But Saffron just looked at Alex, her forehead pinched suspiciously. 'How did you know where to find them?'

'I've been here before,' Alex said. 'A long time ago. It's okay, Saffron. Your Uncle Finn owns everything in the castle. You can use these. I think the former owner would be very happy to see them hung on a tree again.'

Saffron considered Alex's words for one long moment and then she nodded. A second later she was on her hands and knees beside Scarlett, unpacking the treasures and laying them out on the coffee table.

Thank you, Finn mouthed at Alex, unsure whether

he was thanking her for reassuring Saffron, getting the ornaments or just for being there.

'Look!' Scarlett held up a red glass apple. 'It's the twin of yours, Uncle Finn.'

'And so is this angel!'

'And this reindeer.'

'Don't forget I lived here before,' Finn said, his gaze not leaving Alex's.

He couldn't have looked away if he'd wanted to, and the air crackled as he watched her. Her hair had tumbled out of its usual smooth knot and her cheeks were flushed, her eyes soft.

Neither girl found his answer odd, although it didn't really make any sense, and continued to sort the ornaments.

'Here.' He handed Alex one of the glasses and she accepted it.

'Thank you. I can't believe it's got dark already. I used to like the lead-up to Christmas, the dark evenings, but now I'm just holding out for spring.'

'You don't like Christmas?' Scarlett stopped in the middle of unwrapping an ornament, her mouth a perfect O of surprise.

'It's not that I don't *like* it,' Alex reassured her. 'But my Christmases are very quiet.'

'You'll have to come to my school play,' Scarlett told her. 'We're doing it here on Christmas Eve and then singing carols—aren't we, Uncle Finn? I'm a lamb and Saffy is the narrator, which is a really big part. Bigger than Mary, whatever Polly Myers says.'

The last place Alex wanted to spend Christmas was Blakeley, but she forced a smile. 'I need to get back on

Christmas Eve. My friend is waiting for me, and we always spend Christmas together.'

'Invite your friend,' Saffy suggested.

'I'll see. We were thinking of going away for Christmas, so it depends on our flights. But thank you. The party sounds amazing and I bet you two will be excellent.'

'Going away for Christmas?' Scarlett looked up from the box. 'Won't your family be sad?'

'Okay,' Finn interjected. 'Stop cross-examining Alex. Come on, step to it. More tree decorating, less chat. Someone pass me a reindeer.'

Over the next ten minutes Finn finished the tree, after arbitrating a short but fierce quarrel about whether to use tinsel or garlands—a squabble resolved by Alex declaring that she liked both.

'Okay,' he said at last. 'I think we're done here. What do you guys think? No?' His nieces were adamantly shaking their heads. 'We're not finished? What have I forgotten? Can't be the apple…we have two this year. Can't be the tinsel… Scarlett took care of that. Definitely isn't the chocolate because I sorted that…'

'The star!' Scarlett burst out. 'We haven't done the star.'

'The what?'

'The *star*!' Both yelled at once and he covered his ears.

'I think Father Christmas could probably hear that all the way in the North Pole,' he said feelingly. 'Okay. You know the drill. Out!'

Finn sensed Alex watching him as he ushered the girls out of the room. She'd curled up on the sofa, glass of wine in hand. She was contributing little to the conversation, but seemed contented, more relaxed than he'd seen her all week. It was partly the casual weekend clothes—the red sweater dress matched with grey tights and boots, the chunky silver necklace round her neck—and partly the way her smile finally reached her eyes. Maybe it was also partly the way the girls had pulled her into their circle, disarming her defences.

And possibly…probably…the talk they'd had earlier had helped. It had certainly made her presence easier for him, the long overdue clearing of the air, the explaining of misconceptions. The only problem was that without that barrier between them he was remembering all the reasons he'd failed to stay away from her all those years before. Not just her beauty but her empathy, her warm wit. The way she had seemed instinctively to know him better than anyone else. And even now her perceptive glances warmed him through.

Finn had to face the truth: Alex was the only woman he'd ever loved. But that knowledge changed nothing, because in the end she'd walked away.

He needed to remember that. Needed to remember that the girls needed stability. They only had him. Alex had made her choice long ago, and that choice had been to believe the worst of him. Even if she was still interested, even if he wanted to rekindle what they'd had, he couldn't allow anyone with so little faith near his already damaged nieces. Particularly as they both seemed to have taken to her—even the usually wary Saffron.

'Pass me the star,' he said, and Alex uncurled herself, picking up the finely wrought glittering silver star and walking over to hand it to him.

'You're doing a Mrs Atkinson!' Her smile lit up her whole face. 'Oh, how I remember the utter deliciousness of the anticipation, waiting outside, desperate to peek, knowing when I came in the tree would be lit and the star on the top. I think of it every Christmas.'

'You should go and see her. She would love to see you.'

'And I would love to see her. I couldn't before, I didn't want to be anywhere near Blakeley, but maybe now it might be easier.' She pushed his shoulder impatiently. 'Go on, put the tree lights on! I'll switch the main lights off and let the girls back in before they combust.'

Finn obeyed, after making sure the star was straight. The tree lights sprang to life, flickering more brightly as Alex dimmed the overhead lights. She stood silhouetted by the door and Finn had a sudden vision of how his life might have been if she'd believed in him all those years ago...if she'd allowed him to support her through the fallout of her parents' fall from grace.

But that life had disappeared as surely as Lola. All that could ever be was a friendship of sorts. It was all he could risk for the sake of his girls.

CHAPTER EIGHT

ALEX HAD NO idea why people complained about Monday morning. She *liked* Mondays. Too often there was so little purpose to the weekend. She'd clean, run, do some dutiful yoga, maybe cook, occasionally see a film or see a play, but it was all just killing time until Monday, when she could fill her mind and her time with work, reminding herself that she had a purpose, that she was good at what she did. It helped that she worked in public relations and had a legitimate interest in checking her emails and social media channels throughout the weekend, never switching off her phone.

Her life might seem small to some, but it was the life she wanted, the life she'd chosen. Just as she'd chosen London, cacophonous and dirty and full of people. The city surrounded her, protected her. No one saw her there. She was hidden in plain sight, able to sleepwalk through her life untouching and untouched.

Which meant she'd better be careful not to spend too many more cosy evenings with Finn and his cute-as-a-button nieces. There had been moments on Saturday evening when his dark-eyed gaze had rested on her for just a second too long…moments when she'd been über-aware of his every movement…moments when she'd been fixated on the vee of his throat exposed by his shirt, his wrists, the nape of his neck, all those soft, vulnerable spots in such a hard, fit body. A body she'd once had the freedom to love and to explore. The only body she'd ever...

No. She wasn't going there. She couldn't. It didn't matter that Finn hadn't sold those photos—maybe deep down she had always known he wasn't capable of such cruelty. What did matter was that she'd made herself vulnerable and it had backfired spectacularly. She could never allow that to happen again.

With renewed energy, Alex returned her focus to her laptop and the social media plans she'd been reviewing, pausing only to scribble notes and thoughts, the coffee Kaitlin had brought her cooling at her elbow. When she finally looked up the weak winter morning sun had disappeared and the sky had turned an ominous yellowy grey, the clouds low and heavy. A snow sky if ever she had seen one.

The air shifted and Alex knew Finn had walked into the office. She didn't need to look and check if she was right. A sixth sense had shivered through her body, every nerve awake.

'Okay, everyone,' he said. He didn't need to raise his voice. It was clear and commanding it reached every corner of the room. 'The forecast is for snow, and lots of it, so the minibus is waiting outside for those of you who live in Reading and London. I suggest you take work home with you. It may be a couple of days before the roads are passable. I remember being snowed in for a week when I was a boy.'

Alex couldn't stop herself from looking up as he finished speaking, knowing the exact week he was referring to. He was looking directly at her, and their eyes held for what seemed like an eternity as they were caught in their own private world of memories.

It wasn't until someone claimed Finn's attention that she was recalled to her surroundings. Cheeks hot, she checked to make sure no one had noticed their momentary lapse, but everyone was too busy talking about the snow to have paid her any attention.

'Alex?'

Finn strolled over to her desk and she willed her cheeks to cool. 'Hi.'

'I'm aware that you won't have anything suitable for snow with you. I could send you back to London…'

Yes! That would be perfect, and give her exactly the breathing space she needed. So why wasn't she jumping up at his words and grabbing her laptop?

'But if you'd rather ride out the weather here then of course you may,' he continued. 'I can't see the snow lasting too long, and if you do want to stay then I can kit you out. Time you started living the brand.'

Oh, that smile! The way it lit his whole face, turning a slightly aloof handsomeness into something much warmer—and so much more dangerous.

'I'd better stay,' she said, only a little reluctantly. 'There's a lot to do and there's something I want to discuss with you. Work,' she added.

'Of course,' he said lightly. 'What else could it be?'

'Exactly.'

'Give me fifteen minutes to sort everything out and then I'll be right with you.'

'Fine.'

She didn't mean to be so curt, but there were so many things unsaid, so many things she was scared of saying. So many things best left in the past where they belonged.

Alex stayed at her desk as the rest of the staff gathered their belongings, most of them about to leave. She scrolled through various social media feeds, adding notes when something caught her eye, gradually falling back into the absorbed spell of the world she preferred. A world where noise dimmed and people faded and all she knew was her work.

After a few minutes she looked up, aware that the very atmosphere of the room had changed again. It was no surprise when she looked around to see that the office had emptied and there was just Finn, leaning against the wall, watching her.

'You look busy.'

'That's what you're paying me for.'

'So busy that you haven't even noticed the snow?'

He nodded towards the window and Alex turned and stared at the view. The grass had already been covered with a fine dusting of snow, but judging by the big, fat flakes floating down from the sky in ever-increasing spirals it wouldn't be long before the snow was ankle-deep.

'Time to get you some boots. Come on.'

Closing her laptop, Alex followed him down the back stairs. His stockroom was in the old tack room at the back of the stables. It was almost unrecognisable, the rough wood panelling sanded and painted, the tack pegs replaced with neat shelves, the dirt floor covered in grey tiles. Each shelf was filled with folded clothes, labelled by size and type.

'All employees have a generous clothes allowance,' Finn explained as he ushered her in. 'They need to believe in us, live our values and look the part. Hawk isn't just spin and fancy campaigns, it's a way of life. Here, try these.' He held out a pair of sturdy yet oddly elegant leather boots. 'They're lined, waterproofed, and the sole has been especially designed for icy conditions.'

He eyed her up and down in a way that was purely professional and yet still made her feel exposed. She resisted the urge to wrap her arms around herself.

'Okay, and try this, these, this and...let me see... this.'

'So when you say "live the brand", you mean be kitted out from head to toe?' She took the grey trousers and the white shirt, the berry-red fleecy jumper and black down jacket from him. 'I hate to break it to you but I'm a city girl. There's not much use for waterproof trousers in Chelsea.'

'You're back in the country today and you'll be glad to have those trousers by this evening. Try them. They might surprise you. Our Chiltern range combines cutting-edge technology and fabrics with design-led style. And even Chelsea girls need warm hands and feet.' He added socks, gloves and a hat to the pile. 'You know, there's something I've been meaning to ask you since last week...'

'Oh?'

Alex's heart began to hammer, with strong, painful thuds. There had been enough treading old ground at the weekend. She needed to concentrate on moving forward. Being back at Blakeley, spending all this time with Finn, was dangerous. It was reminding her of all she'd used to be, all she'd used to want. They had to get their relationship back on purely professional ground before it was too late.

'Is your agency really called the Happy Ever After Agency? That's its actual name?'

That was his burning question? Alex didn't know whether to laugh or sigh in relief. 'I know. It's unusual, whimsical in some ways, but that was our purpose. We wanted to stand out.'

'You've managed that.'

Alex shifted, balancing the pile of clothes more securely. 'It has a dual meaning. Obviously we want all our clients to have complete peace of mind, and to know that using us means there will always be a successful outcome. But at the same time it's a personal wish. Once none of us had the security we wanted; our futures felt unsure. The agency was our way of taking back control. It's our happy-ever-after.'

Alex looked up and saw such utter comprehension in Finn's eyes it almost undid her. It was as if she were naked in front of him.

She smiled awkwardly. 'Thanks for these, but I'd better get back to work. Let me know when you're ready to have that talk.'

But as she left the room, Finn fell into step beside her.

'There are four of you, aren't there? I did my research before employing you. Obviously the Armarian royal ball was a huge coup, but I needed to know that such a new agency was capable of handling my work. And I have to tell you, Alex, I was impressed. Not only do you have lots of glowing testimonials, but you've also managed to make one archduke very happy. And apparently there's another equally happy billionaire— Deangelo Santos? Not bad work for just eight months in existence.'

Alex couldn't see his expression, but the teasing note in his voice was enough to raise her defensive hackles. 'You're right, our testimonials *are* impressive. And that's because we work dammed hard to make them that way. As for the rest, the love lives of my business partners are really none of your business. What's important is that we offer exemplary service for everyone, whether they are an archduke or a local café wanting some social media advice.'

'As I said, glowing testimonials.' He paused, and when he spoke again there was a curious tension in his voice. 'So how did you end up in Chelsea? Did you stay in touch with your godmother? I often wondered if that was where you went. The two of you were pretty close, I remember. I did try her a few times, but she wouldn't speak to me. It makes sense if you were living there, I suppose.'

They'd reached the top of the stairs and Alex dropped the pile of clothes onto the nearest desk. 'What does it matter, Finn? It's history. None of it is relevant to why I'm here and the job I'm here to do.'

He didn't answer at first, running a hand through his dark hair, expression unreadable. When had he achieved that inscrutability? She'd always been able to read him before.

Shame engulfed her. She should have read him when he'd told her he hadn't sold those photos, should have seen his innocence in his eyes then.

'It matters because I let you down,' he said at last, his voice hoarse. 'You needed me and I let you down. That's why I need to know what happened to you back then. Why I need to know that you were safe and happy. That you fled to your godmother's and were looked after and loved. I need to know that, Alex. Because I failed you. That's why I wanted you back here at Blakeley. I needed to know that you're okay. And I don't think you are, are you?'

The silence was absolute. Just the two of them stood there in the large, cavernous space, his words echoing around them. Alex was still, staring at him, wonder and fear warring in her expression.

'You don't need to worry about me. Not then, and not now,' she said at last.

'That's nonsense. We were best friends. You gave me your virginity, Alex, and I gave you my heart. I loved you, and I think you loved me. And then your life fell apart and I just watched it happen.'

Her mouth quivered. 'You were twenty.'

'I was old enough to do more. Do something.' He should have held on to her, should have offered her refuge and the unconditional love she had needed. But he'd failed her, utterly and completely. 'I let you drive me away because you hurt my pride. What kind of man did that make me? *Does* it make me?'

At that, her eyes softened. 'You were always the proudest boy. You would never accept help with anything. I should have trusted you, Finn.'

She touched his cheek: a fleeting caress, burning through him.

'Never question what kind of man you are. Look at your girls, look at the village—I never knew it so prosperous. And look at this office, full of people willing to move their lives for you and your vision. You're a better man than I ever deserved.'

'Tell me what happened.' It was as much command as plea. 'Tell me where you've been.'

She regarded him for a long few seconds then sighed, a deep shuddering sigh that seemed to come from her soul. 'I don't talk about it, Finn. I try not to even think about it. It's buried deep inside. It has to be. It's the only way I can keep going. But you are right. You of all people deserve the truth. But not here. I need some air, need to breathe properly if I am going to do this.'

Finn glanced out at the still whirling snow, now ankle-deep on the ground, then nodded at the pile of clothes on the desk. 'In that case it's time you got branded up.'

It took Alex less than five minutes to change, and when she returned to the office she was outdoors-ready, the dark trousers showcasing long, lean legs, the berry-red top just visible under the half-zipped jacket. She'd already laced up her boots, and as she reached him she put on her hat before slipping her hands into the gloves.

'You should be on the front cover of our catalogue!' he said.

He was only half joking, but she shook her head.

'My modelling days are well and truly over. I never enjoyed it, but my mother loved it. Loved people saying I reminded them of her. It was something that bonded us. And I needed that.'

'Do you still see her?'

Her gaze fell, but not before he saw the dark shadows in her eyes. 'She prefers not to be reminded of that time.'

There wasn't anything anyone could say to that and Finn didn't try. 'Come on, let's try out those boots. They're a new model, not due for release until later next year.'

The cold hit them as soon as they stepped outside, fresh and icy, momentarily robbing Finn of his breath. By unspoken accord they walked away from the castle and away from the lake, to the parkland at the back of the castle. It was now officially open for business, with nature trails and hikes winding through, a tree-top walk newly installed, bike tracks freshly laid, but he was sure they'd have it to themselves. The weather was bound to deter all but the most hardened of adventurers, and the snow was swirling more quickly now, blocking visibility.

'You know, these jackets are designed for proper alpine conditions. I didn't think they could be tested so close to home.'

Finn turned to look at Alex as he spoke, blinking the snow out of his eyes. She was transformed, cheeks pink with cold, the snow coating her with white glitter, her smile wide and genuine.

'This is bracing!'

'That's one word for it. I was about to call in the huskies.'

It was easier to walk and talk now they were in the woods. The snow was slowed by the branches overhead, and the trees sheltered them from the worst of the wind. Alex looked so much more relaxed, arms swinging as she tramped through the snow, that Finn almost wanted to forget the purpose of the walk and just let her have this time. But he knew getting her to open up was hard, that this chance might never come again, and the curiosity and renewed regret which had hit him so hard in Armaria needed answers.

He had to move on. Once and for all.

'So,' he said, as lightly as he could. 'Tell me about

your transformation from Lola Beaumont to Alexandra Davenport.'

Her smile instantly dimmed, as though it had never been. 'First I need you to tell me something. If Penelope hadn't had to stop working so suddenly, would you ever have told me that you'd found me? Or after looking me up and researching my agency would you have just walked away and forgotten about me again?'

'I never forgot about you, ever. But as for the rest…? I don't know,' Finn confessed. 'I told myself to leave the past where it was. The girls need me now, so what's the point of dragging up the past? But, Alex, seeing you again was like rediscovering part of myself I didn't know I had lost. I picked up the phone to call the agency time after time, only to realise I didn't know what to say. I wrote dozens of emails I couldn't send. When I finally actually had a genuine reason to call you I don't know if I was more relieved or disappointed when Amber answered instead of you. It was clear Amber had no idea where Blakeley was or what it meant to you. When I said we needed you urgently and offered to send a car for you, she agreed. But it wasn't her agreement I should have sought. It was yours. I'm sorry. I shouldn't have blindsided you the way I did, insisting you came straight here. I shouldn't have threatened you to make you stay. I just didn't want you to leave without knowing that you were okay. That you were happy. *Are* you happy, Alex?'

It was the most important question of all.

'I'm content.'

'And that's enough?'

She shrugged. 'It has to be.'

'I don't believe you,' he said roughly. 'The girl I knew would never settle for "content".'

'That girl is gone. You need to accept that, Finn. Lola Beaumont has gone.'

'No.'

He stopped and turned to face her, holding her loosely by the shoulders. She made no attempt to break free, just stood there, her eyes entreating him. To what? To stop pushing? To let her stay in the dream world she inhabited? The one where she told herself she needed nothing and no one and 'content' was as good as it got?

Maybe it would be kinder to leave her there, to let her sleepwalk through the rest of her life. But didn't he owe it to the girl he'd loved, that sweet and sassy and misunderstood wild child, to help her live again? Because, painful and unpredictable as life could be, it was better than barely living at all.

He couldn't make that decision for her. No one could. But he could help her.

'Lola Beaumont was always a chameleon,' he said. 'Maybe that's why it was so easy for you to leave her behind. Because half the time she was just a costume. You modelled her just as much as you modelled any of those designer outfits and perfumes. But there was always far more to you than that costume. I knew it. Mrs Atkinson knew it. Hell, half the village knew it. I'd say that the only person who didn't know it was you. You fooled your parents and your teachers, and most of those toffee-nosed friends of yours, but you didn't fool me then and you don't fool me now. You can call yourself Lola or Alex or Jane, for all I care. But I still see you. And you are worth seeing. You always were.'

Alex didn't answer. She just stood, mute and compliant under his grasp, her eyes swimming with unshed tears.

The tension stretched until he could bear it no longer. He'd promised himself not to get involved, reminded himself that there was no future here, that the girls came first. But the girls were at school and the future seemed like a distant dream as he looked deep into the ocean of Alex's eyes, no longer pebbles but deep, deep grey and full of passion, suppressed and hidden, but there. He knew it, he saw it, it called to him, and his blood thrilled to it.

With a muttered curse he threw his promises and scruples aside and bent to her.

His kiss was neither gentle nor exploratory, but a deep claiming that sent his blood dancing. Her mouth was warm under his, welcoming him even as she made no move to touch him, to close the distance between them. Emboldened, Finn deepened the kiss, his hands still light upon her, feeling the delicacy of her bones beneath the tips of his fingers.

'No.'

The word sent him reeling back. Had he misread the situation? Misread *her*? Surely she'd come alive under his kiss? Or was that merely wishful thinking on his part?

'No,' she said again. 'You wanted a story and I promised you one. You need to understand who I am now, Finn. And then you'll know. I'm not a chameleon. I'm just empty. I always was.'

CHAPTER NINE

FINN GLANCED AT Alex but she stared straight ahead, her mouth set. There was no trace of the warm, yielding woman in the granite hardness of her face, and her eyes were now like stone. What did she think she could tell him that he didn't know? He knew her truth. Had tasted it and loved it and yearned for it. But he had asked for her story and she was ready to tell him. He owed her the listening.

They hadn't discussed their path, but they didn't need to. There was only one destination, and as they tramped through the still, snow-decked woods it seemed to Finn that, despite Alex's desperate words, her past wasn't as done and dusted as she claimed. How could it be when she knew her way better than he?

Finally, a small cottage came into view, chimney first, and then the rest, curious and crooked, more like something out of a fairy-tale than a real, live cottage.

'You haven't let this out as well.'

It wasn't a question.

'No.' Finn deliberately kept his voice low and his tone matter-of-fact, as if the kiss had never happened, not wanting to scare her. 'It's too impractical all the way out here. Hard for people to get to, too much of a trek for regular cleaning. Besides...' his voice was so low he wasn't sure she heard it '...I didn't want anyone else here.'

She didn't respond. Finn couldn't tell if her heightened colour was due to his words and the memories they evoked, or simply a reaction to the biting cold.

He had the key to the front door in his pocket and she slanted a sideways glance at him as he produced it. 'How very Boy Scout of you. How did you know we were coming here?'

'I always carry it,' he said.

The key stayed on his key ring, the original from before. It was a talisman, a symbol, even more than the key to the castle. That one symbolised his change in status. This key symbolised the moment he had truly found what he wanted. The moment he had lost it.

He opened the door and stood aside to let Alex enter. No one knew when the cottage had been built or who had originally lived there. Right in the middle of the woods, with no garden separating it from the trees around, the stone-built old cottage looked as if it belonged on a film set.

The front door led straight into the one original room, a kitchen and living space, dominated by a wood-burning stove which heated both the radiators and the hot water. A later addition housed the downstairs bathroom and scullery; upstairs was just one large bedroom.

'It's been redecorated.' Alex stood stock-still, her keen gaze taking in every detail.

Finn went over to the stove and began to load it with logs from the filled basket. 'One of the first things I had done when I first bought the castle. It didn't need much; structurally it was surprisingly sound, and the damp was because of the lack of regular heating rather than anything more sinister. A damp-proof course, new plastering and painting and a deep clean and it's perfectly habitable, if a little rustic. I come here sometimes when I need time alone, to think. There's always someone who needs me at the castle or in the office, always decisions to make. I built the business on creativity and sometimes I feel that slipping away. Do you mind? Me using it?'

Her eyebrows arched in elegant if disingenuous surprise. 'Why would I?'

'Because this was your special place.'

'No.' Now it was her turn to be almost inaudible. 'It was ours.'

It didn't take long to light the stove. Alex had taken off her boots and curled up in one of the armchairs, pulled close to benefit from the stove's heat. Finn sat opposite her. He'd come out determined to get answers, closure, and yet he still felt as if he were fighting through thickets to reach her. She was as hidden as ever, only her momentary loss of control in the woods hinting that she was reachable if he just kept pushing.

The stove always heated quickly, and within a few minutes it was warm enough to cast their coats to one side. Alex didn't speak for a long time and Finn sat back, letting her set the pace. It was surprisingly soothing, just sitting, watching the emotions play out on her face. She wasn't as in control as she would have him believe.

Finally, she sighed and turned to him, curling up tighter in the chair as if, like a hedgehog, the curve of her body would protect her. 'What are you doing, Finn?'

'I was about to offer you tea. We might have biscuits somewhere too.'

'Not right now. I mean, why are you here, at Blakeley? You could have made a new life for you and the girls anywhere. Why exhume all these ghosts? Why are we right here, right now?'

It was a good question. One he had asked himself several times whilst negotiating a price for the castle and estate and beginning the extensive renovations and investment: an investment that had made a serious dent in the fortune he had so painstakingly built up.

He stared at the polished stove, at the room with its scrubbed table, the comfy armchairs, the bookshelves. He was a thirty-year-old man and the retreat he had refurbished for himself was no man cave. Instead it was an exercise in nostalgia. Because this had been Lola's place. In those days the armchairs had needed reupholstering, the cottage had often been damp and cold, covered in dust and cobwebs, but to them it had been playhouse, palace and freedom.

When she'd been sent to boarding school she'd solemnly presented him with the key—the key he still carried—knowing he needed a sanctuary, away from his father's anger and his sister's unhappiness.

And this was where they had slipped away, nearly ten years ago to the day, on the night of her eighteenth birthday. Memory of that night was in every line of her defensive body.

'Blakeley is my home. It always was. I wanted the girls to grow up here, free and wild and safe. The childhood we so nearly had? I want that for them.'

She nodded, as if she had anticipated his answer.

'Okay.'

She was tense now, ramrod-straight in the armchair as if she was being interrogated. Her hair had slipped out of its coil while she wore the hat and she had pulled it back into a tight ponytail which accentuated the taut lines of her face and her high, haughty cheekbones. She wore the berry-red fleece as if it were cashmere. Still every inch the lady of the manor.

'What do you want to know?'

'Everything.'

She huffed out a laugh. 'You don't ask for much, do you?'

She looked down at her hands, and when she spoke again it was as if she were telling a story.

'No one knows this, Finn. Not even Harriet or Amber or Emilia. Sometimes even I don't know it. Lola belongs to a different time, a different place. She's a story. A fairy-tale or a cautionary tale.'

He didn't argue, not this time. 'How does it start?'

She smiled, a mechanical curve of her mouth with no life or joy in it. 'How does any fairy-tale start? Once upon a time there was a little girl who thought she was a princess. She lived in a beautiful castle and had everything she wanted: an antique dolls' house, a rocking horse, a real horse. She was spoiled and fêted and allowed to roam free and no one was as exciting or as glamorous as her parents. Everywhere they went people took photos of them, and everyone told the little girl how very lucky she was. And the little girl believed it.'

Finn inhaled, desperate to pull her into his arms and kiss the brittleness away, but he held himself still. 'Go on.'

'Sometimes her mummy and daddy seemed to forget about the Princess, and sometimes it seemed like they only liked her if she was wild and beautiful and fun. But she knew that it must be her fault when they forgot her or were impatient, because her parents were perfect, so she made sure she was always wild and free and beautiful. Sometimes it got her in trouble, but her parents didn't mind. They liked it that way.'

It was almost unbearable, listening to her recite the facts of her life in an almost singsong fashion, but again Finn restrained himself from interrupting. He'd asked, demanded to bear witness. He had to follow through.

'The Princess had one true friend, and when she grew up she knew he was her one true love. And so, on her eighteenth birthday, she sneaked out of her party to be with him. That was the last time she was truly happy. Because that night a curse hit her family, and by the end of the week her father was disgraced and dead and her mother had run away. Neither of them remembered the Princess. Not even in their goodbye notes…'

She paused, her throat working, and Finn's fists tightened, his need to give her comfort more acute than ever.

'No one wanted the Princess to be wild and free and beautiful any more. They wanted her to be humiliated—and she was. Unbearably so. It was like being poisoned. Every part of her hurt. Everything she touched shattered, people turned away from her, and she thought the boy she loved had betrayed her. She didn't know how to carry on. For a while she didn't. She just lay there and hoped it was all a bad dream.'

'Alex…'

'For a long time she thought she was broken. She had ended up by the sea, staying in a cottage in a place where no one knew her. There she decided to stop being a princess. She changed her name and used the little bit of money her father hadn't embezzled and the bailiffs couldn't claim to go back to college and get the qualifications she'd been too wild and free to bother with before. And she decided she was never going to let anyone else tell her story again. She was going to be the one who decided how her story was told and she got a job that helped her do that. No one knew she used to be a princess and that was just how she liked it. And she lived quietly ever after and that was how she liked it too.'

She lapsed into silence, almost unbearably still. None of the tale was new. He'd lived it with her. She'd touched on aspects of it over the last week. But to hear her tell it with so little emotion gave her words a power he hadn't imagined. Finally, he understood how broken she had been. How broken she still was, for all her protestations, and he ached to fix her.

'Where did you go to college? Did you live with your godmother?'

She blinked and the spell dissolved. 'Finn, since I left Blakeley I've worked for everything I've achieved the old-fashioned way. No trading off my name or connections. No trust fund, obviously. The debt collectors took care of that. No home, no contacts—I only saw my godmother a couple of times; she was as keen to disassociate herself from the Beaumonts as everyone else. When I found out that she had left me her house I was shocked. To be honest I almost didn't accept it. I didn't want anything from before. But it wasn't just my life the inheritance would change. We'd been planning the agency for a couple of years, my co-partners and I, and I knew I could give the others the home and stability they needed.'

'And you? Has it given you what you need?'

Her smile was brittle. 'Come on, Finn. You know as well as I do that stability is an illusion and there really is no place to call home.'

'You used to pretend this was your home.'

'That's all any of it was. Pretence. I wasn't the girl my parents wanted me to be, they weren't the great love story they told the world they were, the fortune we spent wasn't ours to spend. Everything I was and everything I knew was a lie. That's my truth.'

'Not everything.'

'Everything,' she whispered, and her eyes filled with tears.

He'd wanted real emotion and here it was, raw and painful. 'We were real. That night was real.'

But she shook her head. 'No. That night was as much an illusion as the rest. It was cursed, like everything else. Those photos plastered everywhere…me plastered everywhere…something sweet and sacred and special reduced to sniggers and scandal. The things I said to you. Accused you of. Believed. If it had been real how could I have said those things?'

'It was real,' he repeated. 'The most real thing that has ever happened to me. You want to know why I came back here? Because this is where I was most alive. I have skied down deadly slopes and climbed mountains and kayaked through rapids and seen some of the most sacred and ancient sights in the world, and not once have I felt the way I felt that night. As if I finally understood my place in the universe. And I let that go. I let you go.'

'I shouldn't have come here; you shouldn't have brought me here. I can't do this, Finn. Not now.' She jumped to her feet and rushed to the door, the tears falling freely now. 'You should have let me stay gone.'

'Alex.' It took three strides to reach her, seconds to touch her, to hold her once again, to pull her in close. 'I'm sorry. But I'm here now. Let me in, Alex. Let me in.'

It was too much. The past was all around her. No matter how hard she worked, no matter how far she ran, no matter how much she buried herself, it wasn't enough. She would never be free of the curse.

But strong arms were around her, pulling her in close. Finn's scent enveloped her, warm and spicy and safe. The low burr of his voice vibrated through her as he murmured words of comfort, of reassurance.

For ten years she had stood alone, needing no one, trusting no one, wanting no one. No dates, no relationships, no one-night stands. Just work and purpose and desperately trying to appease whatever malevolent spirit had taken her world and destroyed it, freezing her in pain and loneliness.

She sometimes thought that if she hadn't met Harriet, Emilia and Amber she just might have given up, slipped away into nothingness. Her friends anchored her, and she allowed herself to care for them—but she accepted nothing in return except some company. And she was right to do so, because Harriet and Emilia would soon be moving on, and she couldn't believe that sweet, warm hearted Amber would stay single much longer. Amber yearned for a family, and she deserved one, deserved to be loved.

And then Alex would be alone once more. She knew it, and she was prepared for it. Accepted it. At times she thought she deserved it. But right now it was hard to remember that. Hard to remember why she needed to stand alone when there was someone giving her strength and support. Someone she could lean on.

Not someone. Finn. The boy she'd loved. No longer a boy, a man. A successful man. A good man. A man with a life and commitments she couldn't imagine. Commitments whose needs superseded hers.

Slowly, reluctantly, Alex disentangled herself from Finn's clasp, blinking back still unshed tears, trying to put her mask back in place.

'Finn…'

But then she made the mistake of looking up. Looking up at a face she knew as well as her own, older, honed by life into something more than handsome, more real than the youthful good looks she'd once crushed on. At a firm mouth she knew to be capable of tenderness, dark eyes full of sympathy, yes, but more than that, blazing with heat and want. Heat and want for *her*.

It had been so long since anyone had looked at her that way. Since *he* had looked at her that way. Right here, in this cottage, when she had slipped out of her dress, feeling like a goddess seeing the awe in his eyes, like a supplicant when he had first reached out to run a finger down her arm and she had really, truly known his touch.

She'd wanted him since she was fourteen, but he'd pushed her away, the two years separating them a chasm. But at eighteen she'd been an adult, and he had been powerless to resist her any longer. And she'd never been able to resist him. So how could she now?

'Finn…' she repeated, but this time it was a plea.

For him to let her go or to hold her tighter? She barely knew herself.

But it didn't matter, because he took it as an invitation. Strong hands cupped her face, fingers burning into her cheeks, branding her, claiming her, as he searched her face. She had no idea what he was looking for or what she was showing him, but whatever it was he seemed satisfied. A wolfish smile spread slowly over his face, his eyes heating even more until she was dizzy with the want slowly filling her, warming her, bringing her back to life.

'Finn,' she said again, and this time it was all plea. A plea for something, anything, to happen. She couldn't take the anticipation any longer. It was twisting her stomach, making her pulse pound through her body, a rhythm of need.

'Welcome back,' he said softly, and bent his head to hers.

The moment their mouths met the years rolled back and she was once again an eighteen-year-old in the fierce grip of first love. His kiss was as firm and as sure, as overwhelming, and she melted into it, into him. And, as she'd known he would, he caught her, his grip solid and real. That kiss in the woods had been one of pity, of solace. This was a kiss filled with desire. And she succumbed to it. All the reasons, the *good* reasons, to pull away had flown. There were no thoughts. Her head was blessedly empty of anything but him.

Slowly, skilfully, he increased the pressure, and her mouth opened to him greedily. Heated back to life, back to action, Alex wound her arms around his neck, angling herself until she could deepen the kiss, her hands gripping the sensitive skin at his nape, pulling him into her. Desperately she moved closer, until every inch of her was pressed to every inch of him, ten years of suppressed need and desire and want spilling out of her. It wasn't close enough.

Finally, finally, his hands slipped from her shoulders, travelling with devastating slowness down her ribcage, caressing the curve of her breasts until they came to rest momentarily at her waist. His mouth left hers to skim butterfly kisses along her jaw, down to her neck, and she tilted her head to allow him access, shivering at his languorous journey.

Couldn't he feel her burning up? She didn't want a slow, sweet seduction. She wanted hard and fast and right now, please. To feel and to live.

Impatient, she wriggled even closer, taking a moment to enjoy his tortured groan before slipping one hand down to where his shirt met his trousers, allowing it to explore the hard planes of his stomach, before dipping it lower to the waistband.

He groaned again. 'Alex. Not so fast.'

'Why? Why wait?' She pulled back to examine him, confused. Didn't he want this? It certainly felt as if he did.

'I've waited ten years to do this again,' he said with a crooked smile. 'I want to savour every minute.'

'But,' she pointed out, 'we could do it fast, and then start again and do it slow.'

His eyes flared and her stomach quivered at the look in them, as if he wanted to devour her whole.

'I knew you were still in there somewhere,' he said, gravelly and low-voiced.

For one second Alex wanted to retreat. To deny the part of her sparking into life, hungry and eager and ready. She had been hiding this girl, this woman, for so long, afraid of what might be unleashed if she allowed her to feel and to do. But she was so tired of hiding her. She had told her story and Finn had borne witness. He had looked into her and found her, denied her emptiness and coaxed her back to life. She would not run and she would not hide. Not today.

'I want you, Finn Hawkin.' Alex spoke clearly, enunciating every syllable.

Slowly he reached out and took her hand, strong, cool fingers entwining with hers. 'I want you too. I think I have since the moment you got out of that car, all professional and cold and so damn desirable. I nearly kissed you that same evening. But you weren't ready...'

'I'm ready now. Less talk and more kissing.'

He looked at her, really looked, as if he could see beyond the practical clothes emblazoned with his trademark, could see inside her skin to her beating heart and thundering pulse and aching need.

'Yes, ma'am.'

Tugging her hand, Finn led her to the door which she knew concealed the staircase leading up to the bedroom. Last time she had led him, overcoming the last vestiges of his doubt, proving that she was grown up, a woman. Now it was him leading the way, but she had no doubts. Her blood thundered round her body as she followed him up the stairs. Home at last.

CHAPTER TEN

'WHAT ARE YOU doing?'

Alex jumped as the clear voice sang through the air, and as she did so her feet slipped in opposite directions. She yelped, desperately trying to get them back under control.

'Have you done that before?' Saffron padded through the snow to peer down at Alex's feet, strapped securely into long, slim skis.

'Believe it or not I used to be very good, but I haven't skied since I was seventeen. I'm hoping it's like riding a bike and that when you get your balance you remember how to do it.'

Alex peered down the gentle but lengthy slope which led from the very back of the formal gardens down to the fields that formed the working farm part of the estate. She'd not skied this slope since she was much younger than Saffron. It had been far too tame for her. Now she wasn't entirely sure she could get all the way down.

'Can I have a go?' Saffron looked wistfully at the skis.

Alex nodded. 'If you look in the cupboard in the boot room, you'll find some boots and skis about your size.'

'How do you know?'

'Your uncle mentioned it. There're several pairs of boots, so make sure you get your size. Go on, go and get them, and if I make it down in one piece I'll show you how I did it.'

The boots and skis were Alex's own, long since grown out of and discarded, just as this pair had been. A fraction of her old possessions, her old life, still here in the castle, reminding her of who she'd used to be.

But the memories didn't hurt the way they'd used to. Being at Blakeley didn't hurt the way she'd expected now she was starting to feel again. Instead there was a kind of peace at being here; she'd come full circle. Come home. Back to Finn.

Oh, she was no longer the besotted teenager she had been back then. She had no romantic dreams or hopes of a happy-ever-after. A few happy hours couldn't change a girl that much. Her life was in London, at the agency, building her career. Finn's was here. He had responsibilities she couldn't imagine: to his nieces, to his employees, to the village. Responsibilities she didn't have any share in and didn't want any part of. Better not to dream of any future and leave on Christmas Eve as planned.

But there were still a few days before that happened. A few days of negotiating her way around Finn.

Alex couldn't stop the smile curving her mouth, and her hands gripped the ski poles as she remembered the taste and the feel of him, the fire and heat and life. It had been five days since their tryst at the cottage. Five days since he had breathed new purpose into her. Five days since she had held and kissed him. Since he had kissed her. Since she had touched and been touched.

Because of course he lived with his nieces, so she couldn't come to the castle, and she worked for him, so he couldn't come to the cottage, and it was much better to chalk their afternoon's lovemaking up to emotion and nostalgia and aim for a mutually agreeable professional friendship. Or something.

Only… Alex had seen the way Finn looked at her when he thought she wasn't looking. And she certainly couldn't stop fixating on his wrists, his throat, the firm line of his mouth…

Their business was still unfinished. She knew it and he knew it. The knowledge gave every interaction between them a certain edge, and she couldn't help thrilling to it just as she had all those years ago, when she had sent him those photos.

Full circle, indeed. Luckily she was older and wiser now. The only photos she would be taking were for the Hawk social media accounts…

'Got them!' Saffy appeared on the path, arms laden with boots and skis. 'What do I do now?'

Alex surveyed the girl critically. 'Good, you're in waterproof trousers. That will make falling down a lot easier.' She laughed as Saffy glared. 'You *will* fall down. A lot! So, first things first. Sit on that bench…'

She pointed with her pole to a bench perched on the top of the hill, so passers-by could sit and enjoy the view in more temperate weather.

'And change your boots. Whatever you do, do not put your foot on the floor in just your socks or you are going to have icy toes. Make sure you do the boots up as tightly as possible and then give me a shout to let me know you're ready. Okay?'

She waited for Saffy's nod and then turned to face the hill again, bending her knees experimentally, tilting her body forward. It instinctively knew what to do.

'Like riding a bike,' she murmured as she pushed herself off, keeping her feet tilted slightly together to slow her down as she found her balance again. 'Oh, yes, that's the way.'

She wasn't going to win any prizes for style or speed, but Alex made it to the bottom in one piece, even turning to stop rather than exaggerating her snow plough.

She looked up to see Saffy waving enthusiastically.

'That was amazing, show me!'

'Okay,' Alex called as she began to make her way back up the slope.

This was a lot harder. She was so out of practice she couldn't help sliding about. Any grace or technique was non-existent, and she couldn't help but think longingly of the days when she hadn't even had to think, her skiing technique utterly innate, as had been her horse-riding ability, also long gone. She hadn't been near a horse since Strawberry had been sold.

'Put the skis onto the ground, one in front of each foot and close together, and put one foot into one of the bindings. It should click in. Leave the other one until I get there. Got it?'

'I think so!'

By the time Alex reached Saffron the girl had attached one boot to a ski. Alex checked the bindings and made sure each boot was properly secure and nodded.

'Good job. Right, take my sticks and use them to balance while you put the other ski on.'

She barely remembered her own first ski lesson; she'd been on the slopes and on horseback from the moment she could walk. But she did remember the insistence on self-sufficiency. A good skier knew how to look after her own equipment.

It took Saffron a few goes, but eventually her foot was in and she stood there, wobbling like a baby duck about to take its first step.

Alex held up her phone. 'Smile! Your uncle won't want to miss this.'

She snapped the beaming face and then, as she returned her phone to a secure inside pocket, where it hopefully would survive any falls, realisation hit her. She hadn't seen such open joy in Saffy over the two weeks she'd been at Blakeley. The girl's smile was infectious, and Alex couldn't help beaming back as she instructed her.

'Okay. Shuffle forward, tiny steps…that's it…to the top of the hill. Now I want you to do what I just did: a controlled, slow glide. If you try and point your skis towards each other it slows you. Now, bend your knees… that's it…and let your weight shift forward.'

'It feels weird.'

'I know, and it's so tempting to lean back, but don't! Right. The main thing is to try and keep your balance, but don't worry if you fall. It's inevitable. We all fall. It's how we get up that counts. Right, on the count of three: one, two, three.'

Alex waited until Saffron set off, in a slow, uncertain half-glide, and followed behind her, shouting encouragement.

'That's it. Nice and controlled. Lovely! Oh, well done. Right, let me show you how to get uphill and then we'll do the whole thing over again.'

Laughter was the first thing Finn heard as he walked around the side of the house. Loud peals of pure and unadulterated laughter. His chest tightened and he stopped to listen. When was the last time he had heard Saffy laugh like that? Like the child she was rather than a solemn miniature adult, weighed down by responsibilities and cares he couldn't persuade her to relinquish. Yet here she was, giggling away.

He walked forward, the snow crunching under his feet, taking a moment to take the day in. The air was still crisp but the sky was an impossible blue, the snow millions of bright crystals under the sun's spotlight.

After a couple of days of typical British travel chaos, with gridlocked roads, cancelled trains and supermarkets running out of bread, the country had returned to sheepish normality. With the temperature cold enough to preserve the snow, but the weather fine enough for the roads to be cleared, Blakeley had enjoyed a steady influx of visitors, coming to enjoy the wintry hiking trails or, for the younger visitors, to meet Father Christmas in his real-life sleigh. Visitors of all ages finished their visit with hot chocolate, coffee or mulled wine and delicious homemade treats in the café.

The school holidays had started today, and as a result Blakeley was buzzing. Not that it was apparent here, where there were no signposts or trails to lure visitors.

'Saffy?'

He reached the top of the terrace and looked over the sloping hill leading to the fields of the tenant farm, now snow-covered and bare apart from a scattering of sheep in the distance. To his amazement he saw his eldest niece gliding to the bottom of the hill on a pair of skis, slowly, but with a confidence he hadn't seen before. Alongside her was Alex, her usually pale cheeks pink, whether with cold or excitement he couldn't tell, her eyes sparkling.

'Hi, there,' he called, and both females stopped and turned. Saffy promptly fell over, clutching at Alex as she did so, who tumbled on top of her. Finn held his breath, relieved when they both started laughing again.

'Don't try and join us, Finn,' Alex warned when she'd sobered up a little and helped Saffy get back to her feet. 'The snow has frozen on top and it's really icy. We'll head back to you.'

'Been having fun?' he enquired, and Saffy lifted a glowing face to smile at him.

'Skiing is the best!'

'Is that so?' He grinned as he looked at the tracks in the snow. 'Did you know that I learnt to ski right here too?' With the exact same teacher.

He risked a glance at Alex, all kitted out against the snow, and his whole body heated at the way her hair was slipping out of her hat and at the natural colour in her cheeks. She looked utterly wholesome and absolutely adorable, and Finn couldn't quite remember just why they had decided not to repeat Monday afternoon's activities.

No. He could. And they were all very worthy and sensible reasons. But the main one was that he knew that it was too dangerous. He'd been in love with her once. He so easily could be again. Maybe he was. Maybe he had always been.

But one afternoon didn't cure a lifetime of hurt. He wasn't naïve enough to believe that—although Alex did seem a lot less brittle, more optimistic. But her future wasn't here, where she would be trapped by her past. And his was. The girls were happy here, and he had promised them stability. If he jeopardised that then he would be no better than Nicky.

'Go on, then,' he said to Saffy as she reached him. 'Show me how it's done. Thank you,' he added to Alex. 'This is really kind of you.'

'There's no need to thank me!'

She smiled at him and Finn's heart turned over. Was she feeling it too? This yearning? This sense of belonging?

'I enjoyed it. She's a really lovely girl. You should be so proud of her.'

'I am. Of them both.'

They didn't speak while Saffy set off, then Finn yelled encouragement as his niece sailed to the bottom of the slope. He applauded her enthusiastically and she gave him a shy wave before starting her journey back to the top of the hill.

'She's doing really well. But of course you are an amazing skier yourself. I'm surprised this slope isn't driving you mad with boredom.'

'I haven't skied in years. To be honest I didn't come here for the sport but for work. I had this idea of doing some really short videos of myself, all in Hawk ski gear, out and about enjoying the estate. From my perspective, so it could be anyone. It would be a double reinforcing of the clothes being used in the snow and also all the Christmas things we have on offer.'

The 'we' warmed him through.

She's just doing her job, he reminded himself.

'That's a great idea.'

'I want to do some filming around the castle too, now it's really open and being visited.'

'The place is buzzing. Loads of people are enjoying the Christmas Through the Ages exhibition in the castle and even more are out and about. I've checked that the treetop trails aren't accessible. With this ice it would be a health and safety nightmare if some kid got up there and slipped. But everything else is very much open for business.'

'It's amazing to see the estate so alive. It used to be so exclusive, and in a way I loved the privacy and secrecy of it. But this is good too.'

'It seemed so sad when I first came home. The village neglected and more and more people leaving. The castle all closed up; the gardens barely maintained. It seemed at times like I'd never hack my way through everything that needed doing to get it open for this Christmas. People advised me to wait until the New Year but I knew it could be done.'

'Why was opening for Christmas so important?'

Finn glanced at Saffy as she padded towards them, panting and beaming, and lowered his voice. 'To tackle the elephant in the room straight on. To show that I know what happened here at Christmas ten years ago and move the conversation on. I didn't want a whole year of the anniversary looming on the horizon.'

Alex didn't betray her intimacy with the elephant by even a flicker of her eyes. 'Very sensible. I probably would have advised doing the same. And it's worked. I've been out and about all week and most people are talking about the amazing Tudor marchpane house or the Edwardian tree, not the Beaumonts. Congratulations, Finn.'

She looked over at Saffy.

'That's brilliant, Saffy. You are doing so well. If I were you, I would try and persuade your uncle to take you skiing. I think a few proper lessons and you'd be away.'

'Can I, Uncle Finn?' Saffy's pleading eyes were huge in her thin face. 'That would be the coolest thing ever.'

Finn reached out and tousled his niece's hair. 'Sure.'

'When? This winter? Can I go these holidays? Christmas isn't for five days. We could go now.'

'And miss the play rehearsals?'

Saffy shrugged. 'We already did the play once. Oh, Uncle Finn, please can I go skiing soon?'

'We'll see.' The quintessential adult response.

Her face fell and he cursed inwardly. Oh, to be nine and think that the world was that simple. That you could just decide to go skiing and go. It had been like that for him once, post-university and pre-Hawk, when he had worked his way around the world, deciding direction and timetable on a whim. In those days he'd been as likely to head to the mountains and ski as to the sea to surf. Not the stable life he had promised his nieces, but fun.

Their life with Nicky had been full of their mother's impulse decisions. Finn had vowed to give them the safety of itineraries and timetables and annual planners. Their schoolwork and activities were plotted out on the blackboard in the kitchen. Every appointment was programmed into his phone. He knew clothes sizes and shoe sizes and the name of the woman who cut their hair. They were safe.

But as his gaze snagged Alex's he knew that wasn't enough. He couldn't keep the girls wrapped up in bubble wrap, much as he wanted to. Alex had wrapped herself up and hidden herself away for all her adult life, and maybe she'd been safe, but her life was only half lived. Never sad, maybe, but never truly happy. His greatest gift would be to teach the girls happiness.

'I have to make a quick work call,' he said. 'Keep going, Saffy. I'll time you when I get back.'

'Can Alex film me? And put it online? I'm all in Hawk clothes.'

Finn had a strict no publicity rule for the girls. He had seen what constant exposure had done to Alex, and that had been in a pre-social media age.

He looked at Alex and she shrugged. 'I could make sure her face wasn't in it. Just the back of her head. But it's your call.'

'Let me see it and then I'll decide. Fair, Saffy?'

'I guess… I need to see it too, Alex. I don't want me falling over online, even if you can't see my face.'

'Understood.'

Finn watched for a moment as Saffy set off with a stylish flourish, Alex filming her. Anyone looking at them would assume they were a family. The situation felt so domestic, so right. With a sigh, half for what might have been and half for what was to come, he headed back around the corner to make his call.

Less than five minutes later he was back, to find Saffy and Alex squinting over Alex's phone. They looked up as he hailed them, and Finn was unable to keep the smug smile off his face.

'Okay, Saffy,' he said. 'I've managed to get us a ski lodge for two nights and lessons for you and Scarlett this afternoon and tomorrow morning. Kaitlin is booking us flights right now. So, you need to go and pack for yourself and Scarlett. Warm clothes. I'll get you ski trousers, a jacket, gloves and a hat, but you need clothes for underneath, PJs, and dresses or jeans for the evening. I'll come and check in an hour. Toothbrushes, too.

Scarlett's over at Polly's so we'll grab her on the way to the airport. What?'

Both Alex and Saffy were staring at him, with identical expressions of surprise on their faces.

'I thought you wanted to go skiing?' he said.

'I… I do. We're really going? Today?' Saffy's face was so full of hope it hurt him to look at her.

'If we're ready and don't miss the flight, yes. You'll only get a couple of hours this afternoon, but all day tomorrow and Monday morning. Oh, and don't forget your cossies—the hotel has a hot tub.'

Saffy threw her arms around him, almost overbalancing on her skis as she did so. 'Thank you, Uncle Finn. Thank you.'

'You deserve it,' he said gruffly. 'You had to change schools yet again when we moved here, and you've done really well. And don't think I don't see you looking out for your little sister. Father Christmas thought you deserved an extra early present and I agreed.'

'Father Christmas?'

'Who do you think I was just talking to? Go on, Saffy, get those skis off and start packing.'

'If you leave the skis and boots here I'll put them away,' Alex said. She smiled at the girl. 'I can't wait to hear all about it.'

'Why don't you come too?' Saffy said. 'Can she, Uncle Finn? Alex hasn't been skiing for ages, and she's really good.'

'Oh, I don't…'

'I'm not sure she'd…'

They both spoke at once, and Finn gestured for Alex to go first.

'It's a family trip, Saffy, but thank you for thinking

of me. Besides, I have my work here. I was planning on filming, remember? It will be good to have lots of footage for the next few days.'

'Scarlett and I won't mind you being there,' Saffy reassured her. 'Nor would Uncle Finn.' She looked up at Finn imploringly.

His first instinct was to agree with Alex. She did have work to do, and it was a family trip. But the words wouldn't come. She hadn't skied for years...why not invite her along?

Because you're supposed to be maintaining some boundaries, especially around the girls.

He looked over at Alex and knew that, although she was hiding it really well, possibly even from herself, she wanted to come.

'There's plenty of room for one more. And you could get lots of great footage of Hawk ski-wear. We'll be back Monday afternoon, so you can film here then.'

'I have been meaning to talk to you about featuring you much more prominently online. After all, the brand is all you. You named it after yourself. It's based on your lifestyle. Footage of you out on the slopes would be a great start. But...'

'No buts. That's settled. I'll let Kaitlin know, email her your passport details. Help yourself to anything you need from the stockroom. I'll see you out front in an hour.'

She stood there, bottom lip caught between her teeth as she considered, evidently torn.

'Please, Alex,' Saffy begged from the bench where she was wrestling with her skis.

Alex nodded, more to herself than them. 'Okay.'

'Okay?'

'Yes. Yes, I'll come. Thank you, Finn. Saffy, hand me those skis. Pack warm things. I'll see you soon.'

With a swish of her ponytail she was gone, handling both pairs of skis and boots effortlessly. A small hand stole into Finn's and he looked down at Saffy.

'I like Alex,' she said, with a little wistful sigh that tore at Finn's heart. 'I wish she wasn't leaving at Christmas.

'Me too, kiddo. Me too.' He ruffled her hair again. 'Come on, let's get going.'

And as Saffy skipped towards the house, her movements graceful on the firm snow, Finn knew that by inviting Alex along this weekend he was making her inevitable departure harder for everyone. But he wanted to give her something to remember. He wanted to remind her just what fun life could be. That was his gift to her.

He just hoped the personal cost wouldn't be too high.

CHAPTER ELEVEN

'THAT WAS THE best day ever!' Scarlett couldn't stop yawning as she spoke and Saffy joined in. Both girls' heads were drooping onto the table.

Alex laughed. 'I have never seen two such tired girls. You've not even finished your chocolate cake.'

'Bed for you two as soon as you finish your dinner.' Finn reached out and snagged a piece of cake off Scarlett's plate. She only half-heartedly swatted him away.

'I'm not tired.' She yawned again.

'I am,' Alex said frankly. 'A whole day of skiing when you're not used to it would exhaust anyone. And isn't Anton meeting you two bright and early for your last lesson? You want to be well rested so you can show him how much you've learnt.'

'Yes!' Scarlett brightened.

Both girls had taken immediately to their handsome and engaging young instructor, who was clearly used to children and beginners. After an anxious first hour Finn had relaxed enough to allow Alex to coax him up to the slopes, secure in the knowledge that the girls were in experienced hands.

'Maybe I *will* go to bed, Uncle Finn.'

'Right…'

Finn looked so discombobulated it was hard for Alex not to laugh.

'If I'd known you were going to say those words I'd have had my phone ready to record them, as proof that Scarlett Hawkin chose to go to bed of her own volition. You heard her.'

'You are silly.' But Scarlett didn't demur when Finn lifted her from her seat. 'G'night, Alex.'

'Night, Scarlett. Sweet dreams.'

'I'm off too,' Saffron said, sliding off her chair. 'Night.'

To Alex's surprise Saffron gave her a small, clumsy hug before joining her uncle and sister. From the look on Finn's face, he was as surprised by the girl's display of spontaneous affection as Alex had been—and as moved.

As Finn shepherded the girls out of the room Alex managed to get to her feet, muscles pressed into action all day after being unused for too long protesting at the movement, and gathered the girls' plates to carry through to the small galley kitchen. A kitchen that was mostly for show, as the cluster of lodges situated by a icy lake were supplied with all meals by the hotel to which they belonged.

Small but comfortably designed, the lodges had a heated outer room, for skis, jackets and other winter clothing to dry overnight, and one huge sitting and dining room, with windows at the back looking out over the lake. The floor was heated, but a huge oil burning stove still dominated the room, chucking out impressive amounts of heat. A staircase at the side led up to two bedrooms, both with their own bathrooms, and a further bedroom, where the girls slept, was tucked into the attic. The décor was very minimalist and tasteful, all greys and creams, with splashes of colour, but comfortable and cosy as opposed to stark and modern, and enhanced by the silver and cream Christmas tree in the corner and other seasonal decorations.

After rinsing and stacking the plates, Alex collected her barely touched wine and moved over to the vast sofa, tucking herself into the corner from where she could see the lit-up lake and some intrepid ice skaters in the distance. She listened to the almost inaudible giggles and talk from above as Finn chivvied the girls into bed. Any minute now he'd be down, and then they would have the whole evening together. Alex's stomach clenched at the thought of the torturous intimacy. Of looking but not touching.

Last night hadn't been too bad. After managing three hours on the slopes they'd all headed to the hotel to use the pool and the hot tubs, and had eaten there with a contact of Finn's who owned the resort—and stocked Hawk clothing in his hotel boutique. They'd stayed on to watch the entertainment, and by the time they'd got back to the lodge they'd all been ready to head straight to bed, knowing they had an early start.

But even with the exercise, fresh air, good food and wine it had still taken Alex far too long to get to sleep, knowing that Finn was just over the corridor. All the reasons for staying in her room were as valid as they had been back at Blakeley: the girls, her own imminent departure, the knowledge that the more time she spent with him the harder moving on would be. But his proximity had made those excellent reasons seem less and less persuadable.

Today was no better. All evening she had been hyper-aware of his proximity, of his every word, every movement, her body reacting to each accidental touch. She wanted him. That afternoon in the cottage in the woods hadn't slaked her desire, it had heightened it.

Maybe she should plead tiredness and head up herself, or go out for a walk...

'I've been thinking.'

Alex jumped as Finn spoke. She hadn't heard him come back downstairs, so lost in her thoughts.

'Why don't we go out for dinner? The hotel offers a babysitting service.'

'It might be too late to get someone,' she said, but the thought appealed. Out. Where there were lots of other people. No intimacy, but crowds. 'But it would be nice to see something of the village while we're here. Gorgeous as the hotel is, I'd like to explore a little further.'

'In that case I'll see what I can do.'

Alex took a sip of her wine and gazed out at the lake while she waited for Finn to return. If he couldn't get a babysitter then she needed a plan: she'd order something quick and light off the extensive menu, talk about work until it arrived and then go straight to bed. No more wine, no lingering glances, and no personal chat. It would be fine. She could absolutely do this. Even if she didn't want to.

'All sorted.' Finn stood opposite her, phone still in his hand. 'I'll just go and tell the girls; I'd hate for them to be alarmed if they wake.'

'Great. I'd better put on some lipstick if we're heading out. Maybe a dress.'

She looked down at her jeans and jumper, both from the Hawk range and both chosen for comfort rather than high fashion. Her friends would barely recognise her. She had a reputation for being exquisitely and tastefully dressed, no matter what her budget. But being with Finn and the girls made her feel comfortable, as if she didn't need her usual armour.

When she re-joined Finn downstairs, twenty minutes later, her armour was firmly in place. She'd picked a long-sleeved red flowery midi-dress, nipped in at the waist, teamed with wool tights—it was cold out, after all—boots and a chunky gold necklace. After some deliberation she'd let her hair stay loose, merely brushing it and tucking it behind her ears.

'You look lovely,' Finn said as she picked up her coat.

His tone was mild, but when she turned to smile her thanks the look in his eyes made her shiver.

'So do you. Nice to see you in a suit, not a fleece.'

'When we start a tailored menswear division I'll wear more suits.'

'I'll look forward to it.'

Before he could answer there was a soft knock at the door and Finn opened it, ushering in a capable-looking young woman who, in a strong Australian accent, introduced herself as Michelle, one of the seasonal workers who enjoyed bed, board and ski passes in return for bar work, waitressing shifts and other duties, such as babysitting.

Alex gave Finn five minutes to question Michelle on everything from first aid to fire safety, her stomach twisting all the time. She had thought going out would be the better of two evils, but they both looked so smart it felt more like a date.

Well, why couldn't it be? In just two days it would be Christmas Eve. She'd go home and this time they'd part as friends. But part they would. Why not enjoy one date first, as if they were living that alternate might-have-been life?

The Alex who had first set foot in Blakeley would be horrified by the idea. But that Alex wouldn't be here, in a ski resort in the Austrian Alps, in the first place. She'd been left behind in that cottage in the woods, and her newer, braver incarnation was taking her first cautious steps into the future. Why not start with an evening to remember?

'Come on, Finn.' She slipped an arm through his and smiled at Michelle. 'You have both our numbers? We won't be far. And do order anything you want. There's tea and coffee in the kitchen, and obviously there's room service for food or soft drinks.'

It was cold out, but fresh, and Alex was glad of her Hawk down coat, even if it wasn't as stylish as the long wool coat she wore in London. Her feet were snug inside her lined boots, her hands protected by gloves.

Although snow lay all around, thick and deep, the paths had been either cleared or gritted, making walking easy throughout the hotel grounds and into the small Alpine village. It had been dark for several hours and streetlights lit the pretty chalet-lined streets. Lights beamed out of hotels, cafés, shops and bars, where the après-ski hour was well and truly going strong, ensuring the town buzzed with activity. Christmas lights were strung across the streets, adding a festive air to the surroundings, and as they neared the village square Alex saw a huge Christmas tree, glaring with red, gold and cream lights and baubles.

As they had left the house Finn had taken her hand in his, and after a startled moment she had let him. They were both in thick gloves, no skin to skin at all, yet she fancied she could sense his pulse beating in time with hers.

'So, what do you want to do first? A drink? Or go straight to eat?'

'I don't mind. It's not often I have time to just wander. It's quite nice.'

Finn squeezed her hand. 'Then let's wander.'

They walked slowly through the packed centre of the village, browsing the enticing shop windows and eventually stopping in front of a shop selling traditional dirndls.

'I can just imagine my friends' faces if they opened parcels with those inside on Christmas Day,' Alex said as she took in the intricate embroidery and lace. 'They'd think I'd gone mad. But they're so pretty. I'd love to have an excuse to buy one. Would the girls like them?'

Finn shrugged. 'Where clothes are concerned I have no clue. A T-shirt can be the favourite thing one moment and the most despised the next. I defy the most accomplished data scientist to forecast Scarlett's sartorial choices.'

'I'll still have a look, if that's okay with you? I'd like to get them something and I've been so busy I haven't had a chance.'

The shop was filled with traditional costumes and accessories of all colours and types, and after some thought Alex bought traditional filigree silver heart necklaces for the girls. Scarlett's on a red ribbon and Saffron's on bright yellow.

'I never thought I'd be so clichéd as to match ribbon colours to names,' Alex said as she paid. 'But they can always change them if they hate them. Are you sure you don't want some lederhosen? I'm happy to get them for you?'

'That's very kind, but a gentleman always buys his own lederhosen.'

Tucking the two necklaces into her bag, Alex followed Finn out of the shop, freezing as she looked into the window of the next shop along. The window dazzled, showcasing glass and crystal, wine glasses and vases—and hundreds of Christmas tree ornaments.

She glanced at Finn to find him looking at her, his expression one of nostalgia and regret. 'Do you want to go in?' he asked.

'I haven't bought a Christmas tree ornament since I left Blakeley,' she said, unable to maintain eye contact, fixing her gaze on the sparkling display instead. 'I love it that you did, though. You wouldn't let me buy you lederhosen, but maybe I can buy you an ornament instead. How about that one?' She pointed to a little mouse holding a pair of skis.

'Yes, the girls will like that one. But I have one condition.'

'A condition?' She still couldn't look at him, feeling unaccountably shy.

'That I choose one for you. But you can't open it until Christmas day.'

That didn't sound like too much of a condition. Amber was bound to have put up a Christmas tree in the office. It would be nice to have something of her own to put on it. 'Okay.'

She turned to walk into the shop and Finn put a hand on her arm.

'And one more condition.'

She looked up at him then, and her breath caught at the tenderness and desire in his eyes.

'That you let me thank you properly.'

His kiss was light but, oh, so sweet, and after a moment's surprise Alex kissed him back, uttering a small cry of protest when he drew away, her fingers still entangled in his hair.

'I thought we'd agreed not to?' Her voice shook slightly. She still held on to him, unable to quite let go, and Finn smiled down at her.

'We did. But maybe we were too hasty in our decision-making. After all, here we are in this beautiful place, enjoying each other's company. I'm happy to bend the rules a little if you are.'

Was she? Should she? The sensible answer was no, of course not. But she'd bypassed sense when it came to Finn Hawkin a long time ago.

'I'm all in favour of a little rule-bending now and then.'

His smile widened. 'In that case, let me thank you again. I don't think I got it quite right last time.'

The village was full of restaurants and cafés to fit every inclination and budget. Finn found them a table at a small intimate restaurant overlooking the lake, where the atmosphere wasn't too loud or glitzy and there were no groups of weekenders enjoying shots at the bar, nor tables of bankers ordering bottles of champagne as they lived out their rock star dreams.

The food was simple but good, everything was cooked perfectly, and the décor was a little traditional but not too touristy. It was perfect.

Alex was perfect too. Dangerously so. She was relaxed, seemingly happy. She had no edge tonight, no wariness. She asked and answered questions, chatted inconsequentially about frivolous things like TV programmes they both enjoyed, music and books.

She listened, too, as Finn opened up about how complicated his feelings were about taking his nieces to live with him, about the feeling of guilt that he had deprived his sister of her children and the girls of their mother, the worry that he had acted too soon, the even bigger regret that he hadn't acted sooner. He touched on his father's death, and shared some of the stories from the first year of Hawk, when money had been so tight he'd lived in a student house, only for the brand to soar when a celebrity snowboarder had been photographed in one of their jackets.

'It's been a surreal journey,' he said at last. 'Hard work, but worth it.'

'It's been really interesting today. I filmed you a little, but I was also doing vox pops with some skiers and snowboarders who were in Hawk ski-wear. They all feel a real connection to the brand and to your values. They're making a definite statement when they buy your clothes. It's inspiring, and there's a lot you can do with that. I know Penelope already works with some influencers and successful surfers and climbers, but I'd suggest aligning yourself with people who share your values too. Eco-warriors and environmentalists… people who want to make a difference, to change the world. Have you found someone to cover the rest of Penelope's time off?'

'Not yet. I don't suppose you would stay on?'

He was only half joking and her smile was full of regret.

'I don't think that would be a good idea. Things are already complicated. Besides, I'm needed back in Chelsea. With Harriet's wedding this year, and Emilia's engagement surely on the horizon, there will be a lot to do. And over the last two weeks I've looked at what you've achieved, and I have to say I am a little envious. My goals were smaller, safer. I knew I wanted to work in PR, but I hadn't thought too far beyond being good at my job and where that might take me.'

'You *are* good at your job,' he interjected, and she smiled at him.

'Thank you. It's always good to have happy clients. I wanted to be head of and own my own agency. To have control, to be safe. And the last few months have been more successful than we could have imagined. Emilia is working on huge international events. I was in New York just before I came to you, working with a lifestyle brand who want to expand into the UK. Harriet's been placing PAs all over the world, and the demand for British trained nannies is so huge Amber is seriously considering setting up a section to focus on that area. We could be properly international. A household name.'

'You could.' It was brilliant to see her like this, inspired by the future, lit up with ambition, just as she had used to be. 'What do your partners think?'

'I haven't discussed it with them yet. To be honest, Finn, I don't think they'll be so actively involved in the future. Deangelo travels so much and Harriet likes to go with him. When Laurent proposes, Emilia's life will change completely. And as for Amber... Amber definitely wants marriage and a family of her own. It's just a matter of time.'

Finn desperately wanted to ask about *her* plans beyond work. Did she want marriage too? A family? But he knew what the answer would be. Why would a girl whose life had been destroyed by her family, who had never known unconditional love, aspire to love and marriage? If he'd been free, then maybe he could have tried to help her. To give her the time and love she didn't know she needed.

But he wasn't free.

How he wished he was.

'Tell me about them…your friends.'

He should have been there to help her when everyone had failed her. He couldn't help but be curious about the women who had stepped in where he had faltered. The women Alex clearly thought of as her family.

Alex took a sip of her wine. 'What do you want to know?'

'When did you meet?'

'One Christmas Eve. Not a good day for me, as you know. We all worked together, for Deangelo Santos, but we didn't know each other well—it's a huge company. I was head of PR, Harriet was Deangelo's PA, Emilia managed events and Amber was in charge of looking after visiting clients and their families. We might have been in the same meetings, but we didn't know each other. But on Christmas Eve four years ago we all had reasons not to leave early and bumped into each other on the way out of the office. It was clear none of us had anywhere to be, so we spent the evening together—and met up the next day for a walk. It was the best Christmas I'd had for a long time.'

'Why were the others alone?'

It almost physically hurt Finn to hear her loneliness laid out so starkly. He looked over at her, soft and warm in the candlelight, but with that glittering edge she'd always had, and knew with a shattering certainty that now Alex was back in his life he would never allow her to be lonely again.

He'd thought he was too busy to fall in love before. Too invested in his work, choosing Hawk before relationships time and time again, and only faintly regretful when that choice led to break-ups. But maybe he had never fallen out of love with Alex, the determined girl he'd grown up alongside. The only person he had ever really counted on. No wonder it had wounded him so badly when she'd turned on him.

Their reasons for parting this Christmas Eve were valid. Alex wanted to return to London, and his life was at Blakeley. He'd promised himself no relationships. Not while the girls lived with him, and not unless he was pretty damn sure the relationship would be a for ever one—and who could make that guarantee? But he had known and loved Alex his whole life. There had to be a way to make them work if she wanted to as well. And he was as sure as he could be that she did. He just didn't think she knew it yet.

Alex poured them both some water and sat back. 'Harriet's dad has dementia. She'd been looking after him since school and was really isolated. Emilia didn't get on with her dad and stepfamily, and Amber was estranged from hers. I don't know the details; we don't pry and we don't have to tell. There's an unspoken pact, I guess, not to ask. We've spent the last three Christmases together. It will be weird this year without Harriet and Emilia…' Her voice trailed off.

'Stay with us,' Finn offered. 'Your friend is very welcome too. The girls would love it.'

It was a spontaneous response, but the more he thought about it, the more sense it made.

'We're having a small Christmas too. There's plenty of space. Show your friend where you were brought up.'

'She doesn't know. About before. None of them do. Only you.' She stared down at her empty plate. 'They're the people I am closest to in the world and they know nothing about me. I let no one in, Finn.'

'You've let me in. I'm here. I'm not going anywhere. Whenever you want me you just have to ask. No, don't even ask. Tell me.'

'Finn...'

He laid his hand over hers, their fingers slotting together as if they were made to fit. 'I mean it, Alex. We've wasted so much time through misunderstandings and fear and hurt.'

He took a deep breath, trying to figure out the next step, not wanting to scare her off, but needing her to know exactly how he felt. That this time he was in— all in.

But at that moment the glamorous woman at the table next to them, whom Finn had noticed eying him several times over the last hour, leaned over and tapped his arm.

'Finn Hawkin? Is that you? How lovely to see you.'

Damn. Finn smiled automatically, his brain trying to compute who the woman might be. As he did so he noticed Alex stiffen and shrink back in her seat.

'It's been too long, but you are looking amazing,' he said.

It must have been the right response because the woman beamed. 'The Hawk campaign feels like a lifetime ago.'

He was on solid ground here. 'You look younger than ever.'

'I wish! Five years is a long time, especially in this game.'

'Not at all,' he said. 'We're just lucky to have people like you representing Hawk. Are you enjoying the season?' He turned to the mystery model's companion, hoping for some clues, and was rewarded when she beamed at him.

'Antoinette. Lady Antoinette Anstruther. I was at school with Spiffy here.'

Right. Spiffy.

That narrowed it down. It was like one of those hideous parties Alex used to have, when every girl he met had been called Flopsy or Bunny or Popsy, as if they were characters in a children's book. He'd never understood the upper class penchant for saddling children with a string of long and unpronounceable names and then shortening them to something infantile.

He thought hard and recognition finally dawned. 'So how are you, Sofia? Are you still modelling?'

'Oh, no. I gave it all up when I got engaged to Jimsy. In fact, that's why I'm here—joint hen and stag dos skiing over Christmas. Toni and I are the advance party. I can't believe I ran into you. Everyone is talking about how you bought Blakeley. No one believes me when I tell them that I met you there before, with Lolz.' Her laugh was as high as it was false. 'It's amazing to think I knew you back then. You always did have that brooding Mellors thing going on, even as a teenager. We all had quite the crush, but Lola made it very clear we could look but not touch.'

Alex had become so self-effacing during the conversation she might have turned invisible, and neither woman gave her as much as a glance. Finn couldn't look at her as he replied. 'That was a long time ago.'

'Not that long…'

Sofia stopped speaking, waiting as the waiter came over to remove their plates, and as Alex murmured a quick thank-you her attention shifted. Finn could see the moment recognition hit her, blue eyes widening and mouth opening.

'Lolz? Is it you? Oh, my God, Lola Beaumont. Where have you been?'

CHAPTER TWELVE

'THE SITUATION IS completely manageable.' Finn strode down the path, mouth set.

Alex understood his reaction, even though she didn't agree. He assumed that every situation could be controlled. After all, he was used to calling the shots. Thought a simple 'no comment' would suffice. But he must know this wasn't going to happen this time.

He'd been there when the story broke last time. Had driven through the crowds of photographers, seen the headlines. Did he really think that the sighting of a missing It Girl and the realisation that she'd been working back at her scandalous old home wouldn't create a media storm? That the whole saga wouldn't be raked over again and again? That those photos wouldn't find their way back onto front pages?

Her stomach tightened, nausea writhing around inside her.

It was all going to happen again.

Maybe exposure had been inevitable from the moment she'd found herself at Blakeley. Or from the minute Emilia had been catapulted into the public eye. She should have known that she couldn't hide for ever. But to be discovered at Blakeley on the anniversary of the tragedy was nothing short of a disaster. She was a mistress of spin, but she had no idea how to handle this.

She looked at her hands and realised they were shaking, but she couldn't feel them. She didn't even feel sick any more. She was numb.

'Plausible deniability.'

It was amazing, under the circumstances, how she could sound so calm. As if her carefully put-together life *wasn't* about to be blown into smithereens.

'If Sofia goes to the press, or her friend does, you go with plausible deniability. You employed Alexandra Davenport to work on the reopening of Blakeley Castle. You haven't seen Lola Beaumont in years, and you have no idea if Lola and your temporary employee are the same person, but you doubt it. Meanwhile I'll prepare a statement saying that we provided you with PR support and have no prior acquaintance. Hopefully no one will dig any deeper. Even better, maybe Sofia will forget about seeing me. Either way, we need a plan, and I think it's definitely for the best if I head straight back to London tonight. I can handle the rest of the work from there. You don't actually need me on site. We'll monitor the situation. At least we didn't confirm anything to Sofia. She might just decide she was wrong.'

But she knew that hope was futile. Even when Finn had introduced Alex and explained that she was just a colleague she'd seen the disbelief in her old friend's eyes. The chances of her not telling anyone about her suspicions were slim to none.

Sofia might not go to the press herself, but she wouldn't be able to help gossiping. And, maybe not today, maybe not tomorrow, but at some point a journalist was going to start looking into the co-founder of the

Happy Ever After Agency. The links to her godmother and the address in Chelsea were there for anyone who knew what they were looking for.

'So what if they do dig?'

Alex blinked. Surely she must have misunderstood. 'Sorry?'

'So what if they realise who you are? What difference does it make?'

What difference did it make? How could he even ask that?

'I thought you wanted your nieces kept safe? Any suggestion that Lola Beaumont has been back at Blakeley and they can wave goodbye to a normal life for weeks. There will be cameras at every gate, journalists at every event. Your life, Nicky's, your father's will be exhumed and picked over. Our prior acquaintance— everything. You escaped the scrutiny last time, Finn. Believe me, you don't want to be the target this time.'

'It will be uncomfortable for a few days, but it will die down. Alex, the girls love you. *I* love you. I always have. If the truth is out there, then what does it matter? You could make your home at Blakeley. Figure out who you are and what you want with us by your side. No one will bother you; you'll be safe.' He stopped and turned her to face him, dark eyes burning. 'I love you, Alex.'

Alex couldn't meet his intense gaze. His words echoed around and around her head, and her hands were shaking harder. She clasped them together, trying to still them. He'd said he loved her. Finn Hawkin, her one constant, the boy who had made her childhood happy, the man who had saved her, woken her from a decade's half-life, loved her.

For one moment she felt his heat coursing through

her, warming her, and the tantalising possibility of a future with him flashed through her mind like the end credits of a movie. All she had to do was say the words trembling on her lips, words she had said only to him, and that future could be hers. A life of laughter and companionship and love. A life in which she would fall asleep and wake up next to this man. A life back home at Blakeley. A life with two girls who needed to be shown that happiness was possible.

The words withered and died. How could she, of all people, give them stability? How could she trust that what they shared now would last? How could she even trust in this? Finn said he loved her, but she was a lie. She always had been.

'I can't.'

'Why not?'

She couldn't look at him. Instead she started walking again, almost at a trot. The hotel gates were within view, and that meant the lodge was less than five minutes away. She could be packed and out through the door within an hour. On the first plane back to London by dawn. Home by morning. The thought of the Chelsea townhouse, her own bedroom, safety, was almost overwhelming.

'I've enjoyed this walk down memory lane, Finn, but that's all it was.'

'Nonsense. Don't lie to me, Alex. I know you. What happened earlier this week, this evening, wasn't just nostalgia.'

'You love Lola, Finn. You want me to be her. Well, I'm not. She's gone and she won't be coming back. I'm sorry but you have to move on. I have.'

There was a long silence before he spoke, and when

he did his voice was hoarse with emotion—with passion, with sincerity and with sorrow. Sorrow she had caused. The pain of it ripped through her.

'The boy I was loved Lola, yes. But even then I knew that Lola wore a mask, even with me. And when I met you again you wore a mask too, but I saw through it. I see through it now. You know what I think? I think the real you is somewhere in between. Not as reckless as Lola, not as guarded as Alex. I think the real you sent those photos to me that night and that's why you were so very hurt when they were leaked. Lola would have turned their existence into a PR campaign. I think it was the real you a week ago, in the cottage, and it's the real you tonight. I think that the real you loves my girls and understands them, and they love her. I think I have a chance at a really happy future with you. But I get that you're scared. I get that letting people in is hard. But trust me, Alex. Trust in love.'

'This summer I told Emilia the same thing. I told her to trust in love, and she did. But she's different to me.' She had difficulty speaking, her voice so small she wasn't sure he'd even heard her.

'How?'

She winced at the catch in his voice.

'Why is she different?'

'It's not just us, Finn. It's my past and your girls and Blakeley itself. I can't be there. I just can't. Even if Sofia miraculously tells nobody someone will recognise me eventually, in the local shop or in the village. I can't hide in the cottage and the office for ever. And I can't be recognised.'

'Alex, you did nothing wrong. Your parents' sins are not yours.'

'But I ended up paying. Finn, I've worked so hard to protect myself. Please don't ask me to undo all that work. Please don't ask me to be vulnerable. Please don't ask to be let in.'

'I don't want to ask. I want you to welcome me in. You don't have to do this alone, Alex.'

If only she could believe him. 'I do. I have always had to. It's the only way I'm safe. Don't you see that, Finn?'

'So tonight, last week, all we've shared, all we've been, all we are, means nothing? You are just going to walk away?'

'We could be friends,' she suggested, aware of what a poor offer 'friends' was compared to the love he had so openly offered. 'You and I could see each other sometimes…if we were careful.'

It wasn't much, but it was all she had.

It was Finn's turn to shake his head, his eyes darker than ever with sorrow. 'I've said all along that I can't embark on any relationship that puts the girls' security at risk. Sneaking around to see you sometimes isn't something that works for them or me. We deserve more.'

Alex swallowed. 'It's all or nothing? Is that it?'

'I never said any differently,' Finn said gently.

He stopped again, tugging gently at her hand to get her to stop too. Reluctantly she stilled, allowed him to turn her to face him, allowed his hand to tilt her chin so she met his eyes.

'What we have, Alex, it's pretty special. Not many people get to be with someone who knows them so completely. Not everyone gets to right the past. We can do both. Sure, it's scary. I get that. I'm scared too. There's so much at stake. But I believe in us. I believe in you. I always did. Believe in me, Alex.'

How she wanted to. How she wanted to lean against his broad shoulder and allow Finn to carry her through life.

He hadn't sold those photos, had never betrayed her. He hadn't destroyed them. She had. She was as reckless with people's lives and hearts as her parents. How could a person who had never known stability and unconditional love offer it? She wouldn't just be screwing up her life or Finn's life if she got it wrong, there were Scarlett and Saffron to consider. She recognised a kindred spirit in Saffron, seeing a girl scared that she wasn't good enough, ready for rejection. What if she messed her up even more?

'Damn you, Finn,' she whispered, and his grip tightened.

'Believe in me,' he said again.

She reached to cover his hand with hers. 'I do. I always did. But I don't believe in *me*. I don't know how to and I need to figure that out. Being back with you, loving you, has shown me the way. Shown me that maybe I can reach for more than security, that I can have ambitions and hope. Thank you for that. But I'm not safe, Finn. Not just because I could find myself back on the front pages at any time, or because my very presence could disrupt your home and your business, but because I don't know how to be part of a family. I can't take the risk that one day you'll realise I'm not enough. I don't trust myself to be what the girls need…'

'Alex, we all feel like that. I feel like that every day. There's no rule book—not for parenting or for love. All we can do is our best. That's the secret.'

'Finn. When I'm with you I feel anchored. I always

did. But it's just another act. Nothing about me is real—not even my name. My whole life is about spin, from my job to the way I want people to see me. I want you to love me. I always did. But how do you know I'm not spinning you? Being the person you want me to be? How do I know that?'

'Because I have always known you, and I have always seen you. Doubt yourself, Alex, but don't doubt me.'

'You're my one constant and I can't risk losing that. Not again.' She reached up with her other hand, cupping his cheek, drinking him in. 'I do love you, Finn. I have loved you my whole life. I love your heart and your soul, your courage and your kindness. I love watching you with the girls and seeing how safe they are with you looking out for them. I love your vision for Hawk and the company you've built. I love what you are doing at Blakeley and knowing that my ancestors are respected by you. I love you. If I loved you less I might take a risk. But you deserve more. Your girls deserve more. Let me do the right thing, Finn. Let me go.'

Standing on her toes, she pressed a soft kiss to his mouth, trying to imprint every sensation on her memory: his scent, his taste, the way his mouth felt, firm and yet so tender. She tasted salt and didn't know who was crying, him or her.

'Be happy,' she whispered against his mouth, then turned and walked away.

CHAPTER THIRTEEN

'EMILIA, WHAT ARE you doing here?' Alex jumped up from her office chair to embrace her friend. 'It's so good to see you. But I thought you were in Armaria?'

Alex had been home for a day and a half, but the townhouse wasn't quite the sanctuary it usually was. Amber was busy with a series of corporate Christmas parties, Harriet was auditing another company's administrative procedures before heading straight to Rio de Janeiro, and Emilia had gone to Armaria at the weekend to spend a few days with her father and his family, who had recently relocated there, before her stay at the palace.

This meant Alex had been home alone most of the time, as the receptionist they'd employed a couple of months ago, when they'd realised they needed someone full-time in the office had taken annual leave. The townhouse had never felt so empty. It felt a little like purgatory.

They'd worked so hard to make it a home as well as an office space, knocking down the wall between the sitting and dining room to create a welcoming office and reception area, where the wooden floorboards shone with a warm, golden glow, and the original tiled fireplaces had been renovated to shining glory. Two comfortable-looking sofas sat opposite each other at the front of the room, an inviting space for potential clients or staff to relax in, and the receptionist's desk was on the wall behind.

Their own desks, an eclectic mixture of vintage and modern classic, faced the reception area in two rows, with paperwork neatly filed in the shelves built into the alcoves by the back fireplace. Flowers and plants softened the space, and there was a warm floral print on the blinds and curtains, the same theme picked up in the pictures hanging on the walls.

The door at the back led to a narrow kitchen and a sunny conservatory extension that they used as a sitting-cum-dining room, and they each had a bedroom on the first or second floor—two to a floor, sharing a bathroom. Cosy for four, it was too big a house for one person.

Alex gave Emilia a quick hug. Neither was a demonstrative woman, but they had grown closer during the summer, when Alex had helped Emilia organise the Armarian Midsummer Ball and encouraged her to tell Laurent how she felt about him.

'You do know it's Christmas Eve, right? You *are* supposed to be in Armaria.'

'I came back because we always spend Christmas Eve together,' said Emilia. 'So put the "out of office" on, switch the phones to "off". No one is going to need anyone at midday on Christmas Eve. Let's go. The car is coming to whisk me back to the airport at four, so we have all afternoon.'

'It's so good to see you.'

Alex swallowed the lump in her throat, blinking back

threatening tears. She was the calm and collected one. She never cried, never had emotional crises. She didn't intend to start now, but she hadn't realised how much she needed to see her friends.

Pulling on her coat and grabbing her bag, Alex followed Emilia out of the house into the cold, crisp day. The snow was gone from the London streets, but the temperature was still below zero, the railings and bare tree branches glistening with frost despite the winter sun.

They didn't walk far. Emilia stopped at the small wine bar and restaurant at the top of their street, where they often went for an after-work drink or weekend brunch.

'After you,' she said.

Alex pushed the door and walked into the dimly lit restaurant. Only to stop in surprise, feeling something as close to happiness as she had felt over the last few days rushing through her.

'Harry! Aren't you in Rio? What's going on? Amber—lovely to see you.'

'It's like I said,' Emilia said, squeezing her hand. 'It's Christmas Eve and we spend it together. Harry and I are going to the airport together at four. I'll be in Armaria by six—'

'And I'll land in Rio tomorrow morning, so I'll be with Deangelo and his family for Christmas.' Harriet enfolded Alex in a hug. 'How could I miss our Christmas Eve?'

'And you and I will go for our usual walk tomorrow.' Amber smiled at Emilia as the waiter brought a bottle of champagne over to their table and expertly opened it. 'But first we deserve a Christmas party of our own. We've all worked so hard this year.'

Alex had never told them that Christmas Eve was her birthday, nor how much she appreciated their tradition of meeting up and spending the day together. And yet somehow they knew she needed them. She wasn't as alone as she thought; even with all the changes on the horizon they were still a team.

It had been far too long since all four of them had been together, and the next couple of hours passed quickly as they sipped their champagne and ate a delicious assortment of tapas.

By common assent they decided against talking about work for a while, which meant Alex didn't have to talk about Finn or Blakeley. Instead she listened as the other three discussed their Christmas plans.

Emilia immediately invited Amber and Alex to Armaria when she heard they were planning to book a last-minute deal for the week.

'I should have thought before,' she said remorsefully. 'Of course I'm a guest, both at Dad's and at the palace, so it's not really my place to invite people, but it's not fair for Harry and I to be away and leave you two alone. Laurent won't mind. I'll text him. There's great skiing; you ski, don't you, Alex?'

This would be the perfect time to mention that she'd been in Austria at the weekend, but Alex had no words to touch upon what had happened there. Instead she just nodded and applied herself to her barely touched plate.

The discussion quietened and when she looked up all three of her friends were staring at her.

'What is it?'

'You've been quiet, even for you.'

'And you came back early from your last job and didn't say why.'

'Alex, you look so sad. Please let us help.' Amber spoke last as she covered Alex's hand with hers.

Alex inhaled breath, long and painful, thoughts tumbling around her head. If she told them who she was—what she really was—those words could never be taken back. But she was so tired of carrying secrets.

She stared at her still full plate, her barely touched glass, and felt her resistance shatter into tiny pieces. She couldn't be this alone any more. She just couldn't. And if she didn't let in these girls, these amazing resilient women, then she was doomed for sure.

She looked up at the three concerned faces and tried to summon a smile. 'My name isn't Alex,' she said slowly. 'At least it is now, but I was born Lola Beaumont and I grew up at Blakeley Castle.'

'But isn't that where you've just been?' Emilia asked.

Alex nodded.

Amber's hand tightened on hers. 'It must have been very difficult,' she said softly.

And the sympathy in her voice and in the faces of all three of her friends undid Alex. She couldn't stop the tears gathering in her eyes and falling down her face as she finally told them it all. Every detail of who she was, what had happened—and about Finn.

'Here's your tea.'

Amber handed Alex a steaming mug and Alex accepted it gratefully. They were all back at the house, with Alex placed firmly on the sofa with a blanket and told not to get up.

'Your Finn sounds like a hottie!' Harriet had her

phone in front of her and now she squealed, holding it up so they could all see the picture she'd found of Finn, looking rugged, surfboard in hand. 'Oh, he *is*! Tall, dark and handsome—just the way I like them.'

'And you an engaged woman,' Amber scolded her.

Harriet laughed. 'Deangelo knows I love him completely, but that doesn't mean I can't appreciate a good-looking man when I see one. But, more importantly, he sounds kind. Looking after his nieces the way he does is a wonderful thing, and Hawk has a great reputation as an employer and for its ethos.'

'He is kind,' Alex said. 'He's a very good man.'

And hot too, she silently agreed.

'In fact…' Harriet smiled at her. 'He sounds like a keeper. Alex, why are you here with us and not with him?'

It was a very good question.

'I told you. He needs a stable person for the girls. Not someone who has no idea who she really is.'

'A very wise person once said something to me and I've never forgotten it,' Emilia said, perching on the sofa next to Alex. 'She said: "If the worst comes to the worst we're here for you. We're your family. We'll pick you up and heal you. But going through life too scared to put yourself out there isn't living, it's existing, and you deserve more. We all do." *You* told me that this summer, and you were right. Living fully is scary, Alex. It's much easier to sleepwalk through life. But it sounds to me like Finn woke you up. It's up to you what you do with your life now, but do you really want any more regrets?'

'It's easy to be wise for other people,' Alex said, but her own words, repeated back to her, resonated through her. 'It's not just me. It's the girls, it's being found out again, it's being Lola once more, and the press…' She shivered. 'If they're going to find me I can't bring that to their door.'

'So you're going to hole up here and withstand the siege?' Harriet asked.

'I'm hoping there won't be a siege, but, yes. What else can I do?'

'What would you tell me to do if I was in your position?' Amber asked, pulling up a chair to sit opposite, her large green eyes fixed firmly on Alex. 'I've a secret and there's a good chance it might be discovered. I don't know if the press will descend tonight, or tomorrow, or next week. All I know is that I am going to spend the next few weeks, months, years in fear. What would you tell me to do?'

'I'd tell you to own it,' Alex said reluctantly.

'How?'

'I… I would tell you to get your side out first. To find a friendly journalist and offer an exclusive. And to pick a time of year when the news cycles are busy to minimise the exposure.'

'Like Christmas?'

'Like Christmas…'

Amber didn't say anything else. She just waited. Harriet and Emilia sat still and silent as Alex stared at her tea. Amber was absolutely right. Her advice was always to own the story, to control as much of the narrative as possible. And yet here she was, allowing the narrative of her life to be controlled by fear, by what might happen. Finn was right too. Lola would have laughed at the headlines, turned them to her advantage. Alex was hiding from them.

What if there were a middle way? And, more importantly, if there was, was she brave enough to take it?

A phone beeped, breaking the silence, and Emilia got to her feet, pressing a light kiss to Alex's head. 'The car is here and Harry and I need to go. It would be lovely to see you and Amber in Armaria, so let me know if you're coming. But if I were you I'd be on my way to another castle. Think about it, Alex. Merry Christmas, Amber.'

'I'll see you both soon. Have a wonderful Christmas.' Harriet threw her arms around first Amber and then Alex.

The two women left in a flurry of hugs, kisses and 'Merry Christmases', leaving Amber and Alex alone in the darkening kitchen, looking at each other.

'You know what I really want for Christmas?' Amber said. 'A nativity scene. Any idea where we can see one?'

Alex stared at her. Could she do it? Go to Blakeley and know she would certainly be unmasked, sooner or later. Risk finding happiness knowing it could end at any time, that there were no guarantees? But, more importantly, could she *not*? She'd thought there were no second chances. Not for her. But fate—and Finn—had shown her the possibility of a different life. All that was stopping her from taking it was fear. And she was so tired of being afraid.

'It's a good thing I know where there is one. Pack your bag, Amber, we have an invitation to a castle this Christmas. But first,' she said, resolution filling her, 'I have a phone call to make.'

CHAPTER FOURTEEN

'ALEX PROMISED SHE'D be here.' Scarlett's lower lip wobbled dangerously.

Finn knew how she felt. He still couldn't believe Alex had packed her bags and left that very night in Austria. No backward look. Uncaring of who she left behind. Again.

Heaving a sigh, Finn pulled at one of the woolly ears adorning Scarlett's head. 'She'd be here if she could, Scar. It's not her fault she has to work.'

'No one has to work on Christmas Eve apart from Father Christmas and his elves. Oh, and vicars.'

'Lots of people work over Christmas. Come on, let's get you backstage. Can you imagine the disaster if we didn't hear your "baa" at the right moment? The whole play would be ruined.'

Finn watched Scarlett prance ahead. She was never down for too long. She looked adorable in her white fleecy costume with its little woolly tail and pointy ears—and he had no one to share the moment with.

His sister should be here—he'd sent her an invitation and offered to pay her plane fare from wherever she was, but Nicky hadn't replied. He didn't know if it was a good or bad sign that the girls never asked about their mother, and nor did they expect to see her. But they did want to see Alex. The thing he had promised himself never to let them do had happened: they had got attached to someone temporary.

And they weren't the only ones. It wasn't Nicky he wanted next to him, much as he hoped she'd make an appearance for the girls' sake, he wanted to share this moment with Alex.

The real question, the question which had been nagging at him for the past two days, was what he was going to do about it. Should he respect Alex's wish to live a quiet, safe life or do what he wished he'd done ten years ago and go after her? Show her he was hers, always?

So far he hadn't had any enquiries about the identity of his temporary PR manager. Maybe Sofia had believed Alex when she'd denied any prior acquaintance, but the truth was bound to come out one day. Wouldn't it be better for her to be with people who loved her when that happened? Wouldn't it be better for her to be with people who loved her whatever the future held? Shouldn't that be how everyone lived?

He looked around the ballroom, filled with laughing, chattering people. It was as unlike the Beaumonts' famously decadent Christmas Eve parties as a party could be. Instead of the great and the good, the famous and curious, he'd invited the whole village, owners of local businesses and neighbours, plus all his staff, with coaches laid on to take them back to London and Reading and a shuttle bus prepared to do several station runs for those wanting to catch trains back to family. Some people had come dressed up, others were in jeans. There was no dress code, no expectation., All he wanted was to see the ballroom full of seasonal cheer.

At one end of the ballroom a buffet table groaned under the weight of food, while waiters and waitresses circulated with canapés and trays of drinks. A kids' bar and buffet were in the attached dining hall, along with paid entertainers, to give the adults a chance to relax and their over-excited offspring an opportunity to work off their Christmas Eve energy.

Finn had also arranged for a TV to be set up, with rows of comfortable chairs and beanbags, and a selection of kids Christmas films ready to go. After the nativity play and some carols, the children would have their own party while a band entertained the adults, and the whole thing would finish at eleven to give those who wanted to attend Midnight Mass time to get there.

He'd been planning the event for months. It was his statement as the new owner of the castle, ushering in a new era. He should feel pride at its success, but instead he was just desperately tired. He felt as if he'd let Alex down all over again, that he should have found the right words to make her trust in him, in them.

But if telling her he loved her weren't the right words then he wasn't sure what they were. Would she ever be ready to accept love? Would it ever be their time?

With a start he realised that the small stage set at one end of the ballroom was filling with children and that people were beginning to sit in the rows of chairs placed in front. The school choir stood to one side, self-important in their smart cassocks, and the orchestra was nervously tuning up next to them. Right at the front of the stage, standing to one side, was Saffy, white with nerves, biting her lip.

Finn held a hand up to attract her attention, giving her a grin and a thumbs-up when he had it.

He wanted his nieces to be the best they could be, not to be afraid to love or to go after what they wanted. Didn't he owe it to them to set a good example? Didn't he owe it to himself?

He still had Alex's Christmas tree ornament in his pocket, like a talisman. He should go and give it to her. Tell her he was here for her whenever she needed him. That this time he wasn't going to just watch her walk away. It was up to her what she did with the information, but at least she would know.

Mind made up, Finn strode to a seat at the back, phone out, ready to record Scarlett's big moment, having promised Saffy not to embarrass her with as much as a photo.

As he sat down the orchestra began to play the first strains of 'Once in Royal David's City', and a boy with a cheeky smile and tousled hair sang the first verse with a voice of such sweet power Finn could hardly credit someone so small could manage it. The rest of the choir joined in and then, blushing furiously, Saffy spoke.

'Once upon a time there was a woman named Mary, and she lived in a place called Nazareth…'

Her voice shook at first, but grew steadier as she went on. He could see the relief on her face when the girl playing Mary delivered her first line and attention switched to the actors.

It was the most traditional of traditional nativities. No whales or dinosaurs at this manger. But it had a simplicity that appealed to Finn, with the old carols threading through the narrative, the whole audience joining in with a gusto that clearly amazed the vicar.

Finn sat still, proudly blinking back tears as Saffy, her confidence growing with every word, narrated beautifully.

And then his absorption was broken by low voices and a clatter by the door next to him.

He looked round, annoyed, as the door opened and the sound of high heels announced the entrance of newcomers, their attempts to walk quietly almost comical, before switching his attention back to the stage, vaguely aware that two figures had stopped behind him.

At that moment a spotlight highlighted the back of the hall, in readiness for the shepherds to walk down the aisle, and he heard Saffy let out a peculiar little cry, half-sob, half-unintelligible word, her face shining with shock and happiness as she gazed at the spotlight.

Finn twisted round to see what she was looking at and it was all he could do not to repeat his niece's cry.

It was Alex.

Happiness burst through his body, through his very soul at the sight. He didn't need to go and find her. She had returned to him.

To them.

'Hey…' he whispered.

'Hey.'

At that moment the shepherds ushered their small flock into the back of the hall, ready to be dazzled by an angel on the stage, only for one lamb to utter a loud cry and break away from the herd to fling itself at Alex.

Finn looked at Alex as she bent down and enfolded the lamb in her arms, meeting his gaze with her own steady one. And he knew for certain. She'd come back for them all. For good.

* * *

'Okay, girls. Go and get some food and let Alex and her friend get a drink and some food of their own. It's lovely to meet you,' Finn said to Amber. 'I'm so pleased you are joining us for Christmas.'

'You're really staying for Christmas?' Scarlett asked, still in her lamb costume.

Alex nodded. 'If that's okay with you two?'

'Yes!' Scarlett nodded so enthusiastically her ears were in danger of coming off.

Saffron's smile was more sedate, but her dark eyes shone and Alex gave her a gentle hug.

'You were brilliant. I'm sorry we were so late; it was hard getting a taxi at Reading station.'

'That's okay,' Saffy said. 'I'm glad you're here. Come on, Scar. Otherwise only the yucky sandwiches will be left.'

Alex watched the two girls run off to the dining room, taking in the ballroom as she did so. Christmas Eve at Blakeley, a party. Just like old times. A band up on stage, people milling and talking and laughing. But this was a family occasion—a community event. If people were drinking to excess or taking drugs or engaging in affairs and dares then she couldn't see it. Everyone looked festive, many in party clothes, but no one was in haute couture, costing enough to feed a family for a year, or dripping in diamonds. Her ancestors would probably think it a tame affair, but she liked the simplicity of it.

She knew people were watching her, trying to figure out who she was. Some had noticed her in the last two weeks, but many of the villagers hadn't seen her at all while she'd been working there; she'd done her best to stay out of sight of the village.

With her hair down, and wearing a severely cut black cocktail dress, she knew she looked more like Lola than she had done during her whole stay at Blakeley. It was likely someone would recognise her sooner rather than later. But that was okay.

Alex inhaled, nerves fluttering. With Finn by her side she could handle it.

'I'm going to get some food,' Amber said, touching her arm reassuringly. 'And Saffy tells me that the first film scheduled is *The Muppets Christmas Carol*. So, much as I'm looking forward to the band, I might join the kids for a bit. I can't resist that film.'

Dear Amber. Subtly telling Alex that she was okay and would be fine by herself. 'Have fun.'

Amber's green eyes sparkled. 'You too.'

'Would you like a drink?' Finn smiled down at her and Alex's stomach flipped with nerves mingled with desire.

'You're in a suit again? This is becoming a habit.'

'You look beautiful,' he said softly, and her desire ramped up, painful in its intensity.

'Thank you. Can we go for a walk? I need some air.'

And to talk without everyone surreptitiously watching them.

'Sure.'

Finn guided her out of the ballroom and back through to the west wing, so they could slip out through the side door, avoiding all the other people getting some cool air after the heat of the ballroom, stopping only to collect their coats to guard against the winter chill.

Alex took a deep breath, feeling the shock of what

she had just done enfolding her. 'I called a journalist. A feature writer I've known a while. She's fair. I trust her to be fair. I am going to meet her back in London on Boxing Day and give her the story—all of it.'

Finn took her hand, his fingers warm and strong and comforting. 'Tell her to come here.'

'Finn…'

'Blakeley is embedded in you, in your story. You should tell it here. I want to be with you this time.'

Relief flooded her, and the tension she'd held since making the call melted away. 'I'd like that.'

'You're very brave. I'm proud of you.'

'It was Amber. She made me see that I was ignoring my own best advice, letting the story rule me, not me it. I'm not brave—I am quite frankly terrified—but it's time. How can I have a future if I'm hiding from the past?' She looked out across the moonlit landscape. 'Would you mind if we walked to the lake?'

He raised an eyebrow in surprise. He must have noticed how she had avoided the lake over the last few weeks, but if she was going to do this, be here, there were a few more ghosts to lay to rest first.

The path was lit by lanterns, the same lanterns as those hanging in trees around the castle, and the moon was hidden by low clouds. It smelt like snow.

Finn took her hand as they neared the lake and Alex entwined her fingers with his, glad of his strength. Finally they reached the low platform bordering the lake. The same platform she had fished from, launched boats from and swum from summer after summer. She stepped onto it, looking out into the dark, inky depths, thinking of the young woman who had died there exactly ten years ago and in doing so had set in chain a series of events which had totally changed Alex's life.

'She was high,' she said after a while. 'So out of it that she thought it was a good idea to swim in the lake on Christmas Eve night. The inquest said that if she hadn't drowned she would probably have died of hypothermia. Dad realised she was missing and came to find her. He pulled her body out of the lake. She was only twenty-three, did you know that? Meanwhile my mother was sleeping with that girl's husband back at the castle. We thought normal rules didn't apply to us, that we were somehow above it all. But we were so wrong. And that poor young woman paid the price. Kate paid the price.'

She hadn't spoken the name for years, and doing so now lifted a weight from her heart she had been carrying for so long she'd forgotten it was there.

'And my dad. I never knew whether he was taking the coward's way out or whether he truly thought he was doing the right thing. I've always wondered if he thought about me at all...'

Finn held her close, his clasp firm and reassuring. 'You are not your parents. What happened here was tragic, and it was desperately sad, but it shouldn't define you. You can't let it define you any more. I told you. I don't care if you call yourself Alex or Lola or anything else. Names are just words. What matters is what is in here.' Finn touched his chest. 'You have a good heart. That's what matters. And you have *my* heart, whatever you want to do with it. It's yours.'

He reached into his pocket and brought out a small paper bag.

'I didn't get a chance to wrap it…sorry. Happy Birthday, Alex.'

She recognised the logo on the bag. It was from the glass shop in Austria, where she'd bought the girls' necklaces, now both wrapped and in her bag ready for the morning. Opening it, she saw a tissue-wrapped object. She slowly pulled it from the bag, unwrapping the tissue to reveal an exquisite crystal Christmas tree ornament—a heart.

She held it up to the lantern light, watching the light sparkle off it. 'It's beautiful.'

'Will you take it, Alex? Will you take my heart? I come with a lot of baggage, I know. Memories you want to forget and two pre-teen girls and a castle full of your ancestors. But I love you. I always have. I want to be by your side no matter what life throws at you. You think you need to be alone. You don't. I'm here. I'll always be here.'

Alex looked at the crystal heart a little longer, her own heart too full for her to find words. Then, slipping it into her pocket, she reached out and took Finn's hand, drawing him away from the lake. She looked back at the lake for one long moment and felt the last ghost slip into its depths.

She waited to speak until they were halfway along the path, drawing him close to her under a tree, looking at the castle lit up against the snow-heavy sky.

'I'm scared,' she said honestly. 'Scared that I'll let you down, that I'll let the girls down. Scared that one day you'll wake up and realise I'm not enough. It's almost overwhelming. It's as if I pushed all that fear deep down and hid it, along with every other emotion. That I survived by not feeling and not living, by being asleep in my own life. And then you fought your way back into my life and woke me up, and it's been more painful and harder than I could ever have imagined. But also more wonderful. You, the girls, being back here at Blakeley... It's like all the wishes I never dared to dream have come true. And it's all thanks to you. My knight, the only person who has always seen me. I can't believe you love me. I can't believe I get to be that lucky. I have always loved you, Finn. Always.'

'I know you have your business, and your life in London, and I know you have huge ambition and that's part of what I love about you,' Finn said hoarsely. 'But we can make it work. You can have your own offices here or commute. Whatever you need. All I know is that if you agree to give this a go then I won't be stupid enough to let you walk away a third time.'

'I can't believe that I can be this lucky. That I get to have my agency and my friends, you and the girls and Blakeley. There were so many times when I never thought I'd be happy again. But you do know, don't you, that Hawk and Blakeley don't change anything? I'd want to be with you and the girls no matter where you lived or what you did. Being able to come home is just the cherry on the cake, but you're the cake.'

Finn gave a sudden shout of laughter at her words, his expression turning serious as he gazed down at her. 'Welcome home, Alex.'

He bent to kiss her and she reached for him, entwining her arms around his neck, pressing so close to him she could feel every sinew and muscle, feel the beat of his heart in time with hers.

As his mouth found hers the snow began to fall, settling in her hair, on her arms and shoulders, but she was warm within his arms, warmed by his embrace.

'Merry Christmas,' she whispered against his mouth, and felt him smile.

'Merry Christmas, my love.'

* * * * *

THEIR ONE-NIGHT CHRISTMAS GIFT

KARIN BAINE

For Richard Rankin xx

CHAPTER ONE

CHARLES ROSS-WYLDE WAS a selfish, cold-hearted liar and Harriet Bell was better off without him. At least, that was what she'd spent the last twelve years telling herself.

The reality of seeing him again was very different from the scenario she'd imagined. She'd been shocked to see him here, but so far she'd resisted slapping him, throwing a drink in his face, or announcing to the rest of the conference attendees that *he* was the reason she couldn't risk loving anyone again. Perhaps she'd matured or, more likely, hadn't expected to feel anything other than pure hatred towards him.

She watched him now from the other side of the room as the assembled medical community enjoyed the tea break between lectures. It gave her time to study him unnoticed and decide what she wanted to do—if anything. If she chose to she could walk out of here and he'd be none the wiser, with nothing changing their current status quo.

Impossible when there was so much she wanted to say, so much she wanted him to explain.

Physically, he hadn't changed much from the man who'd once promised her their lives would be spent together except he looked older...more manly.

He was still trying to sweep that floppy dark hair back into a neat style befitting a professional man, though she remembered all too well how it had looked first thing in the morning tousled by sleep. And, as always, he was dressed impeccably, the navy suit tailored to his exact measurements. The beard was new, the dark shadow along his jawline making him look even more masculine, if that was possible. It suited him—as did the glasses he was sporting.

Damn it, he was still gorgeous, and apparently still able to make her heart flutter maniacally as though she'd just run a marathon.

'They really should have an open bar,' she muttered to the bewildered woman serving refreshments to the masses, turning away from the view of her ex-fiancé and wishing for a tot of whisky in her coffee.

Not that she drank often, but she'd make an exception to help her escape memories of her and Charles—good and bad. She'd have to make do with an extra spoonful of sugar in her tea to help with the shock.

'I didn't expect to see you here.' That soft, Scottish burr capable of rendering her into a gibbering wreck tickled the back of her neck. He'd found her.

Harriet fumbled with her cup and saucer, spilling the contents over herself right before she turned around to face him. 'Charles. What a surprise.'

'Sorry, I didn't mean to startle you.' He grabbed

a napkin from the buffet table and started dabbing at the stain darkening the front of her dress.

'I can do that, thanks.' She didn't mean to snap but she couldn't bear to have him touch her after all this time when she didn't know what emotions it would unleash.

'Sorry.' He handed over possession of the napkin so she could tend to the ruined dress herself. 'It was just nice to see a familiar face. How have you been, Harriet?'

There was no sign of remorse for the relationship and future he'd thrown away. He was talking to her as though they were old school friends, who had no real emotional connection and had simply happened to run into each other.

She set the wet napkin and coffee back on the table and took a moment to consider her response. If she kicked off and made a scene it would be clear she'd never got over him and that would most likely send Charles running. She didn't know what she wanted from him, but it wasn't that.

'Oh, you know, keeping busy. You?' She plastered on a smile, willing to play along with this game until one of them broke. Her, probably.

'The same. I took up a placement in Glasgow to complete my medical training and set up a clinic at Heatherglen. It was initially to help army veterans, but we've extended to provide state-of-the-art medical facilities for physical and emotional rehabilitation to a wider range of patients.'

'Sounds impressive.' Inheriting his father's for-

tune and the family estate had signalled the end of
their engagement so it was difficult for Harriet to
be as enthusiastic about his accomplishments as she
should have been.

'I wanted to do something worthwhile to honour
my brother and father, but it takes a lot of upkeep. I
don't get to make as many trips to London as I'd like.'
His older brother, Nick, had served with the military
in Afghanistan. Unfortunately, he'd been killed by a
roadside bomb before Harriet had had the chance to
meet him. That family tragedy, followed by the death
of his father about a year later, had proved too much
for Charles and their wedding plans.

'I'm the same, too many responsibilities here to
even take a holiday these days.' Needless to say, she
hadn't been back to Scotland since his father's funeral, when Charles had gone back on his promise
of making a life with her. At the time she'd believed
grief had driven his decision, but when he'd failed to
follow her back to London she'd soon realised he was
serious about no longer wanting to marry her. It was
difficult to reconcile that man who'd broken her heart
with the one stood before her now, making small talk.

'So, you did stay here after all? I'd hoped you
would.' He was smiling so Harriet didn't think he
was trying to rub salt into the wound he'd inflicted on
her that day. She'd never received a proper explanation as to why he'd called things off. Goodness knew,
she'd been desperate for one, but she'd eventually
had to accept the simple truth that he didn't want her
any more. She'd seen that happen between her own

parents when she'd been young and had watched her mother torture herself trying to figure out what she'd done wrong when her father had walked out on them. There was no way she was spending the rest of her life beating herself up about it, the way her mother had until her death.

'Yes. I'm an orthopaedic surgeon.'

Top of my field, she wanted to add, piqued by the fact he'd never bothered to check up and see what she'd been doing. Then again, she hadn't done that either, afraid she'd start obsessing over him or what could have been between them. In his case it seemed it was merely down to a lack of interest.

'Neurologist,' he countered. 'I thought it made sense to take that path, so I'd be able to better treat veterans.'

What a team they would have made working together but perhaps she wouldn't have pursued her career so doggedly if they had married. When she and Charles had been together she'd imagined she could have it all—a career and a family. She'd thought they were a team, on an equal footing and willing to share the responsibilities of raising children. Except the moment Charles's circumstances had changed he'd backed out and left her to pick up the pieces of her broken heart. She'd paid the price for his actions.

Perhaps she'd had a lucky escape. If he'd proved so unreliable further down the line, he could have left her raising their children alone once he'd decided he didn't want her after all. As it was, she'd poured her heart and soul into her career because that was the one thing she could count on always being there. Things happened for a reason and she had no regrets when it had moved her focus back onto her work. It didn't look as though he had any either.

They fell into an awkward gap in conversation, neither apparently knowing what to say to the other but not wanting to make the first move in walking away.

'Could all attendees please make their way back to their seats for the next talk, please?'

The announcement over the loudspeaker filled the silence on their behalf and left them with the decision of whether to say goodbye temporarily, or for ever.

'Listen, why don't we go for a proper drink? The hotel bar should be quiet enough with all the reprobates locked in here for another few hours of telling us things we already know.' Charles rested his hand lightly at her waist, leaning in so his comment reached only her ears. She could barely feel the pressure of his fingertips on her skin, but it was sufficient to awaken every erogenous zone in her body until she was sure she'd follow him to the ends of the earth.

'Sure,' she squeaked.

Damn, she was in trouble.

Charles didn't know what he hoped to gain by getting Harriet on her own, except having her to himself for the first time in over a decade. When he'd spotted her across the room there had been no great plan, just a need to be near her. Much like the first time they'd met in medical school and had instantly become inseparable. Being each other's first loves, they'd become serious quickly. In hindsight, that youth and inexperience would never have worked in a world where tradition and duty to the family name was everything. He'd just wanted to be with Harriet and had given no thought to Heatherglen back then.

Now he considered himself lucky she'd agreed to go for a drink with him instead of throwing a cup of hot coffee in his face.

'There's a seat in the corner. I'll get the drinks. White wine?' He led her into the bar, where one or two other hotel guests had sought refuge.

'Yes, please.' Even that knowledge of her preferred drink brought back memories of times together it was difficult to ignore. Those early student days of being silly and partying too hard. Later, when it had been a bottle of wine to accompany a romantic meal they often hadn't bothered to finish...

'Charles, what are you doing?' he muttered under his breath, and stole a glance back at Harriet as she settled into the corner.

Those days of acting only in his own interests were supposed to be far behind him. He didn't make any decisions now without thinking through how it might affect those around him. It had been a tough lesson to learn when the consequences of his past actions had come at the price of his brother and father's lives. He'd sacrificed his relationship with Harriet for her benefit—his first act of selflessness when he'd inherited Heatherglen. Not that she'd known, and he couldn't have told her it was because he'd wanted her to stay on in London and pursue her career instead of getting dragged into his mess. She would've insisted on going to Scotland with him.

Although, seeing her now and realising everything he'd lost, regret weighed heavily on his shoulders along with his threefold burden of guilt.

Approaching her this evening and getting her to agree to join him for a drink had been entirely for his own benefit without considering her feelings. Yet, so far, she'd shown him nothing but friendliness in return. It was entirely possible he'd over-inflated the idea of what they'd had together in his head and she'd forgotten him the second she'd got on that train without him.

'You look good, by the way. Have I said that already?' He'd certainly thought it as he'd headed back to her.

Harriet had always been pretty with her slim figure and long, dark blonde hair but now she was a stunningly beautiful woman. The emerald-green dress she was wearing wasn't particularly noteworthy except for the womanly figure it clung to, accentuating her every curve. It was understated and sophisticated, but on Harriet it was as sexy as hell.

'You haven't but thank you.' She sipped her wine, leaving a trace of ruby lip gloss on the rim of her glass, and…he really needed to keep his libido in check. She was his ex-fiancée, not an anonymous one-night stand.

'So, are you married? Any kids?' He took a gulp of lager, making the question as nonchalant as he could.

Why should it matter to him what her marital status was, other than cooling his jets if he found out there was someone waiting for her at home?

'No. I decided my career was the only long-term relationship I needed in my life. I'm too busy to fall for all that again.'

Ouch.

Harriet's brown eyes glittered with a dark challenge for him to bite back. Charles didn't want to go down that route, going over old ground and spoiling the moment they were having now, but she deserved some sort of explanation.

'What about you? Did you settle down?'

'I'm too busy with the clinic and, to be honest, Mum isn't the best advert for marriage. I'm not sure what number husband she's on now since Dad. Three, I think. She spends her days sailing around in his superyacht. We don't see very much of her. I think Heatherglen holds too many sad memories for her.'

'I know the feeling.' Harriet took another sip of her wine, apparently needing to dull the mention of his family home with alcohol.

'Harriet, about all that…' There had to be some way of saying 'It wasn't you, it was me', without sounding completely insincere.

She saved him the trouble, reaching out her hand to still his, which was currently ripping up the cardboard beer mat. 'This is much too serious a topic for this evening, Charles.'

Suddenly his mind was spinning, trying to come to terms with the way his body was responding to her touch after all this time apart and to what she was saying to him.

'I don't do serious any more.' She held him with her ever-darkening gaze, making no attempt to break contact.

'No? What *do* you do?' He leaned in closer, hoping that if she was actually coming on to him, it wasn't simply a ploy to get revenge.

'I have fun, Charles. You do remember how to do that, don't you? If so, I'm in Room 429.' With that, she got up and walked away. Leaving Charles with his mouth open, his heart hammering, and battling with his conscience, which was telling him that following her was a really bad idea.

Harriet's legs shook on her way towards the elevator. She'd never been so brazen in her life and couldn't even blame it on the alcohol when she'd only had a sip. From the moment she'd seen Charles, she'd wanted what they'd had in the past. Wanted him. What she didn't want was to rake over the ashes of the past and be reminded of how he'd rejected her. It was important to know he was still attracted to her. As though that would somehow erase the previous damage he'd caused her self-esteem.

One night with her ex, on her terms, might give her closure on the relationship that had spoiled her for any other.

Except he hadn't immediately jumped up and begged to take her there and then. She'd merely succeeded in humiliating herself and now had an extra chapter to add to their tragic story.

She jabbed and jabbed at the button for the lift, wishing it would somehow make it come faster. Then it would swallow her up and transport her away from view as soon as possible.

'Harriet, wait!' Charles shouted after her as she stepped inside the lift. It was tempting to let the doors shut in his face and be done with him once and for all, but he jammed his foot inside and stole that option from her.

The only scenario worse than being stood up when you'd offered yourself on a plate to a man was having him tell you why he didn't want to sleep with you. She fought off the tears already blurring her vision because she was determined not to re-create their last mortifying goodbye.

'Are you sure you want to do this?' His brow was furrowed, and she could see he was actually contemplating her proposal, not attempting to let her down easily at all.

That reassurance buoyed her spirits once more, along with her intention to seduce him. 'It's not a big deal, Charles. We're both single, hard-working professionals who want to let off a little steam in a hotel room.'

Now that she knew she had his interest, she stepped so close to him they were toe to toe.

'We both know it would be more than that.' There was a thread of resistance left in his words, yet his eyes and body were saying something different.

They'd spent enough time together for her to know when he was aroused, and vice versa.

'It doesn't have to be.' She didn't have to fake anything to convince him she wanted this no-strings fling when her breathy voice was a natural reaction to having him so close again.

'I know I hurt you, Harriet. Sleeping together now isn't going to change that. It isn't going to change anything. I'm still going to go back to Heatherglen and your life is here.' He was pointing out the obvious to her, they weren't getting back together no matter what happened tonight. It wasn't an outright rejection, though, because he was reaching out to her, caressing her cheek with his thumb, letting her know this was her decision. She was all right with that, safe in the knowledge she was in control of what happened next.

'I'm not looking to rekindle a romance. The past is done with but it's clear that the chemistry is still there between us.' She stroked a finger down the front of his shirt, revelling in the desire darkening his eyes until they were almost black. This was what she wanted—confirmation that she still affected him as much as he did her. More importantly, she needed this to give her some closure.

She'd used Charles as an excuse not to let anyone else get close to her but recently she'd begun to wonder if she was missing something in her life. If she was ever to entertain the notion of a serious relationship, or even a family, she had to put Charles's memory to rest first. One more time together and a chance to say a proper goodbye should finally close that chapter of her life.

'As I remember, that was never a problem for us, but we do have a long, complicated history. Is it really a good idea to go back there?'

'Now isn't the time to start getting chivalrous, Charles.' Harriet let her finger trail down until she reached his belt buckle, then started to undo it.

Charles let out a groan. 'I just don't want us to do anything that will end up with you getting hurt again. I can't give you any more now than I could all those years ago.'

'All I'm asking for is tonight. I'm not going to beg.' She popped open the button on his trousers then stopped. If he wanted more he was going to have to say so.

'One night?'

'We never got to say goodbye. Let's think of it as us both getting closure.'

'Going out with a bang?' he asked with a smirk, but he was close enough she could hear the hitch in his breathing. Clearly, he wasn't as composed as he was making out.

'Something like that. A one-time offer never to be repeated or spoken of again.'

'Deal.' His voice was a growl as he wound his arm around her waist, pulled her tight to his body and covered her lips with his.

Just like that the touch paper was lit, their passion reignited in an instant. The kiss so urgent and demanding it took her breath away. She didn't remember

Charles being quite so…masterful. Perhaps it was that knowledge they were being reckless that added an extra frisson to their passion. This was definitely the last time they'd be together and would be a sweeter memory, she hoped, to hold onto than the last one.

He backed her against the wall of the lift, his mouth, his tongue never leaving hers. Arousal swept through her, showing no mercy or regard for their location or history. Harriet felt along the wall for the control panel and hit the button for the fourth floor. Charles paused their amorous reunion to hit the one for the second floor instead.

'My room's closer,' he whispered against her neck, and she felt the effect of his warm breath on her skin all the way down to her toes.

The thing about being her past lover was that he remembered exactly where to strike to make her weak at the knees. He knew all her sensitive spots and she shivered with anticipation at the thought of him using that advantage. Two could play that game and it wasn't long before they were both gasping with pleasure as they began to reacquaint themselves with each other. If either of them had booked the penthouse suite she doubted whether they would've made it out of here without consummating their renewed acquaintance.

The doors opened, and they were soon fumbling their way down the corridor, steadfastly locked in their passionate embrace. Charles smiled against her lips as he tried to unlock the room door behind her. They were giggling young lovers again, driven by their hormones and lust, and Harriet was ignoring her adult brain telling her otherwise.

'Have you got any protection?' As they fell through the door her mind was racing ahead. She didn't want to interrupt a crucial moment to track down some condoms in case it gave either of them time to think about what they were doing and change their mind.

'Somewhere.'

He backed her over to the large bed, raining kisses along her neck and collarbone until she fell onto the mattress in a puddle of ecstasy. With one hand he fished in his pocket for his wallet and produced a foil packet. Harriet was glad he didn't have a drawer full of condoms by the bed stocked up for a weekend of bedroom antics with faceless women. A hook-up had come as much of a surprise to him as it had to her but now it was happening she was glad one of them had come prepared.

She helped him shed his jacket and set to work unbuttoning his shirt, longing for the feel of his skin beneath her fingertips. Finding that patch of hair on his chest reminded her how familiar his body was to her but, oh, how she wanted to get to know it intimately again. Her hands at his fly, she began to undo his trousers.

'Harriet? I want to make this last,' he gasped as she pulled him free from the constraints of his clothes.

'I want you. Now,' she demanded. This had to be on her terms, so she remained in control. The only way she could justify bedding her ex was to treat him as casually as he had her. She had needs and though she'd taken lovers since Charles, only he could give her what she truly wanted.

Charles didn't protest. Instead, he slid his hand beneath her dress and tugged her underwear away. With their clothes half on, half off, and Harriet's dress hitched up around her waist, she waited with bated breath for him to sheath himself. There was something daring and incredibly sexy about the spontaneity of it all. She was risking everything she had by bedding him one more time when he'd had the power in the past to topple her world around her.

'I guess we do have all night to get to know each other again.' Charles smiled at her in the darkness and Harriet arched to meet him at their most sensitive parts. She wanted their bodies to do all the talking tonight. That way there could be no confusion about what she expected from him. This was only about sex. An area she knew he excelled in.

They clung to one another, perspiration settling on their skins as they raced towards that moment of utter bliss they knew they could find with each other. Harriet was already on her way to hitting that peak as though she'd been waiting for twelve long years to do this with him again. Those years apart certainly hadn't diminished their appetites for one another, not on her part at least. No other man had come close to satisfying her the way Charles had. Perhaps because she'd never allowed herself to get as emotionally involved with a man as she couldn't bear the pain that came with it, or perhaps because he'd been the best lover she'd ever had.

He knew exactly where to touch her to drive her crazy and exactly where she needed him to be. Charles too seemed to be making up for lost time, lust setting the heady rhythm of his every stroke inside her. It was as out of control as she'd ever seen him, or indeed had ever felt herself.

When her orgasm came it hit fast and hard, and as Charles's cries echoed hers she knew she never wanted this night to end. There was no more living in the past when the present was so much more enjoyable.

CHAPTER TWO

Two months later

EVERYTHING AND EVERYONE on this road trip had been telling Harriet to have a merry Christmas. From the radio presenters accompanying her on this journey, to the few strangers she'd encountered along the way, to the very weather, they'd been insisting she should be enjoying Christmas Day.

There was a fat chance of that happening, thanks to Charles, and now she was about to ruin his day too. She was happy to do this alone and more than capable. The only reason she was coming all this way was to give him the chance to step up to his obligations this time instead of walking away. He could tell her face to face if he didn't want any part of this, then they wouldn't have to see each other ever again.

The drive to Scotland had been long but uneventful thanks to the lull in traffic. Most people had chosen to stay at home celebrating with family and loved ones. How ironic when she had neither, but next year things would be different. Her whole life was about to change if she didn't take steps to secure the one she already had.

The closer she got to the Ross-Wylde family estate, the harder and faster her heart pounded and her stomach churned. Both from the conversation she had to have with Charles, and the last one they'd had at Heatherglen. She'd never imagined returning to the very place where she'd left her heart.

Road signs directed her towards the clinic that had essentially stolen Charles from her. Where he'd committed to setting up a life as the director there and Laird of the estate, instead of as her husband.

The drive up through the hills to her destination was as familiar to her as the last time she'd seen it, albeit through tear-filled eyes back then. It was dark now, the winter night so all-consuming it had swallowed up the colourful patchwork of countryside she knew surrounded her. All that remained were the inky shadows of the trees towering on either side of the winding road leading to Charles's ancestral home.

Buildings new and old appeared in view but her focus was entirely on the castle itself. With lights blazing in every window and the porch decorated with Christmas wreaths and garlands, it was a welcoming sight. An invitation to visitors that at least one of the residents might come to regret. She hadn't called or texted ahead so she had the element of surprise and could gauge Charles's true reaction to her news.

Harriet parked her car behind the others, which all had a dusting of snow like icing sugar on a sponge cake, and it was obvious no one had left the premises today. They'd been too busy having a good time, to judge by the sounds of music and laughter filtering through the crisp night air as she made her way to the entrance. There was a twinge of jealousy thinking of him celebrating the festive season here with family when she had no one. She rested her hand on her belly—flat for now. In another few months it would be a different story.

This wasn't about forcing him back into her life. She'd managed quite well without him these past years and she wasn't expecting anything from him now. Harriet wasn't that naïve. A baby hadn't been part of the deal, but she wanted to do the right thing by informing him of the pregnancy at least. With his track record she didn't believe he'd want to be involved and so she would let him know she didn't need anything from him. Her plan was simply to tell him and walk away, leaving them both with a clear conscience over the matter.

Before she could make her way up the stone steps, a door further along the castle burst open and all the warmth and excitement from inside spilled out.

'Oh, sorry. I didn't realise there was anyone out here. Are you here for the clinic?' The petite, smiling blonde looked familiar.

'Esme? Is that you?' She'd only been a teenager when Harriet had last seen her, but there was no doubt that was who she was looking at. It was those dazzling blue eyes, so much like her brother's, that gave away her identity.

'Yes? Can I help you?' There was no sign of recognition from the woman who'd almost been her sister-in-law but for all Harriet knew Charles could've had a procession of fiancées over the years. She couldn't be certain Esme would even remember her if she introduced herself.

'Esme, will you close the door, please? You're letting the cold in.' Charles's irritated voice sounded from inside right before he marched out to see what the commotion was on the doorstep.

It was then Harriet wondered what on earth she'd been thinking by turning up here tonight instead of waiting to speak to him on his own. In truth she hadn't been thinking clearly at all the second she'd seen the positive pregnancy test in her hand. She'd simply packed a bag and headed off to Scotland rather than spend the day considering what the consequences of their night of passion meant for her.

'Harriet?' He peered out into the darkness, glass of whisky in hand.

'Sorry. I didn't realise you'd have company.' She was prepared to walk away from the heated conversation she'd imagined having inside rather than discuss it in front of an audience.

'Harriet? Harriet Bell?' Esme let out a squeal and launched herself at Harriet, hugging her so tight she could no longer feel the cold, or much else.

'Esme, put her down.' Despite their more mature years, big brother Charles still spoke to her the way all boys did to their irritating little sisters. And, as all little sisters tended to do, Esme ignored him completely.

'What on earth are you doing here? It's been, what, ten years?' She had her arm around Harriet's shoulders now, steering her past the main entrance to the house to a side door.

'Twelve, but who's counting?' She managed to dodge answering the question when it was apparent Charles hadn't shared any details of even having met her at the convention. There should have been no reason for him to do so when they'd agreed to forget it had ever happened. Something they could no longer afford to do.

'It's good to see you.' Charles kissed her chastely on the cheek as she entered his ancestral home, probably for his sister's benefit. If he'd answered the door he might not have let her over the doorstep. This definitely hadn't been part of the arrangement.

'You too.' The brief contact was enough to fluster her and she hoped she could explain away her reddening skin with the cold.

'We use the main house for the clinic now. Esme and I have private rooms in another wing. We converted the old servants' quarters downstairs into a small kitchen and informal lounge. It affords us a little privacy from the comings and goings at the clinic. Now, can I get you a drink? A mulled wine or hot toddy to warm you up?' He swilled the contents of his whisky glass, filling the air with scent of cinnamon and warm spices.

'No, thanks. I'm driving. I'd take a cup of tea, though.' She didn't want anything, but she was hoping a trip to the kitchen would get her some privacy to speak to Charles alone.

'Ooh, what about a hot chocolate? I can make you a double chocolate with cream and marshmallows.' Esme's special sounded delicious after the poor service-station efforts they'd dared to charge Harriet for during the stops she'd made on the way here.

'That would be lovely, thank you.' This was all so civilised and bizarre. The Ross-Wyldes were acting as though she was a neighbour who'd just happened to drop by, not an ex-fiancée who'd turned up out of the blue after an extended absence. Either they were incredibly well mannered, which she knew, or they were too worried to ask why she'd come.

Lovely Esme slipped off towards the kitchen and Charles offered to take Harriet's coat for her. She supposed she was staying longer than she'd imagined.

'So, you were just passing by, huh?' He was smiling as he helped her out of her jacket.

She'd panicked when it was clear she couldn't blurt out the real reason she was here on his doorstep. He knew there was no 'just passing by' when London was an eight-hour drive away, yet he didn't seem put out by her unexpected arrival.

'I know this wasn't part of our deal and I'm sorry to intrude on you on Christmas night. I didn't realise you'd have a house full of people.' Even alluding to the 'arrangement' seemed salacious outside the anonymity of the hotel now, when they were in his home.

Charles, however, didn't appear perturbed if his smile was anything to go by. 'Oh, don't worry. You've saved me from another game of charades. Esme insists on covering all the clichés of the season.'

'That explains the outfit.' Now they were in better lighting she could see what he was wearing. The gold paper crown suited him, but the ugly sweater was a far cry from his usual dapper suits. Although he did look pretty cute in it.

'A present from little sis. She made it herself.' He rolled his eyes and Harriet knew he'd suffer the indignity of being seen in it rather than hurt Esme's feelings. If only he'd taken such consideration over *her* feelings when he'd broken up with her, she mightn't have been so intent on getting closure with that one last night together.

'That's lovely. It's so thoughtful for someone to put all that time and effort into making a gift.' To her, Christmas had become just another day. There weren't many presents beyond the odd box of chocolates or a bottle of wine from a grateful patient and she didn't bother making an elaborate Christmas dinner just for one. She preferred to work whenever she could, this year's exception giving her the chance to make the journey here.

'I guess. I'm sure she'd have made you one too if we'd known you were coming.'

Harriet could tell he was curious about what had brought her here when they'd severed all contact after that unforgettable night in his hotel room.

She cleared her throat. 'I came because there's something we need to discuss.'

'In that case, we should go somewhere quiet. We're

winding down from our Christmas party and there are still a few people here.'

'That would be better.' She didn't want an audience for what was a very private matter.

'What are you two still doing, standing in the hall? Charles, bring Harriet in so she can have her hot chocolate by the fire.' Esme tutted as she chivvied them towards the lounge, but Charles resisted leaving the hallway.

'I think Harriet would prefer somewhere more peaceful after her long journey.'

She saw the disappointment on Esme's face and didn't want to hurt her feelings when she'd been so welcoming. 'I can always make time for a hot chocolate first.'

Charles seemed to understand what had brought on her change of heart and stood back to let them enter the living room in front of him.

There were a few couples engaged in conversation by the table of food along the back wall and a ruggedly handsome man, who got to his feet when he saw them, sitting by the fire.

'Harriet, this is Dr Max Kirkpatrick. Max, this is Harriet Bell, an orthopaedic surgeon visiting from London.'

Charles made the introductions, giving little detail away, but Harriet realised it would be impolite for him to say she was the fiancée he'd dumped on inheriting the family silver. Introducing her as 'an ex I hooked up with recently at a medical conference' wouldn't have been the ideal ice-breaker either. The extra bodies in the room, however, did mean she was forced to delay her news a bit longer.

'Nice to meet you.' She shook hands with the man, who couldn't keep his eyes off Esme, and Harriet detected a reciprocal attraction between them. He wasn't the last man she remembered Esme being head over heels about, but she knew better than most that love didn't last for ever. These two still had that glow of new romance about them, which suggested they were in that phase when they found it hard to keep their hands off each other.

'You too. Esme, didn't you say you needed a hand with something in the kitchen?' Max wasn't very subtle about wanting some alone time with Esme, but Harriet didn't begrudge them their privacy. You had to take the good times when you could find them.

'Yes, I think I did.' Esme set the hot chocolate on the table and hurried out with him, giggling down the hall.

Harriet couldn't help but glance in Charles's direction, when they'd been as keen to spend time together not long ago. To find he was looking at her with that same longing was unravelling all the tension that had set in on the drive until her limbs felt more like spaghetti. One word and she just knew they'd both agree to another no-strings tryst. Except that word wouldn't be 'baby'. It was going to change the way he looked and felt about her, and probably not for the better.

'I should probably let you meet some of our staff here.' Charles led her over to the source of the chatter she'd heard from outside.

'Harriet Bell.' She shook hands with the group and introduced herself.

'Cassandra Bellow.' The pretty American set down the plate of canapés in her hand to greet her.

'Cassandra is one of our past patients and this is Lyle Sinclair, our medical director.' Charles didn't have to tell her these two were a couple either when they were glued to each other's sides.

'I'm Aksel Olson. I work with Esme.' The large hand pumping hers up and down next belonged to a bear of a man who couldn't fail to make an impression. The muscular build and Scandinavian accent coupled with the long air gave him a definite Viking vibe.

'Nice to meet you,' she said, before Charles moved her swiftly on to the woman standing next to him.

'Flora. I'm a physio at the clinic.'

'Hi.' She was definitely the gooseberry here but, then, so was Charles, who didn't seem to have a significant other in the mix. Something that hadn't gone unnoticed and brought her a sense of relief she hadn't known she needed. It hadn't entered her head that he might have met someone in the weeks since they'd last seen each other. Certainly, it hadn't been part of the deal that they couldn't date anyone else. They weren't supposed to see each other again. Thankfully, things wouldn't get any more complicated than they already were.

'And you've already met Esme and Max.' Charles didn't attempt to hide his disapproval as they reappeared with huge smiles on their faces.

'Are you staying in Cluchlochry?' Charles asked, as she attempted to drink her hot chocolate through the cream and marshmallow topping. It tasted as over-indulgent as it looked, and she just knew she was wearing a cream moustache as a result. As confirmed by Charles's smirk when she lifted her head to reply.

She did her best to wipe away all traces with the back of her hand. 'Probably. I didn't really think that far ahead.'

It would be suicidal to attempt a return trip tonight when she was ready for bed. There was bound to be a B&B in the village where she could put her head down for the night.

Charles frowned. 'Not everywhere would be willing to take guests in on Christmas night and those that do will be booked out. We get a lot of people who come for the Christmas market and stay on for Christmas itself.'

'You must stay with us, Harri. There's plenty of room.' It was Esme who offered her refuge, not her brother. Although Harriet wanted to protest, she couldn't face getting back into her car again so soon.

'Esme, I really wish you wouldn't invite every waif and stray into Heatherglen as though it's your personal rescue centre. We converted the stables for your pet projects.'

'No offence taken,' Harriet muttered.

'Sorry. That was directed at someone else.' He nodded towards the furry bundle currently rolling around at his feet.

'Oh, he's gorgeous. What's his name?' She knelt

down to stroke the curious-looking puppy with tiger-striped brown fur, which was wearing its own ugly little sweater.

'Dougal. He was half-starved when we found him, but Aksel nursed him back to health. Esme's trying to find him a home now.'

It was Flora who filled her in on his sad background, which just made him even more adorable.

'My sister has issues about turning anyone away.' Charles muttered.

'Harriet is neither a waif nor a stray. She's a friend who's very welcome to stay.' Esme overruled her older brother, using Harriet as a pawn in their sibling rivalry.

'I didn't say she wasn't. I was simply making a point, Esme.'

Harriet set down her cup. 'It would probably be easier if I look for somewhere in town to stay.'

This wasn't what she had planned at all. By this stage she'd expected to be on her way home, with Charles thanking his lucky stars for escaping the parent trap.

'No!' Both Ross-Wyldes expressed their indignation at the suggestion.

'I thought you said you wanted to talk to me about something?'

'We have so much catching up to do, Harri.'

The group watched the pair vying for her attention with as much fascination as she was, and Charles discreetly manoeuvred the argument away from the spectators over to the far side of the room.

'Charles is just trying to make a point—badly—about him being the king of the castle here. He runs the clinic and I run the veterinary practice and canine therapy centre across the way.' Esme punched him not so playfully on the arm.

'Oh, I think you mean Laird, Esme—but, yes, this isn't about you. Forgive me, Harriet. I'll take you up and show you to one of the spare rooms. Dear sister, perhaps you'd be so kind as to get Harriet something to eat too?'

He batted his eyelashes at Esme and Harriet knew it would be enough to persuade her to do anything. Especially when he was wearing those glasses and that jumper, which made him look more like the Charles she'd known instead of the suave version she'd met at the conference. She hoped that would keep some of the most recent, more erotic memories at bay so she could stay focused on the reason she'd come all this way.

'I would love to—but I'm doing it for our guest, not you, Chas.' Esme fluttered those same long dark eyelashes in response. They were so alike it was probably why they'd fought for as long as Harriet had known them. Deep down it was obvious how much they loved each other, and she wished she'd had a brother or a sister to fight with, love unconditionally, and have to hold after she'd lost everyone else.

'We keep a few rooms made up just in case of emergencies.' Charles led her up the stairs to one of the bedrooms. She couldn't help but wonder which door led to his.

'Do you get many late-night, uninvited women calling in on you?' she teased, when he was such a stark contrast to the man who'd literally sent her packing in a previous lifetime.

'No, I don't, but sometimes we get patients arriving too late to be admitted to the clinic, so we put them up here for the night.' Her teasing fell flat with him, but she supposed his defence from her insinuations was understandable when she was accusing him of having loose morals. She knew nothing about him any more.

'I'm sure it's most appreciated. As it is by me.' She had to remember he was doing her a favour by letting her stay when she had no right to be here. Their risky behaviour in London had been her idea and as such she was fully prepared to take on the consequences single-handedly.

'Bed, bathroom, wardrobe. All the essentials.' He did a quick tour of the room before turning back to her. 'Do you need help bringing in your luggage?'

'I just have an overnight bag in the car, but I can manage that myself. As I said, this was a spur-of-the-moment visit.'

'Ah, yes. The talk. Is this about what happened in London? I must admit it's been harder to put out of my mind than I'd imagined too.' He was moving towards her and Harriet's heart leapt into her throat at the thought of him kissing her again. She wanted it so much but that's not what had brought her here.

'I'm pregnant, Charles.'

His outstretched arms immediately fell limply to his sides. 'Pardon me?'

She sat down on the edge of the bed, wishing it would swallow her up. 'That night in London… I'm pregnant.'

Charles collapsed onto the mattress beside her. 'But—but we took precautions.'

'The first time,' she reminded him with as much of a smile as she could muster when she was wound up tighter than a drum, waiting for his reaction.

The second time had happened later, when they had both been naked under the covers and he'd reached for her, keen to do things at a slower pace and drive her wild with want before he had his way with her again. The third time, in the early hours of the morning, when she'd reached for him, knowing they would have to part again.

Conception could have happened at any point during those few passionate hours together. They'd simply been too wrapped up in each other, literally, to care. Well, they would now.

He dropped his head into his hands and she waited for him to process the information.

'Are you sure? Have you done a test?'

'Yes, Charles. I wouldn't have driven all this way otherwise.' She understood this was a shock to him, her too, but questioning her common sense wasn't going to make the situation go away.

'I gave up on plans for a family after we broke up. With very good reason. I don't have time to spare for babies and all the baggage that comes with them.' He was on his feet now, pacing the room like a caged animal. Trapped and unsure how to get out.

'Believe me, becoming a mother wasn't in my immediate plans either but here we are. I only came here to tell you about the baby because I thought it was the right thing to do. I didn't say I wanted anything from you. You had no room in your life for me, I wouldn't expect it to be different for your child.' If he thought she'd waited until she was at the peak of her career to seduce him, get pregnant and force him back into her life, he'd really forgotten who she was.

'That night was supposed to be a bit of fun. One last hurrah before we went our separate ways again. A baby means the complete opposite. We'll be tied together for ever now. If I'd wanted that I would've saved us the heartbreak of splitting up twelve years ago.'

'Okay. You've made your point. I don't think there's anything left for us to say.' She should never have come here. Despite whatever flicker of hope she may have harboured for a different response, Charles had proved he hadn't changed. He still had the capacity to let her down. She'd managed this far on her own and she was sure she could raise this baby alone too. It was preferable to Charles feigning interest, only to have him bail out later and make their child suffer too.

Harriet was pregnant. It was his fault for not protecting her, for getting carried away, and not thinking about the consequences of his actions. Again.

When she'd turned up on the doorstep tonight he'd

hoped it was because she'd wanted a replay of that night in London. Perhaps an extended version that would have taken them into the New Year instead of one night. Mostly because he hadn't been able to get that time together out of his head, but this was a whole different scenario.

He was waiting, hating this ridiculous sweater more than ever, for Harriet to give him some sort of clue what he was supposed to do next. Instead, she slowly rose from the bed, crossed the floor and walked out the door. It wasn't the response he'd expected but some space would be good. Esme could keep her entertained and when he'd digested the news they could sit down and plan the next move.

Any second now Esme would come bowling up the stairs and deliver a knock-out punch once she heard what had happened. He was surprised Harriet hadn't done just that after the way he'd spoken to her. It had been a knee-jerk reaction to finding out he was going to be a father and one he'd apologise for once this sank in. He was angry at himself, not her, when his selfish needs had resulted in this life-changing news. The last thing he'd ever wanted to do was complicate her life.

Harriet's response to his outburst was reminiscent of that awful day of his father's funeral. She hadn't slapped him then either, the way most women would have. Silently crying, she'd simply packed her things and walked out. He hadn't seen or heard from her again until that conference.

At the sound of a car engine running outside,

Charles rushed to the window in time to see Harriet driving away. It was déjà vu, except he couldn't claim his actions, or lack of them now, had been in any way for her benefit.

'Charles, what the hell have you done?' Esme arrived, as he'd known she would, temper flaring, fists balling, ready for a fight.

'Not now.'

'You must have said something to make her leave like that. Are you really just going to stand here and watch her go? Again?' That was the ultimate question. What they were going to do about the baby, how he felt about Harriet and what they did next were incidental if he let her go without a fight again. She was a successful surgeon in her own right with no need for him or his money. He was the one standing to lose out here.

'Tell everyone to go home. The party's over.' He left Esme to break up the gathering before dashing downstairs to retrieve his own car keys. His child wasn't going to grow up thinking its father was a disappointment, like the rest of his family had.

This was one time he could do the right thing without waiting until it was too late. He couldn't live with any more guilt and regret. Losing his father and brother had taught him not to be selfish, and unless he wanted to lose his child too he had to think about the needs of its mother. That didn't include being upset by her baby's father. Not when she'd driven the whole way to Scotland to tell him personally on Christmas Day. Something a person would only do if they had no one else to turn to.

CHAPTER THREE

'DID YOU HONESTLY expect him to react any differently? What were you hoping for? A happy-everafter? Stupid woman!' Harriet chastised herself in the mirror as she drove away.

She'd given him the chance to be involved in the baby's life and he wasn't interested. End of story. It was his loss. She knew where she stood and that wasn't with Charles by her side. She could raise this child alone. It would be better for her and the child. At least it was apparent she'd be parenting on her own from the beginning, unlike her poor mother.

Coming here had been a reminder that night in London had been nothing more than a fantasy. The real Charles was entrenched in family tradition and duty with no room for anyone else in his life. Harriet was an independent city girl. She didn't belong here. She hated the fact it still hurt that he didn't want her, whatever the circumstances.

Perhaps she'd convinced herself something had changed between them after their escapade in that hotel room, and not merely on a physical level. Deep down she'd hoped he'd be pleased to see her again because, even before realising she was pregnant, she'd wondered about rekindling their relationship. Sentimentality and lust over common sense, but she hadn't been thinking with her head lately. That's how she'd ended up in this mess.

Charles Ross-Wylde had altered the course of her life again, sending her down a road she'd never planned to take. Now she simply had to make the best of it, the way she had the last time. Only instead of becoming a successful surgeon, her next goal was to become a good mother too.

Bright lights began strobing around her, disturbing the pitch-black night. A glance in her rear-view mirror revealed a car, flashing its headlights at her and now blaring its horn. Someone from the house had followed her and was trying to get her attention. Esme, no doubt, had figured out something was amiss and was coming to persuade her to go back. There was no way Charles would've told his sister about the baby when he didn't want it messing up his life. It was likely to be her good heart making her chase after someone who was virtually a stranger now.

Although Harriet had no intention of going back with her, she would put Esme's mind at ease because she held no bad feelings towards her. She indicated and pulled into the side of the road. The sooner they said their goodbyes, the sooner she could leave Heatherglen behind her for ever.

She stepped out onto the grass verge, but the headlights continued to blind her as she waited for the driver to get out. It wasn't until the very tall, very male silhouette drew closer that she realised it wasn't Esme who'd flagged her down.

'I have nothing to say to you. At least, nothing very ladylike,' she threw at Charles, hurrying back towards her car. He probably wanted her to sign some sort of gagging order to prevent her from claiming her unborn child had any right to the estate.

Her attempt to open her car door was thwarted as Charles grabbed her arm and spun her around. 'I'm sorry, Harriet. I reacted badly.'

'You think?' She tried to wrench her arm out of his grasp. It was going to be harder to continue hating him if he insisted on touching her, reminding her of an intimacy they could never have again.

'Come back to the house so we can talk.' He didn't let go of her, but he did loosen his grip.

'Why? You've made it clear you don't want to be part of this.'

'I'm sorry. It was a shock to the system, that's all. We both know I was a very willing participant that night, and the following morning.' His cheeky grin did things to her insides, which apparently shouldn't be acted on.

Goodness, she needed him to stop teasing her with enough delicious memories to block out the more hideous ones. Twice now he'd let her down in the most callous way. The last time she'd forgotten not to trust him and had let her hormones do the talking she'd ended up pregnant.

'I should've called instead of coming here.' That

was one thing she was sure about and something he'd agree with when she'd spoiled his Christmas.

'No. I'm glad you came. Look, it's late and freezing cold out here. Why don't you just come back to the house? The talking can wait.'

It was tempting when her stomach was rumbling and the tip of her nose was so cold she was convinced it had turned blue. She thought of the lovely roaring fire in the lounge and the banquet of food spread out and going to waste. Pregnancy apparently had lowered the price of her pride. If she went back with him it would be for the baby's sake. They had things to sort out. It was the whole reason she was here. It definitely wasn't anything to do with the man still holding her, dressed in that ridiculous sweater his little sister had knitted for him.

'I don't have anywhere else to go, I suppose.' She didn't fancy traipsing around town, knocking on doors and hoping to find room at an inn.

'That's settled, then. You're coming home with me.' If only he meant that as something other than a polite host she'd be reassured he'd had a change of heart where the baby was concerned. This was more about him saving face in front of his family and friends. She shouldn't get too carried away with the idea that he'd finally stepped up to be the man she'd always believed he was deep down. For now, she'd take advantage of the food and lodgings being offered because it suited her and meant she'd no longer be putting her unborn child at risk out here in the Scottish wilderness.

'Fine.' She got back into her car, but nothing had changed. Except perhaps his conscience getting the better of him at letting the mother of his child disappear into the night.

Harriet followed Charles back to the house, resolving to take herself straight to bed and avoid any further confrontation. When he slammed on his brakes as they approached the house, she almost ran into the back of his car. As it was, she nearly gave herself whiplash having to make her own emergency stop.

'What the hell are you playing at, Charles?' she shouted as she wrestled her seat belt off, about to jump out and give him hell. That's when she saw him bolting across the driveway, not even taking time to close the car door behind him.

She got out and followed him over to the side of the road where the house lights didn't quite manage to reach. It wasn't until she was standing over him that she realised what it was his headlights had picked up along the drive. Charles was hunched over the body of a woman who was clearly having some sort of fit. Stranger still, there was a dog lying next to her, providing some sort of cushion for her head.

'Fenella? Can you hear me? It's Charles, Esme's brother.' Charles checked the woman's pulse while he tried to get some sort of response from her.

Harriet knelt beside them and brushed away the debris of Christmas presents scattered around her, and anything else she could hurt herself on while her body was jerking uncontrollably on the cold ground. 'Is she one of your patients?'

'One of Esme's clients. She's epileptic so we'll just have to wait this out with her.'

When someone was having a seizure it was important not to restrain or try to move them in case of injury. All they could do was make sure she didn't hurt herself and time the fitting in case it developed into something more serious. A fit lasting more than five minutes could lead to brain damage.

'I don't think she hurt herself in the fall. I can't see any obvious injuries.' Harriet checked as best she could and loosened the scarf around Fenella's neck.

'That'll be down to Nora, the dog Esme trained with her. She would've alerted Fenella that the seizure was coming and positioned herself underneath to prevent her hitting her head.'

'That's amazing.' She'd known what Esme did for a living but actually seeing it in practice made Harriet see what a valuable service she was providing to the people who came to her. As was Charles. Despite her personal issues with him, there was no denying the good he was doing at Heatherglen between the clinic and the canine therapy centre he'd set up with his sister.

'The convulsions are slowing now. She should be back with us soon.'

'I'll go and alert the others so we can get her inside out of this cold.' Harriet hurried inside to inform Esme and Max so they could organise a transfer for her into the clinic. When she came round, Fenella would be tired and probably confused about what had happened. She'd be spending the night under medical observation and so would Nora.

By the time Fenella had been admitted to a bed in the clinic for the night and Esme had taken Nora to the kennels, Harriet was emotionally and physically exhausted. Charles had gone out to park the cars and lock them so she thought she could sneak off to bed unnoticed.

With a foot on the first tread of the staircase she thought she'd got away with it until Charles called her back.

'Harriet, you don't have to hide away from me up there. Come and get something to eat. You deserve it after the night you've had.'

Her stomach rumbled and made the decision to stay for her. 'I did miss dinner.'

'It's important for the baby's sake that you don't skip meals.' At least he was acknowledging her condition, even if it was only to scold her.

The house was unfeasibly quiet compared to the raucous atmosphere she'd arrived to earlier. 'Is Fenella okay?'

Charles led her to the kitchen where the worktops were laden with covered leftovers. 'She'll be fine. Apparently, she was coming to deliver a few Christmas presents to the staff but she really shouldn't have been out walking alone in that cold weather. I'm going to look into the medication she's on and see if I can reduce the frequency of the seizures. I'll get onto Clydesbank Hospital again and get a rush on her records. In the meantime, Esme is spoiling the dog something rotten for doing such a good job tonight.' The smile on his face showed the pride he had in his sister's achievements.

'Does Esme know about you-know-what?' She pointed to her belly, afraid to mention the baby again and end this fragile truce, but she didn't want to put her foot in it if she ran into Esme at some point.

'No. One thing at a time. Now, turkey sandwich?' He uncovered the carcass of their earlier dinner and Harriet was so hungry she could've attacked it with her bare hands.

'Yes, please.'

'Help yourself to a drink.' He waved the huge carving knife in the direction of the fridge, where she found a bottle of non-alcoholic grape fizz. She poured two glasses in the hope he wasn't just going to sit there and watch her eat. Thankfully, he placed two plates of sandwiches on the table and they both sat down.

'This is really good. Thanks, Charles.'

'I'm sorry about what I said earlier, Harriet.'

After a couple of bites, they talked over each other, Charles surprising her with his topic of choice.

'You were being honest. A baby isn't in your plans.'

He set down his half-eaten sandwich. Harriet's appetite too had waned at the reminder of their earlier conversation. 'It's been a long day and I wasn't prepared for that kind of bombshell. I shouldn't have been so short with you.'

'Believe me, it came as a shock to me too. Why do you think I jumped into my car and started driving here, Charles? I didn't know how to react any more than you do, but the important thing is where we go from here.'

An apology for his behaviour on this occasion was progress and more than he'd offered the last time he'd spoken to her so harshly.

'Okay, so you're a couple of months gone?'

She nodded, though she'd been so busy she hadn't noticed the first missed period. 'I honestly only came to tell you about the baby so no one could ever say I kept it from you. I mean, joint parenting between London and Scotland simply isn't feasible. Plus, I intend to continue with my medical career.' Motherhood and her job could co-exist if organised properly well in advance.

Charles took a drink as he contemplated his response. 'I want to *be* a father. I just didn't think it would happen. Although seeing everyone around me settling down and starting their own families has made me realise I did want that once. I know this wasn't planned, but it's really a blessing. I mean, this child will be the heir to Heatherglen. This is a legacy that should be passed on to the next generation. I can't let you walk away with my baby when I'd want to be more than just a weekend dad. Family is everything to me and I want my child close.'

It was such a turnaround Harriet's head was spinning. She should've considered the Ross-Wylde obsession with family tradition before coming here. Of course the Laird of Heatherglen would want an heir and she'd made it all so easy for him. There was nothing to say he had to want her along with the baby. As was clear when his first thoughts were about passing on his legacy. She'd left herself open to becoming collateral damage for a second time.

Did Charles think he could somehow get custody of their child and keep her out of the picture altogether? She hadn't anticipated having a custody fight on her hands but if he insisted, she'd do everything in her power to make sure this child had a stable influence in life. Experience had taught her that Charles wasn't reliable enough for that role.

'How do you suppose we do that? It's not practical for either of us to travel up and down the country on a whim and my schedule is not nine to five, Monday to Friday. What are you going to do, kidnap me? Lock me up in the attic until I give birth and dispose of me when I've outlived my usefulness?' She snorted. It might sound absurd but right now he was making her feel little more than a baby-making machine. This wasn't supposed to be about him. She had to fit in a life of her own somewhere, not spend every spare minute making sure Charles was happy.

'I don't think we need to resort to that, but you could move in here. The house is big enough that we could live our separate lives and share child care.' He'd managed to come up with a practical solution to co-parenting that suited him. Her initial suspicion was that he'd only suggested the move because he knew she'd never agree to it. Heatherglen held so many sad associations for her that she couldn't imagine waking up every morning in the very place where their fairy-tale romance had turned into a nightmare.

Then he would be free to make a legal bid for custody and who wouldn't think a child would be better off with his prestigious side of the family and their millions in the bank? A cold sweat broke out over Harriet's skin at the fight she could have on her hands for a baby she hadn't realised she wanted so much until now.

'You know that's not an option, Charles. My life and my career are in London.' Unlike him, she'd never left.

'Hear me out. The country would be so much better to raise a child than the city. You have no family there and look at the land we have around us. At least here you'd be surrounded by family and friends.'

'Your family, your friends, your home and your rules, I expect.' She wasn't going to let him control her. There was no way she was giving up her independence to be locked away in a tower, so the Laird and master of all he surveyed had unlimited access to his heir. What was in that for her?

'Esme would be the baby's family too. Everyone else who lives and works at Heatherglen would soon become a friend to you. Not to mention those mutts my sister keeps around the place. I'm sure a child would appreciate growing up around her four-legged friends much more than I do.' There was a hint of tension surrounding the matter and she could imagine how irked he'd be finding puppies peeing on his antique rugs. She'd be tempted to agree just to see his face when that happened.

'I told you, I'm not flushing away my career because I'm pregnant. Being the mother of your children is no longer enough for me in life, as hard as that might be for you to believe.' His ego had grown to match the size of his bank balance if he thought he was enough for her to turn her back on the success she'd worked so hard to achieve.

'I'm not asking you to give anything up for me. It would be for the baby.'

'Emotional blackmail won't get you anywhere, Charles. I'll raise this child to understand women can have it all these days. You did me a favour, you know, dumping me like that. If you hadn't, I would've left London there and then and moved here with you. I would never have had the career I have now.'

'Why do you think I did it?' he mumbled as he cleared the dishes away. That was the first time he'd offered any explanation for his actions, but he wasn't making any sense.

'You told me you no longer wanted to marry me, that you had Heatherglen and didn't need me once you inherited your father's land and title.' Not his exact words but it was the gist of his rejection after his father's funeral and sufficient to send her back to London alone with a broken heart.

'Did you honestly believe I was able to switch off my feelings for you so easily? I knew you'd insist on moving back here with me and I didn't want you to give up on your medical dreams. This place cost my father his life. I knew the mess and the hard work I had waiting for me here. I didn't want to inflict that suffering on you too.'

Harriet could see he was being sincere and felt as though her heart was breaking all over again. For that young woman who'd believed she wasn't good enough for the love of her life, and for the grieving son who'd had the weight of the world on his shoulders.

'I had no idea.' Her voice was but a whisper as she came to terms with the knowledge it had all been a lie, albeit with the best of intentions. All these years she'd hated him when he'd acted out of love for her. Yet there was a slow burning fire starting deep inside her that he'd taken the choice away from her about her future.

'Yes, well, we can't go back even if we wanted to. This is about moving forward.'

'Wait. You made that decision for me to return to London and now you're dictating I move here because it's more convenient for you? Control freak much? Are you so bored and lonely out here you've decided it might be nice to have an ex with benefits on site?' She couldn't sit here any more when she wanted to smash things, including Charles's face, for he was being so damned noble and breaking her heart without giving her a valid reason. There was no doubt she would've moved to Heatherglen with him because she'd loved him and nothing else had mattered. It was a shame he hadn't felt the same way about her.

'I know you're angry, but it worked out for the best,

didn't it? Until now.' He gave a sad smile, which she wasn't sure was for her or himself.

It was a revelation to find out his behaviour, in his eyes, had been in her best interests. From the outside it would seem his plan had worked. She was financially stable, living in London with a career she'd dreamed of, but she'd never been able to trust again. Despite his scheming, fate had brought them together in the end, expecting the baby she'd always imagined having with Charles. Except now the circumstances didn't include parents who were in love or anything like it.

'My career isn't up for negotiation.' She wasn't budging on that point and he couldn't make her. If he had sent her away to build on her career, that time apart would've been wasted if she was expected to give it all up now.

'We have the clinic here. It would be a real coup to have someone of your calibre with us. Heatherglen could offer you a flexible position to fit around your needs and a home for you and the baby. Come and work here. It sounds like the perfect solution to me.'

'Of course it does. You win this way. It's your home and it doesn't inconvenience you. You get to play daddy on a full-time basis on your doorstep and get an orthopaedic surgeon thrown in too. However, it's asking a lot from me to give up everything at home to move here.' Regardless of Charles's wealth and the unspoilt land around Heatherglen, Harriet didn't know if this was the best environment in which to raise a child, or even to live in herself. She knew nothing of life in the country or how isolated she might feel here. However, she did know that Heatherglen hadn't brought her happiness in the past and the family ties that kept Charles here weren't what she wanted for her baby.

What scared her most, though, was having all those feelings resurfacing for Charles and being trapped here with them. One night had been difficult enough to forget, even before she'd realised she had a souvenir of the event.

'It's not a competition, Harriet. Don't you want us to do this together? It would be a partnership without the inconvenient distance between us.' He made it sound so straightforward, but it was that distance that would keep her sane now they were back in each other's lives.

'Do you really have need for an orthopaedic surgeon here? I mean, I'm not trading in a full schedule for the odd consultation here and there. I'm not taking a demotion.' The whole point of this exercise was to ensure parenting wouldn't affect her working life. She couldn't help thinking this was going to end up with her in that stay-at-home mum role she was trying to avoid.

'As a matter of fact, I have a patient at the moment I could use your help with. If you find clinic life and motherhood aren't enough for you, I'm sure every hospital within a hundred-mile radius will be queuing up to have you on their books. You could consult, run your own clinics. Whatever you need.' He was being so damned reasonable it was difficult to argue with the options he was laying out before her. It was being around other people she found most appealing. Life in London was busy, hectic, and she did everything at breakneck speed, but that was because she didn't have anyone at home to make it worth her while to slow down to enjoy time out from it all. That was going to change in a few months, whether she was ready for it or not.

'Why should I believe you're not going to change your mind again?' There was no way of predicting the outcome if she took this gamble but there was every chance she'd be the one to come off worse out of this arrangement.

'I've lost a brother, a father and a fiancée because of this place. I don't want it to cost me the chance of being a father too. You know I can't leave here, there's just too much responsibility involved, but I want my child to know I'll be there for her or him. Your moving here would give me the chance to do that.'

'It's a lot to put on my shoulders, Charles, and after everything we've been through…'

'Marry me, then. I can provide you both with everything you could ever need. I know you need something in return to offset everything you'd be trading in to come here.'

'Don't be ridiculous.' It was like a slap across the face for him to toss a proposal of marriage in there so casually, as if it meant nothing, when the last time he'd asked her that question it had meant the world to her.

Her mother had passed away not long after they'd

started dating and Charles had represented everything she'd thought she'd have in her new life. Marriage and stability were all she'd wanted then but he had obviously never held it in the same regard when he'd used it as a device to keep her dangling on a string.

'It's not unheard of for a couple to get married for the sake of a baby. I would give you equal rights to the estate, the clinic and anything else you wanted.' He was offering everything except love and devotion, the only things that could ever convince Harriet marriage would be a good idea.

'No.'

His shoulders slumped when she torpedoed his marriage of convenience idea, but he'd a lot to learn about the woman he was dealing with now. This one wouldn't be so easily swayed into the life-changing decisions he made on a whim.

'When are you due back at work?'

'Not until January. Why?'

'You could spend the rest of your break here. A trial run if you like. You could get to know the staff and patients at the clinic and see where you could be working if you gave it a chance.'

'See if you and I can live together in the same place without coming to blows?' She didn't know how to get out of this situation she'd created by coming here in the first place. If she left now, Charles would be sure to look into the legalities surrounding the baby's parentage and she didn't want him or her to get caught in a tug of war between them. It might be best to do as he'd suggested and stay. That way she could do her best to make him see how impossible it would be for her to fit in here. She would be reasonable and, when it didn't work out, she could say she'd tried to do things his way. Once she was back in London and the baby was born it would be too unsettling for them to uproot again.

If she stayed, it wouldn't be the clashes between them she was sure would keep her awake at night but the memories of the passion he'd awakened in her. Something she'd be reminded of with every ounce of gained weight and growing belly. Yet he'd barely mentioned that incredible time they'd had, as if it had never happened, and this pregnancy had been some sort of divine intervention.

This baby had apparently been created from thin air solely to provide him with the opportunity to become a father. A few days under the same roof would give them both an idea of how difficult it would be to carry on that pretence. If she couldn't manage it, they'd have to come up with a plan B. For now, this was the only one they'd come up with.

'What do you say, Harriet? You, me and baby for the rest of the festive season? It would mean you'll be here for our Hogmanay party too. Esme is hosting it this year so it's sure to be a spectacle you don't want to miss.'

She tried to convince herself it was the headache of facing a custody battle that finally persuaded her to stay. Not his smiling blue eyes or the thought of them spending time as a family.

CHAPTER FOUR

'ORANGE JUICE, CEREAL, toast and tea.' Charles ticked off the breakfast checklist as he loaded a tray to take up to Harriet. Since it was early in her pregnancy, he wasn't sure how she'd react faced with a cooked breakfast first thing in the morning and chose the safe option.

He still couldn't quite believe he was going to be a father. For the longest time it had only been him and Esme at the castle, wrapped up in their own careers. Now there would be a new focus. Okay, the suggestion of marriage had been a mistake but since he and Harriet had agreed back in London that they had no future together, he'd wanted something to keep her in his life. He was asking her to give up more than ever to move back to Scotland now, with nothing to offer her in return. For now he just wanted time with her and a chance for them to work this out together.

Family was something he never dared believe he could have after inheriting Heatherglen and knowing his whole life would be tied up in it. It was expected for the Laird to marry and provide an heir, but it had been more important for him to get the clinic up and running. Now he had no choice, and there was going to be a baby, it was a chance for him to be normal and have a role for himself other than running the castle and clinic. No other woman had lived up to Harriet, so it seemed only fitting that she should be the mother of his child.

'Someone looks happy this morning.'

He looked up to find Harriet standing in the kitchen doorway with much the same expression on her face as the one he was wearing.

'I was thinking how nice it might be to have a wee one running around the place.' He didn't need to lie to her when he was trying to persuade her to stick around. She had to know he was looking forward to it all, no longer fighting the idea.

'I haven't agreed to anything yet.' Her frown told him he'd jumped the gun, but he was determined to make her see this was the best place for them both.

'What are you doing up, anyway? I was going to bring you breakfast in bed.' He did his best to dodge another argument, even though he was miffed she'd thwarted his attempt to gain brownie points.

'I'm an early riser. I like to make the most of every day. Thanks, though.' She took a seat at the table and started picking at a slice of toast from the tray. Charles joined her so he wouldn't appear rude in leaving her by herself, then poured himself a cup of coffee and sat down.

'Ah, yes. My little lark. I'd forgotten how much you enjoy mornings.' It was a throwaway comment borne of past familiarity, but it brought back more recent, erotic memories, which made him shift in his chair. Images of their early morning tryst in that hotel bed burst into his thoughts and refused to leave.

Harriet was blinking at him, her toast hovering in mid-air, frozen by the inappropriate reference to her insatiable appetite for him. It wasn't as though they could avoid the subject altogether when she was carrying the evidence, but he realised he'd been indiscreet. Harriet had made it clear she didn't intend to let their past get in the way of a potential working relationship.

'It's only me!' Esme's timely arrival through the back door saved both their blushes.

'Morning, Esme.' Harriet sounded as relieved as he was to have someone break the sudden tension in the air.

His sister was going to lose her mind when she heard she was going to be an aunt.

'I've just been down to the therapy centre to pick up a few things. Charles said you could use a change of clothes so you didn't get yours dirty. I brought you some of our winter gear.' She plonked the pile of clothes and boots on the table, Charles whipping away the breakfast things a fraction of a second before she did so.

'That's very kind of you but there's really no need to fuss.'

'It's only a sweater, some waterproofs and a pair of wellies to wear around the estate. Nothing fancy, just practical.'

Harriet made no further protest. 'Thank you. I don't know how much longer I'll get away with wearing my own clothes anyway.'

She tested the give in the trousers, stretching the elastic waistband. Charles could see the very second she realised what she'd said as her wide-eyed gaze flicked between him and Esme.

His sister didn't miss it either. 'What do you mean?'

Worried he'd put his foot in it more than he already had, Charles left it to Harriet as to what to say next. There would be no going back once Esme knew about the baby. Although, by the excitement he could already see fizzing up inside her, she'd probably already guessed.

'I...er...' Harriet cleared her throat. 'I'm pregnant.'

Esme managed to contain herself a second or two longer until Harriet confirmed the paternity, should it be in question.

'Charles is the father.'

His sister's squeal almost deafened him. 'Oh, my goodness! When did this happen? How did this happen? Wait...don't answer that one. This. Is. *Amazing!*'

Another squeal and she launched herself at Harriet. Charles leaned back against the kitchen worktop, content to let them hug it out, only to have the breath knocked out of him too by an Esme missile.

'Are you trying to kill me?' He laughed as she squeezed him hard.

'I'm just so happy for you, bro.' She paused. 'It is good news, isn't it?'

He supposed neither he nor Harriet appeared to have as much zing as the auntie-to-be.

'Yes, of course.' There was no hesitation in his reply and he wished he'd been as positive about the news the first time around. That knee-jerk, defensive lashing out had damaged what little trust Harriet had left in him, but he hoped he'd have the chance to repair their relationship over these next few days. If only for the baby's sake.

'It was that conference, wasn't it? I knew something had happened. You couldn't wipe the smile off your face for a week. My brother has been emotionally frozen since losing you, unless you count being perpetually grumpy. You're the one person who ever seemed to make him happy.' Esme knew him better than he was comfortable with and the heat in his cheeks confirmed he'd flushed the same shade of scarlet as Harriet.

He flashed Harriet an unspoken apology for his sibling's lack of tact. This was their love life, the supposedly never-to-be-spoken-of-again fling they were now discussing over the breakfast table. A bit much for someone who hadn't set foot in this house in over a decade.

'I'm only here over the festive season so we can work a few things out.' If Harriet didn't see the need to satisfy Esme's curiosity with the details, neither would he.

'Well, I hope you do. Feel free to pop down to the therapy centre and look around or, you know, if you just want to talk.' As subtle as a brick, Esme shot a dark look in his direction that said she'd already pinpointed him as the source of their conflict. He'd prepare himself for an interrogation, followed by an ear-bashing, once they were alone.

'Thanks. I'll keep that in mind.'

'Yes, Esme, thanks for bringing the clothes over for Harriet. We wouldn't want to keep you from your work any longer than necessary.' He didn't need her siding against him too if she thought he'd been in the wrong. Which he had been. Besides, he needed every second he could get alone with Harriet to try and redeem himself.

'It's lovely to have you here, Harriet.' Esme ignored him and kissed her new favourite person— which obviously wasn't him—on the cheek.

'I'm only a couple of months gone, so I'd appreciate it if you keep the news to yourself for now.' It might've helped Charles's cause if Harriet hadn't enforced a news blackout, but he knew Esme would respect her wishes, even if she was fit to bust with the good news.

'I can't believe I'm going to be an auntie.' She skipped back out the door and he envied her carefree position in this situation.

'She's going to make a wonderful aunt,' Harriet mused.

'Esme will spoil the baby rotten.' She was bad enough fussing over those dogs so the second a baby was on the scene the place would be filled with toys and cute outfits. Strangely, the thought of the castle being turned upside down didn't disturb him as much as it usually did. It would be nice for it to be a proper home again instead of a memorial reminding him of everything he'd lost. His sister was right about one thing, though. He had been frozen here, never really coming to terms with his losses, including Harriet. Hopefully now, reconnecting with her would bring him some peace again.

'Yes, well, I'm sure we'll be glad to have an extra pair of hands when it comes to babysitting. *If* I decide to stay.' Harriet was quick to correct herself, but it was a good sign she was thinking about having support here at Heatherglen rather than being on her own. Letting the news slip to Esme could've been the best thing to happen. For him. With his sister on side he'd have double the chance of persuading Harriet to stay permanently.

'Why don't I give you a tour of the clinic and let you see everything we've achieved?' Perhaps if she saw why he'd sacrificed their future it would give them the chance to have another one.

Harriet cursed her big mouth. As lovely as Esme was, she wished she hadn't blabbed about the pregnancy. Now there was more than her and Charles involved it was bound to complicate things. Once Charles realised there was no way she was letting him dictate the rest of her and her baby's lives, a clean break wasn't going to be so easy. Not with a super-excited auntie in the mix.

She could do without Charles being all charming and thoughtful too. He'd thrown her last night by coming after her and begging her to stay. Even if it was for his own selfish reasons. That last-minute plea for a second chance, that offer of a future here at Heatherglen had left an opening for a flicker of hope she couldn't extinguish that he might still be the honourable gentleman she'd once believed him to be.

Their time together at that conference had reawakened feelings for Charles she had no business having when he didn't deserve them. She had confused past Harriet and Charles for their present-day incarnations because her hormones were all over the place.

So, she'd woken up this morning determined to harden her heart against him. Only to find him making her breakfast, smiling to himself about the baby coming, and arranging for her to be more comfortable in this environment. That's why she'd spilled the beans to Esme. She'd been so comfortable she'd started imagining being here as part of a family.

All she could do to save herself now as he led her out for a walk in the grounds was to look at Heatherglen from a professional viewpoint. There was no way she'd be content with swapping the hustle and bustle of London hospitals for a country practice. Working on a casual basis in the middle of nowhere would be a demotion for her. A sure-fire way to ensure her career took a back seat to motherhood. Exactly what she'd hoped to avoid.

'I know the twenty-sixth of December is considered a holiday, but I hope you don't mind if I call in and see my patients? It must suck, being away from home at this time of year.'

They walked to the front of the clinic and it seemed odd to find everything still decorated for the season when Christmas Day had been something of a non-event for her. Christmas night, on the other hand, had been more action-packed than she'd anticipated.

'I don't mind at all. I know as well as you do we're never really off duty.' If she'd been back in London she might've been calling in on some of her own patients. There weren't very many people in her life. At least, none who'd be spending time with her instead of with their own families.

Sometimes those patients having treatment were her comfort as much as she hopefully was theirs. Hospital could be a lonely place with only sporadic visitors, if any. Much like her home life. A simple chat could reassure both sides there was life outside those four walls.

'Sorry, I didn't mean to be insensitive.' It took her a few seconds to figure out what he was apologising for. He'd mistakenly believed she might have been pining for the comfort of her own home when it was strangers in a different medical setting she had been thinking about. Not that she was going to have him pity her by explaining that to him.

He'd given up their relationship to remain here, transforming an ancestral pile into somewhere he and his sister could work and live side by side. Home was never somewhere he'd leave when he'd given up everything to keep it. Whereas her apartment was simply a base where she slept between surgeries and meetings. It could literally be anywhere in the world.

Easily transferable. There was no real emotional connection. If that's what constituted a home, there was more attachment for her at Heatherglen already.

'Don't worry about it. There'll be plenty more Christmases to come.' Once there was a baby involved, things would be different. She was sure she'd want to spend all the time she could with her child rather than wandering around hospital wards.

It had been a long time since she'd felt the excitement other people seemed to draw from Christmas and she was looking forward to experiencing it for herself. Whether it was London or here at Heatherglen, Harriet knew next year would be the best one yet.

'Things might have changed since you were last here.' Charles showed off the renovations with pride, but Harriet couldn't view his achievements objectively when she knew they'd come at the price of her happiness. Every new fixture and fitting had been built on her heartache.

'So, how many patients do you take in at a time?'

'We can manage around twenty residents, but Esme deals with more clients at the therapy centre. We've got a good set-up.'

They wandered past a Christmas tree decorated similarly to the one in the private wing except it was missing those personal touches of home-made ornaments she was sure were Esme's handiwork.

'Didn't this used to be—?' She spun around, finding something familiar about the space they were in, except in place of the heavy velvet drapes she re-called, there were modern vertical blinds.

'Ah, yes, this used to be the lounge. We had to re-place a lot for health and safety reasons, but we tried to keep the original features, like the fireplace. This one is only for the aesthetics now.' It remained grand and ornate in here, although it had been repurposed, but it was in this very room he'd crushed her thoughts of marrying him.

Perhaps that was why he'd gutted it. In the hope of removing all traces of her and what had hap-pened. This place was proof that wasn't possible. You couldn't simply erase history because it suited you. There were always going to be reminders of the past intruding on the present, no matter how hard you tried to cover it up.

'I remember being in here the day of your father's funeral.' She hadn't said it to upset him. The mem-ory of that day, the room full of people and chatter as they'd mourned his loss, was simply too vivid to ignore. It had been clear something other than grief had been plaguing Charles when he'd been so distant they could've been in different cities then instead of standing side by side. He'd done her the courtesy of waiting until the other mourners had departed be-fore he'd ended their engagement, even insisting she keep the ring, but it hadn't lessened her humiliation or confusion.

'It was a long time ago.' Something he obviously didn't want to be reminded of when he was striding on towards the other rooms.

Harriet bit her lip when it wasn't as easy for her to dismiss it but opening up old wounds wasn't going to help either of them. She was supposed to be over it all, that's what she'd told him, or he'd probably never have slept with her again. They couldn't change what had happened then any more than they could alter their decisions, or lack of them, in London.

She wasn't sure he'd even do anything differently when so many had benefitted from the clinic since their break-up. Certainly, she wouldn't choose to change more recent events between them. Motherhood wasn't something she'd wish away now when it was a part of her. If she hadn't fallen pregnant by accident she might never have factored a baby into her life and she had no regrets about the prospect of becoming a mum. It was the most important event in her life she had to look forward to. They simply had to live with the decisions they'd made and make the most of whatever fate had in store for them.

'So, what services do you offer here?' Back onto more neutral ground, perhaps she'd stop getting so emotional about what this place represented to her and begin to see it as just another workplace environment.

'We run our clinics, of course, with state-of-the-art facilities. Along with more holistic therapies and emergency facilities for the community en route to the main hospital.'

'It looks as though you have everything you need here. I don't see what I could possibly add to your set-up.' Harriet wasn't being humble. She was aware that an experienced orthopaedic surgeon would be sought-after in a private clinic. There simply wasn't enough professional incentive in it for her.

While she wanted to help every person she could, she suspected the more challenging patients would be found in city hospitals and that was where she thrived. It was satisfying to improve a patient's quality of life by relieving pain and improving their mobility. Those with more insight into the human psyche might suggest a link to the mother she'd never felt she'd truly helped, and needed to atone for her perceived failure as a daughter. It was just as well she tried not to dwell on those things she couldn't fix and concentrated on those she could. With one exception. While the surroundings of her patients might be different, she wouldn't trade the number of lives she could improve for a matter of comfort or cash.

'You're the best in your field, Harriet. We both know that. Waiting lists for surgery can be backlogged for years and most people come here because they can't face the pain for that extended amount of time.'

'Spit it out, Charles. I know you're building up to something.' It wasn't simply her sparkling personality and unborn child he was after, by the sound of it.

'You know me too well.'

'Once upon a time, perhaps, but I don't presume to predict what's going on in your head any more.' The barb successfully managed to wipe the grin from his face and suggested she could still wound him. Although that wasn't going to achieve anything except make it harder for them to work alongside each other if she kept dragging up past hurt. If she ever entertained the idea of moving.

'The main reason for my visit today, and for bringing you with me, was to meet a few people.' He stopped looking at her as though she'd shot him in the chest and started up the huge marble staircase.

'Who?' Her borrowed boots were squeaking as she hurried to catch up with him down the corridor. She might be dressed appropriately for the Scottish winter climate, or Esme's place of work, but compared to Charles and the clinic she was out of place and under-dressed.

A city slicker transported into the birthplace of nobility, she could do without him trailing her around like a pet. She preferred to be the one in control of the facts and her daily schedule. Something she'd sworn she wouldn't give up for Charles or anyone else. Not even her firstborn.

Flora, the physiotherapist, was leaving the room they'd stopped at. 'Oh, hi. He seems to be moving a little better today. I'm sure he'll be glad to see you.'

'Thanks, Flora. We're just popping in to say hello.' He knocked on the door and waited for the resident inside to permit him entry. It was a simple gesture but showed the respect he had for his patients' privacy, treating them more as house guests than customers.

'Come…in.' A laboured male voice came from the other side of the door.

'I'm taking you in to see Gerry. He's recovering

here after his stroke, so we're still working on getting his speech and mobility back on track.'

Harriet appreciated the heads up before they went in. A stroke could occur when a blockage prevented the blood supply reaching the brain, or because of a burst blood vessel. The resulting injury to the brain caused by a stroke could cause widespread and long-lasting problems. Including communication or irrational behaviour, caused by the psychological and cognitive impact of a stroke. It was always best to be prepared for such circumstances in case a patient became angry or resentful towards those trying to help them. Thankfully, such behaviour lessened as rehabilitation and recovery progressed.

The elderly gentleman was sitting in an armchair by the bed, clad in blue cotton pyjamas and trying his best to run a comb through his thinning white hair with a shaky hand.

'Hello, Mr Moore. I hope you don't mind me bringing a colleague of mine in to see you. This is Harriet.' Charles made the introduction and Harriet stepped forward to say hello.

'Call…me… Gerry. Lovely…to…meet…you… Harriet.'

His speech was slow and slurred. The evidence of his stroke was visible where the left side of his face drooped, but he still had a twinkle in his eye that said he had a lot of life still to live.

'You too, Gerry.' She took his hand and gently clasped it between both of hers.

'How is it going with Flora, your physiotherapist?'

Charles sat on the edge of the bed, giving more of an impression that he was a visitor than the attending doctor.

'Task…master.' Gerry grinned.

'You certainly seem to be improving.' He nodded towards the comb, which was now balancing precariously on the edge of the nightstand. Harriet knew how important physio was to stroke patients to improve muscle strength with exercises. Although recovery could be slow, these small goals, such as picking up objects, were important. They encouraged patients on towards longer-term, more demanding goals such as standing or walking. It was all working towards getting the person's life back where possible.

'Can…feed…myself…now.'

'That's fantastic. I'll see if it's possible to have your meals with the other residents. The company will do you good.'

Gerry smiled at that but even the effort of speaking was obviously already taking its toll on him.

'We should get on and let you practise the exercises Flora has given you. I just wanted to call in and see how you were. I know the team are working with you but if you need to talk to me about how you're feeling, just let me know. This can be a confusing, frustrating time and I'm here, along with everyone else, to help you through this. The same goes for your wife. This is a lot for her to deal with too.' Charles shook his hand and Harriet said her goodbyes too. By the time they reached the door Gerry had already closed his eyes.

It was clear Charles went above and beyond the

call of duty for his patients and if he was doing this to prove to her he was a nice guy at heart…well, it was working.

'He's a lovely man and he certainly seems to be recovering well.'

'I think it helps to have a multi-disciplinary team all under one roof. There are a lot of us working together in cases like this. You know orthopaedics could be used in conjunction with physiotherapy to work towards the best recovery. Surgery could provide stability to increase function in some instances.' Charles didn't have to convince her of the benefits of having a skilled team tailored to the needs of individual patients. She'd witnessed it for herself on occasion. The problem for her in joining the team at Heatherglen lay closer to home.

'Uh-huh?' She didn't give him the satisfaction of agreeing with him, but she was enjoying having him try to convince her. It gave her an insight into the work he was doing here, and the sort of man he'd become in her absence. A noble, conscientious one who only wanted the best for Heatherglen and his patients.

'I have someone else I'd like you to meet. If you want to?' He hesitated, perhaps picking up on her wariness about getting drawn into this.

'Of course.' She didn't want him to think she wasn't interested in his work when that was supposed to be the reason behind this visit.

He led her down the hall to another room and knocked on the door. A cheery, young voice shouted for him to come in.

Charles opened the door and ushered Harriet into the room. 'This is the Dawson family. Everyone, this is Harriet Bell, a friend who's staying with us at Heatherglen.'

'Hi.' The young girl in the bed could only have been about seven or eight with her parents sitting close by. Her adorable gap-toothed smile stole anyone's right to be in a bad mood when she was the one hooked up to hospital machinery.

'Bryony is my favourite patient but don't tell anyone else in case they get jealous.' Charles winked at the little girl, who giggled in response. He was charming a child as easily as he had her when they'd first met. It gave some indication of what an excellent father he would make. One more reason to like him she didn't need.

'Hello, Bryony.' Harriet greeted Mr and Mrs Dawson too, though she didn't know why Charles had brought her here.

'Is Harriet your girlfriend?' Bryony asked. The Charles-crushing apparently started from an early age.

Harriet found herself watching and waiting for his reply as intensely as his little admirer. Ridiculous when she hadn't held that title for a considerable part of her adult life.

'I told you, Ms Bell is a surgeon, like me. Except she works with people's bones instead of their noggins.' He rapped his knuckles on his skull and set off more childish laughter, successfully avoiding answering the personal question.

'Can you fix my legs?' With the directness only a child could get away with, Bryony challenged Harriet directly.

'I'm sorry, I...er...' Put on the spot, she felt compelled to answer without knowing anything of Bryony's medical history, or how long her connection to Heatherglen as a medical practitioner would last.

'Harriet's just visiting but I'd like to share your details with her, if that's okay?' He was checking with Bryony as much as her parents but all three nodded their consent.

Harriet had the ominous feeling of having walked into a trap.

'Bryony has cerebral palsy. At the minute she has a baclofen pump to help with the chronic pain. It's a small device implanted in her abdomen connected to the spinal cord by a thin tube under her skin. It continuously dispenses medication through the spinal column and delivers muscle relaxant to reduce tightness.' Undergoing surgery at such a young age made the children more special to the medical staff involved. There were always risks and no one undertook these procedures lightly on such fragile bodies. Bryony certainly seemed to have a special place in Charles's heart.

As an orthopaedic surgeon she had a lot of experience with CP too. Cerebral palsy—a group of conditions caused by an issue with the brain around the time of birth—led to difficulties with muscle strength and movement. The severity of the condition varied from patient to patient, but many came to her to address problems of muscle spasticity and contractures. With surgery, Harriet was able to help release muscles that were too tight or transfer strong muscles for weak ones. In some cases, she operated on the joints themselves, to aid deformity preventing basic motor function.

All of which Charles would've known before bringing her in here. However, the history of the patient's condition and potential for improvement had to be taken into consideration before surgery. She couldn't volunteer her skills without extensive consultation with a team of carers and specialists to set realistic goals. Something she was willing to do if asked.

'I hope the pump helps you feel better soon.' Although she didn't want to reference it for fear of upsetting the family, Harriet was aware it must've been hard to have gone through this, especially over Christmas.

'Recovery has taken longer than expected. Bryony picked up a virus from her little brother right after surgery, but we hope to have you home soon, don't we?' Charles obviously had been thinking the same thing and Harriet would've been surprised if he hadn't paid a visit at some point yesterday, as he was so fond of her.

'Santa sent me a letter to say he'll make a special stop at my house when I'm better.'

'Because you're such a brave and special girl.' Her mum rested a hand on her daughter's forehead, but Harriet didn't miss the glances exchanged between her and Charles. She got the impression he might've had a hand in that letter. In fact, she'd go as far to say it was probably in his handwriting.

'We're going to have a second special Christmas once Bryony's home.' As Bryony disclosed the contents of her extensive, unicorn-themed Christmas list, her mother looked as though she'd enjoy it as much as her daughter, knowing she'd be home safe.

A sudden jolt of awareness at the role she was about to take on almost knocked Harriet off her feet. Every decision she made from now on, every emotion was going to be tied to this baby. Just as Mrs Dawson's happiness and peace of mind were centred around her child. It didn't matter what happened between her and Charles, Scotland and London, this baby's welfare came first.

Her hand automatically rested on her stomach, already protecting him or her. The movement didn't escape Charles's notice as his gaze followed the action.

'Bryony's suffering twenty percent spasticity in her limbs. She was mobile, but the pain has become too much for her lately. There's no guarantee on how long the pump will last, so that means another operation further down the road.' Charles shared that extra difficult news out of Bryony's earshot.

Harriet's heart broke a fraction more for the family she'd become attached to in such a short space of time. If it was her child she'd want everything humanly possible done to stop her hurting.

'How can I help?' she asked, knowing she'd committed to coming back to Heatherglen.

CHAPTER FIVE

CHARLES HADN'T BROUGHT Harriet here to guilt her into assisting him with Bryony's treatment. He would've been here regardless of his ex's presence, but he wouldn't apologise for wanting Harriet to see the difference she could make at Heatherglen. The little girl had had a tough time of it as had her parents, and he would do everything in his power to make things easier for them.

When he had the ear of an orthopaedic surgeon with Harriet's experience it made sense to get her advice. It was simply a bonus on a personal level if she got involved and maintained an interest that saw her return, or stay for good.

'I'm going to show Harriet around the rest of the clinic, but I'll be back to see you all later.' He shook hands with Bryony's parents, who knew he couldn't spend all day at their daughter's bedside when they had other children at home on a post-Santa high. But he'd do his best to call in and provide some company for Bryony when he could. He knew Harriet well enough to expect her to want to do the same. Perhaps spending quality time with a child would show her what could be gained by sharing parenting responsibility. She could easily walk away, deny him any access to the child she was carrying, after the way he'd treated her in the past, but he wanted her to see they'd be better as a team. That their baby would be better off here, with both parents. A family.

The triumphant smile he was wearing as Harriet was saying her goodbyes to the family died on his lips. A wagging, panting bundle of fur streaked past him as he opened the door to leave the room.

'What the—?'

'Isn't this Esme's puppy?' Harriet scooped up the excitable animal, which had been causing havoc recently.

'He's so sweet. Is he for me?' Bryony's voice matched the excitement of the canine intruder and he cursed his sister's generous heart. If Esme hadn't insisted on keeping this nuisance around, he wouldn't have to upset a young patient.

'Sorry, Bryony. He must've escaped from the house.'

'You can stroke him if you want.' Harriet stepped in with a compromise and took the dog over to her before the tears had an opportunity to fully form.

'He tickles.' Bryony giggled as Dougal licked her face. Charles wasn't pleased that Dougal had made an unscheduled, unsupervised visit but it was good to see her happy. Harriet too. Although the dogs were part of the ongoing therapy around here, he'd still have to have a word with Esme about keeping a closer eye on her four-legged friend. He didn't want Dougal getting in the way when staff were doing their rounds.

He lifted the hand sanitiser and passed it to her mother. 'I'm so sorry about this.'

'Don't worry. He's the best therapy we could have asked for.' Bryony's mother joined the group fawning over Dougal as though he were a newborn baby. Now, that kind of interest he could understand. When their child was born he'd expect the whole world to take notice. But a dog?

He understood their importance in terms of therapy here. He'd seen the results for himself. They calmed patients as well as providing a distraction from illness and treatment. However, on a personal level he didn't know what the fuss was about. He'd never been a dog lover. Probably because his parents had stressed how much mess and destruction they could cause in a place like this where every stick of furniture had historic and monetary value. As proved by their canine companion. Sure, Dougal was cute, but he didn't do anything for Charles except generally make his life more difficult around here.

'We should get him back where he's supposed to be.' Charles stood back and let Harriet and her new friend leave before him.

''Bye, Dougal.' There was a chorus as they left, indicating there was only one of them who'd be truly missed.

'Just wait until I see Esme. I'd prefer he had a bath at least before he starts wandering around the place.'

'Oh, poor baby, don't listen to the nasty man. You

smell like home to me.' Harriet covered Dougal's ears against the insult and peppered him with kisses, completely losing her own professional image to let her soft-hearted mothering instinct take over.

'You lived in a kennel?'

She tutted. 'We always had a dog in the house when I was growing up with Mum. They're great company and totally devoted to their owners. If I wasn't so busy with work, I'd still have one, but it wouldn't be fair to leave one at home alone all day.'

'Exactly why he shouldn't be in the castle, unsupervised, while Esme is at work.'

Harriet had talked about her parents and how difficult her childhood had been, with an absent father and an over-dependent mother, but she'd never mentioned having pets. She took so much joy from being around Dougal, a picture of their little family, complete with raucous pets, flashed into his head and suddenly he didn't mind at all.

'He's only a baby. Esme is the expert and she only has his best interests at heart. How could you be mad at this little face?' She held Dougal out towards him. The dog's tail was wagging so hard his body nearly folded in two.

Charles stared into the pair of soulful eyes begging for his love. A little pink doggie tongue shot out and began slobbering over his face, making it impossible to remember why he was being a grouch.

Then a warm trickle of liquid soaked through his suit and reminded him.

'Dougal!'

'Whoops. I think he got too excited.' Harriet could barely contain her laughter as the puppy promptly forgot all the house training Esme had no doubt instilled in him.

Harriet didn't know how Charles was going to react to a little pee as she laughed at his expense. It was understandable he would be upset at the dog running amok in the clinic but there'd been no real harm done, other than to his suit.

Charles rolled his eyes, took the pup from her, and held him at arm's length as he headed towards the front door.

'You can't abandon him outside. It's too cold.' Even with his jaunty Christmas jumper he'd freeze to death out there. She wouldn't stand back and let that happen. She'd never forgive herself and Esme would never forgive either of them.

'What do you take me for, Harriet? I'm not a complete monster.' Her accusation stopped Charles in his snow-covered tracks. It highlighted how much work was required on her trust issues with him before the baby arrived.

She didn't dispute his intentions were honourable in his desire for them to raise the child here, at least in his eyes, but sometimes that wasn't enough. This time she'd need more than promises to persuade her to change her life for him.

After all, this was only a helpless pup and a baby was going to cause much more disruption. She would do whatever it took for her child to have a stable home life and history had shown Charles couldn't always be counted on.

Nevertheless, she followed him to the canine therapy centre and was blown away by the changes there too. The old stables had been modernised with huge windows, opening the building up to welcome people inside. A huge investment of time, money and love had gone into the clinic and the centre. A commitment Charles hadn't managed to make to her.

'I'm sorry. You didn't seem very sympathetic to him.' If he couldn't put up with Esme mollycoddling an abandoned pooch in her own home, it didn't seem so far-fetched to think he'd chuck it out in the snow.

'The dogs are a great asset here but they're Esme's responsibility. I don't want to spend my days chasing after them when I'm trying to work. It's my job to make sure the patients are comfortable during their treatment and Esme's to train the dogs. I'm sympathetic to a point but I can't have puppies running amok in the clinic. As well as the professional issue I have with what happened today, I guess I'm just not a doggie person. We were never encouraged to have pets in the castle because of the potential mess and damage they could cause and that has stuck with me. That doesn't mean I'm incapable of showing love and compassion to a baby. Despite whatever is going on in that head of yours.'

It sounded so ridiculous out loud she blushed. Charles was justifiably upset by the accusation. She'd overreacted. This was the real reason she'd agreed to spend time here—to find out who he really was now and decide if this was the right environment to raise their child after all. If his ego took a bashing in the process he'd simply have to get over it. As a father-to-be he was going to have to put the needs of the baby above his pride.

'Charles! Harriet! It's nice of you to stop by.'

'I believe this is yours.' Charles presented Esme with the canine criminal who didn't look the least bit guilty as he licked her face.

'What are you doing out here, mister?' Esme nuzzled her face into the bundle and Harriet wondered how the siblings could interact so differently with the animal.

'Good question. You can pay the dry-cleaning bill for my suit.' Charles arched an eyebrow at them both.

'Oh, dear. He didn't, did he? Dougal loves you, that's why he gets so excited to see you.' She too was doing little to hide the laughter at her brother's misfortune.

'Yeah, well, the feeling is definitely not mutual. You're going to have to increase his security detail.'

'He's not some sort of criminal mastermind. He probably slipped out through the door when you weren't looking.' Esme inadvertently tripped Harriet's guilt switch. It was possible she hadn't been paying close attention to anything other than Charles's sunny disposition when they'd left this morning. It seemed such a long time ago now.

'It might be my fault. I think I was the last one out this morning.' She confessed her misdemeanour, glad something more serious hadn't happened if it had been her who'd left the door ajar.

'It's not your fault.' Charles was quick to absolve her of responsibility, though he'd been keen to hold Esme to account for the same incident.

'It's no one's fault. What my brother has neglected to tell you is that this isn't the first time this has happened. As much as I've tried to partner Dougal with Max, he prefers Charles's company. The dog, not Max.'

'Goodness knows why.' Charles brushed off the idea, but Harriet had witnessed the puppy's love for herself.

'We should've called him Houdini. It doesn't matter where we put him, he always manages to escape and track down his favourite person in the whole world.'

'I wish he wouldn't.'

'You're fighting a losing battle, dear brother. Just give in and accept you're the leader of Dougal's pack.'

'Never.' Despite his refusal the scowl had broken on Charles's face, hinting that he wasn't as immune to the cute little mongrel as he made out. It was nicer to imagine him sitting in his armchair with a dog curled up contentedly in his lap than a man capable of leaving a puppy out in the snow. Then it wasn't such a stretch to picture him cooing over a baby.

'He certainly made an impression on Bryony, the young patient whose room he barged into.' Harriet attempted to shift her thoughts to someone who wasn't a part of her soon-to-be family. She wanted to remain objective where a potential work environment was concerned and keep her confused feelings about Charles out of any career decision. He'd taken the last one out of her hands and now she wanted control of the next. Minus his influence.

Esme grimaced as she heard about Dougal's exploits. 'I'm so sorry. Max and I have been checking on him regularly. I don't want to have to lock him into a dog crate. It's important he gets used to a home environment.'

'Preferably without wrecking it in the process,' Charles added.

'Charles and I can take him with us and keep an eye on him until you've finished here. We'll have to go back anyway.' Harriet indicated the ruined suit, which wasn't going to do anything to improve his attitude towards Dougal with the constant reminder of his humiliation.

'Would you? That would be so helpful. I have my hands full here.' Esme passed the pooch parcel again as a dozen others sounded their demands for her attention.

'You owe me one, sis.' Even Charles seemed to realise her workload could do without one more demanding dog as he accepted his fate of puppy-sitting for the rest of the afternoon.

Harriet feared for Dougal's future if he got on Charles's bad side again or damaged more than the Laird's cool façade.

'Excuse me if I'm speaking out of turn, but there was one positive to come out of this mishap.' All eyes were on Harriet now, including Dougal's, begging her to save him from eviction.

'I'm dying to hear this.' Charles folded his arms and waited for the defence.

She ignored the cynicism and the childish urge to stick her tongue out at him. 'Bryony, Charles's patient with cerebral palsy responded well to Dougal and I know you train therapy dogs here. Is there a chance you could partner the two together?' It would solve the immediate problem by finding Dougal alternative accommodation and at the same time provide the young girl with a much-needed companion.'

Charles was so busy laughing it was left to Esme to explain the flaw in that plan. 'Unfortunately, I'm not sure Dougal is going to be suitable for training. Not unless we use Charles as an incentive. We can look into alternatives for Bryony if the family is interested. We train a lot of dogs to help cerebral palsy patients. They seem to get a lot out of having therapy dogs.'

Harriet nodded. She understood the joy of having unconditional love from a pet during tough times. A dog could only aid Bryony through the challenges she endured.

'I can mention it to her parents and get them to come and talk it over with you if they're interested.' Now they were on the subject of his patient Charles resumed his professional manner and took the suggestion seriously. Although it didn't help with the Dougal problem, Harriet was satisfied her idea hadn't been as ridiculous as she'd initially feared.

'Great. I can give them a tour and put them in

touch with some of our other CP families.' Esme gave her brother a swift kiss on the cheek and did the same to Harriet before disappearing back into the kennels, leaving Harriet and Charles to mind her fur baby.

'Stay!' Everyone in the vicinity could've told him it was a pointless command by now, but Charles attempted to assert his authority all the same.

Dougal had that same goofball expression, tongue hanging out the side of his mouth, tail wagging, with no intention of doing anything he was told. Charles had no idea why he was so irresistible when there was a bowl of dog food and a comfy bed waiting nearby. He knew where he'd rather be. Especially when there were belly rubs and Harriet kisses on offer elsewhere.

Naturally, the little mongrel had made a run for it the second Charles turned his back and it was only Harriet's quick reflexes that had saved him from further dog slobber.

'I'll keep him company while you get changed,' she promised, burying her face in Dougal's fur.

'If you wouldn't mind, I think I'll grab a quick shower.' A cold one. Then he might burn his Dougal-scented suit.

'Go. I'll be happy to get some snuggles without you scowling at us.' He thought she was joking but he and the mischievous pup were going to have to get along if he was going to impress Harriet. Besides, if Esme had anything to do with it, Dougal was going to be a long-term resident. Charles was simply going to have to get used to changes around here.

Some breathing space between him and Harriet was good, he realised, casting off his clothes to step into the shower. He'd jumped in with that offer to Harriet to join them at the clinic on the basis he'd be closer to the baby. However, the more time he spent with Harriet the more he could see what he'd given up twelve years ago.

If that one night in bed had reminded him what they'd had together physically—and, boy, it had improved with age—being in her company today had brought out that caring side he'd admired so much in her. She was good at her job, that had never been in doubt, but it was her extra interest in Bryony, and that stupid dog, that took him back to the reasons he'd fallen for her in the first place.

It was a shame she'd made it clear she didn't trust him to commit to more than one night together. He didn't blame her but the reasons for wanting her to stay at Heatherglen were becoming more personal by the second.

He wanted to have it all—a successful career, a memorial honouring his brother and father, and a family of his own, including a partner to share it all with. Yet he knew it was selfish. Something that always spelled disaster for those closest to him. The ones he was supposed to love.

He was pushing her to transfer to Cluchlochry for the baby's sake because *he* wanted her to. Really, what was in it for her? There were better career prospects in London and that was the reason he'd sacrificed a life with her in the first place. It wasn't fair to pressure her. Hopefully they could resolve this with a proper conversation about what was best for all of them. It wasn't the first time he'd had to rein in his feelings for her and he'd survived. They both had.

Once the water had turned colder than he was prepared to subject himself to, he stepped out of the shower and wrapped a towel around his waist.

The en suite bathroom made his wardrobe accessible without having to compromise his modesty.

If he was spending the afternoon with Sir Pees-a-Lot, he wasn't going to risk another good suit. He bypassed the smart shirts and trousers, reaching for the comfy, less expensive option of a well-worn pair of jeans and a sweater.

The bedroom door burst open just as he was about to unfasten the towel. A flash of brindle brown, a tug at the hem of the towel and Charles felt cold air on his naked skin.

He exclaimed in exasperation, 'What the hell...?'

That was closely followed by Harriet's 'Dougal!'

As she ran into the room Charles was left cupping his hands over his privates to save both their blushes. Nothing she hadn't seen before but the way she was staring at him made him feel more exposed than ever. He should've been flattered by the blatant ogling but with a rogue puppy wrestling with his towel on his bedroom floor it was downright embarrassing.

'Well, this is awkward.' He sidestepped towards the clothes he had laid out on his bed, wondering how he could dress without flashing her again.

Harriet blinked at him a few times before she

became animated again. 'Oh, my goodness. I'm so sorry, Charles. He slipped past me when I was putting the kettle on for a cup of tea. He's as fast as lightning.'

'It's okay. You need eyes in the back of your head to watch this one.' What else could he say to make this whole episode less embarrassing for both of them? This dog had a lot to answer for.

'Dougal. Drop it. Drop it.' Harriet attempted to retrieve the towel Charles would appreciate having back. Dougal clamped on tighter to his prize. Charles knew at first hand those little teeth were like needles.

'Leave it. If the two of you wouldn't mind leaving, I might salvage some of my dignity.' An unfortunate choice of words given what he was clutching at the moment.

'No problem. Sorry. Again.' She reached for the dignity-destroyer, who saw this as some sort of game and dashed away every time Harriet came close. Eventually she managed to grab one end of the towel and entered into a tug of war.

It was all becoming ridiculous now. All they needed was Esme to walk in on this farce and she'd laugh herself into a coma.

'Give. Me. The. Damn. Towel.' Harriet gave one last yank and emerged victorious, clutching the now chewed towel. Although she did manage to land flat on her backside in the process. Dougal had bested them both.

'I'm not sure who won that one. I'd help you up but…' He shrugged, unable to come out of this situation as a gentleman.

She stood up and held the towel out to him. Even then he wasn't sure how to accept it without making another show of himself.

'You might want to close your eyes or something.'

'Don't be silly. We're both adults.' The twinkle in her eyes said she wasn't offended, or surprised, by what she'd seen.

She wrapped the towel around his waist for him, pressing her body to his as she did so. Close enough that Charles could hear the hitch in her breath, feel her warmth on his skin, and it was torture that he couldn't do a thing about it.

Harriet sensed his eyes on her before she saw him watching her so intently. So much for remaining emotionally detached. Now here she was standing in his bedroom with her arms wrapped around Charles's lower half with the most recent image of what lay beneath burned on her brain.

Her skin was flushed with the heat of arousal, not embarrassment, remembering the last time she'd had her hands on his naked body. It would be easy to fall into bed with him again and forget everything except how good he could make her feel.

'Harriet…' That husky tone of his desire shot straight to her loins, cutting off all common sense in favour of a more basic need.

She closed her eyes against temptation, but it didn't help her forget the softness of his lips, the memory of him kissing her fresh enough to make hers tingle.

'Don't.' It was a plea for him to stop. If he made a move on her she couldn't resist because she didn't want to. She ached for him and to share his bed again. It was only her long-held insecurities maintaining that last defence.

Sex with Charles would only complicate her life. London had proved that. Her seduction hadn't given her any sort of closure but instead had opened a whole new chapter between them.

He rested his chin on her head and sighed. A reflection of Harriet's own frustration at their situation. She wanted to cry but Charles continued to hold her as though he was drawing as much comfort as she was from this embrace.

Yes, he was wearing virtually nothing, and she was aware of every taut inch of him as she pressed her cheek against his chest. Even if he'd been fully clothed in a room full of people the moment would've been as touching, and intimate.

They'd made mistakes and suffered as a result, but they couldn't go back and change anything any more than they could predict what was going to happen. She couldn't remember the last time someone had simply held her, or when she'd let them. Accepting comfort seemed like a failure to her. As though the stresses of life had defeated her. She'd learned long ago not to give in and admit she couldn't do everything on her own. Growing up with her mother hadn't left room for two to wallow in personal hardship. One of them had to be strong enough to carry the other and in her case, the child had become the parent.

Later, when Charles had broken her heart, she'd been in need of a shoulder to cry on. With none available she'd soldiered on lest she let melancholy consume her as it had her mother. Since then, she'd cultivated pride in her independence and in taking back control of her emotions.

This warmth from his touch even without the physical attraction reminded her of everything she'd been missing in her pursuit of a self-sufficient life.

She sighed, and Charles continued to maintain the simple contact. Given their traumatic history and the break-up he'd told her he hadn't wanted, it was possible he'd been living in emotional isolation too. Even though he mightn't have replaced her in his affections, the thought didn't please her. Rather, sadness settled over her as she realised what they'd both lost.

A sharp yelp reminded them Dougal was in the room and they broke apart.

'I think someone wants your attention.' Charles was smiling at her, but his hangdog expression was tugging at her heartstrings more than the little one nipping at her heel. The fact Charles might crave something more than her attention was something she couldn't afford to indulge.

'He's due a feed.'

'I can see that,' Charles laughed as Dougal caught the bottom of his towel and tugged again. This time Charles was ready and managed to keep a tight hold of his modesty.

'This time I'll lock him in solitary confinement if I have to.' The dog was turning out to be such an excellent guardian against her making bad decisions she might just adopt him herself.

CHAPTER SIX

'IT'S MY WAY of saying thank you for not driving Dougal to the nearest dog pound.'

Esme plated up the dinner she'd insisted on cooking, regardless that she'd only recently finished work. She was another one who didn't submit to a typical nine-to-five schedule but had made an effort to get home to cook this feast.

'Really, you didn't have to.'

Harriet would have settled for something as plain as a slice of toast. Her stomach had been somersaulting since she'd walked into Charles's room to find him naked. The sight of him sitting opposite her at the dinner table in his casual wear hadn't lessened the impact he'd had on her when she'd set eyes on him again.

Now, as well as the memories of rolling around in bed with him, his very presence reminded her of the vulnerability of being in his arms. When she'd let go of everything except the bliss she'd found in his embrace. It was unnerving that she'd lost that much control around him, yet she yearned to do it again and again. It didn't help when the four of them—Esme, Charles, Max and herself—seemed like they were on a double date. At worst, a family meal she was intruding on or anything else she didn't have a legitimate reason to attend.

Charles tucked into the home-cooked meal with gusto, his appetite greater than Harriet's.

'This is amazing.' Max reached across to squeeze Esme's hand in thanks and the pure love in their eyes for each other was so touching Harriet had to turn away before she started blubbing.

It was hard to believe she and Charles had ever been that oblivious to the world around them, though they must've been at some point. Certainly, Charles had blamed their relationship for making him blind to his father's struggles after Nick had died. That was what had made his blunt dismissal so hard to accept when she'd still been loved up. If Max turned on Esme now it would blindside her too, Harriet was sure. Love was a painful business.

'So, what did you guys get up to this afternoon after you left the centre?' As innocent as it was, Esme's question almost made Harriet choke on her dinner as a naked Charles sprang to mind.

He was smirking at her now, daring her to share their adventures in his bedroom, which, although without serious incident, were memorable all the same. It turned out to be something she'd prefer to keep private between them for more than one reason.

'We were…er…busy trying to keep Dougal out of

trouble.' Eventually Charles jumped in with a truthful half-answer.

Harriet couldn't help but smile at him in thanks and because of the memories of the pup running rings around them.

'He'll be out of your hair tomorrow. Max is going to install safety gates. You know, the ones you use for babies. They'll come in handy in the future anyway.' It was at the last second Esme caught what she was saying. Max too, judging by the expression of horror on his face.

'Harriet's pregnant,' Esme blurted out, probably before Max keeled over thinking she was the one planning a baby in the near future.

Charles dropped his knife and fork onto his plate with a clatter. 'For goodness' sake. Harriet asked you to keep it yourself.'

'Sorry,' Esme mumbled into her chest, but Harriet would've been surprised if she hadn't shared the news with Max at some point, given the close nature of their relationship.

'It's fine. Don't worry. We've just found out we're expecting, Max, and we're trying to figure things out at the moment.' She didn't know how much of their history he was aware of but there was no reason to make anyone feel guilty about the situation. The news had to come out some time.

Max nodded sagely. 'Sure. It's a lot to take in. I won't breathe a word to anyone.'

'Thanks.' For all Harriet knew, she'd be gone by

the end of the week, with no need to put Max or Esme under pressure to keep their secret.

'Congratulations.' Max raised a glass to toast them and Harriet clinked her water against it.

'You too, mate.' He reached across the table to shake Charles's hand.

'Cheers.' Charles was beaming, and the simple acceptance of the unplanned pregnancy began to make her feel part of the family. Not the best environment to nurture that sense of isolation she needed to maintain control in her life.

Heatherglen was offering that support to her child she hadn't had growing up, but she wasn't convinced it would be a good move for her personally. A miserable mother, as she knew, did not a happy childhood make. It would take her to get past her feelings about Charles, positive and negative, to be able to face him on a daily basis.

'Harriet and I are going to take a trip into the village tomorrow.' Charles dropped the next bombshell into the middle of their meal.

'We are?'

'You are?' Esme echoed Harriet's surprise at the announcement when he hadn't consulted either of them.

He carried on eating without missing a beat. 'I thought I could show you around. The shops should be open again and I expect you'll need to get a few things.'

'I do.' The trip would take them away from the patients, family and four-legged friends who'd provided a necessary buffer between them today, leaving them alone. A dangerous position as this afternoon had demonstrated. Yet the gesture proved he had been thinking about her, about spending time with her, and anticipating her needs for her unexpected extended stay. She couldn't turn him down even if she wanted to.

Out of the corner of her eye Harriet could see Esme shaking her head.

'What?' Charles demanded to know why she disapproved of his plan. Harriet too wondered why such a thoughtful gesture should warrant the negative response.

'You never take time off. Yesterday was Christmas Day and you spent most of it at the clinic. It's so unlike you, bro.'

He shrugged. 'Maybe I have different priorities now.'

Harriet snapped her head up at that.

'Already? Wow. Fatherhood must be agreeing with you.' His sister teased him, their back and forth relationship dizzying, but it showed how close they were. Only two people who loved each other could generate such strong and varying degrees of emotion. One minute they were at each other's throats, gently joshing the next. If Harriet had had a sibling, she would've had someone on her side supporting her through the ups and downs. She might not have shut down emotionally over the years if she'd had someone giving her a kick up the backside when she'd required it. Annoying her when she hadn't.

It was a nice idea that her little one might have that family support but it made her consider what sort of relationship she had with Charles. Their lives had already been turned upside down without future family planning too. They weren't even together. In case she'd forgotten it, she was supposed to be putting him off the idea of her hanging around so she could return to London. It was ridiculous to go down the road of believing they could have a family together when their circumstances were so unstable.

Yet he was making an effort to convince her and Esme he was going to change and manage his time at Heatherglen so he could devote himself to her and the baby. This wasn't the Charles she'd anticipated finding at the castle, Laird of all he surveyed and un-willing to give up anything for anyone. Now every little thing he did for her, every concession was going to make it harder for her to walk away when the time came.

'Ready?' Charles waited for her to belt herself in, his hand on the ignition key as though he was giv-ing her the opportunity to bale out. This venture was about more than replenishing her wardrobe. He was showing her he would prioritise her when he had to. The significance wasn't lost on Harriet, but anyone could make a promise. It was being true to your word that counted. Only with time and a history of see-ing things through could she be convinced he meant what he said.

She couldn't expect Charles to drop work to take

her on a shopping jaunt when the mood struck, neither would she want him to. It wasn't the commitment to his patients she had an issue with. Raising a child necessitated making small compromises on a regular basis for school runs, holidays or illness. Children didn't run to a schedule and Harriet would rather manage it all on her own than have him complain every time he had to make alternative work arrangements.

'As ready as I'll ever be,' she sighed, and buckled up for the bumpy ride they were about to undertake.

'The roads have turned icy overnight so I'll take it easy. I'm carrying a precious load after all.'

She didn't know if he was talking about her or the baby as he negotiated the frosty lanes with his foot hovering on the brake. They came as a package now but that would change, physically, in about seven months' time.

If she decided not to move and he wanted their child at weekends and holidays it was going to be difficult. Should she have other work commitments, or Charles no longer thought of her as part of the equation, the separation was bound to be stressful. She was already fitting in here way too easily, with everyone being so accommodating. In some ways it was like being a child again, only with people who were taking her feelings into consideration along with their own.

'It's like a scene from a Christmas film where they've thrown in every cliché they could think of to make it look festive here.' In the city, snow was a cold, slushy nuisance, causing accidents and slowing traffic to a standstill. Here in the country she was able to take the time to appreciate the beauty in the weather. The white undisturbed fields, glistening invitingly, made Harriet want to roll around and make her mark where no one else had.

As they approached the village, the cosy fairy-tale cottages coughed wisps of smoke into the freezing air and told of the families inside sitting around the fire.

'Different from London?' Charles would take this vista for granted when he had it on his doorstep. Gaudy lights, over-decorated trees and throngs of harassed shoppers would be as much of a novelty to him as this was to her. It was only the potential hazards of the season that linked the vastly different locations.

They stopped at a junction just outside the village to check for oncoming traffic, only for the car to continue travelling out onto the road after Charles had applied the handbrake.

'We must've hit a patch of black ice.' Very experienced in driving in these kinds of conditions, he did his best to control the vehicle, steering into the skid instead of fighting against it.

The car eventually slid to a halt and Harriet sent fervent thanks to the heavens that they were alone on the road. They would've been helpless should anyone else have been coming towards them. Instinctively she wrapped her arms around her belly, that mama bear already fully formed and protective of her cub.

'Are you all right?' Another hand covered hers.

'No harm done,' she assured him, but it was apparent papa bear was making himself known too.

'I'll take a different route back. It's longer but the roads might be gritted out that way.'

Harriet muttered agreeable sounds as shock began to set in about what could have happened. At that second she realised her baby's life was more precious to her than her own. She'd give up anything to ensure this child was safe. Including her job and her house if she was sure Heatherglen would be the best place to provide security.

It took several attempts to get the car going in the direction they wanted. That was mainly because Charles refused to let her get out and lighten the weight of the car. The result of spinning tyres as he attempted to get traction on the slick surface was the smell of burning rubber.

The spinning motion of the vehicle combined with the acrid air had her clutching her belly now for a different reason.

'I have to get out, Charles.' It was a warning for him to pull over before his car was filled with more than fumes.

'What is it? What's wrong?' He immediately pulled over to the grass verge.

'Air,' she gasped, nausea rising too fast for her to quell with willpower alone.

Charles unbuckled his seat belt and jumped out of the car before she could stop him. He slipped and slid around the side of the car in his hurry to get to her. 'Be careful. We don't want any more accidents.'

With one hand steady on the now open passenger door, he held the other out to her.

'I just need some fresh air. There's no panic.' Embarrassed by the sudden bout of nausea, she ignored the helping hand to stand on her own two feet unassisted. A plan that went awry as soon as her foot slipped on the ice and she had to accept all the support offered.

'I've got you.' He caught her and braced her against the side of the car with his body.

She closed her eyes and wished the world would stop spinning. 'I'm fine.'

'Look at me. Open your eyes and focus on me, Harriet. That's it. Now, take deep breaths. In…and out.' Charles called her back from the brink of oblivion promising to take her somewhere safe.

She followed his instructions, inhaling his familiar scent, so reassuring and irresistible. Despite her return to full consciousness Charles kept a tight hold on her.

'Has this happened before?'

'No, but I don't usually spend my mornings doing doughnuts in the car.' Sarcasm was her only defence when she was at his mercy.

'I'd never have come if I'd realised the roads were so bad. Do you want to go home?' He eased her back into the passenger seat so she was sitting sideways with Charles kneeling at her feet.

His feelings of guilt were almost palpable, but revenge wasn't something she'd ever wanted in coming to Heatherglen.

'No. It's probably just shock, or morning sickness, or motion sickness. It'll pass.'

'You know it's not a weakness to be sick or, heaven forbid, to let someone help you.' He was holding both of her hands and Harriet could picture him in the delivery suite with her with the same calm presence, coaching her through labour. She hadn't realised how much she needed someone like that in her life so she could take a breather once in a while and let someone be strong for her.

However, the birth was a long way off and anything could happen in the interim. It wouldn't do to become reliant on Charles for support if he wasn't going to be there at the crucial time.

'Honestly, I feel a lot better. I'd rather get back on my feet and find something to distract me. Now, you said something about shops?' With steadier movements than before, she exited the car and slammed the door, forcing him to take a step back.

In London the shops would already be bulging at the seams with savvy shoppers seeking bargains in the sales. Cluchlochry was quiet, as though in hibernation, waiting for spring before the inhabitants would emerge back into the daylight.

Charles huffed out a cloud of breath into the atmosphere, but he'd stopped arguing with her. If these past couple of days had shown him anything about the woman she'd become, he'd realised she was much stronger than the one he'd known previously. Headstrong, stubborn, she'd heard it said before from other people whose interference in her life she'd refused to accept. It was that self-defence mechanism that had protected her fragile heart from any further sledge-hammer blows. She had to keep that superwoman cape on at all times. Especially around Charles.

'Christmas is over. People have a living to make. I'm sure they'll be glad to see customers in their businesses and we can always stop for lunch at McKinney's pub.'

Harriet was curious about the shops, which were missing the garish signs the high-street stores usually displayed. If anything, the shopfronts here blended in too well with the surroundings. Especially now it had begun snowing again in earnest and limiting visibility.

'Any suggestions about where we should begin our shopping trip?' Left to her, she was afraid of walking in on some unsuspecting local watching TV in her parlour because she couldn't tell the business premises from the residential buildings.

'There's a wool shop if you fancy taking up knitting.'

'Why would I?' She rounded on him, waiting for the explanation, which was bound to begin a debate about stereotypical gender association.

'It's the sort of thing wo...people do when there's a baby on the way, isn't it?' Charles's face was unreadable as he waved at the proprietor standing by her colourful window display of yarn.

Harriet hoped he was joking.

'Are you honing your carpentry skills so you can knock a crib together, then?' It was a jibe to get back at him for insinuating she should be sitting knitting bootees for the duration of her 'confinement'.

Not one to give her the satisfaction of winning an argument, Charles countered with a chirpy, 'Maybe I will.'

Now she was going to be plagued with a sultry montage of him in her head, his naked torso beaded with sweat as he lovingly crafted a masterpiece with his rough, strong hands. Looking for a distraction from her over-active imagination, she pushed open the next shop door.

'Hello, there.' The shopkeeper didn't need the jingle of the bell to alert her that she had customers.

'Hi, Joanie. This is Harriet, a friend of the family. I'm just showing her around the village.' Charles made the introduction and Harriet wondered for the first time if any of the locals would remember the scandal of the young Laird's failed romance. The rumour mill would be working overtime if they heard she was back, pregnant.

'Nice to meet you, Joanie.' Harriet shook her hand, already getting friendly vibes from the pleasant redhead and her quirky shop.

The shelves were packed with all manner of knick-knacks and cute gifts tourists and children would lap up. Unfortunately, there was nothing in stock that would aid her quest for a bigger wardrobe.

'Your hands are freezing. Let me make you a cup of tea to warm you up.' Joanie wouldn't hear another word on the subject and disappeared into the back of the shop, ignoring any protest.

'Hot sugary tea is exactly what you need.' Charles pulled over a couple of chairs to the counter and gave the impression that impromptu tea parties here weren't unusual.

Despite the suspicion he'd somehow tricked her into this, Harriet took a seat and warmed her hands by the electric fire. The pleasant warmth seeping into her bones reminded her of how it had felt walking into Heatherglen after being so alone on the road from London. It was cosy, homely and she wanted to stay here for as long as possible.

'There you go.' Joanie returned with a tray full of tea things and Charles passed a cup to Harriet before taking one for himself.

'Try some of the shortbread. I made it myself.' She prised open a tartan tin full of sugar-dusted Christmas-tree shapes.

Surmising the sugar hit might help her wooziness, Harriet helped herself. One bite and she was in buttery, sugary heaven.

'You know, I should be sick to death of eating this stuff, but this is really good.' Charles finished his shortbread in two bites.

Joanie blushed, as most women did when Charles paid them a compliment.

'Everyone seemed to like it. Perhaps I should start selling it.'

'You should. It's delicious.' Harriet took another when their host offered the tin around a second time.

Joanie beamed at the praise. 'You two finish your

tea. I'm just going to take the rubbish out into the back yard.'

The sudden chill blasting through the building when Joanie opened the door was a stark reminder of the outside temperature.

Charles set down his tea and rubbed Harriet's shoulders up and down as she shivered, trying to generate some heat back into her body. It was the touch of his hands on her that managed to raise her temperature again.

A thud and the sound of broken glass outside startled them both.

'Joanie? Are you all right out there?' Charles called, on his way to find out for himself with Harriet following close behind.

There was no reply and when they were faced with the scene in the shop's back yard they could see why. She was lying unconscious on the ground, the contents of the rubbish bag strewn around her and a pool of blood staining the ground crimson around her head.

Harriet no longer cared about the cold or the snow as she knelt in it to take the woman's pulse. 'Joanie? Can you hear me?'

'I'll phone for an ambulance. Hopefully there'll be one nearby. Watch out for the broken glass. I don't want you getting hurt too.' His concern for her continued to amaze Harriet when it came so naturally to him to think about her. It took her right back to the time when they'd been in love and he'd have done anything to keep her safe.

Harriet carried out basic checks on Joanie, making sure her airways were clear, while Charles gave their location to the switchboard operator. He came to assist her once he hung up, covering Joanie with his coat to keep her warm.

'She's probably slipped on the ice and hit her head in the fall. We don't want to move her until we can get a neck brace on her.' There were all sorts of complications with head or neck injuries and there was a risk of paralysis if they tried to move her.

'We're going to need a CT scan to see what the damage is in case it's more than concussion. If the roads are too bad to get her as far as Glasgow we can make her comfortable at Heatherglen until it's safe to transfer her to hospital.'

'There's a good strong pulse and her breathing is normal.' Harriet reported her observations, but Charles didn't seem as positive as he checked the head wound.

'She has a compound fracture to the skull. The skin and tissue are broken, leaving the brain partially exposed.' An open fracture presented a risk of bacterial infection. If left untreated it could lead to permanent brain damage or even death. An open head injury also left the patient vulnerable to other conditions such as seizures and paralysis.

They needed a CT scan to assess the extent and severity of the fracture, but it was looking as though Joanie was going to require surgery to reduce swelling in the brain. This was time sensitive.

* * *

Harriet was applying pressure around the wound to control the bleeding, all the while talking to the patient and trying unsuccessfully to get a response. Charles got back on the phone to give an update on the severity of their patient's condition, but he didn't return with good news.

'The weather's bad out there. They don't know how long it will take to transfer her to the hospital and an air ambulance is out of the question until that blizzard outside passes.' He had a decision to make quickly as he could already hear the clinic vehicle drawing near. Joanie didn't even have any family around with whom he could discuss the situation.

'We'll take her back to Heatherglen and do a CT scan there.' If it proved he was worrying unnecessarily, they could take their time with the hospital transfer. However, something more serious would require immediate action. They didn't usually carry out major operations at the clinic, referring serious cases to the hospital, but they did act as a local A and E when necessary.

'Lyle will assess her, but we might have to ask for your skills here if we need to operate.' His fellow Scot was the one called on for any local emergencies, but Harriet was the surgeon here. This decision could prevent them wasting time and improve Joanie's chances of recovery. They could make a difference.

This was exactly the sort of situation he'd helped Lyle set the clinic up for in the first place.

CHAPTER SEVEN

THEY WERE GREETED at the front door of the castle by
Dr Sinclair and Dr Kirkpatrick.

'I thought you might need some extra help on this
one,' Max was offering his services too, which could
only improve Joanie's chances with so many accomplished medical staff available.

Harriet realised she'd already been included in this
band of doctors. She was no longer merely a visitor.

'Do you mind if I take the lead on this one?' Harriet asked as they wheeled Joanie inside.

'Not at all. You're the surgeon here.' There was no
sign of territoriality from Lyle, which went some way
to easing the pressure Harriet was suddenly under.

'We'll need a CT scan to see what we're dealing
with.'

'Would you like me to assist if you do have to operate?'

'The more the merrier, right?' Harriet soon found
herself scrubbed in alongside the others prepping for
surgery once the scans showed their fears had been
justified.

'I'm glad we had so many hands available.' Charles managed to lighten the mood a little as the team came together to provide access to Joanie's injury once she was under general anaesthetic.

He made the initial cranial incision to reveal the extent of the fracture, and he needed assistance to keep the skin flap pinned back out of the way.

Harriet worked quickly to debride the area, cleaning and removing the blood clots that had formed there and repairing damaged blood vessels. Once the bleeding had stopped, she used screws to hold the skull back together in place.

'We'll monitor for infection or secondary complications such as intracranial pressure and brain swelling. Charles, we'll need to keep her on a ventilator until it's possible to move her to a high-dependency unit.' Sometimes patients needed additional surgery to relieve pressure and drain any accumulating blood. In the meantime, she'd prescribe strong antibiotics and medication to reduce possible inflammation.

This wasn't her area of expertise, but she'd spent sufficient time in an operating theatre to be confident in what she was doing. Charles too had put his trust in her skills to make this call. Everything he did was with his patients in mind and whatever would produce the best possible outcome. The easiest option would've been for him to leave Joanie at the mercy of the time it would take to get her to that hospital.

Instead, he'd taken on the responsibility for her initial treatment and everything that would happen once she was at Heatherglen. Harriet was beginning to see there was a role here for her to perform emergency surgery when it was required. Along with the everyday cases which came into the clinic requiring her expertise as an orthopaedic surgeon. It was a good balance of cases which would hold her interest and provide a necessary service to the local community.

All the same, she'd be happier when Joanie was getting specialist care at the hospital and she was relieved of her responsibility.

With the benefit of hindsight, and an explanation for his behaviour, she was beginning to understand what had driven Charles to do the things he'd done in the past. It was a pity it had come so late.

She was the one who'd been selfish over the years, wanting him to herself when he'd devoting himself to improving the lives of countless others.

'I'm sure you weren't expecting to perform brain surgery on your holiday.' Unbidden, Charles brought her a cup of tea and set it on the table beside her chair.

'This was never supposed to be a holiday, remember?' She was keen to remind him that this stay wasn't about her taking some time out. It was for them to make life-changing decisions regarding the child they were to have in a few months' time.

He took the seat opposite, the glow from the fire throwing shadows on his face. It was the first she'd seen him rest since Joanie's accident. After the surgery he'd insisted she come back home while he oversaw Joanie in Recovery. She'd had the chance to shower, change and take a nap before he'd come back.

If this was his regular schedule it was no wonder he didn't have time for a private life, but that didn't mean she was willing to pick up the slack.

'How could I forget when Heatherglen is all about family for me?' He was staring into the flickering flames of the fire, not seeing Harriet at all and making it difficult for her to believe she was part of that sentiment.

'Forgive me, Charles, but I don't understand that. We could've been raising a family together by now, but you turned your back on me and our future. I admire your dedication to your work, but I can't help worrying where you're going to fit a child into your routine? What's going to change?' It was all very well saying the words but what point was there in making promises he couldn't keep? Relegating her in his affections in favour of Heatherglen was one thing but she wouldn't let him do that to their child.

'Nothing. I'm going to remain as faithful to my family as I have been for these last years. That includes my son or daughter.'

A lead weight dropped into Harriet's stomach as he confirmed she'd never been, and never would be, included in that beloved circle.

'Being faithful, providing a home and financial stability is completely different from being a parent. I grew up believing my thoughts and feelings didn't matter in comparison to my mother's. I had to be the strong one and ignore those things every other child took for granted. I didn't have attention, affection or even an interest in what I was doing at school from my mother. So much of my time was taken up with her insecurities and demands for my attention and it was almost a relief when she passed away. I'm not going to subject my own child to the same treatment.'

Losing a parent was anyone's worst nightmare and she still grieved for her mother. It was difficult to reconcile that with the belief that her mother's heart attack had given Harriet her freedom. She would never have reached the heights in her career she had if she was still at her mother's beck and call.

Harriet would do her damnedest to ensure her own child's emotional needs were met. Something she'd missed out on as a child, and as an adult. Sometimes being read a bedtime story or an afternoon spent making cupcakes could be enough to prove to a child it was loved. Since she'd arrived here Charles had gone out of his way to make her comfortable, but it was impossible to know if taking time out when necessary could be sustained long term. There was no way she was going to move here if they'd end up resenting the intrusion into each other's lives, with their child in the middle of the feud.

'I'm aware I'm not part of the family, you made that abundantly clear when you sent me back to London.' It hurt, regardless of his reasons for behaving the way he had after the funeral, or her insistence she was over it.

Charles shook his head. 'Don't you see? I'm the reason my father died. That's why I had to stay at Heatherglen. After we lost Nick I carried on with my life in London without a thought to how my parents were coping. The long and short of it is that they weren't.

'Dad threw himself into work here, trying to blot out the pain of losing his firstborn. If I'd been any sort of son to him I would've come back and helped then, lightened the load or given him something to focus on other than his grief. He worked himself into an early grave and I did nothing to stop it. I was so used to having my freedom, with none of the responsibilities resting on Nick's shoulders, I simply continued doing my own thing. Including proposing to a vulnerable young woman barely into her twenties who'd only recently lost her mother.'

He was clutching at the arms of the armchair so hard Harriet was afraid he'd rip them off.

'We were both old enough to know what we were doing. Yes, we may have rushed into things but don't use me to exacerbate your guilt. As to your father's death, what could you have done? You were grieving for your brother too.' She remembered the tears and sleepless nights in the wake of Nick's death. Unsurprising in the circumstances. What had happened to his brother had been horrific and traumatic for everyone.

Charles stopped worrying the upholstery and began pacing the room, coming to rest his hands on the mantelpiece and staring into the blazing hearth.

'That wasn't grief. It was guilt.'

Despite the heat of the fire, Harriet shivered at the coldness of his tone. So matter-of-fact and emotionless when she knew Nick's death had devastated him.

'How can you be to blame for his death? He was in Afghanistan on patrol. You didn't plant the IED. I know how much you loved him.' He'd always spoken of Nick with such admiration she was sorry she'd never got to meet the man in person.

'You don't understand...we rowed before he was posted. I said unforgivable things that I can never take back. I told him to drop dead when he tried to lecture me about stepping up and doing my bit to support Heatherglen. All because I was jealous of him. I didn't see why I should put time and effort into the place when I wasn't the golden child who'd be inheriting everything.' The sound that came out of his mouth was somewhere between a laugh and a sob.

'We all say things we don't mean in the heat of the moment. We shouldn't spend the rest of our lives beating ourselves up about it.' She was pretty sure she'd said she'd hated Charles on more than one occasion when emotions had run high, but she'd never stopped loving him. It was a way of lashing out, trying to hurt him with words she knew weren't true.

'We can when we'll never get the chance to take the words back again. I thought he was the one who had everything. He was the war hero, the heir to Heatherglen. Esme was the youngest, Mum and Dad's little princess, and I was nothing more than the spare.' There was such raw pain in his every word it was heartbreaking to listen to and Harriet knew deep in her soul he'd never shared his torment with anyone else. She felt privileged but she also hurt for him, and for herself. If he'd only confided in her at the time they might have worked through this together then.

Instead, they'd retreated to their respective homes and locked themselves away to recover from their wounds.

She wouldn't have been human if she'd sat back and let him pour out his heart without offering some comfort. With his mother no longer on the scene either, and his big-brother protectiveness of Esme, Harriet recognised the signs of self-neglect. Thankfully, she was able to prescribe the correct treatment.

Charles angled his body to meet her when she put a hand on his shoulder to let him know she was there, and pulled him into a hug. He was unyielding at first but soon relaxed into her with a sigh, letting that tension escape on a heavy breath near her ear.

They stood for a while, drawing comfort from each other, with only the sound of the crackling fire to break the silence.

'You have to leave the past behind, Charles. Don't let it destroy you. You're still entitled to a life of your own. Especially when you've done so much for others.' Her voice was cracking with the thought of him carrying so much unnecessary guilt.

'I couldn't bring Nick or Dad back, but I thought I could do the right thing by you, Harriet. Thinking I could get married and have a normal life was a fantasy and the nightmare of taking Heatherglen on was stark reality. I envied your freedom when mine had been taken away from me. I didn't want to ruin your life too by dragging you back here and now I've done that anyway. I know I broke your heart, but I broke my own too.' He broke the seal between their bodies to drop his gaze to her belly where their baby was growing by the day.

'I've never done anything I didn't want to do. Except leave you.' She was trying to smile but the overwhelming sadness at the memory wouldn't let her. She hadn't been truly happy since that day.

'I never wanted you to go, Harriet. I thought I was doing the right thing by you, Nick and my dad, by setting this place up.'

'I know.' She rested her forehead against his, wishing someone had bashed their heads together at the time. 'What about you, Charles? What did you want?'

'The only thing I've ever wanted, Harriet. You.' His hands were at her waist now, sending her pulse into overdrive. When she looked into his eyes, saw the blue fire of his truth there, the game was all over.

Her future was undetermined but, at this moment, she knew exactly what she wanted to do. Yet she hesitated, her mouth hovering against his, her breathing ragged, knowing that if she gave in again to temptation she'd never want to leave.

Then Charles closed the gap and made the decision for her, his lips hard on hers as he kissed her. She'd been waiting for this since London. Wanting him to kiss her and obliterate everything else around them. Now she was burning with need for more. Circumstances had kept them apart for too long and now that raw passion for each other was free to burn out of control.

Harriet tugged his shirt from the waistband of his trousers, undoing only a few buttons before yanking it over his head. Much to Charles's amusement.

'Here? Now?'

'Yes.' She didn't recognise the huskiness in her voice demanding Charles take her where she stood. Such was the intensity of her desire to have this man again she'd lost all inhibitions.

She let her hands roam over his torso, getting to know that terrain of hair and muscle. Charles kissed his way along her neck as he tore off her clothes. 'Max and Esme are in bed and Dougal is safely locked up,' he murmured against her fevered skin. So they weren't being totally reckless. This time.

The yearning to join together was as great as it had been in London. Yet that urgency to consummate their reunion before common sense prevailed had been replaced with a different longing. This transcended the physical, it was more than re-creating the best times they'd had together. Now they were going to be parents, making plans for some sort of future together, they were reconnecting on an emotional level too.

Harriet could try and deny it. Blame it on her hormones or a holiday fling, but Charles was the only man she'd ever given herself to completely. Her body and soul had always been his and in sleeping with him again she was playing a dangerous game with her heart.

To her detriment she'd always considered Charles worth the risk.

Hopefully, this time it would pay off. With the baby, the job and an offer to stay at Heatherglen, the last commitment he needed to make to her was himself. It was the only reason she'd stay. She loved him. Always had and always would. Without having that in return from him there was no way she could live here. It would be so much worse than never seeing him again.

'Are you cold?' He mistook her shiver as a symptom of being left clad only in her underwear when she was burning for him from the inside out.

'Nervous,' she answered honestly. Anxious about what was going to happen between them after tonight. She needed to be more than a convenient distraction for him.

'Me too.' His admission surprised her. It suggested there was more on the line for him too than simple physical satisfaction.

Charles took her back into his embrace, brushed the hair back from her face. 'We can take it slowly.'

As if to prove they had all the time in the world, he gave her a long, leisurely, skin-tingling kiss that melted any nerves into a puddle.

He unclipped her bra and let it fall to the floor, freeing her breasts to his attentions. Her nipples were more sensitive than usual, and a shot of electricity zapped to every erogenous zone when he brushed his thumb across one. When he took the other in his mouth and tugged, she almost combusted with desire.

'Charles…' She was pushing away his boxers, ridding her of the final barrier to his body. So much for taking it slowly. Her body had decided she wanted him to satisfy her craving right now.

How could something they'd done a hundred times in the past still feel like the first time? Charles wanted this to last and to make it special. The night they'd conceived this baby had been passionate and urgent because they'd thought they'd never see each other again. Tonight he was going to make love to the mother of his baby, proving his commitment to her. No pressure.

He could already see the subtle changes in her body with the swell and new sensitivity of her breasts. It awakened such a love inside him for her it terrified him that he might hurt her all over again. He wanted to put her needs before his own so he could watch the pleasure on her face and know he'd put it there.

Not that Harriet was making it easy for him. Her confident command of his body as she slid her hands over his backside and around to take hold of him was seriously jeopardising his good intentions.

'Don't worry. I'm going to make sure you get everything you need, Harriet.' He quelled his own throbbing desire to focus on hers.

He dotted feather-light kisses across her midriff, felt her quiver against his lips as he moved lower until he was kneeling between her feet. With a gentle nudge he parted her legs and relocated his focus to her inner thighs, kissing and teasing the soft skin. Her sweet gasp of anticipation and the slight unsteadiness in her stance matched his own growing impatience for that most intimate contact.

She opened to him at the touch of his tongue and cried out as he lapped her sex. Hands braced on his shoulders, she encouraged his efforts and he lost himself in the quest for her orgasm with every venture into her core.

He was so dedicated to his pursuit that when Harriet climaxed he almost came apart with her. Through every tightening and subsequent release of her inner muscles he demanded everything she had, leaving her limp and breathless when the last shudder of her climax subsided.

He didn't give her the time to say anything, literally sweeping her off her feet to carry her over to the settee. Softly, he laid her down and covered her naked body with his. Kissed her until he drove himself to the brink of insanity with desire for her.

'Harriet, I can't wait any longer.'

'Good.' The coy smile was at odds with the wanton action of her legs as she snaked them around his hips. Pressed tightly against him, it was impossible for Charles to resist any more. Finally, he gave in to his own primal urge and took possession of the woman he loved. If he'd thought she'd believe him, he would've said the words. Instead, he wanted to show her the strength of those feelings in his every move.

He claimed her again and again, her soft moans increasing his steady rhythm until his restraint was hanging by a thread. Then Harriet secured her inner hold around him, building that unrelenting pressure inside him to the point where he could no longer hold back.

He roared as his love for her burst free, so loudly he was afraid they might hear him at the other side of the castle. Perspiration clung to his skin as the ripples of his release shuddered through his limbs.

Only then did he see the sheen of tears in Harriet's eyes and his racing heart almost came to a halt.

'What's wrong? Did I hurt you?' He'd been carried away on that wave of ecstasy, but he was sure she'd been right there with him.

She bit her lip and shook her head, letting him breathe again. He'd never have forgiven himself if he'd done something to cause her pain for a second time in her life.

'It was amazing. It's just…' Her throat sounded raw with the unshed tears she was swallowing down for his sake. He understood then why she was so upset. They could have had this a long time ago and no one knew better than he what a great loss that had been.

'I know.' He kissed her on the lips, trying to show her how sorry he was as the salt water of her tears washed over them both.

All this time they could've been living at Heatherglen together, raising their family. The hurt he'd caused them both seemed senseless now in the scheme of things. The separation clearly hadn't diminished their feelings for each other. They were more intense than ever.

Dougal barked somewhere outside the confines of

their reunion, reminding Charles that their privacy wasn't guaranteed. More so when he heard a bedroom door opening and closing, followed by footsteps on the stairs.

Without another word they scrabbled for their clothes like two horny teenagers about to be sprung by his parents. They dressed in silence, but remained undisturbed by his sister or her puppy charge. As he pulled on his trousers, and Harriet fastened the last button on her blouse, no one would've been able to tell they'd just had the most mind-blowing sex. Or that he'd woken up to the fact he loved her more now than he ever had as that selfish young student. Perhaps the time apart hadn't been a complete tragedy. If not for the life he'd gone on to have without her he might not have appreciated how much more enriched it was with her in it.

'We can go to my room. We'll have more privacy there.' Not only so he could share his bed with her but they had to talk about the future. Time was slipping away and he wanted to spend every second of it with her. To make her feel the same way about him so she'd realise this was the best place for her and the baby. With him.

'If you don't mind, I think I'll retire to my own room, Charles. I don't want to confuse anyone.' The willing partner he'd had wrapped around his body only moments ago was now keeping her distance, her hands fidgeting in her lap.

His earlier euphoria dissipated with the rejection,

though he didn't think this was about revenge. It was much something much more serious than that. Doubt.

'I just thought—'

'Please don't put me under any more pressure. It's not fair.' She was on the verge of crying again and he would never willingly cause her distress again.

'I'll see you in the morning, then.' It was almost as difficult to walk away from her tonight as it had been all those years ago. Only this time he was leaving the next move to her. The decision about the future of their relationship was entirely down to Harriet. He was powerless. Something he was no longer used to.

CHAPTER EIGHT

'ESME IS LOOKING forward to meeting you to discuss the possibility of a therapy dog for Bryony.' Harriet had caught up with Bryony's parents in the corridor and taken them aside to discuss their daughter's needs. She didn't want to mention anything in front of her and get her hopes up in case things didn't work out.

'Yes, Charles said he'd make an appointment for us to see her at the therapy centre. We think it's a great idea. A dog will be good company for Bryony.' Her mother was much brighter than she'd been yesterday, and Harriet imagined the prospect of training a dog had caused much excitement.

'I'm so pleased to hear that before I go back to London.'

'I suppose you have your own family there.'

A denial hovered on Harriet's lips, but they weren't here to discuss her personal life. It was already confusing things at the clinic. Instead, she simply smiled, neither confirming nor denying the assumption she had someone to return to. She wasn't sure if it was sadder to admit that or the fact she was running away from the chance to have a family here because the idea freaked her out so much.

Bryony's parents thanked her for her help before setting off back home, leaving Harriet wondering where she could retreat for peace of mind from Charles.

She'd set out early this morning to avoid him. It was silly, really, when she was living in his castle and seeing patients. She couldn't dodge him, or what was happening between them, for ever. It had crossed her mind to do a moonlit flit and leave in the middle of the night. All because sleeping with him again had made her realise she was still in love with him. In reality there was no escaping that, regardless of her location.

She dropped her head into her hands, taking a moment to reflect on what the hell she was doing with Charles. Once she'd had that space from him to think straight last night she'd convinced herself that by refocusing on the professional aspect of her stay she could get away unscathed. It wasn't turning out to be that simple, though. There was no way to keep this solely about the baby now they'd slept together again.

It was one thing to tell herself she'd somehow exaggerated how great their last time together had been and she'd read more into it than she should have for a conference hook-up. The reality of being in his home and work life was very different. Those feelings weren't simply going to be cured by hiding from him.

She'd spent half the morning with Esme, playing

with the dogs and discussing the merits of pairing therapy pets with CP patients, safe in the knowledge Charles was on his rounds at the clinic. She'd only come back here when she'd spotted him going back home. It would be childish, not to mention exhausting, to keep this up. He'd catch up with her at some point.

Then what? She couldn't tell him why she'd run off after their passionate encounter and expect things to carry on as normal. Either he'd try to take advantage of her wasted feelings towards him in order to maintain contact with his child or he could cut off communication altogether. One thing was for sure, he didn't return the strength of her admiration, he never had.

Harriet was stuck, trapped by her own emotions and bad decisions. The worst of it was she didn't regret last night, and she'd do it again given the chance. She was a danger to herself.

The quiet elegance of the lounge called to her. A room where patients were able to relax and interact and which had been empty when she'd passed by earlier.

'Sorry. I didn't realise anyone was in here.' She hadn't expected to see another peace-seeker but there was a man sitting by the fire.

'No problem. It's a good place to collect your thoughts.' Now he'd spoken to her it would be rude to walk out again so Harriet joined him on the opposite side of the fireplace.

'I'm not sure I should be collecting them. I might be better off throwing them in the bin.' That prompted a deep laugh and she instantly relaxed in the man's company.

'Are you staying here?'

'I'm visiting with Charles and Esme.'

'Oh, you're a friend of the family? You knew Nick, then?'

'Unfortunately, I never got to meet him. Was he a friend of yours?'

There was a sad nod of the head, which went a long way to explaining the extent to which his death had affected the man. 'I served with him in Afghanistan. Not an easy thing to get over.'

'I'm so sorry.'

'At least I can talk about it without breaking down now.' His self-deprecating humour was much appreciated by Harriet when she knew nothing she could say would ease the suffering he'd gone through.

'They've been helping you here, then?' If he was a friend of Nick's she knew Charles and Esme would have bent over backwards to assist this man with whatever ailed him.

'They've been life-savers. They literally got me back on my feet and now we're working on getting me integrated back into society. I've still got an issue with loud noises I'm dealing with. You know, with the whole bombs and explosions thing that I can't seem to get out of my head.'

'That must be awful but I'm sure you're making great progress. These things just take time.' It was great to hear first hand the difference they were making here, and she was sure Charles would puff up with pride when she recounted the conversation to him.

'I'm very grateful for the help Charles and Esme, and all of the staff here have given me. We're working up to the ultimate test soon. They're planning a firework display for Hogmanay, so we'll see how I go with that.' He lifted a pair of crutches from the floor and heaved himself into a standing position. Harriet hoped she hadn't chased him away with her arrival.

'Good luck.'

'Thanks. I'm Andy, by the way. Andy Wallace.'

'Harriet Bell.' She couldn't remember the last time she'd shaken so many hands and made so many new friends in such a short time. It was a nice feeling, being part of the community.

'I hope I see you around again soon, Harriet.'

If the lounge was intended to give the residents here a time out from their stresses and allow them a space to simply relax, it had definitely achieved its goal today. It had helped to take her mind off her own problems to think about someone else's.

'I've just spoken to Bryony's parents. They're very excited.' Charles's voice disturbed Harriet's chance of peace and quiet.

'So it seems. I'm glad they'll have something to look forward to.'

'I wanted to speak to you about that.' He sat down beside her on the love seat, which was suddenly crowded now he'd wedged his large frame so completely into the space. There was no room for her to edge away from him when they were sitting hip to hip and thigh to thigh. It was ridiculous that in a castle of this size she couldn't put some distance between them. After all these years apart, suddenly they were drawn together at every turn.

'About Bryony?'

'Partly. I take it you've heard of selective dorsal rhizotomy?' They weren't the words she'd expected to hear from Charles today, but they managed to spark her interest all the same.

'Yes. It's a spinal procedure used to improve mobility. I've been involved in a few.' It involved cutting nerves close to the spinal column, which could not only reduce spasticity but give patients back their independence. However, it came with risks. The operation was irreversible and relied on only cutting sensory nerves. If motor nerves were severed it could result in total paralysis. It was a highly specialised surgery, but she had seen some life-changing improvements for patients who'd had it.

'So you know the difference it could make to someone like Bryony? A lot of CP patients could benefit from it so they're not relying on hoists for the rest of their lives, or they're able to do simple tasks for themselves such as feeding and drinking.'

'Charles, I couldn't make that decision. There's a lengthy screening process for those being considered for the procedure. Patients have to be assessed by physical and occupational therapists on their functionality. My involvement is mostly on a post-op basis should any problems arise with joint alignment. Ultimately the final say would be down to the neurosurgeon performing the procedure and there's no guarantee it would work in her case anyway.' Everyone was assessed on an individual basis and as much as she wanted to improve life for the little girl and alleviate her pain, it wasn't up to her.

'I know I'd have to consult a neurosurgeon too. If I hadn't had Heatherglen to run I might have gone into surgery myself. There's a lot of things I would have done differently given the chance but this is about looking forward, not back. I'd like to give families like Bryony's hope.'

'One of the problems is that there's very little funding out there for the procedure. We're in a Catch-22 situation where they won't approve it universally until they can see conclusive results that it works. Hospitals only have approval for a limited number who meet certain criteria.'

'That's why I want to look into part-funding it myself. Perhaps set up a research facility here, with your help, where we can provide the procedure to those who need it and catalogue the results.'

'Patients need intensive physiotherapy after surgery to help with their mobility too.' This wasn't something to be taken on without considering all the implications and the potential benefits had to be deemed greater than the risks.

'Of course. I'd have to look into extending the physiotherapy department too. I'll sound Flora out about that. What do you think? Would you be interested in being part of it?'

'It's an amazing opportunity, but there would have

to be something more concrete in place before I could consider giving up everything in London. You would have to have a neurosurgeon on board or this whole thing is moot.' They could do so much good for patients across the board and it sounded like an exciting project. Every physician wanted to be part of something revolutionary in the medical world and Harriet was no exception. She simply had to be sure there was something career-wise worth moving for if things didn't work out for her here on a personal level.

'I know a few in the field who are interested in taking part if we have the appropriate after care in place, which would include an orthopaedic surgeon. In the meantime, I'll get a proposal together and get things moving. I'll make some enquiries with Bryony's consultant too and see if she could be a possible candidate.'

'It would be great for her and her family. They've been on my mind a lot.'

'I thought I hadn't seen much of you since last night.' He rested his hand on her knee and though it was an innocent touch compared to last night, her body didn't appear to understand that. Her skittish pulse was reacting as though they were still rolling around naked on the couch. It didn't help when he was expecting her to say something about the progression of their relationship now it was more than resolving custody of their unborn child.

'I've been busy sussing out the career potential here.' It wasn't a total lie. She'd simply been using that research to keep her out of harm's way. When

Charles was close she didn't give any thought to the consequences of her actions. Knew only that she wanted him.

She'd never had much time for relationships, but it was different with Charles. Yes, she had needs, and goodness knew he increased hers every time she laid eyes on him but being intimate with him was about so much more than meeting her physical needs.

Perhaps it was their history, and now their future as parents, but she hadn't realised how incomplete she'd felt until she'd come back to Heatherglen and found that missing part of her. A return to London now would only emphasise what she was lacking in her life. If only she could be truly sure she could trust Charles again she would rather stay here in some sort of relationship with him than go back to a world without him in it at all.

'And? What's the verdict?' He lifted his hand as he awaited her response and even that loss was too great for her to bear for too long.

Harriet cleared her throat, but her mind wasn't proving as easy. She had to work hard to focus on her career prospects rather than on the man beside her. 'I can see the possibilities Heatherglen has to offer.'

'Such as?' His mouth twitched, and it was apparent he knew exactly where her lustful imagination was taking her.

She crossed her legs and attempted to stem the arousal threatening to wreak havoc inside her. 'The clinic provides a good base for my work. As you said, I can consult and operate at the hospital when I'm needed. Working with Esme at the therapy centre is appealing too. I think it would be mutually beneficial for us to confer about patients. Bryony's opened my eyes to the possibility of putting patients in touch with Esme and vice versa. We could do so much together.'

This was what he'd planned when he'd pushed her towards his patients, but she would've seen the benefits for herself eventually. Heatherglen was offering her the chance to continue her career at the same time as raising a family. The only thing casting a shadow over proceedings was that fear of having her heart ripped out again.

'And us?' He took one of her fidgeting hands in his, stroking the inside of her wrist with his thumb and sending shivers of delight across her skin.

A lifetime of denying herself the pleasures he could give her or trying to keep a lid on her feelings was a choice she didn't want to make but Charles hadn't voiced any desire to have a proper relationship. They were going to be parents. They'd already been lovers. It was as much commitment as he was liable to make and only Harriet could decide if that would be enough for her.

'I see no reason why we shouldn't carry on as we are.' The thought of sharing his bed regularly emboldened her gaze on him. Knowing if she wavered he'd see through the bravado and realise she wanted more than he was prepared to give.

'So you'll stay? We'll raise the baby here, together?' The hope and joy she saw on his face should've made her decision clear cut, but it caused a wobble in her confidence. He wasn't declaring his love for her, he was excited about having the baby here.

'I'll stay for now, but I still have to go back to London in the new year as planned.' Despite her unrequited feelings for Charles she knew this was probably a better environment in which to nurture a child than the lonely existence she had in London. As future parents that's what they both wanted.

'What about a permanent move?'

'I'm seriously thinking about it…'

'You don't know how happy that makes me.' To demonstrate, he cupped her face in his hands and planted a kiss on her lips.

If Harriet closed her eyes she could make herself believe this was possible.

When Charles was kissing her, when his hands were on her, she was able to live in the moment. She could move here, raise their child, keep her career, and make love with Charles when the mood took her. The only thing she couldn't have was his love, but no one had it all. Perhaps she simply had to settle for what she could get.

'Morning, sleepyhead.' Charles nuzzled into Harriet's hair, tousled from sleep and their other nocturnal activities.

'Is it that time already?' she murmured, half-asleep.

This was everything he'd dreamed about. Waking up to a naked Harriet at the start of the day, falling back into bed with her at night was the perfect way to begin and end his days. He had the clinic and now, with Harriet here and a baby on the way, he considered himself the luckiest man on the planet.

''Fraid so.'

'Ugh.' She snuggled further down under the covers and Charles's heart swelled because she'd rather be here with him than anywhere else. Long may it last.

These past couple of days with Harriet had been amazing. It wasn't the traditional start to a relationship, beginning with a pregnancy and working backwards. In time he hoped they could repair their personal issues so she could trust him again and someday they'd be living here as a proper family. Not merely together through circumstances. So far Harriet hadn't given him any indication she wanted anything other than having her physical needs met. Although he was happy to oblige, he was still in love with her, he always had been. He hoped at some point in the near future she'd feel the same way about him.

'We do have a bit of time before I have to do my rounds.' Every part of him was wide awake now.

She blinked her eyes open as he nibbled her ear lobes and brushed his thumb across her nipple. He knew all her weak spots and wasn't afraid to use that knowledge to his advantage.

'I look a mess.'

'You look beautiful.' She looked so at peace he wouldn't want her any other way.

'I...have...morning...breath.' She giggled in between kisses.

'I…don't…care.' He didn't. Not that she tasted anything but sweet on Charles's tongue. All that mattered was that she was here with him.

'In that case—'

It was his turn to gasp as Harriet stroked the length of his manhood, making him aware she was up for whatever he had in mind.

His playful growl was answered by her squeal of surprise as he flipped her onto her back. Once he was covering her body with his, all joking was finished. Making love to Harriet was a serious business.

She was so ready for him Charles slipped easily inside her to find that peace he'd only ever found with Harriet. She'd been the only woman he'd ever considered sharing his life with. Although that thought process in the past had been behind the decision to break up, the idea now was akin to winning the lottery. Every touch, every kiss from her was a gift. Someday he hoped they'd both believe he was worthy.

He wanted to say the words, to tell her he loved her, but he didn't have the right. It would scare her off when she'd been wary enough of this set-up. After that first night together, she'd done her best to avoid him until she'd seemed to come to the conclusion this arrangement would be convenient. His feelings for her were anything but convenient. They'd complicated the life he had at Heatherglen and the one he'd planned with the mother of his child. If he kept them to himself, they couldn't hurt anyone. It was only thinking of himself that caused pain to those around him.

'Hey.' Harriet's voice broke through his thoughts.

She took his head in her hands and forced him to look at her. 'Where did you go?'

He had to get better at pretending he could be casual about this if he expected her to stick around.

'I'm right here with you.' He kissed her long and deep, sufficiently that the tension ebbed away from her limbs again beneath him. Passion enough to distract them both from what was going on in his head.

They rocked together, clinging onto what they had in the moment. As Charles followed Harriet over the edge, his last thought before oblivion hit was that since she had come back, his heart had begun to heal again.

In the end they'd had to rush to get ready in time for work, they'd spent so long in bed.

'I'm going to have to get changed. I can't turn up in yesterday's clothes.'

He'd tried to pull her back in for one last smooch, but she wasn't having any of it.

'You could borrow something of mine. I don't think anyone would object if you turned up wearing one of my shirts and nothing else.' He drew a finger down her spine as she leaned over the side of the bed to collect her discarded clothes.

'I would,' she protested, but he couldn't help going back for more when he'd made her shiver. He swept her hair from the back of her neck and danced kisses along that ticklish spot. Her response as she leaned back for more of his touch only added fuel to the fire in his belly. Charles reached around to cup her breasts in his palms, pinching her nipples between thumbs and forefingers so she groaned with appreciation.

'I really have to go,' she tried again as he nuzzled her neck.

'You don't have to. You're free to do as you want, and I hope to hell that includes me.' He knew he'd said the wrong thing when she stiffened beneath him and covered his hands with hers to stop them wandering any further.

'Charles, if I become part of this household I'm not going to take advantage of my position, and neither are you. I'll be coming here to work, not be installed as your mistress.' Harriet pulled her clothes on with such jerky movements Charles could see she was battling to contain her temper.

'I know that. It was a joke. A bad one.'

She wasn't listening as she walked barefoot to the door with her shoes in her hands, no longer content to spend another second with him to put them on.

'I'll see you at the clinic.' The slamming door said everything about the offence he'd caused.

Charles fell back onto the pillows with a sigh. It shouldn't be a crime to want to spend time with her, but it wasn't something she apparently wanted to hear. Perhaps he'd oversold Heatherglen to her when it now held more appeal for her than him.

CHAPTER NINE

HARRIET KNEW SHE'D overreacted to Charles's teasing this morning. Especially when she'd have happily spent the rest of the day in bed with him. It was that niggling fear in the pit of her stomach that sex was all she was good for that made her snap.

'I'm going to have to tell him how I feel.' She ruffled Dougal's ears as he lay at her feet. With Charles caught up in admin work, something she couldn't help him with, she'd returned to his private quarters. It didn't stop him plaguing her thoughts.

Since coming here Charles had dominated her every waking moment, and a lot of the sleeping ones. It was no wonder when he was the reason she'd come here. He was always going to be her baby's father. For her own peace of mind she was going to have to face the consequences of these feelings, even if it meant the end of the affair.

'At least I'm not the only who's fallen for him.' As a last resort to stop Dougal running riot in the clinic in his pursuit of Charles, Esme had suggested using one of his old shirts as a comforter for the pup. It had done the trick. The scent of his reluctant master, lining his basket, settled him until the man himself was available. If things didn't work out Harriet might have to steal some of Charles's clothes to take back to London and do the same.

'It's a poor substitute for the real thing, isn't it?' Although, like the smitten pup, she was sure she'd tire quickly of the imitation.

Dougal snuffled deeper into the shirt, inhaling the scent she knew was intoxicating. They both just wanted to be with him. Unfortunately, it seemed he was only prepared to tolerate either of them on his terms. Yet Harriet had seen him soften towards the dog, sacrificing one of his shirts and fussing over Dougal when he thought she wasn't looking. He was getting used to sharing his space and she hoped that would extend to her. After everything he'd been through with his family, the personal struggles he'd shared with her, it was possible he was simply as scared as she was about getting hurt and losing someone else close.

Dougal let out a pitiful whine.

'It's time to be brave. We've got to show Charles what he could have here. A real family.' She took the dog lead from the hook behind the door and clipped it to Dougal's collar.

'Let's go for a walk.'

Either he'd already learned what the 'W' word meant or he'd picked up on Harriet's renewed optimism, but Dougal was panting with anticipation and jumping at her to hurry up and open the door.

She was going to have a word with Esme about taking Dougal on permanently on Charles's behalf. He'd be the family pet their child could grow up with and a commitment to her future at Heatherglen, where she was more than a staff member or a lover. She wanted to be here as a valued part of Charles's beloved home.

Charles couldn't wait to get back to Harriet after work. Things between them had been strained since his faux pas that morning and he intended to make amends. It had taken a lot to persuade her this was the place for her and their baby and it wouldn't take much for her to change her mind again. Joking that she was moving here to be a lady of leisure, or pleasure, wasn't going to do much to keep her onside.

As he stood at the window he could see Harriet walking Dougal outside with Max and Esme. His sister and her new beau were effortlessly comfortable together, hand in hand. Whereas he and Harriet veered back and forth in their affections.

Although history didn't paint him in the best light, they shouldn't have to struggle to want to be together in the early days of a relationship. It wasn't something that should have to be forced. Yes, they were compatible in bed, they always had been, but outside that confined space there was more than a physical distance between them.

There was always an excuse or a disagreement between them, sending her running after they'd made love. She was holding back from him and that wasn't a good place from which to start a relationship.

'Hey.' He greeted Harriet with a kiss on the cheek. It was all he could do not to pull her in for a full make-out session after spending all day thinking about her.

The slight uneasiness he could detect in the way she was twisting Dougal's lead around her fingers and the sidelong look she gave his sister stopped him. Clearly, she hadn't been pining for him in the same way as the pup pawing at his trouser leg desperate for his attention.

'Hello. I thought I'd take him out for some fresh air this afternoon.' Harriet wasn't as hesitant about showing affection to the other male in her life as she showered the pup with kisses and petting. 'I didn't have anything else to do.'

He caught hold of her arm before she could follow Esme and Max inside. 'We could go out somewhere for dinner, if you like.'

The thing he didn't want was for her to get bored after only a couple of days here. Although he'd forgotten it over the years, there was a world outside Heatherglen.

Harriet moved on past him. 'Some other time perhaps. I have some things I have to sort out with your sister.'

She didn't elaborate or even acknowledge his desire to take her out. He was getting the brush-off.

'Is there something wrong?' He'd rather know now than go on pretending until after the baby was born.

'Wrong? No. I have to take Dougal in and feed him. Excuse me.' She ducked her head under his arm and scooted inside, trailing Dougal, who was fighting to stay by Charles's side. At least someone wanted to be with him.

Charles had that same horrible emptiness inside that he'd had that day he'd realised he was jeopardising Harriet's future happiness by making her follow him to Heatherglen. It was happening all over again. Today should have been proof that neither he nor Heatherglen were good for her.

Her time in London was precious, a whirlwind of activity. By dangling promises of a better life for their child he'd emotionally blackmailed her into agreeing. Only to have her spend her days walking stray dogs and slipping between his sheets when he wasn't at work. He'd virtually bribed her with that promise of a research facility. It was something he'd been considering since Bryony had come to the clinic but the prospect of having Harriet as part of the team made it even more of a priority.That kind of opportunity would grab someone as ambitious as Harriet, but how long would it take to complete? What could he offer her in the meantime?

He banged his head against the doorframe. He'd been the worst kind of fool, a selfish one. This time running the clinic and the estate had made him forget the implications of dragging someone into it along with him. These years in isolation were worth nothing if he hadn't learned his lesson and he stole Harriet's life anyway for his own benefit.

It wasn't for him to tell her she'd be better off here when he knew nothing of her existence beyond these walls. Only what he'd imagined, and that was never going to be something he considered more fulfilling than this when it meant he'd lose her.

This trial run was supposed to have been a test for her to work out what she wanted. No matter how he tried to convince her otherwise, it didn't include him or Heatherglen. Not long term. He was fine for a holiday fling, but her trust in him hadn't recovered and it never would as long as he continued to ignore what was best for her.

It suited him having her, the woman he loved, on site, looking forward to raising their child together at his family home. Exactly the sort of selfish behaviour that had driven his father and brother to their deaths. He couldn't bear responsibility for destroying the lives of any more of his loved ones.

Okay, Harriet wasn't in immediate danger but being somewhere she didn't want to be, with someone she didn't love, would be like a slow, painful death. Like the one she'd told him her mother had suffered. An existence she'd sworn she'd never submit to. He was making her follow in those footsteps and sacrifice her identity for his sake.

Charles had made that difficult decision to end things after his father's death because it had been the right thing to do for Harriet. Now it wasn't her feelings about him clouding her judgement, it was those she had for the baby. At his prompting. He didn't believe she was capable of loving him again and it was his fault she was pregnant. If he'd used contraception or common sense, she would never have tracked him down again.

As much as he hated to say it, the Charles who'd set her free the first time had been a better man than the one he'd been recently.

Harriet would've loved to have gone out on a proper date with Charles. She couldn't remember the last time she'd made time for dinner, or even a movie, with someone. Since reconnecting with him they'd spent their quality time together in bed and though she wasn't complaining, it would be nice to venture out as a couple. That getting to know each other stage was needed more than ever when they were such different people from before.

She was sure they'd get another chance for a bit of fun away from Heatherglen now she was making plans for a permanent move. Taking on the responsibility of a family pet would show Charles she wanted to be here long term with their family.

'I'm so happy for you both.' Esme's eyes were shimmering with happy tears as she hugged Harriet, then scooped Dougal up for a cuddle.

'I'm not sure your brother will feel the same but he's more fond of this one than he'll admit.' Harriet had come to Esme's quarters to discuss the adoption. Her living space at the far side of the castle was perfect for having secret puppy conversations.

She wanted to surprise Charles with the news later. It had been on her mind about Dougal for a couple of days but seeing Esme at work, training and teaching Dougal, and her, a few basic commands had convinced her they could tame this little one. After all, he'd become part of the family too.

'Being honest about his feelings isn't a strong point for Charlie boy, but I can see the difference it has made to him, having you here. I'm not about to interfere in whatever is going on between you two but it's obvious you're in love.'

'It is?'

'It's great having my big sis back again.'

Harriet had been so distracted by her relationship with Charles she'd neglected the one she should've been cultivating with Esme. She'd never supposed the few meet-ups they'd had during uni years would've had any lasting impact on Charles's teenage sister but clearly Esme had seen it differently.

'I'm sorry I didn't keep in touch.' Harriet rested her hand on Esme's, wishing she'd attempted to maintain some sort of communication over the years. She'd simply assumed she was no longer welcome at Heatherglen in any shape or form.

Esme shrugged. 'You weren't to know I'd put you on a pedestal and turned you into the big sister I'd always wanted. I was devastated when Charles said you'd gone, and the wedding was off. I had no idea what had happened. Only that I'd lost you on top of Nick and Dad. I was angry at you, and Charles, for quite some time.'

'I'm sorry. I was so devastated by the break-up I wasn't thinking about anyone's feelings except my own.' Poor Esme had been forgotten about in the midst of the family tragedy and drama. It explained some of the behaviour Harriet had heard about during Esme's teenage years.

'I think we were all floundering back then. Hopefully we've found what we've been looking for.' She glanced at the ring on her pinkie finger.

'You and Max certainly seem very happy.' She and Charles had some way to go yet but there was time before the baby came to work out those issues that got in the way every time they got close.

'It's a promise ring. We want to take our time.' Her excitement was evident, even in Esme's hushed tones. It sounded as though she was afraid to say it out loud and jinx things. Harriet could empathise. She didn't take anything for granted when it came to affairs of the heart.

'Good idea. Congratulations.' This time Harriet instigated the hug.

With Esme confiding in her it felt as though they'd formed their own secret club. A sisterhood. Suddenly thoughts of girlie gossip and shopping trips filled her head. Neither were things she did on a regular basis, but she'd always thought she'd been missing out. It was the promise of spending time with Esme and extending that notion of family that held so much appeal.

'We've all got so much to look forward to and Heatherglen is beginning to feel like a real home again. Can you imagine what it's going to be like when the baby gets here?'

Harriet didn't have the heart to express her concerns regarding Charles's commitment to her personally. She hoped that was something they could work out and signing up as Dougal's new guardians would show Charles she was thinking of them as a family already.

That fizz of excitement Harriet had been trying to keep under control was bubbling to the surface now she had someone else's enthusiasm to expand on.

'I can't wait until next Christmas and being part of everything here. First I need to talk to Charles and let him know about the plans I'm making.' By this time next year, she'd expect to be fully settled. She and Charles would have taken some time off work to spend time with the baby for its first Christmas.

It was impossible not to get carried away by the idea of family in Esme's company, when she thrived on it. Each of them had suffered in their own way over the years but finally the planets were coming into alignment.

'Harriet?' Charles knocked on the bedroom door and waited for a response. He'd already checked the kitchen and lounge, but there was no answer from Harriet's room either. There'd been no sign of Dougal either since their return. He thought that by the time he'd showered and changed she'd have finished whatever she'd wanted to talk to Esme about without him present. A matter that wounded him more than it should.

She could talk to anyone about whatever she

pleased, but it highlighted the growing distance between them if she couldn't confide in him.

He would do his best to reassure her she'd have
whatever support she needed when the baby came,
if that was all that was keeping her here.

'Are you there?' He inched the door open in case
she was simply avoiding him, but the room was
empty.

He took a seat on the end of her bed, expecting her
to come back at some point. He didn't want to invade
her privacy, but the partially unpacked bag was sitting nearby. She was living out of her luggage and
ready to run at a moment's notice. He was hoping his
news would give her a better sense of security here.

The pitter-patter of puppy paws sounded down the
corridor and the anticipation of facing Harriet made
his stomach flip.

'We're going to have to face the music at some
point, Dougal. Let's hope Charles is in a better mood
than usual.'

He got to his feet, suddenly feeling like the intruder he was as he unintentionally eavesdropped on
her talking to the dog. Harriet hadn't always seen him
at his best, but he was doing his best to win her over.

'Charles? What are you doing here?' She pulled
up in the doorway, so startled by his appearance that
she dropped the dog lead from her grasp.

Cue Dougal and his over-affectionate fascination
with Charles's trouser leg. This was one time they
didn't require his canine antics providing some light
relief.

'Can we do something about this dog so we get five minutes' peace to talk properly?' If this moment proved to be a turning point in their relationship, he didn't want it tainted by the memory of her being more interested in the dog than him.

'Okay. Sure.' She stared at him intently for a few seconds before retrieving Dougal and calling on a passing Esme to come and take care of him for her.

'I know I upset you with that stupid comment about being the lady of the house this morning so I put in a few calls to Fort William Hospital. I have a few contacts and I made enquiries on your behalf about transferring there.'

'You did what?' She crossed her arms, challenging him to spit out the words he was now wondering whether he should say at all.

'I wanted you to have a concrete reason for moving here. I thought securing a position for you at the hospital was the best way to convince you there was a life waiting for you here since the research facilities will take a while to get up and running at the clinic.'

'You didn't think to consult me on this first?' Harriet frowning at him was not the reaction he'd expected.

'I thought you'd be pleased. This is giving you the career opportunities you wanted as part of the conditions of moving here.' Unfortunately, neither he nor Heatherglen had been enough to convince her to stay, which was why he'd used his initiative to go further afield. Over time he hoped she'd develop a love for him on the same par as the one she obviously had for her job. Except the impatient tapping of her foot on the floor said she wasn't best pleased with this turn of events.

'Charles, something as huge as changing my career path is for me to decide, not you.' She huffed out an exasperated breath. 'This is you making decisions for me again, without considering the consequences. I know nothing about this hospital, what their practices are like, or what I'd be expected to do in that particular environment. Things that are down to me to investigate, if and when I'm ready to relocate.'

Charles was beginning to think he couldn't do right for doing wrong.

'I was simply trying to facilitate that move for you. All I want is for you to have a reason to want to stay here.'

'Is it me or the baby you want here?'

'I thought you came as a package?' He tried, and failed, to make her smile because he wasn't sure which answer she wanted to hear. Of course it was important for him to be close to the baby but more than anything it was his desire to have Harriet here with him that had prompted his flurry of phone calls today.

'This isn't a laughing matter, Charles. It's my life, my future, and my career you're interfering with. If you can't see that then I really don't think we have a future together.' As she said those words he got some idea of the devastation he'd once wreaked on her. It felt as though someone had taken hold of his heart and squeezed it until the pain was so great he was sure he might die.

She'd been hesitant about starting over again here until she'd seen a commitment from him, telling her he would make a good father and he was no longer that man she'd believed had run out on her with no good reason. He'd thought he'd delivered with the prospect of employment at the hospital. Apparently not.

'I just wanted you to stay,' he muttered, feeling utterly pathetic that he'd failed her again.

'It's always about what *you* want, isn't it, Charles? You know I'd hoped we'd moved on from the past, but this proves we're no further on than we've ever been. Everything has to be on your terms, with no thought to how it affects me. You haven't changed at all, but I have. I'm no longer prepared to be that woman who'll wait until you get bored again.'

'Harriet, please, we can sort this out. I've messed up. Tell me what I can do to fix this.' He wasn't above begging if that's what it would take for her to give him another chance. This time he had much more to lose if she walked out of his life for good. He loved her more now than he ever had. Along with the baby he might never get to meet.

'If you'd changed from the man who ended our engagement without even talking to me about it, I wouldn't have to tell you what to do. We're only going to make each other miserable trying to force this relationship to work simply so you can have us where you want us. If it's okay with you, I'll spend the night and leave tomorrow. I have a few things to sort out and some goodbyes to say. We can work out access arrangements when the baby is born. In the circumstances you'll understand I want full custody. After all, I tried to do things your way.'

He sighed his reluctant acceptance. How could he object when she was right? If she loved him this wouldn't be so difficult, but he couldn't force her to feel the same way he did about her.

He should never have stepped out of his shoes as Laird and medical professional when he knew the heartache that caused from previous experience. Now he'd have to start the grieving process all over again. Grieving for the loss of the woman he loved, his child and the family he wasn't destined to have.

CHAPTER TEN

'I'M SORRY THINGS turned out this way.' Charles walked out the door as though he'd just cancelled a phone contract.

Harriet, on the other hand, had just had her whole world ripped out from under her. Again.

She managed to stay upright until he was out of the room, then her legs gave way and she collapsed onto the bed, too stunned to even cry. The moment she'd decided to seduce Charles in London she'd set herself up for a fall. If she hadn't given in to temptation she wouldn't have to go through this heartbreak for a second time.

Ending it with him was the last thing she wanted to do but she'd done so in self-defence. By making decisions for her without consulting her, it was clear he'd learned nothing. The relationship was never going to work. Especially once the baby was here and he started taking over there too. If he was incapable of changing, of considering her thoughts and feelings, she would end up the one getting hurt. There was a baby to think about in all of this too. The only option she could see now was to walk away and save what little there was left of her heart. It wasn't any easier to do second time around, even if it was through her choice this time.

She lay back on the bed and wondered when she'd started thinking of this place as home when it held so many panful memories for her. Now there was one more to add if she ever had the stupid idea of coming back. Whatever arrangements they made regarding the baby's upbringing, she couldn't put herself through this again.

Harriet curled up into a ball, her arm wrapped around her belly. It was only when she thought about their baby that the tears finally broke free and trickled from the corners of her eyes. It was just going to be the two of them from now on. Like her and her mum all over again. Except she'd make sure she had a job and a home to return to in case of this very eventuality.

Damn Charles Ross-Wylde for making her fall in love with him again. Now not only was she going to be a single mum, struggling to juggle motherhood and a career, but he'd damaged her heart beyond all repair this time. Along with her trust.

He'd offered her a job, a home and a place in his bed. The only thing he hadn't been able to give her was the love she so desperately wanted from him. Charles had waited until she'd fallen in love with the idea of being part of a family here with him, then snatched it away by repeating the same mistakes.

If she'd kept driving that first night and never come

back, she'd be in a different head space than she was in now. A few days over Christmas feeling sorry for herself would've been nothing compared to this. She'd seen the possibilities of living at Heatherglen and becoming part of the family, but she would have to leave it all behind to look out for herself because no one else was going to do it for her.

'You're up early this morning. All that excitement with Harri must have kept you awake.'

Esme was refilling Dougal's water bowl when Charles made his way downstairs to the kitchen. Last night had left him drained but not in the way Esme probably imagined.

'Have you seen her?'

'Not yet. So, how do you really feel about the Dougal adoption plan?'

'The what?'

'Don't tell me you didn't get around to discussing it. Me and my big mouth.'

'No, we…er…had some other things going on.'

Esme stuck her fingers in her ears. 'Ugh. Stop. I don't want to hear what my brother and his girlfriend got up to last night.'

'Then tell me what it is you're wittering on about.'

She grabbed the two slices of toast as they popped up and began buttering them as though this was any ordinary morning and not the day after Charles had lost everything precious to him. 'Harriet had the bright idea that you two should adopt Dougal and keep him here at the castle.'

Charles stopped castigating his sister long enough to consider the implications of that news. 'Harriet wanted *us* to adopt Dougal?'

'Yes.' Esme munched on her breakfast, giving nothing else away about Harriet's secret pet project but it told Charles all he needed to know. Harriet *had* thought about staying on and making a life with him here. Taking on a dog was a commitment for the family they should have become. It was his blundering in, trying to secure her employment, that had messed everything up. If he'd left her to come to her own conclusion about what she wanted, instead of trying to force her hand, she wouldn't be leaving him.

He had been selfish. All this time he'd spent convincing her this was the place to raise the baby, he'd never once considered what would make her happy. He was asking her to give up everything she had achieved in London so he could have her and the baby here without disrupting his life. The truth was he didn't have a life worth living without Harriet in it.

He'd sent her away twelve years ago rather than make her fit into this world and now that's exactly what he was trying to do. She was the one expected to make all the concessions in this scenario he'd conjured up when it was clear it should've been him making the compromises to prove how much he loved her. He hoped it wasn't too late to do that.

With renewed determination to get their relationship on track he headed for the door. 'Esme, if Harriet comes through this way I need you to stall her.'

'What do you mean?'

'She wants to go back to London. I need you to keep her here until I get back, okay?'

'What is going on with you, Charles?' She was waving the remnants of her toast at him and if she knew how badly he'd screwed things up with Harriet, she'd be chucking it at him. He was going to do his best to fix things before Esme resorted to violence.

'I'm trying to get myself a life,' he answered, on his way out the door.

'Well, don't be long. We have a party to sort out.' Esme apparently had faith that he could do that in one afternoon. As Charles got into his car and set off for Glasgow, he prayed she was right. After all, he had everything to lose if he didn't get it right this time.

Harriet had intended to leave first thing, but she'd fallen fully clothed into an exhausted sleep so deep she hadn't heard her phone alarm go off. It had been the sound of a car door slamming outside that had finally woken her. Although she hadn't thought it possible, the sight of Charles driving away saddened her even more. If he wasn't even prepared to fight for her there really was no way back for them.

She took her time getting ready and packing up the last of her things. With Charles gone she didn't have the same urgency. Besides, she still had to say goodbye to Esme. Harriet was surprised to see her still sitting in the kitchen when she was usually at work by this time.

'Hi, Harriet. Can I get you anything to eat for breakfast?' Esme being nice to her was the last thing

she needed. Much more of this and she'd start blubbing and tell her how much she loved her brother.
She'd have to get out of here before she talked herself
back into staying and condemned herself to a life with
someone incapable of putting her first.

'No, thanks. I'm going to head back to London. I
have a lot to sort out.'

She didn't enjoy keeping Esme in the dark, but
she could do without any more drama. She was feeling too raw from the fallout to be exposed to someone else's pain. It was only fair someone considered
Esme's feelings in these matters too, but she had to
work through her own first.

'When?'

'Today. Now. As soon as I've woken up properly.'
She wasn't looking forward to the long drive home,
but she'd have to do it before she was faced with
Charles again. There was no guarantee she'd maintain
her dignity if that happened and her self-preservation
was replaced with the overwhelming love for him she
couldn't seem to bury.

'No! You can't!' Esme's outburst was so loud it
send Dougal scampering back to his bed with his tail
between his legs.

'I have to.'

'But—but it's—Hogmanay. We have our big Hogmanay party tonight. You can't miss that.'

'I'm really not in a partying mood.' It was one
thing to pretend to Esme that nothing had happened
to spoil her time here but putting on a brave face

for a house full of strangers would require an inner strength she no longer possessed.

'It's wonderful, Harriet. Everyone comes together for the party. We have music and enough whisky that we can usually persuade Charles to sing.'

That did catch her interest. It reminded her of the night she'd met him at university. At one of those alcohol-fuelled affairs where it had been too noisy to even think straight. Then Charles had picked up a guitar, begun strumming and that velvety Scottish accent had captivated everyone in the room. It was a long time since she'd heard him sing. The memory of it did nothing to alleviate her pain.

'I'm sure I wouldn't be missed.'

'Oh, but you would. Hogmanay is a time for us all to be together. You haven't seen anything until you've been to our Hogmanay party.'

'I'm due back at work.' She knew the lame excuse wouldn't work but she attempted it anyway, her defences at an all-time low.

'There'll be dancing and fireworks and don't forget all the men in kilts.' Esme sensed her weakness and pounced. There was one man in particular who'd look delectable in the family tartan, but even the promise of that sight wasn't enough for Harriet to prolong her inevitable departure.

'Please, say you'll be there, Harriet. It's our way of saying goodbye to the past and welcoming in a new start.' The way Esme described it, celebrating Hogmanay at Heatherglen was tempting. The closure she needed before starting over as a mother to this baby who needed her to love it enough for both parents. She could always slip away during the fireworks…

'You can't leave anyway. The caterers have stuffed up. I'm going to need you to go shopping for me.' Esme pulled out a pad of paper from a drawer and started scribbling a list on it.

'What? No. Can't you get someone else to do it?' She'd end up with a serious case of trolley rage if forced to endure the hordes stocking up as though they were preparing for the apocalypse on top of everything else.

'There is no one else. I'm waiting for the fireworks guy to set up and Max is helping the band with their sound check. Charles delegated everything to me this year, and I can't have people turning up without food to offer them. I need your help.'

She was getting stressed if she was admitting she couldn't do this alone. If the event turned out to be a disaster Harriet knew she'd blame herself. Esme deserved someone to think of her for a change.

This was turning out to be the worst New Year's Eve in history.

Everywhere Harriet turned she was confronted with families stocking up with copious amounts of alcohol and snacks. Some were arguing over how much they actually needed, others looked bored to tears, but they were all preparing to see in the New Year together. At the stroke of midnight, she'd be getting ready to leave Heatherglen for the last time. Faced with the reality of ringing in the New Year alone made for a depressing picture.

She found herself wandering away from the grocery aisles towards the clothing department. To the baby section. The tiny outfits drew her like a moth to a flame. Her eyes misted as she fingered the soft fabric and thought about preparing for the new arrival on her own. Something she and Charles should be doing together.

Charles no more wanted to host a party than he wanted to go back to a house without Harriet. It was a tradition he usually enjoyed, unlike the recurring break-ups. This year he was prepared to let Esme take over. With any luck she'd throw herself so deeply into preparations he could excuse himself altogether. How could he celebrate the start of a new year when he'd finished this one on such a low? Loving Harriet wasn't something he'd get over as soon as the clock struck midnight. Unfortunately, he didn't have a fairy godmother who could wave her magic wand and make him happy again, or make Harriet love him.

He hadn't seen her today, and he prayed his sister had been able to come up with a plan to keep her there for the few hours he'd been absent. It would be devastating if he didn't get to see her one last time and beg for her forgiveness.

Charles braced himself for the onslaught of Dougal love and whatever else waited for him behind Heatherglen's doors. If Esme was on her own and Harriet had gone, he'd never forgive himself and his sister would kill him once she found out how stupid he'd been. He could only hope with the upcoming party, the ear-blasting would be short-lived.

As predicted, as soon as he set foot inside the family home, Dougal was there to greet him. He reached down to stroke the only one who'd be pleased to see him, no matter what. When he glanced up from his crouched position on the floor he met those anguished eyes that had haunted him since last night.

'Esme wanted me to stay for the party.'

The sight of her when he thought he'd convinced himself he might never see her again hit him so hard it almost knocked him onto his backside.

'Can you give Harriet and me a minute, sis?' He was aware he was on borrowed time with Harriet now, especially if she worked out he'd been behind the ruse to get her to delay leaving for a while.

'I don't think there's any point—'

'Sure.' Thankfully, Esme cut off Harriet's protests and nipped out the door before she got dragged into the conversation.

'Can we talk?' He sat down at the table and pulled out a chair for Harriet. She remained standing.

'I don't think there's anything left to say, Charles.'

'I think there is. I hear you made plans for Dougal to become a permanent feature here?'

Harriet grabbed a cloth and began to clean down the work surfaces, which already looked spotless to Charles. 'It was just an idea I had. I'm sure Esme will find somewhere else for him.'

'You were going to make a decision like that without talking to me about it first?'

She spun around to face him. 'Rehoming a dog is not the same as transferring a person's job to a different country without telling her.'

'I know. I know. What I'm trying to say is that we were both doing things we thought would benefit each other. I wasn't trying to control your life, but I was guilty of not taking your feelings into consideration.'

'Why would you cut me out of decisions like that again after everything we've been through? You know how hard it's been for me to trust you again and then you go and do exactly the same thing.'

'I realise that. Probably too late, but I swear I will do whatever it takes for you to be happy from now on. All that matters to me is you and the baby.'

'I wish I could believe that.'

'Surely the fact you were willing for us to take on Dougal said you were thinking about staying on here? Deep down you must know how much I care about you or you'd never even have considered that sort of commitment.'

'It wasn't my feelings that were ever in question. I love you, Charles. I've always loved you. Why else do you think this has been so hard?'

'Then what the hell are we doing to ourselves?' Hearing her say those words was all Charles needed to know he'd done the right thing in the end. He crossed the floor so he could be closer to her, wanting to take her in his arms, but she dodged around him and resumed her cleaning.

'I'm sorry but, ultimately, nothing else has changed. Except I called you out on your behaviour this time.'

'That's not true. A lot has changed. It just took the shock of potentially losing you to make me realise that. The clinic is up and running. They don't need me here any more. Esme could easily take over Heatherglen.'

'What are you saying, Charles?' Harriet stopped scrubbing invisible stains to stare at him. Knowing he was saying something she wanted to hear gave him the courage to carry on.

He pulled out a piece of paper and handed it to her. 'I went to see my solicitor this morning. This is simply a letter to confirm my intent, contracts are in the process of being written.'

She scanned the letter his solicitor had drawn up this morning under duress. He wasn't happy that Charles was willing to sign away his inheritance so easily, but this was a sacrifice he was only too willing to make if it meant he and Harriet could be together.

'I can't let you do this.' Harriet folded the letter and tucked it back into his jacket pocket. She was so close he could feel her warmth, smell her perfume, and he so desperately wanted to kiss her again. He wouldn't, though. Not unless he was sure he wanted him to.

'Oh? You're telling me what I can or can't do now?' He couldn't help but smirk at the irony in that. Really, he didn't mind when it showed she cared about him.

She gave him a sidelong look. 'This is different. Heatherglen is your life. I can't let you give that up.'

'You and the baby are my life now. I was asking too much of you, expecting you to give up your home, your job and everything else to move here. If you can still picture a future with me I'm fully prepared to follow you back to London. I'm sure I can find work there and we can come back and visit Esme anytime.' The answer had been staring him in the face all along. Harriet wanted him to make a commitment, a gesture big enough that she would stop fearing the worst. That he was going to leave her on her own again.

He'd fulfilled the promise he'd made to honour his brother and father and he'd seen Esme build a business and fall in love. Now it was time to focus on what was important to him. Harriet.

'This is all so...overwhelming.' Harriet wanted to believe she could have it all, but only a few hours ago she'd been getting ready to say goodbye for ever, convinced Charles didn't love her enough to change. Now he was offering to give up everything and go back to London with her. It was everything she wanted yet she was afraid of taking that final step with him again. Her head was spinning with the possibilities awaiting them but there was still something holding her back.

'I'll do whatever it takes to prove to you this family is all that I want. Say the word and I'll quit working altogether to be a stay-at-home dad. I just can't lose you again.'

She would never ask him to do any of the things he was willing to give up, but these weren't things he would say lightly. 'You'd do that for me?'

'I'd do that for us. For our family.' He stroked his thumb across her cheek and placed a ghost of a kiss on her lips. Enough for her to crave more. Except he let go of her again. 'I won't put you under any pressure to make a decision now. You need to do what's right for you.'

Sound advice. If only she knew what that was.

'Esme, this isn't the food I brought back from the supermarket.' Harriet saw the plates of haggis, neeps and tatties and homemade black bun, a rich fruit cake wrapped in pastry, and knew she'd been played.

'There was a bit of a mix-up. The caterers arrived not long after you left.' With the party in full swing, Esme had finally taken a break herself to get something to eat from the buffet laid out in the marquee.

'Uh-huh? You couldn't have phoned to let me know?'

Esme waved her away. 'I was busy. There's no harm done.'

As though Harriet wasn't suspicious enough about Esme's whole part in getting her to stay, she gave Charles a little wink before she disappeared with Max.

'Why do I get the feeling you had a rather large hand in the great catering mishap?' she asked Charles.

'I thought we needed more time to get our act together.' Charles slid his hands around Harriet's waist and kissed her neck.

'Well, one of us did.' She should've been angry that he'd concocted that supermarket trolley dash and wasted her afternoon, but it showed he had been fighting for them after all. While she'd been dispatched on a fool's errand, Charles had been signing his life away in a solicitor's office to prove his commitment to her. It was worth all the cloak and dagger shenanigans in the end when it made them both consider what was most important to them. Right now, she was content to be with Charles. The man who was willing to give up everything just to be with her.

He kissed her again. 'It's almost midnight and I promised I'd get up and sing. Although I'm not sure I've had nearly enough whisky yet to do that.'

'You have to. I've been looking forward to that all evening.' She turned around in his arms and fluttered her eyelashes. This Hogmanay party reminded her of that first night they'd met. Hearing Charles sing again would be the perfect way to end it.

'In that case, I wouldn't want to disappoint you. Now, are you sure Dougal's safely locked away?'

'Yes, and I left the radio on for him so he doesn't get lonely, just as you asked.'

'Thank you.' He dropped another kiss on her lips and went to join the band on the stage. Thankfully, the weather had improved over the course of the day. Although the ground was muddy, the crowd was able to move outside to watch the band. It had the atmosphere of being at a music festival. Especially when most of them were wearing wellington boots to enable them to move unhindered across the wet fields.

Charles looked so handsome up there, singing traditional Scottish folk songs, wearing his kilt and playing the guitar, Harriet had become his number one groupie. Especially when he locked eyes with her and made her feel as though she was the only person here and he was singing directly to her.

'This last song is dedicated to the woman I love. Harriet, this one's for you.' As Charles began singing the slow ballad that had made her fall in love with him in the first place, tears streamed down her face. It was only now she realised she'd been waiting for him to say those words before those last barriers around her heart fell away.

All too soon the song was over, but she'd make sure he kept that guitar and kilt handy. She wanted to see them both on a regular basis.

'Ten, nine, eight…'

The band began the countdown and Charles jumped down off the stage so he could be with her at midnight.

'Seven, six, five, four…' She pulled him close so he was beside her to toast in the new year. Andy, the guy she'd met in the lounge, was standing nearby with Esme and Max and she waved over to him. He looked nervous and was leaning heavily on his crutches, waiting for the cacophony of cheers and fireworks as though he was going into battle.

'Three, two, one.'

The place erupted as the sky lit up with explosions of colour and the crowd burst into a chorus of Auld Lang Syne, linking arms as they did.

'Are you doing okay, Andy?' She moved closer to where she could keep a closer eye on him even though he had people on either side to make sure this wasn't too much for him.

'You know what? I really am. I'm not in Afghanistan any more. Not even in my head. Happy New Year, Harriet. I think this is going to be the best one yet,' he said as he raised his glass of whisky.

'I think so too,' she said, and couldn't resist giving him a hug. It was so heart-warming to see another patient start anew after their recovery, whether from mental or physical impairment. As he joined Esme in letting off the party poppers and covering everyone around them in glitter and string, his laughter confirmed he'd passed his test and finally conquered his demons.

Charles grabbed her by the hand and pulled her towards the house.

'Where are we going? We're going to miss the party.' She looked back with longing at the throng of happy people celebrating without them.

'We can't miss the first footer,' He said as though she knew what he was talking about. Her expression must've given her away as he was compelled to explain.

'The first person to step into the house in the New Year.'

'Oh,' she said, still clueless as to why this was significant.

Sure enough they'd just made it inside before someone knocked. Charles opened the door to a tall, black haired man and welcomed him in with a, 'Happy New Year.'

The dark stranger presented Charles with an array of gifts. 'Whisky, to drink and celebrate the New Year. Coal, so that your house will be warm, bring comfort and be safe for the year ahead. Shortbread, to make sure those in the household won't go hungry and a silver coin to bring prosperity.'

'Thank you. Now go on out back and get something for yourself to eat and drink.' Charles accepted the basket of gifts with one hand and clapped him on the back with the other, ushering him towards the party outside.

Once the mysterious visitor had gone, Charles opened the whisky and poured them two glasses. 'Happy New Year.'

Harriet clinked her glass to Charles's. 'Here's to the New Year, and our new life.'

'I'm so happy you're here to share this with me. There's only one thing that could make the moment more perfect, Harriet. That's why I wanted us to greet the first footer and bless us with good luck for the forthcoming year. Harriet Bell, will you marry me?'

'Yes. A thousand times, yes.' She threw her arms around his neck, uncaring about the whisky spilling everywhere. This was the ultimate commitment and there was nothing she wanted more than to marry this man and have his baby. As long she was with Charles she didn't care where they started their new life.

The truth had finally set them free, enabling them to raise their family in the best possible place. A home filled with love.

EPILOGUE

'DO YOU THINK we should call off the Christmas party?' Charles was doing lengths of the living room with the baby over his shoulder, trying to settle him.

'Thomas is just teething. He'll be fine.' Harriet was more enamoured than ever with her gorgeous husband now he was as attentive to their son as he was to her. They were enjoying their time off together over the festive period, even if sleep had become a thing of the past recently.

'It's not just for Thomas's benefit. I think it would be nice for us to have a quiet evening together.' Once their son had stopped crying, Charles was able to lay him down on the activity quilt he'd received from Auntie Esme for Christmas. The baby's attention now on the bright-coloured jungle animals on the fabric and the noisy attachments, his exhausted father collapsed onto the sofa beside his wife. He still had enough energy to give her a passionate kiss. Thankfully, parenthood hadn't diminished that side of their relationship.

'That does sound like heaven.' Chilling out by the

fire, spending quality time together, was more appealing than the idea of rushing around making sure their guests had enough to eat or drink all evening.

'Surely we could skip it for one year?'

'I don't think people would mind. Aksel and Flora are probably comfortable enough where they are without having to trail out here from the village in the cold. The same could be said for Lyle and Cassandra, even though they don't have as far to travel.'

At this time of year most people were content to stay with the ones they loved. The difference for Harriet this year was that she had people to stay at home with.

'What about Esme?' Charles gave her the face that said their plans for a quiet night had just been thwarted.

'You know she'll want to see her nephew and having Max and Esme isn't the same as hosting a party. We can still have a quiet night in.'

'You think? Just wait until she has us playing musical chairs and hide and seek.' Although he was denying it, Harriet knew Esme's excitement was part of the tradition around here.

'As long as I don't have to start cooking, or even get dressed, I don't care. I'm going to slob out today.'

'Me too.' Charles stretched out along the settee and put his feet up. They were both overdue a good rest after the year they'd had getting her transferred from London and making plans for the research centre. Not to mention their wedding in the middle of it all. Now, with Aksel building an adventure centre on the estate, the year ahead was going to be another busy one for Heatherglen. She would never have expected Charles to give up Heatherglen when it had become a family home for all of them.

They heard paper rustling in the corner and Charles lifted his head. 'Dougal! He's in the presents again.'

Harriet watched with amusement as the two did battle over the new scarf Joanie had knitted Charles for Christmas. She couldn't seem to do enough to thank them both for saving her life.

'Give me that back, you daft mutt.' Charles was growling almost as much as Dougal, who thought he was being treated to a new game, and Thomas was gigging at the spectacle too.

Yes, this was her crazy family, and she wouldn't trade it for anything.

* * * * *

THE ARMY DOC'S
CHRISTMAS ANGEL

ANNIE O'NEIL

This one goes out to the service men and women in our lives.

The sacrifices they make are unimaginable.

The things they see and the work they do can often come at a high cost.

Family life, physical health – even, in those awful cases, loss of life.

And they still go out there.

I hope stories like this one prove we all think their bravery and strength are extraordinary.

CHAPTER ONE

"YOU PLANNING ON wearing a track into the floor?"

Finn looked across at his boss, startled to see him in the hospital given the hour, then gave a nonchalant shrug. "Maybe. What's it to you?"

Theo barked a good-natured laugh. "I paid for that floor. I was hoping we could keep it intact for a few more years before your lunking huge feet are embedded in it."

Finn looked down at the honey-colored floorboards then up at his boss as he scrubbed his hand through the tangles of his dark hair. About time he got a haircut. Or invested in a comb. It had only been…oh…about fourteen years since he'd given up the buzz cuts. Didn't stop him from thinking of himself as that fit, adrenaline-charged young man who'd stepped off the plane in Afghanistan all those years ago. Once an army man…

He took a step forward. The heat from his knee seared straight up his leg to his hip. An excruciating reminder that he was most definitely *not* an army man. Not ever again.

He gave Theo a sidelong look. "What are you doing here, anyway? It's late."

"Not that late." Theo looked at his watch as if that confirmed it was still reasonable to be treading the hospital boards after most folk were at home having their tea. "I could ask you the same question."

It was Avoidance Technique for Beginners and both men knew it.

They stared at one another, without animosity but unwilling to be the first to break. Lone wolf to lone wolf… each laying claim to the silence as if it were an invisible shield of strength.

Heaven knew why. It was hardly a secret that Finn was treating one of the hospital's charity patients who was winging in from Africa today. He just…he was grateful to have a bit of quiet time before the boy arrived. His leg pain was off the charts today and once Adao arrived, he'd like to be in a place where he could assure the kid that life without a limb was worth living.

"Want to talk about it?" Theo looked about as excited to sit down and have a natter about feelings as Finn did.

"Ha! Good one." Finn flicked his thumb toward the staff kitchen tucked behind the floor's reception area. "I'll just run and fill up the kettle while you cast on for a new Christmas jumper, shall I?"

Theo smirked then quickly sobered. "I'm just saying, if you ever want to…" he made little talky mouths with his hands "…you know, I'm here."

"Thanks, mate." He hoped he sounded grateful. He was. Not that he'd ever take Theo up on the offer.

It wasn't just trusting Theo that was the issue. It was trusting himself. And he wasn't there yet. Not by a long shot. Days like today were reminders why he'd chosen to live a solitary existence. You got close to people. You disappointed them. And he was done disappointing people.

Christmas seemed to suck the cheer—what little he had—right out of him. All those reminders of family and friendship and "togetherness." Whatever the hell that was.

He didn't do any of those things. Not anymore.

All the jolly ward decorations, staffrooms already bursting with mince pies, and festive holiday lights glittering across the whole of Cambridge didn't seem to make a jot of difference.

He scanned the view offered by the floor-to-ceiling windows and rolled his eyes.

He was living in a ruddy 3D Christmas card and wasn't feeling the slightest tingle of hope and anticipation the holiday season seemed to infuse in everyone else.

Little wonder considering...

Considering nothing.

He had a job. He had to do it. And having his boss appear when he was trying to clear his head before Adao arrived wasn't helping.

He'd been hoping to walk the pain off. Sometimes it worked. Sometimes, like today, it escalated the physical and, whether he cared to admit it or not, emotional reminders of the day his life had changed forever.

Should've gone up to the rooftop helipad instead. No one ever really went there in the winter. Although this year the bookies were tipping the scales in favor of snow. Then it really would be like living in a Christmas card.

"Why are you here? Was there some memo about an all-staff welcoming committee?" Finn knew there wasn't. He was just giving his boss an out if he wanted it. Bloke talk came in handy for a lot of emotional bullet dodging.

Theo sighed. "Ivy."

Finn lifted his chin in acknowledgement. Her mystery illness had been the talk of all the doctors' lounges. "Gotta be tough, mate."

"'Tis." Theo flicked his eyes to the heavens, gave his stippled jaw a scrub and gave an exasperated sigh. "I hate seeing her go through this. She's five years old. You know?"

Oh, yeah. He knew. It was why he'd retrained as a pedi-

atric surgeon after the IED had gone off during a standard
patrol. The loss of life that day had been shameful.

All of them children.

Who on this planet targeted *children*?

At least he'd had an enemy to rail against. Theo was
shooting in the dark at a mystery illness. No wonder the
guy had rings under his eyes.

"Had anything good today?" Topic-changing was his
specialty.

Theo nodded. "A few interesting cases actually." He rattled through a few of them. "Enough to keep me distracted."

Finn huffed out an "I hear you" laugh. Work was the
only way he kept his mind off the mess he'd made of his
personal life.

*You're on your own now, mate. Paying your penance,
day by day.*

"The diagnostician. She managed to clear her schedule yet?"

Theo nodded. "Took a bit of juggling but she's here now."

Finn waited for some more information—something to
say what Theo thought of her—but received pure silence.
Any topic related to Ivy was a highly charged one so it
looked like his boss was going to reserve judgment on the
highly touted globetrotter until she'd had a bit more time
with his daughter.

"What's her name again?" Finn tried again when Theo
obviously wasn't going to comment further. "I heard one
of the nurse's call her Godzilla."

Theo gave a sharp tsk.

He didn't like gossip. Or anything that stood in the way
of the staff acting as a team. "She's a bit of a loner. Might
give off a cooler edge than some of the staff are used to.
Particularly around the holidays. But she's not yet had a
chance to get her feet on the ground, let alone establish a

rapport with the entire staff." He gave Finn a quick curt nod, making it very clear that he let facts stand. Not rumor. "She's called Madison Archer. Doesn't get much more American than that, does it?"

"Short of being scented like apple pie, I guess not." Finn smiled at Theo, trying to add a bit of levity, but raised his hands in apology at Theo's swiftly narrowed eyes.

More proof, as if he needed it, that Finn was no star at chitchat. He called a spade a spade, and other than that his conversational skills were operating on low to subterranean.

Theo's expression shifted to something indecipherable. "It's at times like this I understand how the parents feel when they walk in the doors of our hospital. Makes it that much more important we treat each other with respect. Without that, how can we respect our patients? Ourselves?" He lifted up his hands as if seeking an answer from the universe then let them fall with a slap against his long legs.

They looked at one another a moment in silence. This time with that very same respect he'd just spoken of.

Theo was a class-A physician and this hospital—the hospital he'd *built*—was one of the finest in the world, and still not one of them could put a finger on what was behind Ivy's degenerating condition. Lethargy had become leg pain. Leg pain had escalated to difficulty walking. They were even considering admitting her full time, instead of dipping in and out, things were so bad.

How the hell Theo went about running the hospital day in, day out when his little girl was sick…it would've done his head in.

Precisely why being on his own suited Finn to a T. No one to worry about except his patients. No emotions holding him back…as long as he kept his thoughts on the future and his damn leg on the up and up.

He gave his head a sharp shake, silently willing Theo

to move on. A wince of pain narrowed the furrows fanning out from his eyes as he shifted his weight fully onto his right leg.

The infinitesimal flick of Theo's eyes down then back up to Finn's face meant the boss man knew precisely what was going on. But he knew better than to ask. Over a decade of wearing the prosthetic leg and he still hadn't developed a good relationship with the thing. The number of times he'd wanted to rip it from his knee and hurl the blasted contraption off the roof…

And then where would he be? In a wheelchair like Ivy? Nah. That wasn't for him.

Helping children just like her—and Adao, who'd learned too much about war far too soon—were precisely why he kept it on. Standing beside the operating table was his passion. And if that meant sucking up the building pressure and tolerating the sharp needles of pain on occasion? Then so be it.

"Well…" He tried to find something positive to say and came up with nothing so fell back on what he knew best. Silence.

After a few minutes of staring out into the inky darkness he asked Theo, "You heard anything about the boy's arrival time?"

Finn was chief surgeon on the case, but Theo had a way of knowing just that little bit more than his staff. Sign of a good leader if ever there was one.

"Adao?"

Finn nodded, unsurprised that out of a hospital full of children Theo knew exactly who he was referring to. Although they didn't have too many children flying in from Africa just a handful of weeks before Christmas.

Then again, war never took much time to consider the holidays.

"Did they get out of the local airport in Kambela all right?" Theo asked.

"Yeah." Finn had received an email from one of the charity workers who'd stayed behind at the war-torn country's small clinic. "Touch and go as to whether the ceasefire would hold, but they got off without a hitch. They say his condition's been stabilized, but the risk of infection—" He stopped himself. Infection meant more of the arm would have to come off. Maybe the shoulder. Flickers of rage crackled through him like electricity.

This was a kid. A little *kid*. As if growing up in a country ravaged by war wasn't bad enough.

There had been a fragile negotiated peace in the West African country for a few months now, but thousands of landmines remained. The poor kid had been caught in a blast when another little boy had stepped on one. That boy had died instantly. The second—Adao—suffice it to say his life would never be the same.

They'd been out playing. Celebrating another renewal of the ceasefire. The horror of it all didn't bear thinking about.

Not until he saw the injuries, assessed damage limitation, talked Adao through how he would always feel that missing arm of his, but—

Don't go there, man. You made it. The kid'll make it.

Hopefully he wouldn't actively push his family away the way Finn had. If he had any leanings toward giving advice, he'd put that top of the list.

Keep those you love close to you.

Pushing them away only made the aching hole of grief that much harder to fill.

He knew that now.

Theo pulled his phone out of his pocket and thumbed through the messages. "He was meant to have been choppered in from London a couple of hours ago, right? The charity texted a while back saying something about paper-work and customs, but you'd think a boy with catastrophic injuries would outweigh a bit of petty bureaucracy."

Finn brought his fist down on a nearby table. That sort of hold-up was unacceptable. Especially with a child's wel-fare at stake.

"Hey!" Theo nodded at the table, brow creased. "You'd better apologize."

"What?" Disbelief flashed across Finn's features then a smile. "You want me to say sorry to the table? Sorry, table. I don't know what got into me." He held his hands out wide. *Happy now?* the gesture read.

Theo closed the handful of meters between them with a few long-legged strides, crossed his arms over his chest and looked Finn square in the eyes. "Are you all right to handle this?"

His hospital. His terms.

Fair enough.

"'Course." Finn said. "But if you think I'm not up to it? Take me off. Bear in mind you'll have to drag me out of here and nurse the black eyes of whoever you think can operate on Adao better than me."

No point in saying he'd have to deliver the punches from a wheelchair if his knee carried on mimicking a welding iron.

He ground his back teeth together and waited. Theo knew as well as he did that the last thing he'd do was punch someone. But it was Theo's hospital. Theo's call.

Theo feigned giving Finn a quick one-two set of box-ing punches, making contact with his midsection as he did.

Finn didn't budge. He had a slight edge on Theo in height, weight and age. The Grand Poo-bah of Limb Spe-cialists, they'd once joked.

"Look at that." Finn's tone was as dry as the Sahara. "I'm turning the other cheek."

Theo widened the space between them and whistled. "Have you been working out again?"

Finn smiled. Always had. Always would.

Pushing himself to the physical limit was one of the things that kept the demons at bay.

Theo gave Finn's shoulder a solid clap. "You're the one I want on this. The only one." He didn't need to spell out to Finn how his time in the military had prepared him more than most for the injuries Adao had sustained. "Just want to make sure you're on top form when the little guy arrives."

"What? Nah." Finn waved away his concerns, gritting his teeth against the grinding of his knee against his prosthesis. "I just save this curmudgeon act for you. Someone's gotta be the grumpy old man around here."

"I thought that was Dr. Riley."

They both laughed. Dr. Riley had yet to be seen without an ear-to-ear grin on his face. The man had sunbeams and rainbows shooting out of his ears. The children adored him. Most people called him Dr Smiley.

Finn nodded toward the Christmas tree twinkling away in the dimly lit reception area where they stood. "A bit early, isn't it?"

"Not if you're Evie."

Finn grunted. Evie was the resident Mrs. Claus around Hope Children's Hospital. Especially now she was all loved up. Just being around her and Ryan made him…well…suffice it to say it brought up one too many memories he'd rather not confront. Love. Marriage. They'd never got as far as the baby carriage, he and Caroline. Now he supposed he never would.

Guess that made him the resident Scrooge. Not that he had anything against Christmas in particular, it was just…

seeing these poor kids in hospital over the holidays always bugged him. He may not want to hang out with his own family, but he was damn sure these kids wanted nothing more than their mums and dads at the end of their beds on Christmas morning.

"Anyone else about for Adao's arrival?"

Finn shook his head. "Not that I know about. I've got the usual suspects lined up for tomorrow so we can give him a proper assessment." He listed a few names. "Right." He clapped his hands together. "I'm going to get on up to the roof, if you don't mind. Clear the cobwebs before Adao arrives." He stood his ground. Theo was smart enough to take the absence of movement as his cue to leave and turned toward the bank of elevators.

"Hey," Theo called over his shoulder as he was entering the elevator. "You know we have a team of experts who look after that sort of thing."

Theo didn't have to look at Finn's knee for Finn to know what he was talking about. He knew the offer was there. He just didn't want to take it. Pain equaled penance. And he had a helluva lot of making up to do. Parents. Brother. Ex-wife. Friends. And the list went on.

"Good to know." He waited until the elevator doors closed before he moved.

A string of silent expletives crossed his lips as he hobbled over to a sofa, pulled up his trouser leg and undid the straps to ease the ache in his knee, not even caring when the whole contraption clattered to the floor.

One breath in…one breath out…and a silent prayer of thanks that he had this moment alone. He didn't do weak.

Not in public anyway.

The handful of moments he'd let himself slide into self-pity over the years…those would remain buried in his chest as bitter reminders of the paths he shouldn't have taken. The lessons he should've learned.

He gave his prosthesis a bit of a kick.

"It's just you and me, mate. Guess we'd better start finding a way to make nice."

CHAPTER TWO

"ARE YOU HANGING about for a meet-and-greet with Adao?"

Naomi went wide-eyed at Evie's question. She hadn't said anything, but that had definitely been her plan. A volley of responses ricocheted round her chest and lodged in her throat because she didn't want Evie to hear any of them.

I know how he feels.

He's probably as scared as I was.

I wanted him to know there's someone here who understands what it's like to live in a world ruled by guns and fear.

But Evie knew nothing of Naomi's past. Having Adao here would be the biggest emotional challenge she'd faced since arriving in Britain at the ripe age of fifteen. Scared. Utterly alone.

Two things she never wanted Adao to feel.

At least he knew his family was waiting at home for him.

Naomi pinned on her bright smile—the one she ensured her patients and colleagues knew her by—and asked, "How'd you guess?"

Evie shrugged in her elfin way. She just did.

Naomi liked to think of Evie as the entire hospital's resident Christmas faerie. She had a canny knack for intuiting things. That and a heart the size of Britain. She smiled as Evie shifted Grace on her hip, the baby who'd been abandoned at the hospital a few months ago and who was to be adopted by Evie and her soon-to-be husband, Ryan.

"I have a really ridiculous question." Evie looked at her a bit bashfully.

"Shoot."

"I'm not exactly sure where Kambela is."

"Adao's home?" Naomi knew what Evie was really asking. *Is it anywhere near where you're from?* Her English, no matter how hard she tried, was still lightly accented. "It's on the coast of Africa. Near the Horn."

Right next door to her country. Zemara.

"Hey…is everything all right with you?"

Uh-oh. Evie's emotional intuition radar was beep-beep-beeping like a metal detector in her direction…not so good.

"Fine! Great." Naomi tipped her head toward the glass doors leading out of the front of the hospital and grinned. "Did you see that?"

"Violet being discharged early? Amazing. You did such good work with her." Evie grinned and shifted Grace from one arm to the other. "*Oof!* This little girl's putting on weight at a rate of knots! I'll have 'mom arms' soon."

Naomi smiled and gave the tip of the baby's nose a tickle. Hope Hospital had hit the headlines with this little girl and would again soon with Adao…if the surgery went well and the rehab was successful. So much of recovery had to do with a patient's will. The will to fight. The desire to survive. The stamina to confront what had happened to them head on.

She crossed her fingers behind her back for Adao, ignoring the tight twist of nerves constricting the oxygen in her lungs.

"Are you waiting for Ryan?"

Evie nodded, her smile hitting the ear-to-ear register. If a couple of red-breasted robins flew in the front door and began adorning her with mistletoe, she could easily be the poster girl for Cupid's arrow. "He's just come out of surgery. I'm swotting up for nursing college in the new term and he's promised to talk me through all the signs, symptoms and early treatment for scarlet fever if I make him an early Christmas dinner."

"Turkey and all the trimmings?" Naomi couldn't hide her shock. She knew they were in love, but Christmas dinner on a "school night"?

"Giant prawn cocktails and pavlova." Evie shrugged and shifted Grace in her arms again. Whatever her Australian-born fiancé wanted…

Naomi giggled. "You are well and truly loved up, aren't you?"

Evie blushed in response. Her whole world had changed. "It's not just me, is it? Have you seen Alice lately? Sunbeams. Everywhere she goes. And Marco can't stop humming opera during surgery these days." She drummed her free fingers on her chin and gave Naomi a mischievous sideways look. "I wonder who's next?"

Naomi put up her hands and laughed. "Not me!" That ship of possibility had sailed long ago.

"Why not? You're beautiful. Amazing at your job. You'd be a real catch."

If cowardice was something a man could ever love, sure. But it wasn't. Which was precisely why she kept herself just out of love's reach.

She was just about say "Finn Morgan" to be contrary, but stopped herself. The man had scowling down to a fine art. At least around her. But the season of good cheer was upon them so she stuck to what had served her best when her past pounded at that locked door at the back of her mind: a positive attitude. "I reckon Mr. Holkham down in the cafeteria could do with a bit of a love buzz."

Evie threw back her head and laughed. "A love buzz? I don't know if that's a bit too energetic for him. What is he? Around seventy?"

"I think so. I love that Theo hired retirees who wanted to keep active, but…if anyone needs a love buzz it's him." She made a silly face. "Anything to make him chirpier when he serves up the lasagna. Who wants garlic bread with a side of gloom?"

"Good point."

Naomi could almost see the wheels turning in Evie's mind…already trying to figure out who she could couple with the sweet, if not relatively forlorn, older gentleman. She'd tried to tease a smile from him every day since the hospital had opened, to no avail. Perhaps she should ask him for a coffee one day. Maybe he was just lonely. A widower.

She knew more than most that with love came loss and that's why being cheerful, efficient and professional was her chosen modus operandi.

"Ooh, Gracie, look. It's Daddy!" Evie took her daughter's teensy hand and made it do a little wave as Ryan approached with a broad smile and open arms.

Naomi gave Evie's arm a quick squeeze and smiled. "I'd better get up there."

"All right. I'll leave you to it, then," Evie said distractedly, her eyes firmly fixed on her future husband.

Naomi took the stairs two at a time all the way up to the fifth floor, as she usually did. She put on the "feel good" blinkers and refocused her thoughts. She was feeling genuinely buoyed by her last session. A cheer-worthy set of results for her patient followed by a discharge. What a way to end a work day!

Watching a little girl skip—*skip!*—hand in hand with her parents straight out of the hospital doors and away home, where she would be able to spend Christmas with her family. A Christmas miracle for sure. Four months ago, when Violet had been helicoptered in from a near-fatal car accident, Naomi had had her doubts.

It was on days like this her job was the perfect salve to her past. Little girl power at its finest. And knowing she was playing a role in it made it that much better.

If she could keep her thoughts trained on the future, she could hopefully harness some of that same drive and determination in Adao. This was definitely not the time to let her own fears and insecurities bubble to the surface.

Then again, when was it the time?

Never. That was when.

So! Eyes on the prize and all would be well.

She hit the landing for the fifth floor and did a little twirl before pushing the door open.

Happy, happy, happy— *Oh*.

Not so happy.

The doctor's hunched shoulders and pained expression spoke volumes.

And not just any doctor.

Finn Morgan.

Of all the doctors at Hope, he was the one she had yet to exchange a genuine smile with. Well…him and the cafeteria chap, but she had to work with Mr. Morgan and he made her feel edgy. The man didn't do cheery. Not with her anyway.

Some days she had half a mind to tell him to snap out of it. He was a top surgeon at an elite private hospital. He worked on cases only the most talented of surgeons could approach with any hope of success. And still… King of the Grumps.

It wasn't as if he wasn't surrounded by people doing their

best to create a warm, loving environment at Hope Hospital, no matter what was going on in their personal lives.

Not that she'd ever admit it, but most days she woke up in a cold sweat, her heart racing and arms reaching out for a family she would never see again.

If she could endure that and show up to work with a smile on her face, then whatever was eating away at him could be left at home as well.

She pushed the door open wider, took a step forward then froze. Her breath caught in her throat at the sound of the low moan coming from his direction. As silently as she could, she let the door from the stairwell close in front of her so that all she could see of him through the small glass window was his rounded back moving back and forth as he kneaded at something. His knee? His foot? She'd noticed a slight limp just the once but the look he'd shot her when he'd realized she'd seen it had been enough to send her scuttling off in the other direction.

Even so…

He was sitting all alone in the top floor's central reception area, his back to her, the twinkling lights of the city beyond him outlining his broad-shouldered physique.

Her gut instinct was to go to Finn… *Mr. Morgan*, she silently corrected herself…but the powerful "back off" vibes emanating from him kept her frozen at the stairwell door.

She'd been flying so high after finishing with Violet she'd thought she'd put her extra energy to use helping Adao settle in. She'd already been assigned as his physiotherapist—work that wouldn't begin until after his surgery with Finn Morgan—but she thought meeting him today might help him know there was someone who understood his world. His fears.

She pressed her hand against the glass as another low

moan traveled across from the sofa where Finn remained resolutely hunched over his leg.

Something about his body language pierced straight through to her heart. A fellow lost soul trying to navigate a complicated world the best he could?

Or just a grump?

From what she'd seen, the man wouldn't know a good mood if it bit him on the nose.

She pulled her gaze away from him and searched the skyline for Adao's helicopter. She'd come here to find her patient, not snoop on a doctor clearly having a private moment.

She had little doubt the little boy was experiencing so many things that she had all those years ago when she'd arrived in the UK from Zemara. The language barrier. The strange faces. No family.

She swallowed against the lump forming in her throat and squeezed her eyes tight.

It was a long time ago.

Eleven years, two months and a day, to be exact.

Long enough to have moved on.

At least that's what logic told her. But how did you ever forget the day you saw everyone you loved herded into a truck and driven away off to the mountains? Mountains rumored to be scarred with pre-dug mass graves for anyone the rebels deemed unfit for their indiscriminatingly cruel army.

Blinking back the inevitable sting of tears, she gave herself a sharp shake and forced herself to paste on a smile. Her life was a good one. She was doing her dream job. In one of the most beautiful cities in the world, no less. Every day she was able to help and nurture children who, against the odds, always found a way to see the good in things.

So that's what she did, too. Focusing on the future was

the only way she had survived those early days. And the only way she could live with herself now.

She pressed her forehead to the small, cool window in the door. In the dimly lit reception area—the lights were always lowered after seven at night—Finn had turned his face so that she could clearly see his profile.

He was a handsome man. Not storybook English— blond and blue-eyed, the way she'd once imagined everyone looked before she'd arrived in the UK. More…rugged, as if he'd just stepped off a plane from a long, arduous trek across the Alps rather than a doctor who had taken the elevator up from the surgical ward where he could usually be found. Not that she'd been stalking him or anything. Far from it. He was an arm's-length kind of guy judging by the handful of terse encounters they'd had.

Come to think of it, every time their paths had crossed since the hospital had opened—either going into or coming out of a session—he'd bristled.

Physically bristled.

Not the usual effect she had on people but, hey…she didn't need to be his bestie, she just needed a quality working relationship. That…and a bit of professional respect would be nice. Having seen his work on a near enough daily basis, she knew he respected her work…it would just be nice if that respect included the occasional smile or "Thank you."

His hair was a rich, dark brown. A tangled mess of waves that could easily turn to curls if it grew out. He was a big man. Not fat. No. Tall and solidly built. A "proper" man, as her birth mother would have said. A real man.

She swallowed back the sting of tears that inevitably followed when she thought of her mother. Her beautiful mother, who had worked so hard to pay for her extra lessons from any of the aid workers who had been based out of her hometown for as long as she could remember.

And then, of course, there was also her foster mother. The one who had taught her that she still had it in her to be brave. Face the maze of applications she needed to complete to get into medical school one day and, eventually, fulfil her dream of working as a pediatric physiotherapist.

Touch, she'd come to realize, was one of the most curative things of all.

Finn shifted around on the sofa and— Oh!

Her fingers wove together and she pressed her hands to her mouth to stem her own cry. He wore a prosthesis. She'd had no idea.

And from the looks of things, his leg was hurting. A man as strong and capably built as Finn would have to be in some serious pain to look the way he did now. Slightly ashen. Breath catching. Unaware of everything else around him.

Instinct took over.

Before she thought better of it, she was by his side.

"Please. Perhaps I can help massage…" The rest of her offer died on her lips as she saw equal hits of horror and anger flash across his gray eyes.

She stood, completely frozen, mesmerized by their near-mystical depths.

How had she never noticed them before? So…haunted. She wondered if her dark eyes looked the same.

"What are you doing here?" Finn hastily grabbed his prosthesis and strapped it back on, despite the redness she saw engulfing his knee.

"I was just— I…"

I wanted to help.

"Well?" Finn rose alongside her, the scent of cotton and forest hitting her senses as he did.

She was tall so it took a lot of height to make her feel small. If the irritation radiating from him wasn't making her feel as if she'd invaded an incredibly private moment, she could almost imagine herself feeling delicate in his presence.

Delicate?

What was that about?

Finn scanned her uniform for her employee badge, though she was sure he already knew her name. It was his signature on the forms requesting her as Adao's physio.

She sucked in a breath. This was about Adao, not about Finn. Although…

Not your business. You have your secrets. He has his.

"Sorry. Please. I didn't mean to interrupt."

"No." Finn stared at her for a moment then swiped at the air between them, causing her to flinch. "What do you need?"

"I-I was here to help with Adao," she stammered. "I thought perhaps I could help settle him in."

"What?" Finn bridled. "You think I'm not up to being my patient's welcoming committee?"

She tilted her head to the side and pinched her lower lip with her teeth. Was he hoping for an honest answer? Or was this the famous British sense of humor at play?

Her silence seemed to give him the "No" he was expecting. His swift change of expression told her he was already dismissing her.

So much for trying to go the extra mile! She was about to tell him Adao was her patient too when, mercifully, Finn's phone buzzed and those penetrating, moonstone-colored eyes of his relaxed their spotlight grip on her.

He was as chatty on the phone as he was with her. A few responses of "Yeah. Yeah. Got it…" later and he was beckoning her to join him.

Okay.

He swiftly crossed to the bank of elevators—so quickly it was difficult to see how he hid the pain—and punched the illuminated button as he pulled his key card out of his pocket. Only staff were allowed up onto the roof and the magnetic key cards were the only way of taking the elevator up there. "Adao's ten minutes out. You done any helicopter arrivals before?"

She shook her head. Not here anyway. She'd seen more than her fair share before she'd left Zemara, but usually those helicopters had been filled with rebels wielding machine guns. Not charity workers with patients about to undergo life-altering surgery.

"Right." Finn pulled a crumpled bit of notepaper out of his pocket. "Adao's seven years old, suffering from—"

"Multiple injuries as a result of a landmine explosion," Naomi cut in. She'd read the case. Memorized it. It had all but scored itself straight into her heart if the truth be told, but that wasn't what this showdown was about. She kept on talking as the elevator doors opened and the hit of wintry air all but took her breath away. "Adao's injuries include loss of his right arm. Efforts have been made to keep infection to a minimum, but our goal is to ensure he retains as much use of his shoulder as possible so that any use of a pros—' She stopped, her eyes clashing with Finn's—*Mr. Morgan's*—as he wheeled on her.

"Fine. Good. I see you're up on the case. How's about we have a bit of quiet time before the chaos begins, yeah?"

Naomi nodded and looked away, forcing herself to focus on the crisp, starlit sky above them.

No problem.

She'd obviously seen far more than Finn—*Mr. Morgan*—had wanted her to. An incredibly private moment for a man who clearly didn't do vulnerability.

Vulnerability and strength were two of the reasons she'd chosen to work at Hope. Most of the children here were going through something frightening. Loss of a limb. Surgery. Illnesses that meant they would be facing a future that would present hurdle after hurdle. And despite all the pain and all the suffering, the bulk of the children confronted their futures with a courage that amazed her on a daily basis. If she could be a part of making their future something to actually look forward to, then she was going to give it her all.

She tipped her head up and let the wind skid across her features as she sought out the Milky Way. The night was so clear she spotted it almost instantly. She was constantly amazed by the band of light made up of so many stars, so faraway, they were indistinguishable to the naked eye. In Zemara, they called the spiral galaxy they were such a small part of the Path of Spirits. This was where her family must be now…far above her…looking down…

A rippling of goose-pimples shot across her arms, but it wasn't the cold that had instigated them.

Guilt had a lot to answer for. Here she was at one end of the galaxy while her family were…only heaven knew where. It wasn't fair.

"Look." Finn's rich voice broke through the thick silence. "Over there."

She turned and followed the line of his arm and saw the helicopter emerging from the darkness.

CHAPTER THREE

NAOMI'S EYES WERE trained on the helicopter but all Finn could focus on was her.

Why had he snapped at her like he had?

It wasn't her fault she'd seen him in the lounge…without his leg…exposed as the embittered man he'd become ever since the future he'd thought he'd have had literally been torn away from him.

It also wasn't her fault that every time he saw her his senses shot to high alert. There was no way he was going to put a name to what he felt each time their paths crossed, but his body was miles ahead of him on that front.

A white-hot, solitary flame had lit that very first staff meeting when they'd all gathered together in the hospital's huge atrium and he'd first seen her. Even at—what had she been? Fifty meters from him? Twenty? Whatever. The impact had been sharp, forceful, and, if today was anything to go by, unabating.

From the response his body had had to her, she may as well have sashayed up to him in a curve-hugging negligee and wrapped him round one of her long, elegant fingers.

Not that he'd thought about her naked.

Okay, fine. Of course he had.

But it had just been the once, and the woman had all but floated out of the hospital's therapy pool in a scarlet swimsuit that had made him jealous of the droplets of water cascading down her body.

What else was he meant to do?

Treat her with respect, you numpty.

Everything about her commanded a civility he could tap into for the rest of his colleagues, but Naomi? Whatever it was he felt around her it meant he simply wasn't able to extend it to her. Not in the manners department anyway.

Naomi's entire essence sang of grace and an innate sensitivity to both her patients and her environment. Her movements were always smooth. Fluid. Her voice was carefully modulated, lightly accented, but he didn't know from where. He'd thought of asking once or twice, but that would've verged on curious and with half the hospital staff staggering around the hospital with love arrows embedded in their hearts…bah. Whatever. He should just stuff his hormones in the bin and have done with them.

And yet…even now, with her head tipped back as it was, the wind shifting along that exquisitely long neck of hers, there was something almost regal about Naomi's presence. Not haughty or standoffish, more…wise.

Where he shot from the hip, she always took a moment before responding to his sharp comments and brusque reactions to her.

She wasn't to know his brush-offs were the age-old battle of desire versus pragmatism.

Where he felt big and lunky, she was lithe and adroit.

Long-limbed. Sure-footed. High, proud cheekbones. Skin the shade of… He didn't know to describe it. A rich, warmly colored brown? Whatever shade it was, it was beautiful. The perfect complement to her full, plump mouth. Not that he was staring at it. Much.

There was something fiercely loyal shining in those dark eyes of hers. He saw it whenever she was with a patient.

But he could also see it now as she trained her eyes on the sky above. For whom or what it shone, he would never know, because he didn't do personal. Didn't do intimate. Not anymore.

As if feeling his gaze on her, she turned and met his eyes.

"Is there anywhere we're meant to stand when they land, Mr. Morgan?"

Finn scowled. Why'd she have to catch him mooning over her? And what was with this *Mr. Morgan* business? Made him sound like a grumpy old man.

Humph.

Maybe that was the point she was making.

"It's Finn," he said. "Over there." He pointed toward the covered doorway where a porter was wheeling a gurney into place then turned his focus on to the approaching helicopter…willing the beats and syncopation of the blades cutting through the thin, wintry air to knock some sense back into him.

Bah.

He hadn't been mooning. It had simply been a while. Once he'd cut ties with his past, he'd thought that part of him had all but died.

He should be relieved his body was still capable of responding to a woman like a red-blooded male. So many of the soldiers he'd met during his stint in hospital…hell…he didn't wish their futures on his worst enemies.

All these thoughts and the raft of others that inevitably followed in their wake fell to the wayside as the helicopter hovered above them for a moment before executing a perfect landing.

And then they all fell to what they did best, caring for their patient.

* * *

There were too many people in Adao's room. It was easy enough to see from the growing panic in his wide, dark eyes as they darted from person to medical contraption to yet another person.

When they landed on her, all she could see was fear.

He was strapped to the gurney, completely surrounded by medical staff from the charity and the hospital all exchanging stats and information at a rate of knots that would have been impossible for him to comprehend.

Short, sharp counts dictated the swift shift from the gurney to the hospital bed and yet another stream of instructions flowed over him as they hooked him up to fresh IVs and peeled out another ream of information as they pressed monitors to his skinny, bare, little-boy chest. And when he called out for his parents it was all she could do not to tear her heart from her own chest.

"It's too much!"

The room fell silent as all eyes turned to Naomi.

"I beg your pardon?"

Finn hadn't moved a muscle, but his voice may as well have been a drill boring straight into her chest for the pain it caused.

She lifted her chin and met his steel-colored gaze. Yes, she was still smarting from his curt form of issuing orders.

"Not on that side."

"Not too close."

"Not too far."

There didn't seem to be a single thing she could do properly under his hawk-eyed gaze. But when it came to the child—*this child*—enough was enough.

"Please. Give the boy some peace. He's known nothing but chaos. This place—this hospital—must bring him peace. Comfort. Not fear."

Finn's eyebrows lifted a notch. It was written all over his face. She'd overstepped the mark.

Just as she was about to run out of the room, find a computer and start composing her letter of resignation, he spoke.

"You heard Naomi." He pointed at one nurse and one doctor, both of whom were on the overnight shift in Adao's ward. "You two stay. The rest of you…" He made a shooing motion with his hands. "Out you go. And you…' He pointed directly at Naomi. "You come with me."

Finn's eyes were glued to Naomi's throat. The tiny pulse point, alive with a blaze of passion he'd not seen in her before.

Their paths had never really crossed in this way. Neither had their temperaments.

Fighting for a patient.

It showed her high-energy, positive approach to work was more than skin deep.

But what he wanted to get to was the *why*. Why this little boy? Why the specifics? Her slight accent intrigued him. Maybe it was from a French-speaking country? He wasn't sure. Either way, there was something about Adao that had got under her skin and was making an emotional impact.

Problem Number One.

Finn flexed his fingers, hoping it would rid them of the urge to reach out and touch her throat, smooth his thumb across her pounding pulse point. From the meter or so he'd put between them, he could still tell her skin looked as soft as silk. But her spirit? Solid steel.

The combination pounded a double hit onto his senses. Primal. Cerebral.

Problem Number Two.

He bashed the primal response into submission and channeled his thoughts into figuring out what made her tick.

Work.

That much was obvious. Not that he kept tabs on the woman, but he'd only ever seen her in work clothes. Never did she shift to casual or night-out-on-the-town outfits as loads of other doctors did when they threw their scrubs in for washing. Then again...he wasn't exactly a social butterfly either.

She was top of her game. No one came more highly recommended in her field of pediatric physio than she did.

Snap. He was up there in the top-rated limb specialists.

She was opinionated.

Snap again.

Fair dos to the woman, she hadn't blinked once when he'd all but marched her to an empty room a few doors down from Adao's and wheeled on her.

He counted to ten in time with her heartbeat before he'd steadied his own enough to speak.

"So." He crossed his arms and tipped his head toward Adao's room. "What was that all about?"

She gave her head a quick shake as if she didn't understand.

He waited. His failsafe technique.

Far more effective than saying the myriad of things he could have:

"There's only one person in charge in that room and it's me."

Not his style.

"Since when is a physio a psychiatrist?"

Ditto. He wasn't into tearing people down, but he did like explanations for outbursts.

The seconds ticked past.

Naomi threw a quick look over her shoulder, stuffed

her hands in the pockets of her Hope Hospital hoodie then said, "Okay. Fine. I just feel for the little man, you know?"

He loved the way she said "feel"—even if it was a verb he didn't include in his own vocabulary. She said it as if the word had heft. Gravitas, even. As if it *meant* something.

What a thing to have all that emotion churning round in your chest. Way too much extra baggage to haul around the hospital if he wanted to do his job properly. If he professed to know one solitary thing about himself it was this: Finn Morgan did not do baggage.

Ha!

He coughed into his hand to hide a self-deprecating smirk.

If his ex-wife could read his thoughts, she would've pounced on them like a mouse on cheese.

One of the last things she'd said to him before he'd left his past where it belonged was that he was "*Made* of baggage." And one day? "One day," she'd said to him, "all of that baggage will tumble open and wreak havoc with the man you keep telling yourself you are."

How about that for a "let's keep it friendly" farewell.

On a good day he recalled her "prophesy" as tough love.

On bad days? On bad days he tried not to think of her at all.

He shifted his weight off his knee and brought his thoughts back to Adao and Naomi. "How do you 'feel' for him? Are you from Kambela?"

"No, I'm…" She started to say something then pressed her lips together and started again. "I know what it's like to arrive somewhere new and feel…overwhelmed. Not know who to trust."

"Oh, I see. So you're the only one he can trust here, is that what you're saying?"

Why was he being so confrontational? She was clearly

doing what any employee of Hope Children's Hospital should be doing: Holding the patient's needs first and foremost in their mind. At all times.

Take it down a notch, man. She's trying to do right by the kid.

He shrugged the tension out of his shoulders and adopted what he hoped was a less confrontational pose. "I see what you're saying. The kid's been through a lot. But the one person he's got to trust is me." He let it sink in a minute. He was the one who would be holding the scalpel tomorrow. He was the one who would be changing Adao's life forever.

"You're the one who will help him live. I'm the one who's going to help him rebuild his life," Naomi shot back.

Wow. The pronouncement was so loaded with barbs he could take personally he almost fell back a step. Good thing he didn't take workplace slanging matches personally.

The surgery and recovery Adao required was a step-by-step process. And they weren't anywhere near rehab. No point in popping on rose-colored glasses at this stage. Whether she liked it or not, Adao had a *long* road of recovery ahead of him, and the first step was the operating table. Finn's operating table.

"You got the order right," Finn said. "Life first."

And that was the simple truth of the matter.

Naomi didn't respond verbally. But the pursed lips followed by a swift inhalation told him all he needed to know. She knew the facts as well as she did. She just didn't like them.

"C'mon." He steered her, one hand pressed to the small of her back, toward Adao's room. "All the basics should be taken care of right now. How 'bout you sit in while I talk Adao through his first twenty-four hours here at Hope?"

If she was surprised, Naomi masked it well. If she noticed he dropped his hand from her back about as quickly as he'd put it there, she made no sign of it either. As if the moment had never happened.

The tingling in his fingers spoke a different story. When he'd touched her? That flame in his core had tripled in size.

Leaning against the doorframe, having refused Finn's invitation to join him, Naomi had to silently admit the truth.

She was impressed.

As cranky and gruff as Finn was with her…with Adao?… he was gentle, calm and capable of explaining some incredibly complicated facts in a way that didn't patronize or confuse. When Adao spoke or asked questions, she recognized the same lilting accent she'd acquired when learning English from American missionaries or aid workers. Hers, of course, was softened by years in the UK and was now predominantly British English. His was still raw—lurching between the musical cadence of his mother tongue and wrestling with all the new English words.

"We can go over all of this again," Finn was saying, "whenever you want. But the main thing is we're here to help. Okay, little man? Anything you need?"

Adao shook his head now, his small head and shoulders propped up on the big white pillows. He was a collection of bandages with little bits of his brown skin peeking out at intervals. And his eyes…those big brown eyes rimmed with tears…spoke volumes.

Fear. Bewilderment. Loneliness.

He nodded at Finn but said nothing.

She got that.

The silence.

Admitting there was something or someone you missed so much you thought your heart might stop beating was as good as admitting a part of you wished it would. And despite the anxiety creasing his sweet little brow, she also saw fight in him. He wouldn't be here otherwise.

She ached to go to him. Be by his side. Tell him all the things she wished she had been told when she'd arrived in the UK. That these were good people. And while they weren't family...

Her eyes unexpectedly misted over as Finn and Adao did a big fist, little fist bump.

You couldn't ever replace family. Could you?

Finn crossed to her.

"I think it's time we let him get some rest." Finn tipped his head toward the staffroom. "His minder from the charity is just getting some coffee. She'll stay with him tonight. The chair in the corner converts to a bed, so...we'd best leave him to settle in quietly." He gave her a weighted look. "As you suggested."

Nothing like having your own words come back to bite you in the bum.

He was right, of course. And Adao was in the best possible place. But leaving the little boy was tugging at a double-wide door to her heart she'd long jammed shut. It felt wrong.

"Now," Finn mouthed, when the woman from the charity appeared from round the corner and Naomi's gaze inevitably skidded back in Finn's direction as if he were some sort of homing beacon. It was madness, considering Finn Morgan was the last set of arms she'd throw herself into if she needed comforting. It would be like skipping up to a hungry grizzly bear and asking if he minded if they shared a den. Not. Going. To. Happen.

He had his hand on her elbow and was filling up the rest of the space in the doorframe.

There it was again. That cotton and forest scent. And something extra. She looked up into his slate-colored eyes as if they would give her the answer she needed.

Her heart pounded against her ribcage when it did.

That other scent?

Pure male heat.

Naomi scooped her keys off the ground for a second time.

What had got into her?

She blew out a slow breath, waited until the cloud dissipated, then put the key in the lock and turned it.

See? There.

All she needed to do was blank any thoughts of Finn Morgan and— *Doh!*

There went the keys again. At least she was inside this time.

She jogged up the stairs to her flat, opened the interior door, flicked on the lights and popped her keys into the wooden bowl that rested on the small table she had at the front door.

Home.

She grinned at it.

The studio flat was dinky, but she loved it. Her cocoon. A twenty-minute walk from the hospital. Fifty if she took a run along the river on the way, which, let's face it, was every day. Going to the river had become a bit of a pilgrimage. If only one day she would come back from the river and find everything was—

If only nothing.

She toed off her trainers—against her own advice!— and pushed her door shut with her elbow.

Brightly lit. Simply furnished. Secure. Two floors above a bookshop/coffee shop that catered to students and, as such, was open all night. All the things she needed to get to sleep at night.

She shrugged out of her padded gilet then pulled her

hoodie, her long-sleeved T-shirt and her wool camisole off, all but diving into her flannel jimjams that she'd laid out on the radiator when she'd left in the morning.

The one thing about England she'd failed to get used to was the cold. This winter was particularly frigid. Rumors of a white Christmas were swirling around the hospital like…like snowflakes.

She gave herself a wry grin in the bathroom mirror as she let warm water run over her freezing fingers. At least the sub-zero temperatures helped keep her heart on ice.

She shivered, thinking of that hot, intense flare of heat she'd seen in Finn's normally glacial gaze.

Did it mean that he…? No. The man was like a snapping turtle. Don't do this. Do that. Not here. There. Me right. You wrong.

She thought of his athletic build, his bear-like presence. Maybe he was more… Abominable Snowman than snapping turtle. Could one make love to a yeti?

She gave her head a shake. Clearly she'd lost a few brain cells on the cold walk home. Even if Finn wrapped a ribbon round his heart and handed it to her on a velvet cushion… *Pah-ha-ha-ha!* Can you imagine?

She tugged on her wool-lined slipper boots, padded across to her tiny strip of a kitchen and opened the fridge.

Yup! Forgot to go shopping. Again.

She stared at the handful of condiments she'd bought in yet another failed moment of "I'll invite someone over" and wondered what it would be like to open up her fridge and know that she'd be making a meal for herself and her family. She closed the refrigerator door along with the thoughts.

Being in a relationship wasn't on the cards for her. Each time she'd tried…*whoomp.* Up had gone the shields holding court round her heart.

She laughed into the silence of her flat.

At last! She'd found something she and Finn had in common.

Now all she had to do was find a way to get along.

CHAPTER FOUR

"DID YOU MANAGE to get some sleep?" Finn looked over at Adao's case worker from the charity when all he elicited from the little boy was an uncertain mini-shrug.

"He slept a little." She gave the boy's creased forehead a soothing stroke with the backs of her fingers before crossing to him and holding out a sheaf of paperwork. "I'm Sarah Browning, by the way. I'm afraid we're short-staffed and I've got to get a move on." Her features creased apologetically.

Finn nodded and took the paperwork. "Not a problem. We've got plenty of folk who are looking forward to spending time with this little guy. Myself included." He looked over at Adao for any sign of emotional response.

Nothing.

Hardly surprising considering what he'd been through. It was a shame the charity's financial reach couldn't have extended to bringing at least one of the family members over. Then again…from what he'd read prior to the boy's arrival, both the mum and dad worked and his teenage sister was still in school, so…not easy to uproot an entire family.

He slapped the papers against his thigh. Too loudly, from the sharp look the charity worker sent him.

"Right." Finn gave Sarah his best stab at a smile. "Looks

like you need to get a move on and I need to assess Adao before we get him into surgery this afternoon."

He went to the doorway and called to the small team of doctors and nurses who would be in surgery with him. "Righto, mateys. Let's get a move on, shall we?" A twinge of déjà vu hit him as the team moved toward the door as one solid mass. Naomi had been right. Too many people standing around Adao might render the kid less responsive than he already was.

"Hey, mate." He looked Adao in the eye. "We've got a bunch of people who are going to come in, but they're all here to help you, yeah? We're all on your side."

The little boy pursed his lips and then nodded. He understood. He didn't like it. But it wasn't exactly as if he was in a position to argue.

Finn's heart went out to the little man, but he needed to keep his cool. Clean, clear precision was what was required when he stepped into surgery today. Anything less wasn't acceptable.

Finn went out into the corridor as the team crowded into the smallish room to hear the details of Adao's case and help set up a battle plan for the afternoon's surgery.

Battle plan.

The cruel irony of it…

He heard a laugh and his eyes snapped to the nurses' station. The hairs on his arms prickled to attention and a deep punch of heat rocket-launched itself exactly where it didn't belong.

Dammit.

Last night's gym session clearly hadn't drilled his body's organic response to her out of his system.

Who knew a woman's scent could linger in the physio gym hours after she'd left the hospital?

He did, that's who. He didn't know if she wore perfume

or body spray or what…he just knew that jasmine and va-nilla were forever lost to him as plain old smells now.

"Mr. Morgan? I was wondering if I could have a quick word."

"Yes?" Grabbing his work tablet from the counter, he looked back up at her then instantly regretted it. Those dark eyes of hers were blinking away his brusque greet-ing as her hands rose to tug on each of her loosely woven, below-the-shoulder plaits.

They made her look fun.

And sexy as hell.

"Hi. Um…hello." Naomi stepped behind the high coun-ter of the nurses' station, putting a physical buffer between them.

So she felt it too. Or was avoiding the "back off" dag-gers he was sending her way.

Fair enough. He'd hardly been Prince Charming last night. Or the day before that. Or…yup. Patterns. He saw it, but she messed with his focus and he didn't like his highly honed "this way trouble lies" vibes being messed with.

"What is it? I've got the team waiting for the pre-surgery assessment."

"I…um…" Something flickered in those dark brown eyes of hers. Had he ever noticed they were flecked with gold?

Yeah. Just like she'd probably noticed his eyes were flecked with amber when the sun hit them. Not. Can it, Romeo. Those days are over.

"You coming in to listen or is the idea to break up the as-sessment mid-flow with more of your touchy-feely stuff?"

Why are you being such an ass?

Naomi's dark irises flashed with disbelief at his narky question. Even the ward sister shot him a sharp look. Great. Just what he needed. More fodder for the nurses to continue the tar-and-feather job they no doubt had begun in the break room.

And it was deserved.

All of it.

If Naomi turned on her heel and marched straight up to HR to report him, he wouldn't blame her.

He was at war with himself and no one was coming out the victor. His body wanted one thing, his head wanted another. His heart was being yanked from side to side and therein lay the crux of the matter.

Good thing he didn't do feelings. Or poetry, for that matter. Ode to a smashed-up, battered heart didn't have much of a ring to it.

To his surprise, and the charge nurse's, Naomi shook her head and gave him a gentle smile. "No, no. Please. Go ahead. I'm here to listen."

He gave her a curt nod. "Fine." Then he turned and walked into Adao's room.

"Looks like someone's gunning for a lump of coal in his stocking this Christmas."

Naomi willed herself to smile back at Amanda, the charge nurse, who was always ready with a quip. She could tell from Amanda's expression it looked as forced as it felt. It appeared all she needed to do to rile Finn Morgan was exist!

"Don't let him get to you, Naomi." Amanda gave her shoulders a quick squeeze as she handed her a mini gingerbread man. "We all bank on you and your sunny smile to keep us cheery, so don't give him the satisfaction of taking it away."

Naomi blinked in surprise.

"Don't look so shocked. We're all in awe of your energy."

"My energy?"

"Of course. Who else around here runs up the stairs after running to work and running round with patients all day. Just watching you is exhausting! We all call you the Fizzy Physio." Amanda laughed then leaned in close after giving a swift conspiratorial look around the reception area. "He's all grizzly on the outside and perfectionist on the inside. We've all decided there's a bit of gold in there somewhere but someone has yet to unearth it."

"Unearth it how?"

"The usual way." She performed a teensy sexy dance. "Romance."

Naomi blew a raspberry. As if. The last thing she could ever imagine Finn engaging in was a hospital romance. She winced. She was hardly one to judge.

"Maybe you could be the one to tease it out of him."

"What? Me?" A solitary laugh escaped. "I don't think so." Her eyes did a quick flick in his direction and in the millisecond she allowed herself to look at him she did think…well…he's not *all* bad.

"Hmm. Well, it's not exactly as if anyone catches him out on the razzle anyway." Amanda picked up a tablet and started tapping away with some patient information.

"What do you mean?"

"He never—and I mean never ever—accepts invitations to go out. And that's weird."

"It's not that weird," Naomi said, instantly realizing she was defending her own penchant for staying in at night. She'd gone out for the odd night, but had always sneaked off early. She never seemed to be able to let herself go the way the other women did.

"'Course it is!" Amanda protested. "New hospital. New staff. New chance to meet friends, fall in love if you want— Oh. Uh-oh! Did I hit a nerve?"

"Ha! No."

Yes. Definitely yes.

Amanda inspected her for a minute then grinned as if she'd pocketed a state secret.

"What are you doing up here on the surgical floor anyway? Adao won't be ready for physio until after the surgery."

"I know. I— Well, I…"

Amanda's entire demeanor changed, her expression softening with compassion. "Ah. One of *those*."

Naomi bit down on the inside of her cheek. Hard. She needed that "Fizzy Physio" cover more than anyone here knew.

"Hey. Don't worry. Some of them get to you more than others." Amanda tipped her head toward Adao's room. "Just don't let Mr. All Work and No Play rile you. He's all right as long as you wear your crocodile skin when you're in the same room."

"Got it." Naomi smiled, relieved to have dodged more questions about Adao.

"Collins!" Finn barked from the doorway. "Are you going to join us or are you too busy with the gossip brigade?"

Amanda gave her hand a quick squeeze then nudged her toward the room with a whispered, "Don't worry, his bark is worse than his bite."

She followed Finn into the room, staying put at the doorway as he shouldered his way through the seven or eight physicians and nurses already around the little boy's bed.

Finn obviously didn't want her there but that was tough. She'd seen Adao arrive last night and wanted him to know she would be there for him when he came out of surgery. After all, she and Adao would be working intimately together in rehab.

Rehab wasn't just tough physically.

It put many of her young patients through an emotional mangle. Adao was bound to have a truckload of emotions come in wave after wave as they worked together.

He had numerous cuts and nicks on his face. None were so brutal they had blinded him or reduced his facial motor function, but there would be scars. Inside and out.

"Right, everyone!" Finn gave a theatrical throat-clearing noise as he took pole position at the head of Adao's bed. "Adao Weza, seven years old and fresh in from Kambela on the west coast of Africa."

He gave the boy a nod and...well, she guessed it was a smile. Hard to tell, coming from someone who clearly had gone to the Neanderthal School of Social Skills.

Ugg. Me surgeon. Me have no feelings. Ugg.

Naomi tucked herself behind one of the junior doctors so she could hide her smile as she pictured Finn wielding a wooden club while wearing a caveman's leopardskin ensemble.

She could still see Adao but was just out of that steel-gray eyeline of Finn's. Meeting his piercing gaze was too unnerving when all she really wanted to do was focus on the little boy.

Perhaps Finn was every bit as upset by Adao's case as she was and this whole Cro-Magnon act was just that...an act. He definitely wasn't the touchy-feely type.

She gave her head a quick shake, her plaits shifting from shoulder to shoulder as she did so, looking up only to catch Finn glaring at her before he rattled off the facts.

Adao had been in a field when his playmate had stepped on an anti-personnel mine. The mine had instantly exploded. She pressed her eyes closed tightly as he continued. She knew, more than most, how easily landmines could go off. The rebels in her own country had taken particular pleasure in littering them throughout the small vegetable patches most families had behind their homes. Two-for-ones, they called them. The blasts knocked out the women and the food supply in one cruel blast. Each morning she and her sister had gone out to the vegetable patch with a long stick, poking and prodding any upturned earth… hoping…praying that today they would be safe.

"Am I boring you, Miss Collins?"

"Sorry." Naomi snapped to attention, horrified to see all the eyes in the room were on her. "No. Not at all."

"Then can you please indulge me and the rest of the team with what you would see as the best solution for the tissue damage Adao has sustained?" Finn's eyes were bright with challenge.

If only he knew. She hadn't been blocking out his words, she'd been trying to block out her own memories.

She pressed her heels into the floor and looked him straight back in the eye. "Well, as you know, I am a physio, not a surgeon, but my understanding is that free tissue transfer can aid with repairing extensive soft tissue defects if the limb has endured serial debridement."

Finn nodded. He wanted her to continue.

Murmurs of curiosity rippled through the team as they cleared a little space around her.

"After a series of pre-operative diagnoses—'

"Which diagnosis? Be specific."

He wanted specifics? Fine. He could have specifics.

She rattled off the list of tests she knew Adao would have to go through prior to surgery—all of which were geared toward finding just how much of his arm they could save while providing his body with optimum chances of healing. She concluded with the overall goal, "The greater the blood flow, the better the healing."

Finn nodded. "So we're looking at measuring his blood flow. What else?" He scanned the room."

"Oxygen tension," said a nurse.

"Good. What else?"

"If the pressure is zero, no healing will occur," jumped in one of the surgical interns. "Ideally, we're looking for the pressure to read higher than forty mils."

"Excellent." Finn scanned the room. "What else?"

Naomi's eyes flicked to Adao's. The pain and fear she saw in them as the medical terminology flew across the room pounded the air out of her chest. A fierce, primal need to do everything she could for this little boy seized every cell in her body, giving her the extra jolt of courage to cut in again.

Finn had been through a trauma of some sort. Surely he had some compassion for this little boy.

Eyes locked with Finn's, she suddenly felt as though they were two prey animals, each wondering who would be the first to pounce. "What's most important for Adao is getting him to a place where he can begin gentle physio—'

"Yes. Fine." Finn cut her off. "We're not there, yet."

"But…" Wasn't giving Adao something to hope for every bit as helpful as doing a skin fluorescence study to measure his microcirculation? He was a little *boy*! A terrified little boy!

"But nothing. We've got the theatre booked in a few hours' time, Miss Collins. He's got to be as strong as possible going into surgery and time's awasting."

Finn gave the back of his tablet a few swift raps with his knuckles and carried on talking his team through the finer points of the surgery, fastidiously ignoring Naomi's shocked expression.

How could he have done that? Interrupting her was one thing, but making that noise?

He didn't even notice how Adao had started at the sound, but she had.

The sharp rat-a-tat-tat had the same effect on her nerves as it obviously did on Adao's.

To them it wasn't knuckles on plastic.

It was the sound of gunfire.

Finn felt Naomi's presence up in the viewing gallery before he confirmed it with a quick sidelong glance.

Her fingers were in prayer position up at that full mouth of hers. A line furrowed between her brows as he meticulously worked his way through the initial phase of the operation before he began shaping what remained of Adao's arm in preparation for a prosthetic device.

What was it with her and this kid? It wasn't as if the hospital hadn't had amputees before. It was, after all, his specialty.

He blanked the gallery viewing room and returned his focus to Adao's small form.

"Skin temperature's slightly different." He nodded to the nurse by the instrument tray. He really didn't want to have to take off more than he had to, but he knew better than most that providing a solid foundation for the prosthesis was crucial.

There'd been no way to save the elbow joint. A layperson could've figured that out. But he had been hoping for an elbow disarticulation rather than the more blunt approach of a proximal amputation. By employing a fastidious millimeter by millimeter approach, he prepared Adao's arm for separation at the joint, thereby providing a solid platform for his prosthetic device. He'd read about some electric elbow prostheses that could potentially set the boy up for a relatively normal life. He might not become a pianist, but...

With any luck, he'd be ready for some gentle physiotherapy in a handful of days.

An image of Naomi massaging Adao's shoulder with her

slender fingers blinded him for an instant. Blinded him because it wasn't Adao he was picturing receiving her sympathetic care. It was him.

It may have been a millisecond but it was a millisecond too long.

"Clear the gallery!"

His growl of frustration sent everyone from the gallery flying. If there was one thing that held true in Hope Children's Hospital it was that the surgeon got what the surgeon wanted when it came to offering a child the best care possible.

Pop music?

No problem.

A favorite scrubs cap?

Same again.

A gallery free of invested onlookers?

That was fine, too. As long as everything came out good in the end.

Muscles, connective tissue, skin all played a role in creating the foundation of what would be Adao's arm from now on.

Sometimes he thought he got the easy part and the physio was actually the one who took the brunt of the patient's pain. Thank God his own physiotherapist had been unfazed by blue language because he had painted that therapy gym the color of a sky heading toward the blackest of midnights for his first few sessions. If by "few" he meant six months. Anyone and everyone who'd crossed his path—and that included family—had been soundly pushed away. The only way he'd survived those dark days had been with grim determination.

Phantom limb pain.

A poor-fitting prosthesis.

Infection.

A second surgery.

He'd had them all.

And he hadn't wanted anyone who claimed to love him within earshot. If ever he'd felt like a wounded animal—made of little else other than rage and fear—it had been then.

It was what had driven him to retrain as a pediatric surgeon after he'd finally got out of rehab and had pushed his past as far away as he could. No one—especially children—should have to go through what he had. And under his watch they wouldn't.

Which was why he did the hard part—the part that required a methodical, emotionless approach—and positive, forward-thinking people like Naomi did the aftercare.

Two or three back-achingly painful hours later he stood back from the surgery table, knowing he had done his best.

"Good work, everyone." He pulled off his surgical cap and threw it in the laundry bin by the swinging theatre doors. "Make sure I'm paged when he wakes up, yeah? One of you stay with him at all times. I don't want the little guy on his own. Not tonight."

His eyes shifted up to the empty gallery.

Idiot.

He should've let her stay.

His gut told him she was the one Adao should be seeing as he blinked his eyes open when he woke from the anesthetic.

His head told him to just butt out and carry on as always. No attachments. No guilt. He was already dragging around enough of the latter, thank you very much, and the last thing he was going to do was add a leggy physio to the list of people he'd wronged.

That list was already full up.

CHAPTER FIVE

NAOMI BURIED HER face in the dog's curly coat and gave him a hug. Much to her delight, he sat back on his haunches and put his paws on her shoulders as if giving her a proper hug.

"He's gorgeous!" She looked up at his handler… Alana, was it?…and opted to ask the surgeon beside her instead. "What's his name, Marco?"

"Doodle," Marco Ricci answered, as if it was patently obvious that the golden-brown labradoodle should be called Doodle. The surgeon gave the pooch's head a quick scrub then wished Alana well.

The pair of them watched as Doodle and his trainer made their way along and out of the hospital corridor.

"Alice thinks he's brilliant. Would use him for all her patients if she could. Whether they needed them or not," Marco said, as they disappeared round the corner.

"Wow." High praise indeed, coming from Alice Baxter, one of the most driven, dedicated surgeons she'd met at Hope Hospital. Then again, having recently fallen in love with Marco, it was little wonder Alice was loving life and seeing the positive side of everything.

Unlike Finn Morgan…the Caveman of Doom.

Naomi shook the thought away—along with the image of Finn back in his caveman togs—and pulled out the small notebook she always carried with her. "That sounds amazing. I think I know someone who would really benefit from a therapy dog session."

Finn, for one.

Might help the man grow a heart.

Not that she was still smarting from being kicked out of the surgery. Or was acutely aware that she was the reason it happened. Flashes of connection didn't strike like lightning then just fade away. They burnt.

"Who's it for?" Marco asked. His tone was friendly. Curious.

Unlike Finn, who would've flung the question at her combatively.

Urgh! Stop thinking about Finn!

"Adao. You know, the boy in from Kambela for an arm amputation."

"Yes. Of course. Yesterday, wasn't it? I heard the operation went well."

Naomi gave her best neutral nod. "That's what I hear."

"Sounds like we all *heard* and none of us *saw.* Rumor has it the Beastie Man of Orthopedics kicked everyone out of the observation gallery." He laughed as an idea struck him. "You sure you aren't booking the therapy dog for him?"

"Positive." The more space between Mr. Finn Morgan and her, the better. She'd popped into Adao's room a couple of times after checking the coast was clear. The first time he'd been asleep. The second she had given his shoulders a gentle massage, eyes glued to the door in case she needed to make a swift exit. Official physio wasn't meant to start until tomorrow, but when she'd drawn up enough courage to go to Finn's office and check if that was still the plan, he'd already gone for the night.

The deflation she'd felt at not finding him there had

shocked her. It wasn't as if she'd been actually looking forward to seeing him.

Well.

No one liked conflict.

Besides, the man was clearly battling demons on his own. She dealt with hers by putting on an extra-cheery façade and pretending she didn't have a past and he… Well, he growled at people like a grumpy grizzly. So to each his own. Who was she to judge?

"If you're after booking some time with Doodle and Alana, the woman you're after is…" Marco rocked back on his heels and did the air guitar version of a drumroll. "Evie Cooper! The source of all wisdom at Hope Hospital."

Naomi smiled. Evie. Of course.

"I'll go hunt her down."

"Two guesses as to where you'll find her."

"NICU or PICU?" Naomi smiled. Evie was not only the resident elf, she was the hospital's resident baby whisperer. The whole staff had swelled with pride when word had gone out she was going to fulfil a lifelong dream of finishing her nursing degree.

"Or wherever Mr. Walker might happen to be." Marco smiled then glanced at his watch. "Speaking of which, there is a certain blond surgeon who's no doubt wondering where I am. Good luck with the therapy dog. Hopefully he'll be the secret weapon you were hoping for."

She gave him a wave and headed for the stairwell, jogging up the stairs to see if she could find Evie before she headed off.

Everyone's schedules had gone absolutely haywire with the arrival of the holiday season. No one was waiting for the first of December to get their holiday groove on. It was as if the opening gala at the hospital had unleashed an entire year's worth of magic fairy dust. Half the hospi-

tal seemed to be falling in love and decorating Christmas
trees or piling nurses' stations with gingerbread men while
cross-checking diaries that drinks dates, department din-
ners and Secret Santas were all accounted for.

And the other half?

Her own evening diary was as pristine as a snow-covered field. Not that she minded. Much.

The truth was, she had only ever dated men with whom
she'd known she had no future. They had tended to be serious, more interested in science than sex. Which was fine
with her.

Being with someone…being *happy* with someone…
physical with someone…it didn't seem fair. Not when everyone she'd loved had had their lives cut so short.

On the flipside, she saw just how unfair life was every
day at work and, for the most part, her young patients just
got on with it. They accepted that life threw grenades at all
sorts of people. There was no rhyme or reason to it. That was
just the way it was. So they chose to focus on the positive.

She did on the outside. But inside? It felt as though she
was frozen. And in order to survive she needed to stay
that way.

When she pushed through to the NICU reception area
there was scarcely a soul about.

She looked at her watch. It was after seven. It explained
why Finn hadn't been in his office. Not that she'd seen him
wandering round the hospital after hours, as she had a ten-
dency to do. What sort of life did he lead after hours if he
wasn't part of the "meet for a drink" set? Was he hacking
piles of wood to bits with a huge, hand-honed axe?

Or needlepointing tapestries of intricate flower patterns
to help him with the delicate art of surgery at which he so
clearly excelled?

Pah! Yeah, right.

"Can I help you?" The nurse manager, Janine, looked up from her computer screen where she was updating some charts.

"I was just looking for Evie. I wanted to see if I could get some contact details for Doodle." She laughed and corrected herself. "Alana, his handler, I mean."

"Evie's gone for the night, I'm afraid."

Naomi must have looked downcast at the news because Janine quickly added, "You know, a bunch of the nurses have headed down to the White Hart. If you're looking for something to do…"

Naomi pretended to consider the offer. Maybe it would be a good way to distract her from her thoughts. "It's just off the King's Parade, right?"

"That's the one! Go on," Janine urged. "They're a friendly group. They'd love to have you join them. I think the city's even turned on the Christmas lights so it'll be a lovely walk." She peered over the edge of the nurses' station at Naomi's "uniform" of trainers and athletic wear. "Or cycle? Or run?"

"Walk sounds nice." Naomi smiled. They had turned on the lights. She actually lived nearby and had heard all of the oohs and ahhs as the lights had been switched on, followed by a good hour of excited chatter and laughter.

It would do her good. Even if she just went to see the lights. Give her a reminder of life outside the hospital. She looked down at her trainers. Not really going-out gear, but… why not give it a go? Who knew, maybe she'd take a new route and discover something else about Cambridge to tell Adao about when they began their proper treatment the next day.

Twenty minutes later Naomi was lost. With the medieval twists and turns of the city center and all the twinkling lights, she'd allowed her thoughts to drift away and had lost track of where she was.

She could hear laughter and the sound of a ball game being played nearby. A group of children were obviously playing footie, with someone teasing and cajoling them from the spirited yelps and guffaws traveling round the corner. A sports center, maybe? A small green?

She made a promise to herself to ask the first person she laid eyes on. What she didn't expect was to discover the laughing, fun-loving man powering along the floodlit football pitch with a child hanging off each of his well-built arms was Finn Morgan.

She froze, unable to reconcile the dedicated curmudgeon she knew from the hospital with this bright-eyed, chuckling human climbing frame! He looked positively alight with joy.

Spurring herself into action, she turned to go just as he lifted his head and met her eyes. Their gazes crashed together and locked tight.

Naomi's heart pounded against her chest as she saw his eyes brighten, then just as quickly turn dull with recognition as the smile faded from his lips.

"Naomi! Hang on a minute."

She looked as surprised as Finn felt. And the look of dismay on her face when he had let his features fall into a frown had touched something deep within him.

He knew hurt.

He knew pain.

And he'd caused both in Naomi.

"Don't go." He scanned his ragtag team of footie mates looking up at him for guidance. He'd never brought a "stranger" to sports night. Hell. He'd not brought anyone anywhere for years.

"Do you think she wants some hot chocolate?" asked Ashley. She was the undisputed leader of the group. One crook of her arm and every single one of those kids followed in her wake.

He glanced back across at Naomi, who was still rooted to the spot.

Yeah. She'd "caught him" in his private place, but it *was* a public playing field. That, and he really had to do something to break the ever-increasing tension building between them. There were only so many alternative routes a man whose patients all required physio in a hospital with one exquisitely talented and beautiful-without-knowing-it physiotherapist could take.

"C'mon." He waved her over, two scrawny six-year-olds still hanging from each arm and—he looked down—yup, two kids on his good leg. At least they had the sense to leave his "robot" leg alone.

The uncertainty in her eyes got to him. He wasn't an ogre.

Well.

Not all the time.

"It's freezing out. Let's get you a cup of hot chocolate. What do you say, lads and ladettes? Hot chocolate all round before I beat you all in the second half?"

Cheers erupted round him and he couldn't resist joining in. These kids were awesome. Some of them had special needs. Some of them were just lonely. For all the beauty and brains Cambridge had on offer, there was also a poorer, lonelier side. Parents working overnight caretaker shifts. Single mums earning just enough to pay the rent and not quite enough to get food on the table. More latchkey kids than there should be. More pain than there should be.

If he could put a two-hour dent in their loneliness and give their cheeks a flush from a bit of a run-around and get some healthy grub into their bellies, then he was all for it. The hot chocolate was just a bonus. So week in, week out, this was his home away from home.

He probably needed them as much as they needed him. They kept him from falling back into that pit of self-loathing that he'd used to ill effect. It had turned out that driving everyone you loved away had a flipside. You were on your own when the demons attacked.

He looked across at Naomi and took an invisible punch to the chest when her features lit up with a genuine smile. A grin, actually. Had he noticed she had dimples before?

Damn. That smile of hers pierced right through to bits of him that hadn't so much as shown a flicker of interest in years. He was no monk, but even his home—a houseboat he'd picked up when he'd been retraining in London—was something he could unmoor and just…float away.

It's hot chocolate, you idiot. Not a proposal.

He gently shook the boys off him, doing his best to avoid Naomi's inquisitive looks. His hand was itching to reach out to the small of her back, see if touching her with four-teen layers of clothes on still elicited fireworks. Instead, he grabbed a little curly-haired moppet under his arm and gave him a quick fist bump. That sort of contact he could deal with. "All right, matey. Time to learn a little some-thing about showing some hospitality."

Finn steered everyone directly toward the sports center's kitchen, which had its own outside entrance. There was a game going on in the gym he didn't want to interrupt.

"All right, everyone. To your stations!"

The children all ran to their pre-assigned spots and Finn couldn't help but feel a surge of pride. Not because he wanted to show off in front of Naomi or anything—well, maybe a little—but it was nice to see these kids so keen to please. When he'd met them, most had lacked the social skills that would help them on a day-to-day basis.

"Excuse me, miss?"

Finn grinned. His star "pupil," Archie, was standing in front of Naomi with a little pad of paper in his hand as if he worked at a Michelin-starred restaurant. "Please, miss. May I take your hot chocolate order?"

Naomi squatted down so she was about the same height as Archie.

It was a nice move. Not many people treated these kids with respect. He shouldn't have been surprised Naomi would be one of them.

"What are my options?" she asked, her eyes twinkling with delight.

"Well…" Archie looked up at Finn with a flash of panic on his face. There weren't really options. It was hot chocolate or…well, hot chocolate. Squash never really got a look-in this time of year.

"Why don't you ask the lady—whose name is Miss Collins—if she'd like it hot or cold, and whether or not she might like marshmallows on top?"

"There are marshmallows?" Archie looked around at his playmates in disbelief. A ripple of excited whispers turned into a sea of high fives and whoops when Finn reached up above one of the cupboards where he'd stashed a tin of Christmas-tree-shaped marshmallows and revealed them to the children.

Wide-eyed, Naomi reached to the floor to steady herself.

What? A man wasn't allowed to indulge in a bit of home economics?

A soldier—an *ex*-soldier—had to feed himself. Especially when he'd told everyone who was dear to him to bugger off.

Turned out water biscuits and cheese did not maketh the man.

"But, Finn!" Archie shook his hands in exasperation. The kid had Asperger's and always had to get things exactly right before he could move forward on any project. Even putting home-made marshmallows into hot chocolate. "Marshmallows are made from horses' hooves, which also bear a similarity to reindeer hooves, which, if you consider the season—"

"Whoa there, mate." Finn gave his shoulder a reassuring squeeze then lifted one of the little tree-shaped confections and popped it into his mouth. "These little babies are as pure as the driven snow. No horse hooves. No reindeer feet. Get your pen ready. I used vegan gelatin." He ticked off the ingredients on his fingers slowly because he knew Archie would want to write them down. "Water. Sugar. Fairtrade." He threw a look in Naomi's direction, not entirely sure why he cared that she knew he bought Fairtrade, but…whatever. Proof he had a heart, he guessed. "Icing sugar. Salt and vanilla."

"My mother says sugar is evil," one of the children jumped in.

"Only evil if it's your only food group." And he should know. He'd survived off a stale box of party rings for a week once when his knee had been giving him jip. Weeks like that one had been the beginnings of finding the fight again. The will to live versus survival.

So he'd cracked open a recipe book and—*voilà*. Turned out he could cook.

"Extract or flavoring?" asked Archie.

"Extract. Only the good stuff for you lot."

He reached up again and pulled down another tin, revealing a couple of dozen flapjacks dotted with cranberries and dried apricots and whatever else he'd found in his cupboards before his shift this morning.

Archie cleared his throat and started again. "Miss Collins, would I be able to interest you in one of Cambridge sports club's finest instant hot chocolate sachets with a topping of home-crafted marshmallows?"

Naomi gave the ends of her red woolen scarf a tug and gave a low whistle. "Wow. That's quite an offer. I would be delighted. Now…" she reached out a hand to Archie "…what did you say your name was? Mine's Naomi."

Archie looked up at Finn—a clear plea for permission to shake the pretty lady's hand. Finn nodded.

"Can I make it?" Ashley shot her hand up into the air as far as it would go.

"I don't know, can you?"

"*May* I make it," corrected Ashley. *"Please?"*

"I want to pour the water!" Jimbo—their littlest warrior—leapt to the hot water urn.

"Whoa, there, soldiers. Who's the only man on campus who does the boiling water?"

"You!" all the children shouted, their arms moving as one toward him followed by a little cheer that always cracked him up.

These kids were nuts.

He gave a couple of their sweaty little heads a scrub and as he turned to get to work caught Naomi looking at him with an expression of pure warmth. It disappeared so quickly when she saw he was looking at her it was akin to seeing a falling star.

Little short of a miracle.

Naomi felt as if she'd walked into an alternate universe.

Finn Morgan made marshmallows and flapjacks?

She tried to picture him wearing a frilly pinafore and

oven mitts and came up with… Oh, my, that was all she pictured him in.

Unexpected.

Was that what a glimpse of the "heart of gold" could do to a girl? Turn a man naked in her imagination?

Crikey.

She gave her head a shake and watched as all the children fell into place for what was obviously a finely tuned routine.

The littlest kids pulled out mugs from the lower shelves of the sports center's kitchen. Bigger ones emptied packets of hot chocolate into the mugs—about a dozen all told. One—who seemed to be the mini-matriarch of the pack—slotted herself in and around them to wipe up any stray chocolate powder.

One scuttled up to Finn, who was holding court at the hot-water urn—wise, considering the sign on the metal urn warned that the water was at a boiling temperature at all times—and beckoned to him that he wanted to whisper something in his ear.

Finn knelt down, his eyes shifting up to the ceiling as the little boy cupped his hands round Finn's ear and whispered. Finn's gray eyes traveled to the two mugs in the little boy's hands and said something in a low rumbling voice then tipped his head in Naomi's direction. "Go on."

The little boy shook his head and pressed the mugs into Finn's huge hands. Had she actually noticed how big his hands were?

He rose to his full height and turned to her.

Gulp.

About as big as the rest of him.

"Miss Collins, would you like the flowery mug or the ladybird mug with a chip in it? Jamie is sorry in advance about the chip, but he can recommend use of the ladybird mug from personal experience." He held them out to her, his features looking as serious as if he were offering her a choice between food for the rest of the month or famine. From the look on Jamie's face, it was on a par.

"Well…" She rose so that she could examine the mugs with proper consideration then gave Jamie a serious nod. "I think I'd like the ladybird mug, if that's all right? Seeing as it comes so highly rated."

The little boy's face nearly split in two with an ear-to-ear grin as he tugged at Finn's shirt. "I told you."

"Well, then, Jamie. Maybe next time you can be brave enough to ask her yourself."

Finn's eyes never left hers as he spoke.

Next time?

She was astonished there was a first time, let alone… Was this an olive branch? His way of saying he was sorry for raking her over the coals at the hospital?

Her heart skipped a beat.

"Finn, look." A little boy came over to him, a marshmallow stuck on each of his index fingers. "I am the ghost of Christmas past!"

And just like that the moment was gone and a new, sillier one had begun. Naomi didn't know whether to be grateful or wistful.

After a few minutes of fussing about with stirring hot chocolates into mugs, doling out the remaining marshmallows and filling kitchen towel squares with a flapjack each, the motley crew were told to head toward the benches in the gym to watch the game.

"Game?"

Finn was shuttling a couple of the children past her as she asked. He dropped an unexpected wink her way.

"You'll see."

* * *

When the door to the gym was pushed open, Naomi's eyes widened with delight.

A full-on game of wheelchair basketball was under way complete with heated banter and the non-stop squeak and squeal of wheels on the gym floor. It was mesmerizing.

About a dozen men and women—all in low-slung, wide-angle-wheelchairs—were careening round the gym with all the focused intent of a professional sports team. The atmosphere was absolutely electric.

"All right, chaps and chapesses." Finn issued a few instructions to his team, holding a couple of the steaming mugs of chocolate aloft as they clambered onto the benches to watch the game. From the gleams of excitement in their eyes this was clearly one of the highlights of their night out.

"Want to grab a pew or are you happy here?"

Finn stood beside Naomi, eyes glued to the game, but his presence… It was weird to say, but…it felt like their bodies were *flirting*. Which was completely mental.

Particularly considering she didn't flirt.

She did happy.

She did bubbly.

Flutter her eyelashes and blush like a maiden on the brink of a kiss?

Nope. That wasn't her. Not by a long shot. Because if she were to allow herself to feel good things, she'd inevitably also feel all the bad things, too. And she never wanted to go back there. Because the bad things came cloaked in a bone-deep fear that was too terrifying to even consider confronting. Once had been more than enough.

"Naomi?"

"Happy here, thanks." She took a sip of her chocolate and gave Finn a bright grin. "These marshmallows are amazing. You should sell them at the hospital café."

Finn barked a laugh. "Yeah. I'm sure Theo would love me upping the obesity rate right there on the hospital mezzanine."

Stung, she looked away. "I was hardly suggesting—" She stopped when she felt Finn's hand on her arm, the heat of it searing straight through the triple layers of her outdoor wear.

"Sorry. I didn't mean it like that."

"You never do, do you?"

Finn stepped back and shoved his free hand through that tangle of dark, wavy hair that was all but begging for someone who looked a lot like her to do the same. He never broke eye contact and it took just about all the willpower she possessed not to look away.

"No," he finally said. "I don't."

She had absolutely no reason to believe him. But she did. Something about the flashes of light hitting those steel-gray eyes of his...they spoke volumes. He knew pain. He'd seen it in her eyes just as she'd seen it in his.

At least she now knew they shared some common ground.

His home-made marshmallows were also ridiculously lovely.

Silver linings and all that.

They watched the rest of the game in silence. It was a revelation, watching the hard-core stamina of the wheel-chair users in action.

A few minutes later when the whistle was blown he strode across to a man with a pitch-black buzz cut and piercing blue eyes. When both of them looked her way she checked behind her to see what they were looking at. When she looked back, Finn was beckoning her to come over.

"Naomi, I'd like you to meet one of my oldest—'

"Hold up!" The man interrupted. "Longest term—

not oldest. Let's keep this accurate." He laughed good-naturedly. "You may continue."

Finn gave his friend a punch in the arm then, still smiling, began the introduction again. "Naomi the Physio meet Charlie the Basketball champ." The change in his tone and demeanor was as warming to her belly as the hot chocolate had been. The two men obviously shared a deep friendship. It was nice to see Finn had so much more to him than gruff bluster and, of course, his incredible reputation as a surgeon.

"Champ?" she asked, truly impressed.

Charlie waved off the title. "Just a couple of regional matches where we beat the pants off the other county teams. Funding's always a problem, but we're hoping to get to the Commonwealth Games next time they come round in the UK. I might be a bit long in the tooth by then, but some of these whippersnappers might still be up to it." He raised his voice and aimed it in their direction. "So long as they all keep listening to my outstanding coaching!"

They sent back their own set of razzes then took the children up on their offer to pour water for them all from the big cooler at the end of the court.

Naomi stood with Charlie as Finn jogged across to oversee the "catering."

"You two together?"

Naomi sucked in her breath and gave an incredulous laugh. "No. I was just walking past and saw them playing. We work together. That's all."

"Huh." Charlie pinned his bright blue eyes on her, as if to say, *I'm more than happy to wait it out until you come clean.*

It didn't take long.

"Honestly. We don't really know each other. The hospital's still relatively new. I do my thing. He does his."

"Yeah, well. I think there might be a little bit o' the lady protesting too much." He chuckled and gave the beads of sweat on his brow a swipe. "I've known Finn a long time and he's never brought anyone in here to see him do his thing before."

"Oh." Seriously? Then again…the man played his cards so close to his chest she sometimes wondered if he'd even seen them. But the only one to ever see him do this amazing work? "Well… I did just happen to be walking past, so…"

"So nothing. I haven't seen him look at anyone like that since the divorce went through."

"Finn was married?"

You could've knocked her over with a feather.

Maybe that explained why his male-female relations were so…rusty. Not that she wanted him to flirt with her or anything. Her eyes traveled across the gym to where a gaggle of children were clamoring to get his attention.

Her heart did a little skippity-hop as their eyes met and he dropped her a quick wink before returning his focus to the children.

Maybe she did.

"Oops. My bad. Open mouth, insert foot!" Charlie grinned unapologetically. "Look. Finn and I go way back. Did our basic training together when we were fresh out of school. Never met anyone who wanted to be an army man more. He started young with everything, precocious upstart that he was." Charlie grinned, his voice warm with genuine affection. "Finn comes from a long line of army men so the second he could enlist he did. Would have lied about it if that sort of thing were possible these days. He married young, too. Then got himself blown up after just a couple of tours in the Middle East, but…" he paused for effect "…not before he saved my life."

What?

An action hero on top of everything else?

Still waters did run deep. At least in the case of Finn Morgan.

"That one?" Naomi pointed across the gym to where Finn was teaching the children how to turn their hands into "pilot goggles" then scanned Charlie's face for signs of a wind-up. "That Finn Morgan saved your life?"

"Too right he did." He gave her a quick glance as if trying to get a gauge on her "combat story readiness."

He wheeled his chair closer to her, looked her straight in the eye and said, "If Finn Morgan hadn't thrown himself on top of me that day, I wouldn't be here."

His tone was enough for Naomi to decipher what he was really saying. Finn Morgan had sacrificed his leg to save his friend's life.

She was about to ask how he'd ended up in the chair but Charlie beat her to the punch. "This happened later. On my next tour. I shipped out while Finn was in rehab. He took it hard. Pushed everyone he loved as far away from him as he could."

Naomi could hardly get her head around the fact that Mr. Grumpy liked to play footie with kids with special needs who he handcrafted seasonal treats for, let alone take in the huge news that not only was he a hero, he was also a broken-hearted divorcee.

"Including his wife?"

It felt such an intimate question to ask.

"Including his wife. She moved on but Finn hasn't. May never forgive himself. He was a seething ball of fury by the time I came back for my own stint in rehab." He shrugged it all off. "He just poured all of his energies into retraining as a pediatric ortho king and...' he blew an imaginary trumpet fanfare from his hand '...*voilà*! Look who is one of the country's top limb specialists. An amazing guy."

This was more than peeling away the layers, like an

onion, and finding out there was a diamond in the rough. It was like opening up an enormously intimidating book, only to find the binding and outer layers disguised an enormous and generous heart.

CHAPTER SIX

"FINN! ARE YOU coming along to the Christmas quiz night
at the Fox and Hounds?"

Finn scrunched the paper he was drying his hands with
into a ball and threw it into the nearby bin. "Nope."

"Now, there's a surprise." Amanda rolled her eyes and
laughed good-naturedly. "Don't think a handful of 'nopes'
is going to stop me from trying, though."

Finn bit back his usual retort—*good luck with that*—
and did his best to give her a better-luck-next-time smile
before heading toward the stairs. It wasn't her fault that
ducking out of social gatherings was his forte. Especially
at this time of year. Everything seemed infused with extra
meaning. Intent. He figured Amanda would catch on soon
enough. Finn Morgan wasn't a social creature.

So what the hell was he doing, heading down to the
physio gym with a bit of extra fire in his step?

No prizes for guessing the answer there. A sweet, soft
smile.

He was hoping for a dose of both.

He may not win Hope Children's Hospital's Most Sociable Doc Award, but it seemed as though he'd done a one-
eighty on how he felt about "Naomi run-ins."

The encounter at "his" sports center had changed everything. Letting someone see his private self, the side he al-

lowed to have fun—to *care*—hadn't been the horror show he'd thought it would be.

His world hadn't shattered into bits. He hadn't flared up in anger as he had at his family and wife. His heart still beat. Beat faster, if he was being truly honest.

And, of course, it wasn't just any old someone.

It was Naomi.

Instead of rubbing him up the wrong way, he was experiencing an entirely new breed of agitation.

He actually caught himself *smiling* when their appointments overlapped. Feeling concern when he saw her shoulders tense up in advance of going into Adao's room. Actual, honest-to-God pleasure shot through his veins when she clapped and hugged a patient who'd achieved a new benchmark.

Curiosity teased at his nerve endings. What would it feel like to be on the receiving end of one of those hugs? One of those smiles?

Which was why the deserted physiotherapy gym was getting a bit more after-hours attention from him than usual.

One man. One gym. A perfect night. The best way to pummel all the feelings straight out of his system.

At least that's how it had worked in the "before Naomi" days.

Now that he'd let himself see beyond the beautiful, chirpy façade of hers, and he'd realized she seemed to have every bit as much going on beneath the surface as he did, the gym felt empty if she wasn't there. He'd almost grown to anticipate the quiet way she had of looking at him when he'd been a bit too gruff. The slip of her gaze from his eyes to his hips then his knee on days his leg was giving him jip. The way her cheeks had pinked up when he'd winked at her that night at the gym.

Winked!

What the hell? The last thing his ex would've accused him of was being soppy and yet…each time he walked through the deserted corridors and pushed through the doors to the physio gym, he caught himself hunting for signs of her. A stray clipboard, a little cloud of her perfume, a Hope Hospital hoodie hanging in the small office she used in the corner of the gym.

True, he could've gone to any gym, anywhere in Cambridge, but something about coming to the playground atmosphere of the hospital's physio ward appealed to him. A reminder that if children could push themselves to work harder, achieve their goals, then he could, too.

There were the standard weights and cardio machines any adult physiotherapy center would have. Running machines. Static bicycles. A small set of steps. Massage tables.

But the walls were painted with colorful murals. There was a climbing wall. It was too small for him but it never failed to capture his interest. All of the "rocks" were shaped like dinosaurs. Each time he came down here he traced a new path to the top. And there was also— Ah! A zip wire. And tonight it was in use.

"That's right, Ellie." Naomi was helping a blonde ponytailed girl establish her grip on the bar. "Now, off you go and hold, hold, hold, hold… Hooray!"

Naomi applauded as the young girl—maybe around ten—landed on the huge gym mats at the far end of the zip-wire run.

"Looks like fun."

Naomi snapped to attention, obviously unaware he'd been watching them.

"Yes." She looked at her young charge for confirmation, as if she wasn't entirely sure whether to be happy or wary to see Finn. Wow. That stung. Guess he only had himself to blame.

"What do you think, Ellie? Have you been having fun?"

"Definitely." The girl's eyes shone with pride. "Especially now the distal radius epiphys…epiphysss…"

"Epiphysititis," Naomi and Finn said as one.

Ellie laughed and called out, "Snap!"

Finn just stared. Naomi's eyes were about as deep brown as a woman's eyes could get. A man could get lost in them if he had nothing but time.

She drew in a quick breath and turned back to her young charge.

"I think there should be a rule that until you can say the word, it's not completely gone." Naomi nudged the girl with her hip and Ellie giggled.

"Okay. It's not *gone* gone…but now that the cast is off and I can use my wrist again, I can get back to gymnastics practice, right?"

"Well…that's what we're here to establish, young lady."

The way Naomi's dark eyes twinkled and the corners of her mouth were twitching, it was easy to see she was teasing the girl. He liked that. Having patients think they're playing rather than working was half the battle on the rehabilitation side of things. Naomi was obviously excellent at her job—and enjoyed doing it.

"C'mon, please?" Ellie put her hands into prayer position. "That's the first time I've done the zip wire without letting go."

"A zip wire's one thing. Vaulting is another."

Ellie scanned the room, her eyes alighting on Finn. "I bet I could vault him."

Naomi's eyes widened and a hit of the giggles struck her hard and fast.

"What?" Finn gave a mock frown. "I put Ellie's cast on, if memory serves." With a huge grin, Naomi nodded. "I also took the cast off, which would indicate it was healed.

So…tell me, Miss Collins, what exactly is the problem with Ellie here using me as a human vault?"

"Er…health and safety for one?" She crossed her arms playfully and gave him her best what-are-you-going-to-say-to-that-one-pal? look. "Her muscle strength would have deteriorated."

"Not that much!" Ellie pointed at the zip wire as if it was proof she was ready for the next phase. "Look! I can do handstands on the mat, no problem."

They watched and, yes, she could indeed do handstands perfectly well.

"Well." Finn turned to Naomi when Ellie put her hands into prayer position again and gave them both a doleful round of puppy-dog eyes. "I doubt she was planning on vaulting all six foot two inches of me, were you, Ellie?" He pressed himself up to his full height and actually—oh, good grief—he'd actually swelled his chest a bit. Like a cartoon character.

Why are you showboating like this?

Mercifully, Ellie was oblivious to his lame attempt at flirting with Naomi. She was already dragging a mat over alongside the ball pit. "Look, Naomi, I won't do the splits version. I'll just do a simple handspring. If Finn kneels on here…" Ellie eyeballed him for a minute and he tried not to laugh. He'd never really been considered as gymnastics equipment before. Ellie pointed at Finn to relocate himself. Stat. "Mr. Morgan, you have to kneel here and then I'll do a quick run-up on the mats here and when I do the handstand over you, I'll land in the ball pit so it'll be totally safe."

Naomi tilted her head to the side and stared at him. If he thought he was being considered for anything more than a stand-in vaulting horse he would've read something into it. But this was work and it was easy enough to see Naomi's focus was one hundred percent on her patient's safety. As his should be. Which did beg the question…

"You ready, Finn?"

"If we have Naomi's stamp of approval."

Finn and Ellie turned to Naomi as one and the smile that lit up her face at both of their expectant expressions was like the sun emerging from a cloud on a summer's day. Pure light.

Damn, she was beautiful.

"Fine!" She threw up her hands. "Under two conditions. One…" She gave Naomi a stern look. "I will stand by to spot you. And two…" She looked at Finn and then quickly shifted her gaze to his knee. "If you think you're up to it."

He did a squat, as if that was the ultimate proof he could kneel on all fours.

Hmm… That was what her expression said. She drummed her fingers on her lips for a moment then put up a finger. "Hang on a minute." She jogged to the far end of the room and rummaged through a drawer for a minute. She brandished an elasticated wrist brace as if it were a long-sought-after treasure. "Put this on first."

"Thank you, Naomi!" Ellie threw her arms around Naomi then pulled on the brace and eyed Finn with the cool acuity of a girl who knew her way around a competitive gymnastics tournament. "Are you ready, Mr. Morgan?"

"As I'll ever be." He went down on all fours and steadied himself, wondering how the hell he'd gone from wanting a quiet workout on his own to being part of a ten-year-old's gymnastic ambitions.

He looked straight ahead of him to where Naomi had relocated herself to spot Ellie if she needed it.

Her dark eyes shimmered with delight for Ellie as she executed the move to perfection and, much to his satisfaction, when he rose to his full height in front of Naomi, there was an extra flash of pleasure just for him.

After Ellie's mum had come and collected her and she'd been signed off to go on her gymnastics tournament— "using the brace!"—Naomi returned to the gym, surprised to find Finn was still there.

"Did you need anything?" She'd not been alone with him since he'd bitten her head off before Adao's arrival, but seeing him at the sports center the other day seemed to have softened the tension that often crackled between them. Further evidence that gold heart the charge nurse had alluded to wasn't a myth.

"Nope." Finn looked around him as if sizing up the place. "I sometimes sneak down here after hours for a bit of a workout, but having stood in as a human gymnasium was good enough for tonight."

Naomi laughed. "I suspect it wasn't really on a par with your normal workouts."

She saw him start to say something, his eyes alight with fun, and then bite it back, his expression turning back to the thunder face she was more used to.

She turned away so he wouldn't see the disappointment in her eyes. And the shock. Who would've thought a chance sighting at a sports center and a brief encounter in the gym would've brought out a side to him that made him…well… really attractive. If she hadn't been mistaken, he'd been on the brink of flirting with her. But the part that had shocked her? It was that she had wanted him to.

Flirt! With *her*. The one woman in the whole of Hope Children's Hospital who seemed to rub him up the wrong way just by appearing.

She dug rhe fingernails of one hand into the palm of

the other. The woman who liked to keep her own heart as locked away as he seemed to.

Whether she liked it or not, they just might be birds of a feather.

At least it explained the tension.

"Here. Let me help you with that." Finn reached out for the same mat Naomi was lifting and their hands brushed. He pulled his hand back as if she'd branded him with her fingers. She rolled her eyes.

Here we go. Back on familiar territory.

The Mark of The Evil Physiotherapist.

She pulled the mat over to the stack alongside the wall, laid it in place and tried to shake off the grumpy thoughts.

Maybe it was simpler than like attracting like.

Maybe it was a case of a man dealing with his own frailties. Someone as physically capable-looking as Finn—an actual war hero—would not like to be seen as weak, and she'd caught him in an incredibly private moment the other day. Or maybe he'd had an evil physiotherapist back in the day. Not that she was going to ask but physiotherapy wasn't always as fun as it had just been with Ellie. And recovering from an amputation surgery was tough. Just seeing the abject misery on Adao's face brought tears to her eyes.

Finn was a big, strong, physical man. Before his injury she could just imagine how fit he must've been. A young man at the height of his strength and fitness, only to have it taken away by the horror of war. What the man deserved was compassion—not huffs of frustration. It didn't stop her from smarting that he'd rolled back on the flirty behavior he'd shown when Ellie had been in the room. Maybe having her there made it safe. A buffer to ensure nothing would ever really happen.

She knew that feeling. Keeping people at arm's length

was her specialty. Except her patients. Her patients *always* went straight to the center of her heart.

"I'm good here if you wanted to get on," she eventually said when all the mats were back in place.

"I was thinking of heading down to the sports center. I owe Charlie a pint after the game the other day."

"Ah." Was she supposed to be inviting herself along or telling him to get a move on?

"You live in town, don't you?"

Was he feeling as awkward as she felt? Because this whole chitchat thing was… Neither of them was really excelling at it.

"Yes."

Why don't you invite yourself along, you idiot? He's clearly trying to ask you if you want to come.

"Would you like to walk into town? Together?" He shifted his weight and kicked up the pace. "And then, of course, I'll go and meet Charlie."

She smiled. It was strangely refreshing to be with someone as awkward at the "making friends" thing as she was.

"Sounds good. I'll just grab my jacket." She jogged across to the small glass office, willing it to magically get curtains or one-way glass so she could bang her head against the wall. *What was she thinking?*

Her heart was pounding against her chest as white noise filled her head.

C'mon, c'mon, c'mon! Behave like a normal human.

It was a walk.

Just a plain old walk. As she stared at her thickly padded winter coat she smiled. Plus point. It was cold enough that they didn't even have to talk if they didn't want to.

Oh, good grief. If they lived at the North Pole maybe. Not Cambridge.

What on earth was she going to talk to Finn Morgan

about for twenty whole minutes? How he made her insides turn into an entirely new weather system? How she didn't normally blush when men winked at her? Or how, even if the blush led to something more, he could never follow through because she'd left her heart behind in Africa?

"Everything all right in there?"

"Yeah. Great!" Wow. She didn't know her voice went that high. "'Course. Why?"

"Well…" Finn looked at her through slightly narrowed eyes. "You're just…standing there. Have you lost something?"

My sanity.

"Nope! All good." She pulled on her hoodie and then her puffer jacket over it, yanking the zipper up so fast she nearly caught her chin in it when she hit the top. "Ready to go?"

Finn was really beginning to question his own grip on reality. What was he *doing*?

First, acting like a first-class show-off idiot in the gym.

Second, asking to walk a girl home like he was a nineteen-fifties teenage boy.

And, third, making up a story about meeting Charlie for a drink when he knew damn well his friend was at home, helping his children decorate the Christmas tree.

What a doofus.

Way to show the pretty girl you like her. Walking mutely along the festively lit streets of Cambridge as if you couldn't wait to shake her off.

Which he couldn't.

He pretended he had to scratch his chin on his shoulder so he could see if she looked as uncomfortable as he felt.

Yup! Pretty much. Romeo of Cambridge strikes again!

Not that he was courting her or anything like that. They were just colleagues, walking down the cobbled streets of a particularly attractive-looking university city on a frosty, clear-skied, festively lit night. Just the type of night that would be perfect for holding one of her mittened hands.

If he liked her that way.

Which he didn't. Not least of all because his dating track record after his ex totaled a handful of one-night stands that never should've happened. Turned out the chicks didn't dig a surly one-legged bastard intent on becoming the best pediatric limb specialist in the UK.

He gave his face a scrub and groaned.

"Oh, my goodness!"

Though she whispered it, Finn heard Naomi's exclamation.

He dropped his hand, hoping she hadn't seen his what-the-hell-am-I-doing-here face. The last thing he needed to introduce into his life was romance. Saying that, he'd be little short of an idiot to ignore the chemistry between the pair of them.

Then again, he was pretty skilled at being an idiot.

What a nightmare.

"Is that...? Is that *Santa*?"

Finn looked to his left and saw Santa appear around a corner. He turned back to Naomi, only to see she was looking the opposite direction...at another Santa.

They and the Santas were just entering Market Square in the city center. The temporary vendors had taken the "deck the halls" edict to the fullest definition. There were long swags of evergreen caught up in bright red velvet ribbons twirled around the lampposts, giving them a North Pole effect. The shopfronts all glittered and twinkled with their own festive displays. The daytime vendors had handed over to the temporary Christmas market stalls that were positively bursting with seasonal delights—edible and otherwise. Someone was roasting actual chestnuts over a crackling fire and from just about every street that led onto the small square was a Santa. And another and another until it finally dawned on them.

"We're in a Santa flash mob!"

They blinked at one another.

Again they'd spoken in tandem. And something about the synchronicity of the moment felt like fairy dust and kismet. Just like the atmosphere in the square. Someone had put on some music and was piping it through speakers Finn couldn't quite locate. Maybe in the vicinity of the huge Christmas tree lit up in a swirl of tiny golden lights.

"C'mon. If we go over here, up onto the church steps, you should be able to see."

"See what?" Naomi jogged a few steps to catch up with him.

"The dancing. I've seen this type of thing on the internet. The Santas all get together, do a dance or sing a carol."

Naomi stopped and blinked her disbelief. "You watch flash mobs on the internet?"

"Moi?" He feigned horror at the thought then shrugged a confessional, "Yeah, maybe…"

Naomi was more than familiar with his roughty-toughty grumble-guts routine. Not that he put it on or anything, she just…there was something about her that spoke to him and somewhere along the way he'd lost his ability to speak back. Growling was a go-to reaction. Overreaction, from the look of things. When she smiled…something he'd seen far too little of…it felt as though his whole world was lighting up from the inside out.

"C'mon." He held his arm out to block the crowds so Naomi could get through and find a good spot to watch as the Santas did, in fact, fall into formation and perform a street dance to a new Christmas song that had whisked its way to the top of the pop charts.

Finn was enjoying watching Naomi every bit as much as he was enjoying the Santas. Her smile was bright and genuine. She clapped along with the crowd when all the Santas encouraged them to do so. She even threw in a few "Woos!" when the dancing elves who'd joined the Santas pulled off a particularly athletic dance sequence. At one point, she dropped her hands after a brisk rub together and one of them shifted against Finn's. Her eyes sped to his as if she'd felt the exact same thing he had when they'd touched. Fireworks.

Naomi was grateful to have found mittens in her pocket for a number of reasons.

One. It was freezing.

Two. They gave her something to fiddle with when Finn looked at her so intently she thought those gray eyes of his were going to bore a hole straight through her and see the myriad sensations that went off in her head when their hands had brushed.

And, three...

There wasn't really a three, other than they were a similar shade of gray to Finn's eyes, which she could not stop staring into, so she needed to make her excuses and go.

"I'm really sorry, I need to—"

"I suppose Charlie's probably waiting for me at the—"

They stared at one another for a moment, their breath coming out in little white puffs, the music and excitement of the flash mob buzzing around them like a blur of fireflies.

"Neither of us are particularly good at finishing sentences tonight," Finn finally said. He tipped his head toward the opposite end of the square but didn't explain why.

"No." Naomi's lips remained frozen in the "O" they'd formed as she looked up at him.

It would be so easy to close that small gap between them. If she just rose up on to the tips of her nearly frozen toes…

"I guess you'd better get to your meeting," she said.

"What?"

Yeah. What? You were having a moment.

"With Charlie? Aren't you meeting Charlie for a drink?" she reminded him.

What are you *doing*? The man was obviously trying to get to know her. He probably just needed a friend. It would be mean to shut him down. Especially since she could do with someone to talk to as well. Someone who understood the types of feelings patients like Adao elicited.

Guilt.

Fear.

Bone-deep sorrow.

Finn shoved his hands in his pockets and cleared his throat. "Yes. Absolutely right. Charlie's probably on his second pint by now." He flicked his hand toward the dispersing Santas. "Easily distracted tonight."

His gray eyes returned to hers, his look so intense she blinked and had to look away.

"Right, well. Thanks for the escort. I mean…company walking back."

"You're all right to get to your flat on your own?"

She looked at Finn as if he'd grown wings and popped on a halo. What was he doing? Going for boy scout of the year to make up for being such a grouch the other day? Or was he actually a genuinely nice guy outside the hospital walls? Maybe he was a bit like her. Wore a mask to work and took it off once he was alone. Only they seemed to have chosen opposite masks to cope. He'd looked so content, so happy with the children at the sports center and even now there were glimmers of that guy standing right in front of her, waiting for her to say something. Do something.

She simply didn't know how to access the "old" Naomi. The one who had never once imagined a world without her parents or boyfriend in it.

"I'm fine." She gave him a tight smile and a little wave and left before they drew out what was quickly becoming a shambles of a farewell.

It wasn't until she'd run up the stairs to her flat, opened the door, thrown her keys into the bowl on the table by the door, just as she'd done every night ever since the hospital had opened, and flicked on the light that she realized she wasn't fine at all.

She had been thrown off balance.

By the unexpected fun of the flash mob.

The impending session she was going to hold with Adao, who still had to crack a smile.

But most of all by Finn.

It had been a long time since someone had unnerved her in this way. And she wasn't entirely sure which way she was hoping it would go.

CHAPTER SEVEN

"DON'T WORRY, ADAO. It's still early days." Naomi rubbed her hand across the little boy's shorn head and tried to coax a smile out of his somber little face.

She'd been giving him a massage and manipulating his shoulder joints to try and prevent any blood clots. This type of physiotherapy was critical at this phase of his recovery. And painful, too.

Adao dropped his head and it all but broke Naomi's heart to see two fat tears fall onto his blanket.

"I want Mama and Baaba." Adao's voice caught on the final word and he barely managed to stem a sob.

Naomi ached to pull him into her arms. Tell him everything would be all right. His loneliness and grief tore at her chest with a ferocity she hadn't felt in years.

She wanted her mother and father, too. Not a single day had passed since they'd been stolen away that she hadn't ached for their presence in her life. And that of her boyfriend. All lost to a foolish war that had, ultimately, come to nothing. Her country was run by the military now. It was a place she'd never be able to call home again.

"I know, love. I know." She gave his head a soft caress and before she could think better of it dropped a kiss on top of his head and pulled him to her for a half-hug, doing her best not to put any pressure on his loosely bandaged wound.

"Hey!"

They both looked up as Finn appeared at the doorway. His hair looked like he'd just come in from a windstorm and his eyes were bright with energy. He gave the door-frame a couple of polite knocks after he'd quickly taken in the scene. "Mind if I come in?"

Adao didn't even bother to disguise the tears now pouring down his gorgeous plump cheeks.

Finn's eyebrows instantly drew together and he crossed the room in three quick long-legged strides. "Are you in pain, little man?"

Adao shook his head. Then nodded. Then shrugged as the tears continued to fall. It was all Naomi could do not to burst into tears herself.

Physio was often difficult. Often produced tears. Tears of frustration. Tears of pride on a good day, but this was different.

He was a lonely, lost, terrified little boy who wanted his parents.

"Naomi's not been putting you through her torture chamber, has she, mate?"

A few days ago Naomi would've taken umbrage at the question, but now, having seen a new side of Finn, she took it for what it was. A playful attempt to draw a smile from a frightened child. To be honest, she was grateful for the intervention as she was struggling to find anything to say that would make him feel better.

Finn pulled a chair up alongside Adao's bed across from Naomi. He held out his hand for Adao's. When Adao didn't move his, Finn took it in both of his own, ducking his head so he could catch the little boy's eyes.

"Listen, bud. I know this is tough. You know I know, right?"

Adao nodded.

"I showed you mine…and pretty soon you'll be able to show me yours."

"But…all I have is…is…" Adao whispered, tears falling everywhere as he turned to look at his heavily bandaged shoulder. He was still a good week—maybe even a fortnight—away from trying out a prosthesis.

"I know." Finn shot a quick look at Naomi, who pulled a fresh packet of tissues out of her pocket and put them in Adao's lap, keeping one for herself. Just in case.

Definitely, more like. She was already scanning her brain for a private corner just as soon as was humanly possible.

"Bud, look at me. You're talking to someone who's been there and has come out on the other side. The good side. You've got a while yet with the compression garments. They'll support your arm—"

Adao let out a small whimper and then began to cry in earnest.

Just then one of the local hospital volunteers—a lovely grandmotherly type called Mabel—came in with a cup of steaming tea cradled in her hands. She'd assigned herself the task of reading Adao stories since the charity that had brought him here was unable to provide "on the ground" support.

"Oh, Adao!" She threw a quick inquisitive look at Naomi and nodded at the spot where she stood. Obviously it was "her" spot. "Do you mind? I think maybe we need a bit of quiet time."

A swarm of responses jammed in Naomi's throat. All of them were a muddled ache to help and the conflicting, urgent need to push everything back into place that this moment was unzipping.

"Of course." She stepped away from the bed. There was no point in telling Adao she'd be back the next morning.

And the next. He was leaning into Mabel's arms and giving himself over entirely to his grief.

Finn took up Adao's charts and quietly explained to Mabel about when to call the nurses for pain management or, if things took a turn for the worse, when to call him.

Naomi felt invisible. Worse, actually. She felt powerless.

Just as she had on *that* day nearly fifteen years ago when her heart had pounded so loudly she could barely hear the shouts and screams. Shame washed over her as the memories slammed to the fore. Her hiding place. The gunfire. The stench of hot metal filling her nostrils as she'd clenched her eyes tight against what she'd known was happening.

Everyone she loved had gone when she'd found the courage to open them again. Fear had turned her into a coward—not a hero like Finn. And with that knowledge came another bitter home truth. She did not deserve unconditional love. She'd thought she'd loved her parents and boyfriend unconditionally, but she had failed at the first hurdle and had just saved herself. And for that solitary selfish act, she could never forgive herself.

"Naomi! Wait." Finn jogged to catch up to her. Damn, she could crank up the speed when she wanted to. No doubt all that running she did along the river.

Not that he'd clocked her doing her stretches outside the hospital most days before shift. No…he didn't do things like that. The less you knew about someone, the easier it was not to care.

And yet here he was, actively avoiding his own advice. Maybe Christmas was a time of miracles.

"Let me take you to lunch."

Her eyes went wide. He fought not to do the same. He didn't ask women to lunch.

Colleague.

A colleague wrestling with the age-old dilemma. Getting too close to a patient. Most of the time the essential emotional distance needed just clicked into place. It didn't take a brain surgeon—or someone who'd been forced to go through a shedload of PTSD counseling as he had—to see this little boy had wormed his way straight into her heart. And he knew he wasn't the only one to have noticed.

"I've already had a sandwich, thanks." Her tone was apologetic rather than dismissive. And if he wasn't mistaken, the swipe at her eyes wasn't a bit of primping. She was fighting tears.

"Coffee, then." He steered her toward the elevators and put on his best stab at a jaunty salesman's voice. "I hear they've got some festive pastries down in the atrium café. I could grab some and meet you down by the river."

"What?" she snapped, dark eyes flashing with a sudden flare of indignation. "So you don't have to be seen being nice to me in public?"

"Hey." He lifted his hands up in protest. Talk about wrong end of the stick!

She carried on over him, clearly having found her voice again. A very cross voice. "There's no need. I'm more than happy to carry on working. Unless you think I'm not up to the job." She squared herself off to him, eyes blazing with challenge.

"You're crossing a line." He cut her off cold, the smile dropping from his face. He knew she was upset, but he'd never questioned her professional skills. "No one's doubting your ability to do your job."

She harrumphed. "Are you sure about that? This little talk of yours isn't actually some sugar-laced ploy to let me down easily? Tell me you've decided to put someone else on the case?"

"I will if you carry on like this." Finn meant it, too.

There was more than an impassioned plea to do her job crackling in her eyes. Adao's presence here had turned her normally chirpy demeanor raw with emotion.

"Are you *kidding* me?" For a moment Naomi struggled to come up with the best retaliation. "This is what I *do*. It's *all* I do. No hidden talents here. No secret skills in the kitchen. Or special volunteering projects. Sorry to disappoint, *Mr.* Morgan."

"Finn," he corrected her, trying to shake the defensive reaction that shot his shoulders up and around his ears. "And let's leave the sports center out of it, shall we? Those kids are…"

They meant the world to him. Reminded him he had a heart.

"What I do there is different. There's no need to try and rack up bonus karma points to prove you're good at your job. You already are."

She wheeled on him as the elevator doors opened then closed. "You mean you can act like an actual living breathing human being with them but not with me? Fine. Suits me. Once these elevator doors open feel free to take it in whichever direction you like—except *mine*."

Where the hell had that come from? He'd only been trying, in his usual clumsy way, to… Wait a minute. This was all-too-familiar terrain.

Defensiveness. Evasion. Flare-ups followed by pushing the ones you cared about away while deep inside all you really wanted was to be pulled into a deep, reassuring hug and told everything would be okay because you were in a place so dark it was impossible to believe in anything good ever happening again.

She was at war with something that lived deep within her.

Had he become her "someone" she could rail against? The one she was testing?

Despite the fact her entire body was radiating fury, Finn didn't move. He knew how lonely it felt when a person finally succeeded in pushing everyone who cared about them away.

Damn. He cared.

Despite the twitches to fall back into old habits, he held his ground.

His patience paid dividends.

As quickly as Naomi's temper had detonated, a few moments of "I'm not going anywhere" eyes from Finn saw the remaining sparks fizzle and all but disappear. She dropped her head into her hands and huffed out a full-bodied exhalation. After a deep breath in, she let them fall.

"Sorry. I—I didn't mean…" She floundered, trying to find the right words.

His heart softened another notch. Flare-ups were inevitable when the stakes were so high. And there was no doubt about it. Something about Adao had got right under her skin.

Just the same as she had slid right under his.

Two lost souls doing their best to make the world a better place. Sometimes they did good. And sometimes they made a hash of things. Sometimes they did both at the same time.

"C'mon," he said. "Coffee." He punched the elevator button again before tipping her chin up so she was looking him straight in the eye. "And a festive pastry. Doctor's orders."

He turned back to the elevator, trying to disguise his pleasure at eliciting a smile from her. A small one. But it was a smile, nevertheless.

Naomi was one part mortified to one part mollified.

Thank goodness they were outside, walking along the river where there were all sorts of other things and people to look at besides the tall, dark-haired, increasingly intriguing doctor she'd just verbally flayed.

Whoops.

Having a meltdown in front of someone—especially a surgeon—wasn't really her style. Particularly as it hadn't even been about something to do with a patient. This was a hundred percent personal and he knew it. He hadn't rubbed it in, though. For someone whose forte wasn't "cuddly bear"—at least at the hospital—it touched her to see that kind heart she knew he buried under his bluff and bluster rise to the surface.

She blew on her latte before taking a sip of the cinnamon-and-nutmeg-sprinkled drink, sighing as the warm liquid slid down her throat.

"Hit the spot?" Finn asked.

"Yes. And thank you. I'm really sorry—"

"Uh-uh." Finn tutted. "You've already apologized seven times. That's my limit." He stopped and pointed off the path toward a wooden bench made of green sleepers nestled in a sun-dappled copse of silver birches. "This is a good spot."

"You know all the good ones?" A feeble joke, but he gave a little laugh nonetheless. Generous, considering she'd not been showing her best face for the past half-hour. A rare slip.

He gave a vague wave along the towpath. "I live a bit further down the river, so I do actually know all the good spots."

"You live on the river?"

"Literally." He grinned. "Houseboat."

"A houseboat?" She didn't even try to hide her shock. "You."

"Yup. My family moved a lot when I was a kid—military—and I guess life on the move suited me."

"A houseboat?" Naomi couldn't even begin to picture

it. Finn was so tall and powerfully built and…well…it was easier to picture him striding across the sprawling slate floors of a huge stone castle than a houseboat.

Finn laughed a full, rich guffaw. "What? You don't think little old me could fit on a houseboat?" He gave her a quick scan then dropped his volume a notch. "You'd be surprised what I can do when I set my mind to it."

Naomi flushed and looked away. Courtesy of Finn Morgan, she'd been surprised quite a few times recently. She had little doubt he could achieve whatever he wanted when he put his mind to it. He'd already pulled at the seams of her perfectly constructed life and exposed her weak spots. No one had done that since she'd arrived in the UK. Not even the emergency refugee staff who'd seen her at her shell-shocked worst when she'd arrived from Zemara. It was as if from the moment she'd arrived she'd had to prove she was worth even the tiniest kindness.

Her foster mother, Charlotte Collins, had been the only one in those early days who she'd felt hadn't been judging her. Her compassion and support had meant so much to her it was why Naomi had legally taken her surname. At that point, to survive, she had needed to look forward. And Charlotte had given her the strength to do so.

Which had been why standing by and doing nothing when Adao had been crying had near enough destroyed her. Little wonder she'd gone on the defensive when Finn had followed her out. She'd been braced for all sorts of words to come hurtling at her: coward, failure, weak, worthless.

But he'd not said a single one of them. Instead, he'd shown her patience. Kindness. And now this…a chance to talk without any pressure.

Following his lead, she took a seat on the bench and sat back to take in their surroundings.

The little woodland nook looked as though it had been

designed by Hollywood. Frozen beads of water clinging to the silvery bark shone in the watery sunlight. The river quietly susurrated in the distance as joggers wove their way around couples—old and young—walking alongside the river's towpath. A hoar frost had coated everything overnight and it had yet to melt. Even though the sky was a clear blue today, it was cold and everyone was wearing hats with fuzzy bobbles or silly Christmas jumpers. Or both. No doubt about it. There was a festive buzz in the air. So different from the chaos swirling away in her chest.

"He got to you." Finn's voice was warm. Kind. "Sometimes that happens."

He fell silent, clearly waiting for her to fill in the blanks. Explain why Adao in particular had rattled her otherwise happy-go-lucky cage.

She couldn't go down that path. Not when it already felt as if she was being sucked into a black hole that would lead her straight back to that horrible day when her entire life had changed forever. A hit of iron-rich earth and palm fronds filled her nostrils so powerfully she bit the inside of her cheek and drew blood.

After a few minutes of sitting in silence, Finn, no stranger to keeping himself to himself, realized he wasn't going to get her life story. He hitched his good knee up on the bench and propped his arm on the back of the bench, chin in hand, so he was facing her.

"Next time you need to lash out at someone, maybe you can leave my baking skills out of it? I don't want that secret getting out onto the hospital's gossip train, otherwise the entire surgical staff will be demanding marshmallows like clockwork."

His comically stern expression teased a smile out of her. The second since she'd lost the plot.

How embarrassing to have just snapped like that. And in front of *Finn*, of all people.

"I'm really sorry—" She stopped herself. "I've never done that before."

"It's okay. Better in front of me than in front of Adao, right? And look." He reached out and laid his hand on her arm. "Like I said, it happens."

She stared at his hand, wondering how such a simple touch could have such a powerful effect on her. Just a colleague giving another colleague a bit of kindness.

But this was Finn Morgan they were talking about. Resident grumpy bear and...well...she was seeing all sorts of differing hues in his "rainbow" these days. In fact, he *had* a rainbow...not just a set of crackling thunderclouds!

She stared out toward the towpath and tried to collect her thoughts. What he'd said was true. It was impossible to be completely neutral at all times. After all, he'd cleared the entire viewing gallery during Adao's operation. Even so, she wasn't feeling particularly proud of herself right now and being on the receiving end of his surprisingly gentle touch was disconcerting. She shrugged her arm away from his hand, disguising the move as a need to give her arms a brisk double rub.

"Cold?"

"No. I mean yes." She rolled her eyes. "I'm always cold here."

"Cambridge or the UK?"

"Both." She frantically thought of a way to nip the direction this conversation was heading in the bud. "But I have an affection for thermalwear so, really, living here suits me to a T!"

Thermalwear? What are you talking about?

Finn didn't press. Either he was completely repulsed by the idea of her in woolen underwear or...oh, no. Was he thinking of her in her underwear? Worst conversation dodge ever.

"So…how do you deal with it?" Naomi tucked her hands into her pockets.

"What? Not let my heartstrings get yanked out of my chest each time I deal with an emotional patient?"

He wasn't patronizing her. He was stating a bald reality of being in the medical profession. Emotions were high. Keeping one's cool was essential. They were health care providers, not family.

"Tell me. What's the 'Morgan Technique'?" She genuinely wanted to know. For the first time in her professional life it seemed impossible.

He didn't even pause to think. "Easy. I think of my dad."

Naomi's heart squeezed tight at the faraway look in Finn's eyes. He didn't elaborate, but he didn't have to. It was enough to hear the warmth in his voice to know he loved him.

Her dad was the reason she'd pushed herself so hard when she'd moved to the UK. "Me too."

The admission was out before she thought better of it. What an idiot. Saying something like that only invited more questions.

"Mr. Collins?" Finn asked. Inevitably. "Was he a physio as well?"

Naomi shook her head. "And Collins wasn't his name."

Why do you keep telling him private things?

"Wasn't?" Finn asked quietly.

Yes. Past tense. She was the only surviving member of her family.

She ignored the question and instead said the family name she'd not spoken in over a dozen years. "Chukwumerije."

"That was your original surname?"

Yes. It had been.

"A tough one for the British tongue to force into submission," she said, doing her best to keep her tone light. She put on an English accent and mangled her name a few times. Finn's laugh echoed throughout the little clearing. He had little crinkles by his eyes. She'd never noticed those before.

An intense need to tell him the whole story took the laughter from her voice.

"There was actually a woman. A lovely woman. Charlotte Collins. She was my foster mother when I came here. Without her…" Naomi's voice cracked and she pressed her fist to her lips to stem a sob of gratitude.

Finn nodded. He got it. She didn't need to spell out just how important compassion was. Kindness.

"Say it again," he asked gently. "Your Zemarian surname."

It was strange, feeling the taste of her own name on her tongue.

For years using the new name had felt like the worst kind of betrayal and also the most generous of blessings.

She'd been granted a new life. A chance to become everything she'd ever dreamed of. But it had only come to pass because of the deaths of those she'd loved most.

Now? Here with Finn? The name felt like a disguise. All part of the chirpy, got-it-together facade she wore day in, day out to keep the demons at bay.

Finn had been mulling over her name. He gave a few aborted starts on mimicking her pronunciation before miming throwing in the towel.

She laughed softly. "When my mother said it, it sounded like poetry. Stella Chukwumerije. She used to say it as if she were royalty."

He raised his eyebrows. The question in his eyes asked one thing and one thing only: Where were they now?

The fact she'd probably never know haunted her dreams every single night.

"My mum's name means star, so sometimes…" She let the rest of the thought remain unsaid as her gaze lifted upwards. Looking up at the stars and believing that maybe, just maybe, her mother was looking down at her offered her solace. Most of the time.

At least Adao's family was alive and well.

An idea sparked. "What if we went onto the internet? Or asked the charity if they have a picture of his parents—maybe them all together as a family. We could put it in a frame for him. I could run and get something from the charity shops now."

Finn smiled as if she'd just handed him a present. "That's a great idea. I'll leave you to the running bit." He pointed at his knee.

"Is it acting up?"

He tipped his head side to side.

The gesture could've meant any number of things.

Yes. No. It always hurts, but I'm a man, so…

"You know—" An offer to give him a massage was just about to fly off the tip of her tongue when he held up a hand.

"I know. I *know*." Unlike the last time she'd offered help, his defenses didn't fly into place. There might have even been a bit of gratitude in those hard-to-read eyes of his.

In this light they were like sparkling like ice crystals with amber hits of flame…

Oh…

Naomi's body heat shot up a few degrees as their gazes caught and snapped the pair of them into a heightened awareness that blurred everything around them.

Heart. Lungs. Throat. Breasts. Lips. Her *hair* was aware of Finn. Even more so when he turned toward her on the bench, his knee gently shifting against hers.

It was one of the most sensual feelings she had ever experienced.

Which was ridiculous.

Right?

But it didn't feel ridiculous at all. Not with his face so close she could reach out and trace a finger along the fullness of his lower lip before—

No.

She didn't do this. She didn't *deserve* this. And especially not with a man who came with a complicated past.

His gaze on her own lips was virtually palpable. Her body responded against her will, the tip of her tongue dipping out and licking her lower lip, vividly aware that the only thing separating them was a handful of centimeters and air.

Abruptly, she swiveled so that she was facing the towpath and pressed her knees together.

"It must be nice to have Charlie to confide in after all you've been through."

"What?" Finn shook his head as if not entirely understanding what had broken the spell.

An all-too-familiar deadweight of anxiety began gnawing at that indescribably beautiful ball of heat in her belly and turned it into a churning mass of guilt.

"You know." She heard herself continue, regretting each word as it arrived. "After things changed with your wife."

"*Ex*-wife," Finn bit out, his body language instantly registering the change of mood. "We're divorced."

A cold wind blew in off the river, grazing the surface of her cheeks. A welcome sensation as they were burning with embarrassment.

Finn pushed himself off the bench, his good leg all but launching him toward the towpath.

She remained glued to the bench, in shock at her own—what was it? Stupidity? Common sense?

No. It was worse than that. It was fear. Fear of allowing herself to feel true happiness.

"I'm heading back. Going to do a quick check on Adao before I go into surgery for the rest of the afternoon."

He didn't ask her if she was going to join him, but he didn't power ahead as she'd imagined he might.

Silently they headed back to the hospital.

"Aren't you going in?" Amanda flicked her head in Finn's direction as he went into Adao's room.

Naomi shook her head. She was more off kilter than when she'd left the room half an hour earlier.

Had she and Finn almost kissed?

"He's not been Captain Grumpy again, has he?"

"Finn? No. Not all. He's—"

"Uh-oh… I see the tides might've shifted where Mr. Morgan is concerned."

Naomi gave Amanda her best "are you crazy" look then went to hover at Adao's doorway, where Finn was talking with Mabel.

"Absolutely we do, Finn. What a lovely idea. I'll just send a little message through on this thingamajig here and see if they can't do it today." The gray-haired woman pulled a mobile phone out of her cardigan pocket and held it out to him, clearly having no intention of sending the message herself.

Finn gave Naomi a quick nod where she was hovering in the doorway. "You still up for getting Adao a frame?" He looked at the little boy whose tears had now dried. "Would you like that, pal?"

Adao nodded, his tear-laced eyes wide with anticipation.

"Right. I guess we'd better send the office a message."

She watched as he made a show of trying to get the tiny phone to obey his large fingers, even managing to draw out giggles from both Adao and Mabel.

When he was done, he handed the phone back to Mabel then chatted a bit more with Adao. Told him how he was still toying with the idea of becoming an astronaut one day. Pointed out what fun going through airport security was now that he had an "iron" leg. Told Adao how lucky he was they were both lefties. Some of the best people he knew were lefties, he said with a wink, before turning to give her a meaningful look.

She was a leftie.

Was there anything the man didn't notice?

Finn was so good with him. It was mesmerizing to watch the pair of them as Finn ever so casually noted Adao's heart rate. Blood pressure. A little bit of swelling that had developed around the joint. There were multiple factors to consider in these early days after the surgery. Joint contracture. Pathological scars. Cardiovascular response to what had been, ultimately, a traumatic event. Residual limb pain. Phantom sensation, edema, and the list went on. All of which Finn nimbly checked while keeping up a light-hearted conversation about Adao's favorite British football players.

It turned out Adao didn't have any. His heart lay with the Spanish.

"What?" Finn feigned receiving a dagger to the heart and only just managing to pull it out. "Not *one* British player?"

Adao shrugged and grinned. He liked who he liked.

Standing there, watching the pair of them banter, Naomi felt an acute sense of loss. She could've kissed this man. This gorgeous, warm-hearted bear of a man.

Would it have been a mistake?

Most likely.

She didn't deserve a fairy-tale moment like that, let alone the promise of the happiness that could follow in its wake. From what little she knew about Finn, and the stony silence he'd maintained as they'd walked back to the hospital from the river, he wasn't exactly in the market for love. Neither was she, for that matter.

Lust. That's what it had been. A hit of seasonal lust that had taken them both by surprise.

That he was able to treat her as if absolutely nothing had happened between them was proof he compartmentalized his life. Just as she did.

Work.

The sports center for him. The riverside runs for her.

Home.

She tipped her head to the side and scrunched her eyes tight, trying to imagine him in a houseboat, and came up with nothing. The first thing that popped into her mind was a huge man cave carved into the side of a soaring mountainside. Accessible only by foot. Or yak. She easily pictured it all decked out in shaggy woolly mammoth hides and zebra skins. Did it make sense? No. But then again... A huge fire would be roaring in the center of it, with Finn presiding over the place as if he were the king of the jungle. Or the mountain range?

"What's got you so smiley?"

"What?" Naomi shook her head, startled to find both Finn and Adao looking at her as if she'd lost her marbles.

Oh, crikey. She'd gone all daydreamy right in front of the man she was meant to not be daydreaming about.

"Nothing. Just thinking about..." Her eyes darted across the ward to where a Christmas tree was merrily blinking away "I was just thinking about the Christmas party and how much fun it will be."

"Christmas party?" Adao spoke the words as if he'd not let himself imagine such a delight.

Naomi grinned.

"Absolutely." Evie was really outdoing herself if the rumor mill was anything to go by. "It's in a couple of weeks, I think. And…" she held up two sets of crossed fingers "… if everything goes well with your recovery and we get your physio under way, I don't see any reason why you wouldn't be able to go."

Adao looked to Finn for approval.

Finn smiled and gave the little boy's short head of hair a scrub with one of his huge man hands. "You heard the lady, mate. You focus on getting better and in a couple of weeks' time you might be showing Santa your new prosthesis."

For the first time the mention of the false arm elicited a smile from Adao. "I would very much like to shake Santa's hand," he said.

"Well, then." Naomi's heart was buoyed at the fierce determination lighting up the little boy's eyes. "That's what we shall focus on."

Her gaze shifted to Finn, whose eyes were already on her, his expression unreadable. What had she expected? Him to be all doe-eyed? Hardly. She'd turned him down. He was getting on with his life as if it had never happened and what lay deep in those moonstone-colored eyes of his would remain a mystery. No matter how much curiosity was getting the better of her.

She gave Adao a quick wave goodbye and headed toward the stairwell, fighting the growing sensation that running away from Finn could be one of her biggest mistakes to date.

CHAPTER EIGHT

AN EMPTY GYM.

No music.

Just the pounding of his heart and the sound of his breath.

The best part about an exhausting workout was that there was no room in Finn's head for anything other than the weights in his hands and the resistance his body was or wasn't giving as he pushed himself to the next level.

There wasn't one spare second to consider just how close he'd come to kissing Naomi the other day.

Or if he'd been counting: six days, twelve hours and a handful of minutes ago.

But he hadn't been counting.

Or popping round when she was giving Adao one of his physio sessions, taking careful note of how gentle she was with him. Sensitive to how lonely and lost the boy was feeling.

Neither had he been so much as giving the slightest thought to those beautiful, full lips of hers. The slight tilt of her eyes rimmed by lashes so thick and long he could almost imagine them butterfly-kissing his cheek.

Almost.

But he wasn't thinking about things like that.

He wasn't letting himself notice that when she walked into a room the world felt a little bit nicer.

Or the soft curve of her neck.

How watching her work with patients was seeing someone answering a calling, not doing a job.

Or the gentle swoops and soft curves her body revealed even in the athletic gear she almost always wore to work.

Finn strode over to a press-up bench and took off his prosthesis. A challenge. That's what he needed. He dropped to the floor and did a few press-ups, unsuccessfully trying to rid his brain of that instant—that bit of other-worldly time and place—when he'd been absolutely sure they'd both moved toward the other.

Two lost souls finding solace in each other.

Only he had no idea if she really was a lost soul or not. Something about Adao had well and truly shot her emotions up to explosive level. Then again, he never saw her raise her voice or offer anything less than a smile to every other member of staff.

Maybe it was him. Maybe it was the combination of the pair of them. Maybe it was the fact he'd never come to terms with pushing his ex-wife so hard the only choice she'd had in the end had been to leave him.

"Mr. Morgan!" The door to the gym was pushed open and Theo appeared. He was dressed in running gear. In his usual swift, efficient manner he took in a sweaty senior surgeon, a discarded prosthesis, a look that could kill and said, "Want a spotter?"

No. He wanted to be left alone to wallow in his misery. Only…he didn't really.

Blimey. Since when did misery *actually* love company?

Theo crossed to the press-up bench and eyed the weights

Finn had loaded on the bar. He clearly knew better than to wait for an invitation.

"Looks like you're weighted light tonight."

Theo had the world's best poker face and he was playing it hard right now. He knew Finn only pressed weights that challenged him at the highest level.

"I could lift this with my pinky," Finn grunted, not even caring that Theo was his boss. Not right now anyway.

"Well, then. Show me."

Finn craned his neck before lying back on the bench. Rather than address the obvious—his unusual decision to work out stripped back to his true self—he threw a question at Theo. "You look like you could pound out a few frustrations yourself."

Theo sucked in a sharp breath. "That obvious?"

"Only to a seasoned doctor."

Theo huffed out a mirthless laugh. "You mean like all the other doctors we've got wandering round Hope?"

"Something like that." Finn lay back on the bench and wrapped his hands round the bar. "Only…to…the…rest… of…them…you…look…achingly…handsome."

To Finn's relief, Theo took the jibe as it was intended and chuckled. Something to break the tension that had added more than a silver hair or two to Theo's temples.

Ivy wasn't getting any better. Quite the opposite, in fact. No amount of testing, Doodle visits or letters to Santa Claus were making a blind bit of difference.

Theo's hands floated just under the bar as Finn cranked out three rounds of three lifts before pushing himself up. "You want a go?"

Theo eyed him for a minute as if he were being asked to a duel then did the standard guy response. "Get up, then. You're on my bench."

"Your bench?" Finn guffawed loud and hard then made

a show of wiping it clean and presenting it as if it were a throne. "Your majesty."

Theo flicked him a look that said, *Enough with the servitude, mate*, then settled on to the bench.

True. It was Theo's bench. His gym. His hospital. But the last thing he'd ever seen the man be was proprietorial or smug about his financial status. Billionaire. What the guy was was a worried dad. And letting off steam had to be hard when your little girl's health was deteriorating right in front of your eyes.

"How's the diagnostician getting on?"

"Madison?" There was a bite in his voice when he said the name and he ripped off three quick rounds, pressing the same weight Finn had.

Impressive.

Or emotion-fueled.

Easy to see there wasn't much point in asking him if Madison had made much progress. His heart went out to Theo, seeing his little girl, the only one left in his family, go through so much pain right in front of him and feeling utterly powerless. It was one of the reasons he'd stripped himself of his own friends and family. No one to lose. Then, of course, there was the flipside…nothing to gain.

"Want to do another round?"

Theo lifted the bar and began pressing again. The determination on his face reminded him of his own once he'd decided to retrain as a pediatric surgeon. He'd poured everything he'd had into becoming the best. Apart from work, he'd barely imagined wanting to properly live again—let alone love again. And while he was nowhere near loving Naomi, he barely knew the girl, he felt more connected to her on a visceral level than he had with anyone.

Maybe it had taken this long for him to figure out who the hell he was. His whole life he'd worked toward becoming a soldier. Then he had been a soldier for five incredible years. Then in one solitary instant everything he'd thought he'd become had been taken away from him.

Why would his wife and family want a fraud?

And then this beautiful, mysterious, happy, sad, talented and obviously conflicted woman had walked into his life and another bomb had gone off.

For the first time in over a decade, taking the risk seemed better than going back down that soul-sucking rabbit hole he'd swan-dived into after his life had changed forever.

Theo clanged the bar back into place, sat up and stared right through Finn.

Um...

"Christmas plans?" Finn asked.

What the—?

King of casual chitchat he was not.

"You're looking at them," Theo said, lying back down, pressing out one more round then getting up and whirling round on the bench. "This, and trying to find my daughter a Christmas miracle. What about you?" He glared at Finn as if daring him to have better plans.

"Ditto." He opened his wide arms to the gym.

They stared at one another then laughed. "Couple of real players on the social circuit, aren't we?" Theo pushed himself up from the bench, gave it a swipe with the towel he'd grabbed on the way in. "I'm going for a run." His eyes flicked to Finn's good leg. "Want to come?"

"Nah." He had a prosthesis that was great for running, but he wasn't in the mood. He'd come here to test himself. See if he was ready—not just physically—to move away from the past and see how he got on with the future.

Naomi heard the weights drop to the rubberized gym floor before she entered the room. It wasn't unusual for staff to use the large physio gym, but it was definitely rare to hear such heavy weights in use. Aware that being startled could throw whoever was in there off their stride, she slipped into the gym as innocuously as she could.

The sight she saw actually took her breath away.

Finn Morgan.

Bare-chested.

Athletic shorts exposing a leg so toned it would've made Michelangelo gasp.

She pressed her fingers to her lips to stop herself from doing the same.

Finn's body glowed with exertion as, without even wearing his prosthesis, he alternated between single leg barbell lifts and pull-ups.

His back was to her, but she could see his focused expression in the mirrors on the far side of the gym. She'd never seen such a display of precision and resolute determination.

Despite the use of heavy weights, Finn's body wasn't over-pumped, like some of the zealous gym rats she'd seen throughout the years.

No. Finn's tall form had heft, but it was toned to absolute physical perfection. She could see clear definition in his shoulders and biceps as he pulled himself up and over the pull-up bar with the fluid grace of a gymnast. The muscles in his back rippled with the lithe strength of a lion.

Parts of her own body lit up as if she were a freshly decorated Christmas tree. She hadn't felt warm tingles of response below her belly button in just about forever and now Finn seemed to have some sort of remote control on her internal fireworks display—just one solitary glance could detonate an entire evening's worth.

When he dropped to the floor and took a double hop across to where he'd laid the heavily weighted barbell, she watched quietly as his internalized focus manifested itself in an extraordinary show of physical strength and courage. Not every man would put himself to the test like this. Not every man would win.

He'd obviously been working out for a while and when he crouched to pick up the barbell she saw him hesitate before heaving the sagging bar up and over his head. As he held it aloft and looked toward the mirror to monitor his form, his eyes shifted across to her and he threw the weight to the floor with a crash.

"I'm sorry, I didn't mean to interrupt. I was just going to set something up for a patient."

Finn turned to her and said nothing as he reached out an arm to steady himself.

He dipped to the floor and scooped up a white towel and wiped his face.

She'd never seen him without his prosthesis. Well. Not glossed in sweat and half-naked, anyway.

He certainly didn't need it, or anything else to prove that he was anything less than a powerfully driven man.

She'd never wanted to touch someone more in her entire life.

"Do you need these for your next patient?" Finn asked.

"No." Naomi held up her wrist as if her timepiece-free arm would remind him it was well after hours. "I thought I'd just get a head start on tomorrow and set up some equipment for my first appointment."

Neither of them moved.

Tension crackled between the pair of them as if a power line had been torn from its stable housing and set loose in a wind storm. Sparks flying everywhere. No clear place to hide.

"I've got a trick that might help you with your dead lifts."

Finn arced an eyebrow. Go ahead, the gesture read. Improve on perfection if you can.

He wasn't smug. He was just right.

Well. Almost right.

"Your hips. You're not using them as the power thrusters they're designed to be."

Naomi flushed as she spoke. If he were a patient she would normally move up behind them and…well…they would go through the motions together, but…

Her throat tickled. She was suddenly feeling really *parched*.

Her hand moved along the length of her throat as if it would ease the dry, scratchy sensation. A drink of water would be good about now.

As if mirroring her thoughts, Finn dipped to the floor again and grabbed a bottle of water, unscrewed the cap and, eyes still on her, began gulping down the water as if he'd just emerged from the desert.

Her eyes were glued to a solitary trickle of water wending its way through his dark stubble on his throat, shifting along his clavicle, heading toward that little sternal dip between the bones, only to be swiped away by a towel.

She caught Finn's grin as he dropped the towel on a nearby bench and shot her a surreptitious glance. He'd seen her ogling him. And he'd enjoyed it.

"That's a pretty intense workout you have there."

"No excuses," he said.

Wow.

It was that simple.

Of course it would be. For a man who worked with amputees, not to mention his time at the sports center where the wheelchair-bound athletes pushed themselves to achieve more, do better, try again, and never give up, no excuses sounded like a pretty solid motivator. He was making himself an example for his patients.

Only…she wondered if they could see the dark shadows flickering across those eyes of his. The man knew loss. The man knew pain. Whether or not she wanted to admit it, they were kindred spirits. But could two souls who had known devastation create something good?

He hopped over to the press-up bench and strapped on his prosthesis. When he rose again, squaring himself off to her as he pulled on his long-sleeved T-shirt, about a million butterflies took off, teasing her body's erogenous zones as if he were tracing his fingertips along the surface of her skin as his eyes drank her in.

"Well, then." She gave her hands a brisk let's-get-to-it rub. "If you're up for it, let me add some notches to your bow."

Finn stood absolutely still, his eyes cemented to hers. "I don't think that's what you meant to say."

"Of course I—" Naomi stopped. Had she?

Sometimes, even though it had been over ten years, she still muddled up British expressions. Her eyes widened as she realized how the expression could have been taken. Sexually.

"Oh, I didn't—"

Before she could form a coherent thought, Finn crossed to her and she was in his arms, his mouth descending on hers as if the world's most powerful magnets had drawn them together. When he first came up for air he looked into her eyes as if this had been the moment he'd been waiting for. The moment when his life would change forever.

She recognized the fire, because she felt the very same heat incinerating her every intention to remain immune to him. To protect her heart.

Her hands flew to his face, the pads of her fingertips

enjoying the contrast between the hot, needy demands of his mouth and the masculine prickle of his stubble.

There was not a single cell in her in body with the power to resist. Neither did she want to.

One of his hands slid round her waist and pulled her tight to him. As if she wasn't already arching into the solid heat of his chest. No one needed to tell them her body had been designed for his.

Finn slid his free hand up the nape of her neck and pulled back for a moment, looked deep into her eyes then changed tack, descending once again, to taste her in slow, luxurious hits of teasing kisses. He threaded his fingers into her loosely woven solitary plait and tipped her head back, dropping heated kiss after kiss on her throat.

Staying silent wasn't an option.

It was the first moan of pleasure she had ever heard roll from her throat.

These were no ordinary kisses. This was no ordinary connection.

Desire. Hunger. Need.

They were slaking all of them, their bodies and mouths moving intuitively as if the universe had aligned its entire history for this very moment.

In the center of her fiercely pounding heart Naomi knew this moment would be forever branded on her soul.

And she also knew it could never happen again.

Not unless she made peace with her past—and fifteen years on it still seemed an impossible task.

Finn sensed the change in Naomi's body language before she pulled away. They were the matching pieces of the puzzle of his life. He knew that in the very marrow of his bones.

When she stepped back, he didn't try to stop her. He couldn't.

His entire body was jacked up on adrenaline and hormones and one single move toward her might betray just how powerfully—how *intimately*—she had touched him. Had touched his heart.

"Don't let me keep you if you need to set up your equipment."

Naomi shook her head as if he were speaking a foreign language.

"No. It's fine. It can wait. I was just being hyper-prepared."

"Avoiding your life, you mean?"

Her expression became shuttered, her eyes protectively dropping to half-mast.

"I do exactly the same thing, Naomi. Take every shift going. Work out here just in case my phone goes. Tell myself, *Look. Someone needs me.* I'm trying to find proof, I suppose." He looked her straight in the eye. "Proof there's a reason why I exist."

She didn't even bother to protest. Didn't need to. He could see it in her eyes. She shared exactly the same fears he had.

A gut-clenching fear that he hadn't done enough to be worthy of the life he had.

It was the most honest he'd been with anyone in years. And every word he'd uttered was nothing less than the plain truth.

Hard to confront. Abrasive even. But *real*.

The door swung open and Evie appeared with an elf's hat on her head and a Christmas wreath dangling from her arm. She was all smiles these days and today was no different. "Hey, you two! Coming upstairs for the carol concert in the foyer? Free mince pies and mulled wine for the over-eighteens who aren't on duty!"

Naomi just stared at her as if she were a ghost.

Mercifully, Evie whirled around with a wave and a merrily trilled "Fa-la-la-la-la" before registering the shock of being interrupted on their faces.

"Carols?" Finn asked, as if it were the natural progression of snogging the woman of your dreams— Wait. *Woman of his dreams?* That was going to take some processing.

Naomi shook her head and pointed vaguely to another part of the hospital. "I've got to check on someone."

No, she didn't.

The message was clear. She was saying something, *anything,* to get as far away from him as possible.

"Fine."

His stiff, abrupt movements as he pulled on his outdoor gym clothes spoke volumes. He didn't want this to end. He wanted it to be the beginning. The frustrated yanks he gave his hoodie as he pulled it over his head and down across his torso—yes, he caught her looking when his shirt hitched up, *ha!*—were all far too familiar reactions for him. He'd behaved the same way with his ex-wife. Pushed her away when the going had got tough.

Well, he wouldn't give Naomi the chance. Not tonight. Not ever.

He pretended not to watch as she went over to the duffel bag she'd brought in and pulled out a bright red picture frame with a tropical theme embossed along the edges. She turned around with a shy smile and showed him what looked like a family photo. "For Adao."

Ah…

She actually was going to see someone.

He pressed his fingers to his eyes and gave his head a good shake. What an idiot.

He raised a hand to wave goodbye, but when he looked toward the doorframe she had already gone.

CHAPTER NINE

PACING ON A houseboat wasn't much of a tension-reliever.

Finn loved the place even though he near enough brained himself on the doorframes every single day. The warm wooden planks. The compact but modern kitchen. The old leather sofa he'd wrangled in through the small rooftop hatch by sheer force of will.

The ability to untie himself from the mooring and set off whenever the mood struck.

It's how he'd ended up here in Cambridge. He'd bought the portable home when his stint at rehab and his marriage had come to mutual and abrupt endings. He'd stayed in the Manchester area for a while to keep up with his rehab. But really? Once he'd cut ties with his past, he'd liked the idea that he could just cast off whenever he wanted and just go.

He stared at the phone for a minute, then picked it up, checking that he still had his ex-wife's number. His mum had sent it to him "just in case." She never nagged, but about once a year she asked if he'd "heard anything on the grapevine."

The way he'd treated Caroline gnawed at his conscience.

They'd not been a match in the end. They'd been kids who'd married too soon, all caught up in the romance of him going off to war. The last thing they'd been equipped for had been for him to come back at the ripe age of twenty-four with one good leg and a seething ball of fury where the other one had been.

He'd been angry with everything and everyone back then. Most of all himself. But his immediate family had taken the brunt of it.

His parents had retired to Spain a while back and, before they'd gone, the three of them had made their peace. They got it.

It wasn't simply the loss of his leg. It was losing the army as well. It was his family's chosen profession. His family's *history*. And for the first time ever…a Morgan was stepping away from the front line.

Sure. It had been bad luck. No one looks to get injured.

But Caroline…bless her…she hadn't been who he'd needed at his darkest hour.

And now, fourteen years after coming out of that pitch-black tunnel, he was beginning to think he'd found the woman he could open his heart to.

Someone who understood a core-deep sense of loss.

When Naomi looked into his eyes she seemed to see all of the trauma he'd endured and more. The pain. The doubt. The urgent, primal need to do better. To *be* better.

All the things he saw when he looked into Naomi's eyes. She *knew* him.

And for the first time since he'd cleared his social calendar of anything more than a casual fling he wanted more.

He wanted Naomi.

He stopped his pacing and snorted out a laugh as he remembered Theo warning him about wearing through the floorboards at the hospital. To do so on a houseboat would be little short of a disaster. He scanned the cabin, looking for something, anything, to do.

A stack of cookbooks lay front and center on his dinky kitchen island.

When in doubt?

Bake.

And while whatever he'd decided to rustle up was in the oven, he'd call Caroline. It was about fourteen years over-due, but…maybe he'd needed the time.

He began pulling ingredients out of the cupboards.

Excuses. Everything he thought up to say to her was an excuse.

The truth was, he'd met someone.

And if he were going to be in any sort of place to even try having a relationship, he needed to make peace with his past.

A quick look at the ward clock showed it was just after eight.

Naomi had ended up getting wrangled into listening to a few of the carols by a very happy Alice and Marco who'd let it slip they'd set their wedding date for just be-fore Christmas.

She hoped they hadn't noticed her fingers leap to cover her kiss-bruised lips as they'd spoken of their excitement about spending the rest of their lives together.

She'd made her excuses, something easily done in the hospital, and had come up here to see Adao. Chances were he was asleep, but even if she was able to tiptoe into his room and place the framed photo of him with his family near him, it would be nice for him to wake up to.

It wasn't as if she was going to get much sleep tonight.

Kissing like teenagers!

No.

She shook her head.

What had happened with Finn had been two consenting adults ripping open a pent-up attraction. And from the looks of things, neither of them had any idea what to do next.

She'd had a couple of boyfriends, but nothing with this level of passion. If the gossip was anything to go by, Finn was a renowned lone wolf so… He was such a mystery to her and yet…a part of her felt like she'd been waiting her whole life to find him because she'd known him all along.

Those *kisses*.

Fireflies danced around her belly at the thought.

She'd kissed like a teenager with her boyfriend back in Zemara. It had been sweet. Innocent. Two young people focused on school, getting into university and then, when war had broken out, surviving.

She glanced at the photograph she'd managed to get from the medical charity.

In it Adao's face was alight with an ear-to-ear grin. He was holding a puppy in one arm and had his other arm flopped round his big sister's shoulders from his perch atop a large wooden barrel. His parents were behind the pair of them, also smiling. It was a perfect family photo and reminded her so much of how happy she had been with her own family that a prickle of impending tears teased at her throat.

She shook it away as she approached Adao's room. She was here to comfort him, not cry about her own past.

Her eyes shot wide open when she reached the room. Far from asleep, Adao was wide awake, with a huge, cuddly labradoodle sprawled across his lap.

Alana, Doodle's minder, was sitting in a chair a couple of meters away, reading a book.

Naomi tapped on the doorframe.

"Okay if I come in?"

Alana nodded toward Adao. It was up to him.

He looked at Doodle and the dog wagged his tail so he smiled and nodded.

"I've brought you something I thought you might like to put by your bed."

"Really?"

The astonishment in his voice tugged at her heart.

She pulled the photo out from behind her back and showed it to him.

Tears instantly sprang to the little boy's eyes. Naomi held her breath, suddenly worried it was the worst possible thing she could have given him. She hadn't been able to look at any photos of her own family since they had been taken away that horrible day. They existed. In an envelope buried deep in the back of her cupboard. But to look at their smiling, beautiful faces every day and know she'd never see the real things again? She didn't know that she had the strength.

"I love it. I love it so much. Thank you, miss."

"Naomi," she gently corrected.

He repeated her name as if tasting it, his eyes still glued to the photo. He pulled the photo close to his chest and hugged it, then lifted it up to his face and gave each of his family members a kiss.

Out of the corner of her eye Naomi saw Alana reaching for the box of tissues near her chair.

She didn't blame her. The moment was about as powerful as they came. She was struggling to keep her own tears in check.

Adao's face brightened as an idea struck. He showed the photo to Doodle. The dog sat up and listened as Adao pointed out his mother, father and sister. Then listened to a detailed explanation of where the picture had been taken—outside their home—when it had been taken—after they'd come home from church—what they had eaten afterwards—a huge meal with the rest of the members of their congregation—and how he had played and played with his friends that day. Played until the sun had gone down, when all their mothers had called them in and made them go to bed so they would be fresh for the next day at school.

His voice had cracked a bit at the end, but it was the happiest he'd ever sounded.

In fact, it was the most Naomi had ever heard him speak.

From the astonished look on Alana's face, it was the most she had heard as well.

"Good idea," the blonde woman mouthed.

"Naomi?" Adao was holding the photo out to her. "Could you please put this up so Doodle and I can see it from the bed?"

"Of course." She made a bit of a to-do about rearranging the scant items on top of his bedside table and put the photo front and center as Adao lay back on his pillow. "Is this good here?" She gave it a tiny shift closer toward him.

He looked at Doodle for confirmation. The dog lifted his head and tilted it to the side as if checking it from the same angle as Adao, then gave a little woof.

Adao beamed. "Thank you."

"You're welcome. I'm so pleased you like it."

There was a light knock on the door. Navya, one of the night sisters on the ward, was wearing The Look. It was gentle but firm, and it meant it was time to go now.

Naomi dropped a kiss on Adao's head. "See you tomorrow, okay?"

For the first time he didn't look at her fearfully and a huge warmth wrapped around her heart.

She walked to the elevator with Alana and Doodle, amazed at seeing the change in the little boy.

She gave the dog's head an affectionate rub and smiled. "Does everyone tell him their secrets?"

"A lot of people do. Mostly the children," Alana conceded with a smile. "But you know what they say."

Naomi shook her head and entered the elevator along with the pair of them. "What do they say?"

Alana cocked her head to the side at the same time as Doodle. "A problem shared is a problem halved. Or something like that. Maybe it's burden." She shrugged and grinned. "Better out than in is what it boils down to. Isn't that right, Doodle?" She gave the dog a loving stroke. "This guy knows far too much about me. I'm surprised he doesn't put his paws on his ears and start to howl half the time."

Naomi laughed along with her, but the words were hitting home. She'd never shared her story with anyone. Not even the girls and women she'd first bunked with at the refugee facility she'd stayed in when she'd first moved to the UK. She'd nicknamed the facility "The House of Secrets."

Naomi had convinced herself it was best to keep her story close. Hidden. But between kissing Finn and watching Adao pour out his life story to this adorable pooch…it was like the universe was offering her sign after sign that now was the time she needed to share her story.

And she knew exactly who she wanted to share it with.

The elevator doors opened and Alana and Doodle began to head toward the main exit. "Are you walking to the car park?"

Naomi shook her head. "I think I'm going to take a little walk along the river."

"It's freezing out there. Make sure you wrap up warm."

Naomi watched as the pair ambled out of the hospital and toward the car park then set off with a gentle jog along the riverbank.

She'd know Finn's place when she saw it.

Something told her the universe was working in her favor tonight and it was time to start reading the signs.

* * *

Finn was pulling the cake out of the oven when he heard the knock on the door.

What the—?

No one visited him. Ever.

He opened the door, feeling almost as shocked as Naomi looked to see him there.

"I need to tell you something. To explain." She spoke low and urgently, as if she might implode if she didn't get whatever it was she had to say out soon.

"I have one cake, two forks and a bottle of red."

Wow. He was a real Romeo, wasn't he?

Her brows drew together as if he'd just told her he was from the planet Zorg. Her short, quick breaths told him she was running on adrenaline. Maybe he should've offered the standard cup of tea and a biscuit. The rest could wait.

"Come on in."

A few minutes later, coat off, but with a woolen blanket wrapped round her shoulders, Naomi sat across from him at the small wooden table with a fork in her hand, a cup of steaming tea in front of her—she'd refused the wine—and a cake between them.

"Um… This all right?" Finn gave his dark tangles a scrub. "I don't really do hosting. No one really ever calls round."

"I've never been offered an entire chocolate cake before."

"Guess this is a day of firsts."

They looked at one another, their gazes catching and clasping tight. Of course it was a day of firsts.

First kisses being the most memorable of all.

But she wasn't here to talk about kissing, so he sat back and waited.

The air between them was alive with pent-up energy

and yet…somehow it felt right, Naomi being here in his man cave.

"I saw Adao just now."

"The picture? How did that go?"

"He loved it. Alana was there with the therapy dog, Doodle. He told Doodle all about his family. His life…" Her gaze shifted down to her hands where she was rubbing her thumb along the spine of the fork as if trying to remold it into an entirely new shape.

Something clicked. He saw where this was going. She wanted him to be her Doodle.

"I'll take the first bite, shall I? Save you the embarrassment."

"Embarrassment?"

"Of wanting to wolf down the entire cake in one go." He took a huge forkful and made a show of really enjoying it. Which, even if he had made it himself, didn't require much acting. Who didn't like warm chocolate cake?

Following his lead as he plunged his fork into the large cake, Naomi took a daintier portion, her eyebrows lifting as she tasted the cake. "Oh, wow! Mmm… This is delicious."

"I've been competitive baking with a television show," he confessed. "So far I think I'm winning."

Naomi put her fork down, her expression sobering. "I need to explain why Adao means so much to me."

"You don't need to explain anything you don't want to."

"I want to." Her gaze locked with his and everything he saw within those dark brown eyes of hers seared straight into his chest cavity. She was a kindred spirit. A fellow lost soul who, if he was strong enough for her, just may have found her mooring.

He pulled his own mug of tea toward him, took a drink, sat back and listened.

"Many years ago…fourteen and a bit…"

He nodded. It was about the same length of time since he'd lost his leg.

She stopped, drummed the table with her fingers then backtracked. "When I was seventeen, my country was disrupted by civil war. Up until then I had lived a happy childhood. Just like anyone else. Maybe just like you."

Finn nodded as confirmation. He'd had a great childhood. Military through and through. Moving every few years. New countries. New parts of the UK. Always "on mission" to make himself the best possible candidate for army recruitment when the time came…

"It all changed so quickly. One day my boyfriend and I were going to school like normal teenagers—"

"Your boyfriend?" Finn prompted. There was no point in editing her story on his account.

She gave him a weak smile. "It was a teenage romance."

"Hey." Finn raised his hands. "I'm not going green-eyed monster on you. Everyone has a past. I have mine. You have yours." He laid his hands on top of hers and gave them a light squeeze. "The only thing I am here to do is listen."

And learn. And something told him right then and there he'd stay and be there for her as long as it took. Everyone had a past. And everyone had a future. It took moving on from one to get to the other, and that was precisely what he was hoping to do.

CHAPTER TEN

NAOMI SEARCHED FINN'S intense expression for any fault lines.

Not a single one.

Just a solid, warm-hearted, generous man sitting across from her with nothing other than her own well-being in mind.

It was painful. But she began to speak.

"For the most part, the rebels hadn't been around our small town. It was about the size of Cambridge, actually. It had a river. And a hospital." She suddenly became lost in memories of just how much she had taken for granted before the war had begun. A quiet, bustling market town where her father had run a hardware store and her mother had been a teacher. She'd always had food. Clothes. They'd had a happy, perfectly normal life.

"Had you always wanted to be a physiotherapist?" Finn asked, dipping his fork into the cake and indicating she should feel free to help herself.

She smiled but shook her head. She couldn't eat cake and tell this particular story. "I knew I always wanted to help people, but I wasn't sure how. I used to volunteer at the hospital as… I'm not sure what you call them here. In Zemara we had a lot of American missionaries, so we were called candy-stripers. We worked in pinstripe pinafores to identify us as volunteers. It was good fun. I loved it whenever I could help a patient smile or laugh."

"I bet you were great at it."

Her smile faded. "I had only done it for about a year, but it was long enough to discover physiotherapy. I really enjoyed seeing the rehabilitation side of working with patients."

"Sometimes that's the hardest part."

"Exactly!" She felt the original spark of passion for the job still burning bright within her. "That's what drew me to it. The challenge of instilling a sense of pride in the patient. Changing the parameters. Looking at things from a new perspective."

"That's how it works all right." Finn put his fork down and took a gulp of tea. "There were about a thousand times I wished I could've unscrewed my head from this old lunky body of mine and screwed a different one on it."

She gave him a sidelong look. From where she was sitting he was looking pretty close to perfect.

"One with a positive attitude," he explained.

Ah. Well. "Everyone has their down days." She took a sip of her tea and lifted her gaze to meet Finn's. He really was an extraordinary man. A flush crept to her cheeks but she ploughed ahead and said what she was thinking. "For what it's worth? I'm glad you kept the one you had."

They looked at one another in the soft light and if Naomi hadn't come here for another reason entirely she would've been hard pressed not to lean across the table and start kissing him all over again.

Though she'd seen his fiery side, she knew now his temper was usually directed at himself. He was fiercely loyal. That was much apparent. And brave. Her thoughts skipped to Charlie and the look of true respect and admiration he'd given Finn when telling Naomi how Finn had saved his life.

She hadn't saved anyone's life.

And therein lay the crux of the matter.

He was a hero. She was a coward. No wonder she was drawn to him.

She played with her fork for a minute. Took a sip of her tea. She wasn't here to talk about physio. Or her childhood. She was here to explain to Finn why she'd become so emotional about Adao. Too much emotion fueling too many memories.

"The rebels came when we were least expecting it."

Finn nodded, showing no sign of being surprised they'd changed from talking about his head to her home town being invaded by armed rebels.

"I was down at the river, seeing if there had been a catch that day. Food had been...scarce in the previous weeks. We weren't starving but the country had slowly been falling under their reign of terror."

A shiver juddered down her spine at the memory of the helicopters flying overhead, the wild-eyed recruits practically hanging out of the open doors and firing their machine guns indiscriminately. Men, women, children. They hadn't cared. Most of the rebels' so-called cavalry had been poor men bribed with alcohol and drugs. Men who, in another world, could have been convinced to turn their energies to doing good had they been offered food and shelter instead. She tugged the edges of the soft cashmere blanket Finn had draped round her shoulders closer together.

"C'mere." Finn rose and gestured to the comfortable-looking sofa. Worn, golden leather. When she sank into a corner and pulled a cushion onto her lap she felt protected, safe. Finn threw a couple of logs into a small wood burner she hadn't noticed earlier. An image of Finn chopping the precisely cut woodpile by hand flickered through her mind before his silence reminded her she needed to get through this story.

"I heard the helicopters first. My instinct was to run home. I'd asked my boyfriend to meet me there so that we could all eat together that night, but when I heard the shooting and screaming… I…" She pressed her hands to her ears, still hearing the cries of disbelief and fear coming from the normally tranquil country town. "I hid." The words came out as a sob. "I hid underneath some palm leaves I found drying at the edge of the forest because I could see from there. They were loading everyone they could into trucks. Men in some. Women and children in others. They were screaming at everyone to hurry. Telling lies. Saying that they were taking them to refugee camps where they would be safe, but everybody knew where they were really going."

"The mountains?" Finn asked softly.

She nodded, swiping at the tears cascading down her cheeks. From the grim look on his face he knew exactly what a trip to the mountains would have meant for her family and the rest of those other poor, innocent people. The excavation of the mass graves that had been found there only warranted one or two lines of mention in the newspapers these days, but Naomi lived with the knowledge that those she had loved most dearly were very likely amongst the bodies slowly being recovered.

Finn handed her a handkerchief from his pocket. "It's clean."

Their fingers brushed as she accepted the cotton square and the hit of connection felt like a lifeline. A chance to believe in the possibility that one day the weight of guilt might not be as heavy as it was at this very moment.

She swiped at her tears and when she'd steadied her breath she finished her story as quickly as she could. "I hid under the palms for three days."

His eyes widened. "What about food? Water?"

She shook her head. "I was too terrified to move. It rained at night anyway…a warm rain…so I drank what I could from the palm fronds. Even if there had been food I am sure I would have not been able to eat it." Her hands balled into two tight fists in front of the cushion she'd been hugging. "My stomach was tied in knots that day. Permanent knots of guilt and sorrow and shame that I did nothing to help my family."

"Do you still feel that way?"

Pain lanced through her heart. "Of *course* I do. They're still gone. I know the chances of them ever reappearing are minimal. No. They're not even that." She scrubbed her hands through her hair and looked Finn directly in the eye. "They will never come back. And I will have to live with that guilt for the rest of my life."

"Guilt for what? You wouldn't have been able to save them. If anything, you would've been killed trying or…"

He didn't finish his sentence. He didn't have to. If she'd run and joined her mother on the truck, she would have died with her. But what was the point in living if everyone you loved died knowing you did nothing?

"Have you spoken to anyone else about this? There are professionals who deal precisely with this kind of trauma."

He should know.

"When I first moved here there was counselling." She rattled off a few truisms from those early days. "There wasn't anything I could do. I would've been killed, too. Look at all of the good I've done now."

"You *do* know all of those things are true." Finn's eyes were diamond bright with emotion. With compassion. It wasn't pity. And for that she was grateful.

"I do. On an intellectual level." She pressed a hand to

her chest. "It's knowing it here that I find just about impossible."

Finn reached across and took Naomi's hands in his own. He looked into her eyes so intensely she was certain he was seeing straight through to the very center of her soul.

"Naomi Collins," he began, his voice gruff with emotion. "There is so much that is wrong with the world. You have seen more of it than anyone should have to. Take it from someone who's seen more than his fair share too. But let me tell you this. The light and the joy that you bring to your patients and to the people who work with you—hell, to anyone who's lucky enough to see that beautiful smile of yours…"

He paused, giving one of her cheeks a soft caress with the back of his hand while rubbing the back of her other hand with the pad of his thumb. Her stomach was doing all sorts of flips and it was just as well Finn opened his mouth to keep on talking, because she was positively tongue-tied with disbelief.

"The light and joy you bring to *me*—and, let me tell you, I'm a pretty grumpy character, so that takes some doing—is more than enough to lighten the burden of any guilt that you bear."

The tangle of emotions that, for so long, had been a tight knot in Naomi's chest felt the first hit of relief. A slackening in the constant tension that she should be doing more, or better. Telling her story to someone who understood and who didn't judge or blame her for the decisions she'd made all those years ago released something in her she hadn't realized was locked up tight. For the first time in fourteen years she felt it just might be within her power to receive affection.

"Finn?"

He cupped her cheek in one of his broad hands, the edge of his thumb gently stroking along her jawline. "Yes, love?"

"Thank you." And she meant it. With every pore in her body she meant it.

Finn didn't know if it was he or Naomi who had leant into the kiss, but semantics didn't matter at this point. Neither did the fact that finally being able to hold her in his arms was lighting up every part of him like the center of London. One minute they'd been holding hands and the next they'd been kissing and he'd pulled her up and onto his lap. She was straddling him, one hand cupping his face, one hand raking through his hair as if she'd been made to be there. Made to be with him. Gone were all the shy inhibitions he'd thought he'd seen in her earlier.

The same fierce attraction that had pulled them together at the gym was alight. Touch, taste, scent were all threatening to overwhelm him as their kisses moved from tentative and soft to a much deeper exploration of their shared attraction. He wanted this. He wanted *her*. But it had to be right.

What mattered was Naomi and ensuring she wasn't letting the powerhouse of emotions she'd just shared with him lead her into doing anything she would regret.

Using all the willpower he possessed, Finn pulled back from the deep kiss then tipped his forehead to hers, vividly aware of Naomi's soft, sweet breath on his mouth as he spoke. "Are you sure this is what you want? That *I'm* who you want?"

She put her finger on his lips. "Yes."

He captured her hand in his and gave the tips of her fingers a kiss. He wanted this—he wanted her—but not if it was misplaced emotion fueling her desire. "And you'll feel free to stop or tell me if there's any point you don't want to con—"

She dipped her head to kiss him lightly on the lips. "I will." She spoke again, her lips still brushing against his. "There won't be."

She pulled back so he could see her eyes. They shone with certainty. And desire.

Finn's internal temperature ratcheted up a hundred notches as he ran his hands down her sides, enjoying the shift and wriggle of her body's response as he pulled her in close. Two people reveling in the simple pleasure of holding one another. It had been so long since he'd done this and had been emotionally present. She ran her cheek along his stubble then nestled into the nook of his neck for a few slow kisses along his throat.

He heard himself groan with pleasure. And they weren't anywhere near naked yet. As far as he was concerned, they could keep going as slowly and luxuriously as the long winter's night would allow.

"Do you have a bedroom hidden somewhere around here?"

Her smile was one part timid, another part temptress.

"Yes, I do." He rose and took her hand in his, laying a kiss atop her head as he showed her the way to the bedroom in the stern.

This wasn't pure lust at work. He *cared*. He genuinely cared for this woman and all the beauty and pain she held in that enormous heart of hers.

The night might be a one-off. It could be the start of something more. Either way he would finally know what it was like to be with her after months of wondering. He'd deal with the fallout in the morning.

As she opened the bedroom door and turned to him, eyes filled with questions, he knew that from this moment on, starting with the softest of kisses, the most tender of caresses, he would do everything in his power to make sure she never felt heartache or fear again.

When Finn entered the bedroom, the two of them stood for a moment, frozen between fear and desire. Need trounced tenderness. Hunger savaged restraint. The air crackled with electricity, as if the space between them was a taunt—a dare to see who would be brave enough to make the first move.

Finn's touch was powerful enough to fill the void Naomi had ached to fill ever since her family had been stolen away from her. As he turned the distance between them to nothing, his scent—a heady wash of pine and man and baking—unleashed a craving in her for more. His caresses, more tender than she had ever known, told her she was no longer alone.

With Finn, she felt invincible. Like a queen who had finally met her true intended after years of isolation and loneliness. With the invincibility also came an unexpected sensation of peace. Cell by cell, her body registered the change.

Their kisses were weighted with intent. With longing. As if they'd known one another far longer than the handful of months Hope Children's Hospital had been open. Their bodies seemed to know one another as if this whole union had simply been a matter of time. Kismet.

She'd never known what it was like to feel whole again.

And when they lay back upon the pillows, a tangle of limbs and duvet and satiation, the tears came. Tears of relief that she still had it in her to love. To believe in a future. Tears of sorrow for the family she would never see again. And through it all Finn held her tight, the beat of his heart keeping time with her own.

* * *

A few hours later, Naomi tucked the thick duvet close round Finn's sleeping form, doing her best to work with the gentle sway and rock of the houseboat to quietly tiptoe out of the bedroom, scooping up her discarded pieces of clothing from the floor. Atop a lamp. Hanging from the door handle. Her pants had somehow ended up latched to a hat-rack shaped like a pineapple attached to the wall.

Wow. Finn had some aim.

A slow shimmer of sparkles rippled its way through her bloodstream as she pulled on layer after layer of outdoor clothing in advance of going back to the real world.

Dawn wasn't anywhere near appearing, but already what had happened felt like a moment preserved in aspic. A moment so magical she'd picture it in one of those magic snow globes in her heart because there wasn't any chance something like that could happen again.

Not because she didn't want it to.

In the few hours they had shared in the night she had felt complete. And it terrified her. It felt like leaving her family behind all over again.

She couldn't burden him with her history. Finn clearly possessed the strength to forge ahead, see the future for what it was—a kaleidoscope of possibility. She wasn't there yet. Not by a long shot. And Finn deserved someone stronger. Someone able to forgive themselves for valuing her own life above others.

She pulled the zip up on her puffer jacket, tugged on her woolly hat and slipped her fingers into her gloves before realizing she was hardly breathing. As if exhaling would make part of the magic of what she'd shared with Finn go away.

She forced herself to breathe out and in again. Reality was only a few short steps away.

She slipped out of his houseboat, crossed the gangplank and urged herself into a gentle run. The cadence of her feet pounding on the footpath drummed in reminders of who she was. Physiotherapist…survivor…

The next word was usually coward. It was her daily process of building herself up only to break herself down again, only this time…this time she kept hearing Finn's soothing words ease away the sharp edges of the accusation she usually hurled at herself.

And yet…trusting that…believing she could still honor the memories of her family and loved ones as well as open her heart to someone and experience such *joy*…it didn't seem possible. It didn't seem *right*.

She pushed herself to run harder, faster. Until she could no longer feel the touch of Finn's fingers on her bare skin. The tickle of the bristles on his chin against her stomach. The warmth of his lips pressing against her own.

Until all she felt was that familiar ache of loss. Only this time it was bigger. This time it wasn't only for what she had lost. But what she would lose if she couldn't release herself from the guilt of having survived what her family had not.

CHAPTER ELEVEN

FINN WOKE UP HAPPY.

Head to toe.

Realizing he was on his own had come as a bit of a shock, but he brushed off Naomi's absence since, for the first time in years, he'd actually slept in. She'd always struck him as an early to bed, early to rise type. Neither did she seem the type to show up in the hospital wearing yesterday's clothes, so…fair enough. Hospital gossip was hard to shake and it had been one night. It was hardly as if they were at the adorable notes on the kitchen table phase of things.

After a brisk shower, he dressed and went back out to the main room, where he stared at the empty kitchen table again. Had he really convinced himself he was cool with the one-night-only thing? Or was this the seismic shift Charlie had warned him would come one day?

Once he'd heard Naomi's story…understood how deep the waters ran beneath that eternally kind smile of hers… he'd known their paths had crossed for a reason. She was the beacon he'd needed to shine a light on his own life. Show him the bridges he still needed to cross. The truths he needed to confront.

He hit the towpath and walked quickly toward the hospital. An urgent, primal need to see her possessed him.

He hunched against the wind and pressed forward. It was cold out. Cold enough to snow if the weather report on his phone was anything to go by.

He followed a group of nurses into the main hospital doors, wondering when he'd last felt this hyped up.

For a surgery?

Months.

Years, maybe.

For a patient?

More recent, but this was different.

For a co-worker he'd just crossed the line from professional to personal with?

Never.

But he'd cross it a million times over if it meant holding Naomi in his arms again.

He knew it as a truth like he knew the thump of his own heartbeat in his chest.

He walked through the hospital's front doors and scanned the huge atrium at the entryway to the hospital. There was no escaping the fact the festive season was creeping up on them fast and furious. Just over two weeks until the big day and the hospital was, courtesy of Evie and her magic elves, reveling in the lead-up.

Two enormous Christmas trees flanked the large glass sliding doors, giving the impression visitors and patients were walking into something more akin to Santa's grotto than a children's hospital, which—he scrubbed at his freshly shaved jaw—he supposed was a good thing.

These poor kids. None of them wanted to be in hospital. Especially at Christmastime. Despite the early hour, he'd bet Naomi was seeking refuge here for exactly the same reasons he'd thrown himself into retraining as a pediatric limb specialist. To forget about herself and pour her energies into her patients.

"Are you planning on making yourself part of the scenery or are you actually going to work?" Marco gave him a jolly thump on the back as he and Alice took off their winter coats and joined him in soaking up the festive atmosphere.

"I don't know. I'd make a pretty cute Santa's helper, don't you think?"

Both Marco and Alice looked slightly surprised to see Finn waggle his eyebrows and do a mini-jig. Well. It was a stationary jig but, hey, he was new at this "jolly chap" thing, so…

"Hey, Finn. While we have you here, you've not got yourself booked up before Christmas, have you?"

He shook his head, though he had a fair few things he knew he'd like to fill his social calendar with and they all sounded a lot like Naomi.

"Go on." Marco gave Alice a loving squeeze. "Show him."

"He doesn't want to see this."

"See what?"

"This." Marco held out Alice's hand just as the sun broke through the clouds. It hit the ring to glittering effect.

Finn pretended to be blinded by the ring's brilliance. "So it's official, then."

"It will be even more so by Christmas. Here…" Marco scribbled a date and a location onto a sticky piece of paper and pressed it on to Finn's chest. "Consider this your early invitation."

Alice laughed and rolled her eyes. "There will be something a bit more official than a sticky note in a few days."

Finn took off the note, put it in his pocket, watching as Alice and Marco wandered off toward the wards, arm in arm. It looked nice. It looked…solid.

"Finn!"

He whirled round and saw a grinning Evie. She was

wearing a silly reindeer jumper complete with glowing nose on it.

Why was everyone so *happy* today?

Wait a minute.

He was happy today.

Evie brandished her watch at him. "Countdown to Christmas is officially under way!"

He resisted the curmudgeonly urge to point out that the countdown to Christmas was *always* under way…that was how time worked…and smiled instead.

"Are you still planning on helping out at the Christmas party?" She scanned her clipboard as if suddenly doubting herself. "I've got you down as a yes."

He gave her a distracted yes, not entirely sure if he remembered when the long-awaited party was.

"Bringing anyone?"

That got his attention. There was only one person he'd like as a plus one. Not that he knew where she was. The entire staff of Hope Children's Hospital seemed to be swirling in and out of the atrium, buying coffees, getting first dibs on the fresh-out-of-the-oven mince pies, admiring the decorations. Everything but telling him where Naomi was.

"Finn?" Evie prompted. "Are you bringing anyone tomorrow or are you lending a hand on your own?"

"Why? What's tomorrow?"

Evie gave a faux sigh of exasperation. "What we were just talking about. The Christmas party? For the children?"

"Yes. Right. Of course. No. Maybe." He looked at Evie's list, which appeared to be as long as Santa's list of toys. "Does it matter?"

She gave him a curious glance then shook her head and smiled. "No. Of course it doesn't. Just as long as we're all there to show the children just how big the Christmas spirit is here at Hope."

"Count me in. You've done an incredible job, Evie. The place is looking magical."

And he meant it, too. The whole world looked different today. Now, if he could only find the person who'd helped change his perspective.

Finn could feel Evie's curious expression on his back as he strode away toward the surgical ward. He had a full roster today and needed to get his head screwed back on straight.

This whole "looking forward" thing was not only messing with his ability to focus, it was adding a bit of a kick to his step.

"Hey, Alana. You and Doodle are looking well today. Hi, Adao."

Naomi waved to Adao from the doorway, waiting for Alana and Doodle to finish their session. Adao's demeanor was still pretty forlorn, even with the curly-haired pooch nestled up beside him on the bed.

Her spirits sagged.

The photo of his parents might've done the trick for a minute or two, but the little boy, now that she had a moment to watch him talk with Doodle, wasn't much chirpier than he'd been that very first day. And who could blame him? He was in pain. He was adjusting to an entirely new way of dealing with his body. The whole hospital was bedecked and beribboned with all the Christmas festivities and he was here all alone.

She knew that feeling so well and yet…for the first time in her adult life she knew she didn't have to. Finn had thrown her a lifeline. A chance to live and see life from an entirely new perspective.

A flight of butterflies took off in her belly as she thought of Finn. His big bear body all tucked in under the duvet looking more peaceful than she'd ever seen him. His arms tightly around her as they'd slept. Well, *he'd* slept, she'd fretted.

The last thing she was going to do was set herself up for more loss.

"I'm afraid it's our time to go, Adao." Alana picked up Doodle's lead and clicked it onto his collar.

Tears welled in the little boy's eyes. "Can't he stay?"

"Not all day, I'm afraid. We've got to go visit some other children and then Doodle's got to go for a walk. Perhaps…" The therapist looked to Naomi for support. "Perhaps when you're feeling a bit stronger, you'll be able to come out for a walk with us."

Naomi smiled. "As long as we get you wrapped up nice and warm, that sounds good to me." She grinned at Adao. "What do you think of that?"

He gave a lackluster shrug.

Poor little guy.

Perhaps going outside was exactly what he needed. Her runs along the river were far more therapeutic than just a bit of physical exercise. Maybe if she could get Adao outside at the party tomorrow…

Alana and Doodle stopped in the doorway so Naomi could give the pooch a cuddle. His furry face was so lovely and open it was little wonder the children felt safe telling him their secrets. She was seriously beginning to think of getting her own dog, seeing how wonderful Doodle was with the children.

Then again… Finn was easy to speak with. And he gave good advice, too, whereas Doodle's talents peaked at furry cuddles. She buried her face in Doodle's curls for a moment, trying to turn her own expression neutral. It was almost impossible to believe the Finn she had just spent the night with was the same man who'd practically bitten her head off every time she'd seen him over the past few months.

To think…all that time it had been attraction holding him at bay.

Mutual attraction.

And it went so much deeper than the physical. Last night she had wanted nothing more than for him to know her. Understand her.

And when she'd taken that risk and told him the raw truth about her past—how shamefully she'd behaved— he'd painted an entirely different picture. He had been so thoughtful. And kind. Not to mention the best kisser she'd met. A ripple of pleasure shimmied down her spine at the memories. Kissing on the sofa. In the kitchen. In his bedroom.

What had possessed her? She'd never behaved like that before with a man. She'd never been so open with *anyone*. Urgh! She wasn't meant to have let herself fall head over heels—

Wait a minute.

Was she in love with Finn?

The thought threatened to overwhelm her so completely she shut it down immediately. Of course she wasn't. She barely knew the man.

Well, that wasn't true. She knew a whole lot more about him now than she had just a handful of days ago. He was generous. A good listener. Amazing with children. Had an ex-wife. Had saved a life. Had an excellent reputation as a surgeon.

What on earth was he doing, wanting someone like her? Someone who'd let her entire family down at the time they'd needed her most?

"Naomi? Is everything all right?"

Alana was peering down at her as she all but kept a stranglehold on the poor therapy dog.

Naomi popped up to standing and gave her leggings an unnecessary swipe. "Yes. Good. Perfect." A crazy laugh burbled up and out of her throat. "Clearly in need of a hug."

"Who needs a hug?"

Her spine slammed ramrod-straight as her heart started jumping up and down as if it had just won the lottery.

Finn.

The man had a way of being there exactly when—when she did and didn't need him.

"No one." She smiled, doing her best to ignore the confusion in his eyes. Steering clear of that intense gaze of his might be the only way she could get through this day. "Adao and I were just going to have a session and Doodle was kind enough to give me a hug on his way out."

"Very generous of the old boy." Finn's tone had slipped from congenial to neutral and, despite the fact Naomi had hoped for things to stay professional, she already missed the warmth in his voice. "Mind if I have a quick word with the lad about his prosthetic casting before you begin?

"Not at all. Adao?"

Adao nodded somberly as Finn talked him through how a team from the prosthetics department would be coming in and taking off his bandages. "But it's nothing to worry about, all right? They're going to cast a mold of your shoulder area and measure your residuum."

"Residuum?" Alana whispered to Naomi.

"It's what's left of his arm. They'll need to measure the shape perfectly so that his prosthesis works well with what he's got left."

"Such a brave little boy." Alana absently stroked Doodle's head as she spoke, but to Naomi the gesture spoke volumes. She was seeking comfort. Seeing someone you

cared about endure pain—no matter how big or small—
was hard. Just as her instinct had been to go to Finn when
she'd seen him that first time without his prosthesis. Everything in her head had all but screamed out for her to go
to him. To help. To help him through his pain.

Now that she actually could go to him—to talk, for
a hug, for another one of those spine-tinglingly perfect
kisses—acting on it was even more frightening than it had
been when he was a virtual stranger.

Because now it mattered if she lost him.

"Right, then. I'll leave you to your session with Naomi, but
we'll see you in an hour or so, all right?"

Finn crossed the room to Naomi, who was shifting some
paperwork around in a folder. Presumably something to do
with her session with Adao.

"Hey." He kept his voice low. "Everything okay?"

"Yes, of course. Why?"

We spent the night together and you disappeared.

"Nothing." They were at work. He wasn't going to press
it. "Hey." He gave the door a light pat to get her attention
before she began her session. "Do you fancy meeting up
for a coffee later or something after work?"

She gave an apologetic shake of the head. "Sorry. Full
day today and I promised Evie I'd help get things ready
for the party tomorrow." She reached for the door as if to
shut it.

"The Christmas party?" He held it open. She nodded,
her eye contact hitting all the points around him but never
solidly meeting his gaze.

*Had he done anything? Said anything to upset her? If
so, he wanted to fix it.*

"I've really got to get on." She pressed the door again
and this time he dropped his hand and watched it shut.

How was that for poetic justice? A door closing right in his face just when he'd thought a new path in life had just opened to him.

Right.

He glanced at his watch. An hour until his next surgery. A poor little girl born with curly toes. Sounded cute. Was actually very painful. Now that they had exhausted all the physiotherapy routes and waited for her to reach the ripe old age of four to see if her tendons were going to offer her any relief, he was hoping to put an end to that pain today.

He headed to his office, mulling over Naomi's cool re-action to seeing him after last night. He suspected there was a lot more to Naomi's lack of eye contact and polite thanks but, no, thanks to his invitation to meet up than a simple case of "buyer's remorse."

Quite the opposite, he was suspecting.

Intimacy was the one thing he'd been unable to bear when he'd been hurt. A lot of his mates from the military had also struggled to make a start on a relationship—or, even more to the point, hold onto one. Help it flourish and grow.

He grabbed the back of the wheeled chair in his office and let it take his full weight as he picked up his phone from his desk and thumbed through the address book. There was one person who knew exactly what it was like to be an open and loving soul on the receiving end of a person going through hell.

He stared at the phone for a moment then, after years of promising himself he would press "call," he pressed down on the little green receiver icon and lifted the phone to his ear.

Hearing her voice say hello was like being yanked straight back in time—except this time he had perspective. This time he wasn't a raging ball of fury. This time there was gratitude she had been as kind to him as she had.

"Caroline. It's me. Finn."

The line was silent for a moment and he was just about to explain who he was again when she spoke.

"You think I wouldn't recognize your voice after all these years?" There was no acrimony in her voice. No bitterness. He heard children's laughter in the background and a dog bark, followed by Caroline's muffled instructions to take the dog outside while she spoke on the phone. An old friend was on the line.

An old friend.

Generous of her.

"You've got kids."

"Observant as ever." She laughed easily then gave a little sigh. "I've landed on my feet, Finn. I hope the reason you're calling is to tell me you have, too."

"Tell me about you some more first." He pushed his chair back from his desk and threw his good leg up onto his desk and gave his knee a rub as she told him how she'd transferred schools after things had fallen apart with him so she could be closer to her family in the Cotswolds. She was a primary school teacher and had stuck with it. After keeping a close guard on her heart for a while, the gentle persistence of a certain black-haired, blue-eyed teacher across the corridor from her classroom had eventually persuaded her she should let herself love again.

They had two children now—Matty and Willow—and a dog named Mutt.

"So-o-o-o…." Caroline persisted. "I'm presuming you're not calling me to tell me bad news or you would've said it by now. Are your parents all right?"

He smiled at the receiver. Even all these years later she

still knew him pretty well. As for his news? He was...*by God*...he was pretty sure he was in love again.

"The parents are fine. Tanning like lizards down in Spain." He'd rung them last week and would ring again. Let them know he finally had news on Caroline and that things might have changed for him a bit as well. "I'm sorry," he said.

"For what?" Caroline's hand went back over the receiver as she issued some more instructions to her children, who had burst back indoors again. He heard something about Santa keeping close tabs on them followed by a sudden, obedient silence.

"That usually keeps then in check," Caroline said in such a way he could practically see the smile on her face. She'd always wanted to be a mother and he'd always wanted "just one more tour" before they began a family. Sounds like things had panned out for her just as she'd hoped. Eventually, of course. What was the saying? After the storm came the rainbow. Something like that. Whatever it was, he hoped her rainbow was a double.

"I'm sorry I was such a git," he said. "After...you know... everything."

"You weren't exactly seeing silver linings when you got back, Finn." Caroline's voice was soft. Forgiving. "And it's me who should be thanking you."

"What? For being a right old ass and pushing away the one person who loved me most?"

"Your parents probably had the market on that one." Caroline laughed then fell silent for a moment. "Look, we were kids when we were married. Did I hope and pray it would work out? Of course I did. I loved you."

"Loved?" He knew he was being cheeky, but it was nice to know the vows they'd taken had meant something. They'd meant something to him, and tearing them apart as he had—ruthlessly—had been like destroying part of his own moral code.

"You know what I mean. I'm happy now. Really happy. And I wouldn't be married to this great guy or have these fabulous, extra-noisy kids of mine if things hadn't gone the way they had with us. It took a while, but I see now that I wasn't the person to help you get back up. You were the only one who could do that and you were determined to do it alone."

"That I was." Finn huffed out a laugh. "Turns out it takes a lot longer if you do it on your own."

"Yes, it does." He could picture her nodding and smiling in that endearing way of hers and was heartened to realize the place he had in his heart for Caroline was very firmly in the "cherished friends" section.

"Are you in love, Finn? Is that why you're ringing? I hope to God you're not going to ask my permission, because you've always had my blessing to find joy."

He barked a laugh. "How the hell did you figure that out from a few 'what's been going on for the past twelve years of your life' questions?"

"Ha! I'm *right*. Love that. Totally easy to figure out." He heard her blow on her knuckles and knew she was giving them a bit of a polish on whatever top she was wearing. Most likely a goofy Christmas jumper if she was anything like she used to be.

"Easy how?"

"Easy because you've never rung me before and your voice has a certain puppy-dog quality to it."

"What? Roughty-toughty me? I don't think so."

"I do," Caroline said firmly. "So what's holding you back? You'd better not say it's me, because that ship sailed long ago, my friend." She spoke without animosity and Finn knew she was doing her best to tell him that whatever guilt he had about the past wasn't necessary anymore. She was in a great place and she wouldn't be there if he hadn't left her.

Finn thought for a moment. Losing his leg had ripped him from his past in one cruel instant. He'd never be the lifelong soldier he'd planned on becoming. But it was different for Naomi. She'd not had any sort of closure as far as he could make out. Her internal life still seemed dominated by what she thought she *should* have done. An impossible position to live with when your choices had been life or death.

"I think she might be afraid that if she lets herself love me, she'll lose her link to the past." He didn't tell her Naomi's story. It wasn't his to tell, but it gave Caroline the lie of the land.

"Well, then. I guess someone had better find himself a way to prove to her that it is possible to love again, and still be true to yourself."

"Good advice, Caroline."

"Yeah, well…" She could've said a lot of things here. She'd learned from bitter experience. Life could be cruel when you least expected it. But she didn't. Because she obviously also knew that life could be kind and full of richly rewarding happiness that made near enough anything seem possible. Even convincing the woman he loved that she wasn't betraying her family by opening up her heart again.

"Happy Christmas, Finn," Caroline said.

"Happy Christmas to you, my friend. And thank you."

"Couldn't think of a nicer Christmas present than to hear you've finally found yourself again."

"Took long enough."

"Well, you're tall," she said. Then laughed. They garbled a farewell as her children's quiet time erupted into a spontaneous round of "Jingle Bells."

He said goodbye, not even sure if she heard him, but the

warm feeling he had in his chest told him all he needed to know.

Caroline had forgiven him and moved on. All the proof he needed that miracles existed.

Now all he needed to do was show Naomi she could trust him to be there for her. He was ready now. Ready to live his life to the fullest. And the one way it would be the best life possible was to know he would have Naomi by his side.

CHAPTER TWELVE

NAOMI PUSHED HER tray along the counter of the hospital cafeteria, not really seeing the food options. Normally she loved it here. The social atmosphere. Doctors, families, hospital employees all taking a break from "the medicine business" to enjoy a meal. When it wasn't absolutely freezing out, like today, the cafeteria's concertina doors opened up to a small garden that was scattered with picnic tables.

"Do you mind if I take that?"

Naomi turned to see Madison Archer, the diagnostician from America, reaching for the last bowl of Christmas pudding drowning in a puddle of custard. Truly healthy fare for a hospital.

Her shoulders hunched up around her ears as she inhaled and let out a sigh. It was Christmas. People deserved a treat.

"It's all yours," she said to Madison, even though it was a bit of a moot point at this juncture. "Enjoy." She tacked that on to make herself sound cheerier than she felt.

"Is that what you're eating?" Madison asked as they shuffled up the queue a couple more steps.

Naomi stared at her tray as if seeing it for the first time. A bowl of applesauce. A plate of spaghetti. And a yoghurt.

"Nothing on there really looks like it matches." Madison reached across Naomi toward the fruit bowl and pointed at a banana just out of reach. Naomi handed it to her. "So. Are you pregnant?"

Naomi's eyes went wide. She and Finn had used protection and it wasn't like she wanted children right away anyhow— Wait. No. This whole line of thought was completely going in the wrong direction.

Madison unleashed a triumphant smile. "Am I right?" She gave a little air punch. "God, I needed a win."

Naomi winced an apology. "Sorry. I'm just distracted. Not pregnant." She stared at her tray of mismatched food and bought it all anyhow. She could put the yoghurt in the staff fridge for later when she was filling up gift bags for the children…also known as avoiding Finn so he could forget about her as soon as possible.

She gave Madison a quick smile then wound her way through the lunchtime crowd to the one free table in the room.

A bite or two into her spaghetti she laid down her fork. Nothing was right today. Ever since she'd left Finn's houseboat without leaving so much as a note, the entire day had felt off kilter.

"Sorry. All the other tables are full and I've not really found an office to claim as my own yet. Do you mind?" Madison was already settling down in the chair, so Naomi scooched her tray over a bit to make room for her. More quizzes on whether or not she was pregnant were definitely not what she was after. She would've eaten in the gym, but every time she'd walked in there today all she'd been able to think of was Finn…a shirtless Finn…and being kissed by him and held by him and— *Urgh*.

Stop. Thinking. About. Finn.

"Enjoying your stay?" Naomi asked, to cover the fact that she was playing with her food and the few bites she had taken had tasted like cardboard.

"Not particularly," said Madison, stabbing at one of the small roast potatoes that had come with her chicken and vegetables.

Naomi sat back in her chair and looked at the forthright woman across from her, then laughed. "You've definitely not let the English way of covering up how you really feel get to you, then."

Madison shrugged. "Why would I do that? Wastes time. And energy." She cut off a piece of chicken and brandished it in Naomi's face. "If I could just get disease to be as forthright as I am, I would be one happy customer." She ate her chicken.

"If only life could be that simple."

"But it isn't, is it?" Madison pounced on the statement. "It's a complex, difficult and solitary business." The diagnostician didn't seem angry about it. That was just the way life was. She stabbed another potato with her fork and popped it into her mouth.

Naomi was about to protest when she realized she had actually been living her own life precisely as Madison had succinctly put it. Definitely the solitary part. But who at the end of the day was she protecting? Certainly not her family. Whether she was happy or sad, single or falling in love, it would never change what had happened to them.

"Do you think it has to be? Solitary?"

Madison's green eyes widened at the question then softened. "Maybe not. I just find it's easiest." She stared at her plate for a moment then stood. "I think I'll finish this pudding thing on the ward. See if the ensuing sugar high gives me any insight."

"Ivy?" Naomi asked.

"Hmm." Madison scanned the room as if looking for an escape route.

"The trays go over there. Against the wall." Naomi rose

with her own tray. She didn't have much of an appetite either.

"Too many mince pies?" Madison asked, as her final stab at conversation.

"Something like that," Naomi said to Madison's back as the redhead slid her tray onto the rack and headed toward the cafeteria's main doors where an all-too-familiar figure appeared.

"Butterflies, more like," Naomi whispered, as she turned and headed for a side exit. "Definitely butterflies."

Finn glanced through the glass doors into the gym and saw Naomi putting away some equipment from a session with a patient. A pretty strong one, from the looks of the weights she was hoiking about. Now that he was finally being honest with himself, admitting that he loved Naomi, it was a true pleasure to watch her pootle about the gym, slipping things into place, having little conversations with herself—presumably about one patient or another.

When she looked up, those warm eyes of hers lit up when she saw him, and just as quickly dulled.

He pushed through the swinging gym doors. No point in standing outside like a creepy stalker. Besides, he had to get down to the sports center.

"Hey, there."

"Hi." Naomi started rearranging the weights he'd only just seen her settle into place. Unnecessary busy work.

"I'm just going to put it out there. It seems like you're avoiding me."

A nervous laugh formed a protective bubble around Naomi, telling him all he needed to know. "No. Of course not."

"So…" He sat down on one of the large balancing balls

in the room and stared at his hands for a moment. "Why am I getting the opposite impression?"

"I'm not avoiding you," she said, dodging meeting the clear gray of his eyes as she spoke. "I just… It's been busy."

"Too busy to come out for a mug of hot chocolate?" He pointed in the direction of the atrium. "My shout."

"No. Sorry. I…"

Finn watched as she floundered for an excuse and decided to put her out of her misery. He rose from the balancing ball and cupped her shoulders in his hands. "I liked what happened between us the other night. Did it scare the hell out of me? Absolutely. Do I want it to happen again? Definitely. Will I encounter some stumbling blocks in unveiling the true Charm Machine that lives somewhere under this grumpy bear exterior? I hope so. For you. For me. For what I think could be an 'us'… I really hope so."

Naomi wriggled out from beneath his hands. "Thank you. I've just— I've got a lot to do tonight."

"This wouldn't have anything to do with feeling guilty about letting yourself actually enjoy your life, would it?"

From the sharp look of dismay that creased her features Finn knew he'd hit the nail on the head.

"Hey." He brushed the back of his hand along her soft cheek. "I know what you're feeling. And if you believe you can trust in that, trust in me. I will be here for you when you're ready."

An hour later, down at the sports center, the feeling that he might've pushed too hard kept losing Finn point after point.

"I hope she's worth it," Charlie called out as he threw the basketball through the hoop with a fluid swoosh.

"Who?"

Playing dumb had been one of his fortes during the dark years. But it didn't always work with Charlie.

"The woman giving you a taste of your own medicine."

"And what medicine is that exactly?" Finn grunted as Charlie threw the ball at him. Hard.

"The kind of medicine a man deserves when he's pushed and pushed every woman who's ever tried to get close to him as far away as he can and then, when he falls hook, line and sinker, is made to work for it."

"That obvious?"

"That obvious."

Charlie wheeled to the side of the court and chalked up his hands then came back to give Finn a quick once-over. "You've got The Look."

"The Look? What the hell is that?"

"All doe-eyed and soppy-faced—"

Finn punched him in the arm. "There isn't a doe-eyed cell in my body."

"Rubbish. You're one of the most romantic men I've ever met. It's why you fell to bits after..." Charlie tipped his head toward Finn's leg, his expression as sober as a judge's. "You wanted things to be perfect. Your vision for how you saw your life, army, marriage, the whole shebang had been all planned out. You hadn't planned on this happening. Not ever again. Well, my friend, it's happened. So how are you going to deal with it? Fight or flight?"

Despite himself, Finn laughed. There was no point in acting the fool in front of Charlie. He dropped onto the bench next to where Charlie had wheeled his chair. "All right, then, O Wise One. What do you prescribe to make sure I don't follow old patterns?"

Charlie leaned back in his chair and stroked an invisible beard. "Listen, my son, to the wise man who has been married many years. To win this woman's heart, you must be there."

"Be there?" Finn had been prepared for a half-hour lecture on understanding the finer points of a woman's psychology, but this was clearly all he was getting.

"That's the one." Charlie nodded, the idea of a beard clearly growing on him as he continued to "stroke" it, waiting for the light bulb to ping on with Finn.

Finn scrubbed a towel over his head and draped it across his shoulders.

Be there.

Charlie was right. Naomi had not only lost her family and boyfriend that day. She'd lost her home town. Her country. Her birthright.

No wonder it was hard to commit to him. Falling in love with someone so different, so far away from the life…the light bulb went on…*the life she'd thought she'd have.* To fall in love with him, Naomi would have to let go of every single childhood hope and dream and allow herself to believe in a new Naomi. A new life. A new set of dreams. All at the expense of everything she'd ever believed would be true.

He snapped Charlie with his towel. "Who made you so wise?"

Charlie gave his invisible beard a final stroke then grinned. "A really good friend saved my life once. Puts a lot of things into perspective." He popped a wheelie in his chair. "That. And I married a woman who told me if I so much as thought of checking out on her when the going got tough I was going to wish I was dead once she'd got through with me!"

They laughed.

"You got a good one," Finn said.

"And so is Naomi. I could tell that the moment I set eyes on her."

Finn gave him a how-the-hell-did-you-know-it-was-Naomi? glare and Charlie guffawed. "Mate. Your face was puppy dog from the moment she entered this sports center. You are a goner." He wheeled around him and pointed at him. "But not in the real sense. Remember. Be there. That's the most important thing."

CHAPTER THIRTEEN

DESPITE ALL THE confusion knocking around her head about Finn, Naomi couldn't help but feel a growing fizz of excitement over the Christmas party at the hospital today.

Evie had seriously outdone herself. She had stayed with Naomi for two extra hours at the hospital last night to sort out some of the final decorations. Naomi had watched, transfixed, as she'd handed over her precious little one, Grace, to Ryan with a thousand words of warning on how to care for her. He'd laughed and kissed her, reminding his future bride he was a doctor and, as a pediatric heart surgeon, had a rough idea how to care for infants.

Naomi pulled on the silly Christmas jumper Evie had given her last night in thanks for helping. When she pulled on the ivory top, edged round the sleeves, hem and neckline with holly-berry-red stitching, she had to admit, she'd drawn the lucky card.

Where other doctors were being doled out jumpers complete with blinking lights or designs that made them look like miniature elves or pot-bellied Santas, hers was almost elegant. A pair of gold antlers was stitched into the fabric and "floated' above a perfect red nose.

She considered her reflection in the mirror, twisting this way and that, only stopping when she realized she was being this vain because she was wondering what Finn would think.

Her heart was already telling her. Finn was looking to the future...a future with her...if only she would take his hand and join him.

Had he spelled it out? No. Had she seen it in his eyes each time she'd dodged his attempts to talk? Without a doubt.

This was up to her now. She looked into the mirror again. Without having even noticed, she'd woven her hands together in front of her heart as if they were providing some sort of shield. But what was it she really wanted protection from? Happiness?

It seemed ridiculous and yet... Allowing herself the true happiness of falling in love and all that could follow in true love's wake, was that bigger than living with the constant fear that she'd never be entirely present? That part of her would always be in Africa?

Her phone buzzed on the little table by her front door.

Evie. She was already down at the hospital, wondering if Naomi fancied coming along to help get the ball rolling.

A few hours later and Evie finally admitted there was nothing left to be done, apart from have the actual party.

The small green in front of the hospital had been utterly transformed from a frost-covered, plain expanse of grass to a winter wonderland.

"All we need is snow," Naomi sighed.

"That," agreed Evie," would be the icing on the cake."

Together the pair of them looked up at the sky then took in the party scene spread out before them. A bouncy castle shaped like an ice palace was nestled in amongst about a dozen stalls all giving away warm, spiced apple juice or hot chocolate. Others had platters filled with amazing glittery cake pops shaped like miniature Santas and snow-men. There were star-shaped cheese crackers and even a huge Christmas-tree-shaped vegetable platter with a pret-zel "trunk" surrounded by all sorts of tasty-looking dips. An enormous tray of reindeer-shaped sandwiches was al-ready doing the rounds with curly pretzels standing in as antlers and a perfect roundel of red radish taking the role of the nose. At the far end of the smattering of stalls host-ing games for the children was a carousel! Where on earth Evie had magicked that up remained a mystery. Whenever Naomi asked, Evie would just tap the side of her nose and say, "I've got love on my side. Anything's possible when you're in love."

Anything except changing the past.

It felt discordant to have such a gloomy thought when everything about her was all sparkles and glitter and twin-kling magic. Maybe a bit of Evie's "love magic" would rub off on her.

Only if you let it, you numpty.

And she wasn't ready to let go. Not yet. Maybe not ever.

"Want a gingerbread man?" Evie held out a cheerily decorated biscuit to Naomi, dancing it toward her with a zany jigging movement. She looked every bit as excited as the children who were starting to arrive from the main entrance of the hospital, all bundled up in their warmest winter clothing, with nurses, parents and scores of others.

Naomi laughed and took the biscuit, holding it slightly aloft as Evie shot past her to attend to a red baubles or sil-ver baubles crisis while Naomi went through the age-old conundrum of deciding whether to bite the gingerbread man's head off or start with his foot.

"I bet you go with the foot first. Then he'll look like me."

Finn's deep voice crackled like a warm hit of electricity along her spine and, despite the urge to run away, Naomi forced herself to turn around and smile. She couldn't imagine him making a joke about his leg a few weeks ago.

A few weeks ago she hadn't been able to imagine him being *nice* to her, let alone setting her entire body alight with a single brush of his hand. The least she could do was afford him a festive smile. She made a show of biting the hand off, knowing it was a contrary move, but he was disarming her. His gray eyes seemed to hold an extra luster today, jewel-bright against the dark clouds gathering in the distance. He was wearing a scarlet-colored hat that made the dark curls peeking through seem even more mahogany rich than they did without it.

He had what looked like a hand-knitted scarf, dark blue, wrapped round his neck and was wearing a light blue jumper with…gold antlers and a single red nose.

"We match." Finn stretched out his jumper as proof.

Oh, yes, they did. In so many ways.

A warmth lit up her belly as her body took its time remembering just how much they did match.

Unable to hold his gaze, her eyes flicked away from his, scanning the large green, hoping an excuse to run away would jump out at her.

"This is all looking pretty spectacular."

Finn reached out and put his hand on the small of her back as a woman led an immaculately groomed Shetland pony past them and toward a small trap that had been reconfigured to look like a sleigh.

A part of her was desperate to bolt and seek refuge somewhere quiet and solitary, while another part of her wanted to feel that lovely, large hand of his touch her back until the end of time. Despite the layers of fabric between them, heat radiated from the spot where he held his hand and it took all the power she possessed not to lean into it. Heck. It took all the power she possessed not to go up on tiptoe and throw her arms around him and tell him she knew she was being strange, but she was scared and her fear was her problem and hers alone.

"Naomi." Finn shifted round so he was facing her. "I know things have been a bit awkward between us since…" His eyes flicked down toward the river with enough meaning in them to indicate the night they'd spent in his houseboat. "What do you say we start again with a clean slate?" He performed a courtly bow. "Would you do me the honor of coming to this afternoon's party with me as my date?"

Her heart skipped a beat at the invitation. The warmth in his eyes told her so much. He was willing to take it slowly. Go at her pace. *Be there for her.* That someone could be so kind, so generous threatened to change the cadence of her racing heart. It was a risk she simply found too terrifying. Patients came and went. That she could cope with. But loving and losing again?

Is it worth losing him without having even let yourself try loving him?

The ache in her heart threatened to tear her in two. She simply didn't know and choosing to be alone seemed the safest option. Always had been. Always would.

"I've got to go and get Adao," she finally said apologetically, when the intensity of Finn's gaze became too much. "I promised him I'd be his date."

A flash of something all too easy to read shot across Finn's eyes.

Hurt.

It twisted her heart so tightly she could barely breathe. "Excuse me." She gave his arm a quick squeeze then set off at a jog toward the hospital entrance, weaving in and out of the crowds of children, their parents, their doctors and nurses, all wreathed in smiles and bathed in laughter as they saw the magical world Evie had created for them.

Questions assaulted her with each step she took.

Why couldn't she let that joy into her own heart?

Why couldn't she allow Finn to shine some light into her world after such a very long time of living cloaked under the weight of guilt and sorrow?

Because they were your family *and you left them behind.*

"Oops. You going in or coming out?" Alice Baxter was wheeling a child out of the front door.

"In. To get a patient," she hastily explained, stepping out of the heavy flow of traffic heading out to the green. From where she was standing, there was already a queue forming at Santa's grotto.

"Have you seen Marco?"

Naomi smiled. She knew Marco Ricci was the one who had put that non-stop smile onto Alice's face.

"I'm pretty sure I saw him with a set of twins. Twelve-year-old boys, both of them on crutches."

A slip and fall on the ice hockey rink in a spat over a home goal, if she remembered correctly. They were both scheduled to come in to have some physio when their casts came off.

"Excellent. See you out there!" She dropped Naomi a quick wink as she passed. "With any luck, I'll find Marco under the mistletoe!"

Wow. Everyone seemed to have sunbeams shooting out of their ears today.

Little wonder.

Alice was in love.

Evie was in love.

Obviously the same was true for Marco and Ryan.

It was as if the mistletoe fairy had come and sprinkled her fairy love dust over the whole of Hope Children's Hospital...

Was there anyone in this place who wasn't in love besides…?

Her shoulders drooped as her spirits plummeted to the bottom of her boots. *You could be too if you let yourself.*

She gave herself a quick shake and slipped through the traffic coming out the main door.

Adao.

She needed to get Adao and spend the day with him. That would keep her nice and distracted. No more thoughts about love or tall, gorgeous, ex-servicemen turned surgical geniuses needed here. Especially not ones with hands that drove her body wild when—

Naomi pressed her lips together hard and jabbed the elevator button so hard it hurt.

Served her right.

For everything.

Her focus should be on Adao. And after that there'd be another patient and another and another until… How long would she have to keep paying penance for something she couldn't have changed?

Fourteen more years?

Never?

Forgiveness came in many forms. She'd said that once to a parent chastising themselves for taking their eye off their child who had fallen and broken their arm.

Forgiveness comes in many forms.

The question was, would she ever be ready to forgive herself? Until that happened, she would always be alone.

Finn lifted the three-year-old off the carousel and gently deposited her in her mother's arms.

"Have a lovely afternoon."

What the hell? He sounded like one of his mum's friends after they'd popped round for tea.

"Thanks so much." The mum smiled and whirled around, both her and her daughter's cheeks pink with a combination of the fresh winter air and the exhilaration of the afternoon. If they were giving out medals today, Evie deserved a gold. No doubt about it. The party was a through and through success.

"Oops. Easy there, Adao."

Finn whirled round at the sound of Naomi and Adao's voices.

"Need a hand getting onto the carousel?"

Naomi's dark eyes flicked up to meet Finn's. He hated seeing the panic in them when she saw it was him.

"Yes, please, Mr. Morgan," Adao piped up. "May I ride the black one?"

Finn smiled down at Adao. It was nice to see the little guy up and about. Apart from the rumored smile when he'd received the picture of his parents, he remained as somber as ever. His arm was healing nicely and within a few days he should be fitted for the prosthetic that was being made at a special factory that supplied them.

"Absolutely. We just need to let it come to a stop so we can get you safely up there and then you can have a ride. Sound good?"

Adao nodded as if he had just agreed to accept responsibility for Finn's most prized horse.

Finn enjoyed watching Naomi interact with the little boy. Kneeling down when she spoke to him so they were eye to eye. Assuring him that "proper riders" only used one hand for the reins.

When the carousel came to a halt again, Finn helped Adao up and onto a glistening ebony stallion, avoiding jogging his arm as much as he could. The stallion's mane was painted a shimmering gold with a saddle painted on in shades of deep reds and oranges.

Naomi walked round to the far side to help offer Adao support if he needed it, but for now he was holding on tight to the stallion's reins, his face serious as the carousel began to turn and the horse began to "gallop" up and down.

Still avoiding eye contact with Finn, Naomi began to jog in place, pretending to try and keep up with Adao as his horse "galloped' forward.

"I'm just about there! I'm coming to get you."

The corners of Adao's mouth began to twitch as Naomi carried on with her jape, dropping her hands to her knees to pant for a moment then straining to "catch up" as the horse leapt and dipped with the rhythm of the festive music.

Finn watched, delighted, as, at long last, Adao's face lit up with a genuine smile. His smile spread like sunshine and lit up Naomi's features as well. He knew it had only been a few days since he'd seen her share a genuine laugh with someone, but it felt like it had been weeks.

Naomi leant in to ask Adao a question.

He didn't quite catch what she'd said, but the words "Christmas" and "wish" leapt out at him.

He could've told Naomi in a second what his was. But this was Adao's time so he watched as the young boy's expression grew very still as he considered his options.

The music began to slow, along with the movement of the carousel, just as Adao seemed to make up his mind.

"For Christmas," he began, "I would love to see my parents. And I would love to see snow."

Tears sprung instantly to Naomi's eyes when Adao mentioned his parents. It was a wish neither of them could grant. And no doubt was doubly painful for Naomi to hear, knowing she would most likely never know what had happened to her own family.

As for the snow... He looked over his shoulder at the gray clouds moving in from across the fens. He looked straight up to heaven and threw in a silent request that at least one of the boy's two wishes could come true. As for Naomi…he needed her to know the truth about him. See how far he'd come before she completely wrote him off. He was living proof that life was full of second chances.

"Let's get you off there, mate." Finn lifted Adao up and off the horse, noting how light he was, and how receptively he responded when Finn pulled him in close for a bit of a hug before he put him down.

Evie rushed up all smiles and twinkling eyes. "Adao! Just the man I was looking for. Do you think you'd like to come along and meet Father Christmas?" She shot a quick look at Finn and Naomi. "Would it be all right if I steal him for half an hour? We could meet at, say…how about at the Pin the Tail on the Reindeer stand at half-past?"

"Absolutely." Naomi's voice was bright, though Finn sensed a note of reluctance to let the little boy out of her sight.

"How 'bout I take care of this one?" Finn pointed to Naomi. "And you take care of this one." He pulled his own knitted cap off his head and tugged it onto Adao's. "And we'll meet up for apple cider doughnuts and a warm drink after."

"Sounds great." Evie grinned at the pair of them then stuck out a mittened hand to Adao. "Ready to meet the big guy?"

Adao's eyes shone with delight as he slipped his hand into Evie's.

"Right!" Finn clapped his hands together and gave them a brisk rub before putting them gently on Naomi's shoulders. "You and me. We need to talk."

CHAPTER FOURTEEN

NAOMI TRIED HER best to look relaxed as she and Finn strolled away from the party and down toward the river.

"From the look on your face people are going to think I'm kidnapping you!" Finn gave her a playful nudge with his elbow and tried to rouse a smile.

He wasn't successful.

She felt nervous and as if her heart was being yanked from one side of her chest to the other.

Sure. The angst was all of her own making, but...why couldn't Finn just let sleeping dogs lie?

"It's so cold I think we'd better forgo the bench and just keep on walking, if that's all right."

"Of course." She glanced back at the party scene behind them.

"Don't worry, love." He wrapped an arm around her shoulders and gave her a light squeeze. "I'll get you back to Adao." He dropped his arm from round her shoulders and instantly she felt the loss of contact.

"I want to tell you a bit more about me after my accident."

"You don't have to," Naomi quickly jumped in. She knew how painful trips down memory lane were and yet...she'd wanted him to know about her past. "I'm sorry. Please. Go ahead."

Finn gave her a thin smile of thanks, clearly already halfway back on his journey to the past. "After I lost my leg I was in a rage with the world. As you know, I was married at the time and the truth of the matter was I didn't handle it well. Not at all. From a young age I had everything all planned out. I would be in the army like my dad. I would teach my kid brother to do the same so I could look after him—"

"You have a little brother?"

Finn's smile was tight and his eyes didn't meet hers, so she knew the memories were painful. "I do. And there are still some fences that need mending on that front. He's a career military man. Always traveling. Mostly peacekeeping tours, but...he's out there, doing the family thing."

Naomi shook her head. "What do you mean?"

"Morgans have always been military. As far back as we can trace. When I became the first one to drop the baton—"

"You didn't 'drop the baton'!" Naomi was indignant. He'd sacrificed himself to save a fellow soldier. A friend. A life.

Finn took her hand in his and gave it a squeeze. For the first time in days it felt right and she gave his fingers a squeeze back so he would know she was there, listening.

"It felt like it. I thought I'd let my family down. And my wife. It wasn't the future I had promised her. Wasn't the future I had promised myself, and the only way I thought I could deal with it was on my own so I pushed and pushed until there wasn't anyone around me anymore and I'd got exactly what I'd wished for."

"And?" Naomi knew there was a big "but" lingering out there and felt a twitch of nerves, wondering what it was.

"But..." Finn grinned at her as if he'd been reading her thoughts. "Being alone, going through what I'd been through on my own was about the dumbest thing I think I'd ever done."

"So...do you regret getting divorced?"

"Yes. No." He quickly shifted course. "Our vows meant a lot to me. To both of us. And not coming good on them was a lot to face up to. So, for a long time, I didn't. Just pushed her and everyone else who mattered away." He looked up to the sky for a minute before continuing. "Caroline's in a great place now, and to be honest? I don't know that she and I would be a match...the people we are now. We were married very young and neither of us was ready to take on the challenges that my injury brought along with it. The minute I'd decided to retrain as a pediatric surgeon, that was all I had room for in my life. I simply shut her and anyone else who cared right out of the picture."

"What about Charlie?" Naomi was completely lost in Finn's story now. She knew exactly what he meant. The same drive he'd used to retrain as a surgeon sounded so similar to how she'd poured herself into her physiotherapy studies. Like it had been a mission. And yet...she had a feeling Finn's tale came with a lesson. One she might benefit from learning herself.

"Charlie?" Finn laughed. "Charlie was the one who knocked me on the head and demanded I start being more sociable. As far as I was concerned, doing surgeries and skulking round my houseboat were good enough for me. But when he introduced me to those kids and the lads on the wheelchair team, I slowly began to see what an idiot I'd been. But I was still compartmentalizing."

"Until...?" There had to be an "until" because Finn was completely different from the gruff, standoffish man she'd met at that first staff meeting.

He turned and faced her, eyes alight with emotion. "Until I met you."

"Me?"

"Yes," he said softly, stroking her cheek with the back of his hand. "You. You made me want to live again."

"What are you talking about? You're the one who went to the sports center. You…you…made marshmallows!"

"That wasn't living, love. That was going through the motions. Charlie used to harangue me like an old harpy. 'Come down to the gym! Do this! Do that! If you don't come for tea the trouble and strife'll have my head!'"

Naomi laughed at his spot-on imitation of Charlie, then looked up to the sky, trying to collect her thoughts. "Why are you telling me all this?"

"I think you know damn well why I'm telling you," Finn said gently. "I'm in love with you and I think you feel the same way, but you're scared."

Tears sprang to her eyes and she was half-tempted to ask if he'd also been retraining as a psychic. "How do you know?"

"Because I know what it feels like to carry a burden of guilt around. I know how terrifying it feels to let yourself be happy when you hold yourself responsible for causing the ones you loved so much pain."

He took her hands in his and dropped kisses on her knuckles. "Naomi, what happened to your family is not your burden to carry. What you can and should carry in your heart are all the happy memories. The joy."

Tears began to trickle down her cheeks. Finn tugged a handkerchief out of his winter coat pocket and held it out to her. "I brought extras just in case."

She giggled through her tears, despite herself. "You came prepared?"

"I try to always come prepared." He gave her a cheeky grin.

"Army boy," they said in tandem then stopped, frozen

in each other's gazes as if they'd been given a heaven-sent reminder that they were and should be together.

"You're right, you know," Naomi finally admitted.

"About what?"

"All of it. The guilt. Not wanting to let go. Not wanting to let myself admit that…" A hint of shyness overcame her. Finn, once again, seemed to read her mind and dropped a kiss on her forehead.

"It would be the first time in a long time anyone admitted I was worth loving."

"I want to be that person." Naomi spoke in a rush, acutely aware that if she let this pass with Finn—this love that really could grow into something wonderful—she would be letting an enormous part of what it meant to be alive pass her by. Because what was the point if there wasn't love?

"I love them so very much," she admitted. "But I can't do anything to change what's happened."

Finn nodded along as she spoke. "It's the double-edged sword of loving. Loving and losing," he clarified. "Look, I was determined to spend the rest of my days on my own. I didn't want to hurt anyone the way I'd hurt Caroline ever again, but you know what? I rang her the other day and wouldn't you know it? She's as happy as Larry."

"Who's Larry? How do you know that he's happy?"

Finn threw his head back and laughed a full-bodied laugh. A warmth grew in her chest, a happiness that she'd been the one to set him off.

He pulled her close to him, so close she could feel his heartbeat through his winter coat. "Larry is a very happy guy," Finn said. "And I will be too if you'd agree to give this thing a shot with me. I want to live again, Naomi. I want to love and laugh and…" his voice went all rumbly "…make love. And I'd like you to be the woman I do all those things with." He held her out at arm's length. "You deserve happiness, Naomi. You deserve to live a full, rich, incredible life. What do you say? You and me doing our best to make our peace with the past and give ourselves a shot at a happy future?"

She stared up into Finn's gray eyes and knew she could look into them forever. He truly understood her. Her fears, the terrifying experiences she'd been through. Her reluctance to let herself experience unfettered happiness. And yet…he was willing to try it. And when she was with him, she felt brave, too. She'd already had a glimpse into the joy of being with someone who made her insides fluttery and her heart skippity. She already knew she was in love. It was simply a question of saying… "Yes."

Finn stared at her as if in shock. "Yes?"

Her grin widened along with his. "Yes!" She shouted it out and a pair of swans took flight from the river.

"Well, then, my little flower blossom…" Finn pulled her close to him and cupped her face in his big hands "…I think we'd best seal this deal with a kiss."

"You think?" Naomi teased.

"I know," Finn growled, kissing her with a sensual confidence that came with truth and honesty and love.

"He's over here!" Finn hadn't felt this happy in he didn't know how long. A beautiful woman by his side, a chance to look forward rather than dwelling on the past and, best yet, snow!

"Adao!" Naomi waved her arms when the boy turned to them, a cup of steaming hot chocolate in his hands.

"Finn! Naomi!" Evie waved them over. "I jumped the gun when the snow began and ordered some hot chocolate. You in?"

"Of course." Finn looked up at the sky, enjoying the sensation of the big, fat flakes falling on his face, then knelt down so he was eye to eye with Adao. "What do you think, little man? Does it live up to its reputation?"

"Even better."

Naomi laughed and gave the knitted cap on his head a bit of a tweak. "Looks like it's definitely a day for Christmas wishes to come true."

She laughed, enjoying the comforting sensation of Finn nestling in close to her, then leaning in even closer so that he could whisper into her ear.

"Was I *your* Christmas wish?"

"Something like that."

He feigned looking affronted. "Just something?"

"Exactly." She gave his hand a squeeze, already excited for the next time they could be alone and share more of those luxurious, life-affirming kisses. "Exactly what I wished for."

And he was. Finn had helped her see the only person she was hurting was herself. She scanned the party area as she sipped her hot chocolate and listened to Adao tell Finn all about his time with Father Christmas. The only thing she needed to do now was find a little sprig of mistletoe and then all her Christmas wishes would come true.

CHAPTER FIFTEEN

A year later

"Mum… Baaba…" Adao beamed at his mother and father as they stepped into the hospital's foyer, which was decked out with two huge trees the hospital had decorated in their usual incredible fun-loving style. "This is Naomi. And this is Mr. Morgan."

"Finn," Finn corrected, as he stepped forward to shake hands with the couple who had just been flown in. "Lovely to meet you, Mr. and Mrs. Weza. And you must be…"

"Imani." Adao's sister didn't suffer from shyness in the slightest. She shook hands with Naomi and Finn and beamed. "I can't believe it is snowing!"

"These are just the types of miracles that happen here at Hope Children's Hospital." Naomi shrugged and grinned. The place was magical. Especially under a thick blanket of snow.

"It's amazing to see you here in your working environment," said Mrs. Weza. "After the village, I mean. You seemed so at home there as well."

Finn wrapped his arm around Naomi's shoulders and gave her a kiss on the cheek. "That was an amazing trip. I don't think I've ever had such incredible seafood before."

"It was wonderful of the charity to organize for us to

come out and work with Adao. He's progressed so much with his prosthesis. And grown, too!"

Adao beamed. "Nine centimeters in one year!"

"Well above average. In many ways," she added, giving his head a scrub. Seeing his parents again had really brought out the spark in him.

Naomi smiled up at Finn. She couldn't believe how much the pair of them had changed in just a year. Evie had even taken to calling them the Grin Twins.

Well…

When one was in love, why not spread the joy?

The prosthetics specialists spotted them and joined their group. After a quick discussion about what Adao would have to do to get the mold for his new prosthesis, they suggested his family join him so they could all see.

"It was really lovely meeting you."

"We'll see you again before we go, right?" Adao threw his arms round Naomi's waist and gave her a huge hug. His new prosthesis seemed a part of him now. Proof, as if she needed any, of just how important their work at the hospital and overseas was. She smiled down at him. "Of course we'll see you again. And next year when Finn and I come out again with the charity, we'll see if you can manage to grow as much as you have this year."

"As tall as you!" whooped Adao. "Then the next year as tall as Finn!" The thought struck his entire family as hilariously funny and Naomi felt nothing but warmth and joy in her heart as she watched them laughing their way down the corridor.

"They're a lovely family." Finn slipped his hand round hers and gave it a squeeze.

"That they are."

"Want to go out and have a snowball fight with me?"

Naomi looked at him in disbelief. "I bet you think you'll win."

"I think a lot of things," Finn riposted playfully as he pulled her into a hug.

"You do, don't you?"

"Yes," Finn said airily. "And I'm usually right."

Naomi went up on tiptoe and gave him a quick kiss. "You have been right about a lot of things."

"I know."

He tried to keep a straight face for as long as he could, but Naomi knew the trick to make him break now.

"Tickle fight!"

She ran out the front door, chasing him as he begged her not to tickle him. His weakness, she'd discovered one day when she'd worn nothing but a feather boa to bed.

Finn tripped when he reached the green and Naomi fell on top of him breathless with laughter and joy.

When they had caught their breath, she beamed at him. "I love you, Finn Morgan."

"I love you, too, pretty lady. You make the world—my world—a better place."

"And you helped me see what a lovely place the world is."

They shared a tender kiss before getting up and shaking the snow off themselves. She hoped Finn knew how much she had meant what she'd said. Over the course of the year he had shown such patience and tenderness that sometimes it was hard to believe he was the same man who'd barked at her to leave him alone.

Finn knew her inside and out. Her fears. And now, more importantly, her hopes and dreams.

"Fancy a cup of hot chocolate by the Christmas tree before we get back to work?"

"Absolutely."

Finn reached out his hand and took Naomi's in his. This was the moment he'd been waiting for all year.

Luckily, the hospital "fairies" had waved their magic wands over the green outside the hospital yet again and... Yup! Just over by the enormous candy cane...a mistletoe stand.

"C'mere, you." Finn led her over to the stand.

"What are you up to, you rascal? I thought we were going for hot chocolate."

Finn tipped her chin up and looked straight into her eyes. "I can do you one better than that, my love."

"Better than hot chocolate on a snowy day?" She laughed. "I don't think so."

He reached into his pocket and pulled out a little light blue box. "How 'bout an early Christmas present?" He flicked open the box and showed her the diamond solitaire he'd been carrying around in his pocket for the last three months.

"A—? What—?"

Finn dropped to one knee, not caring who saw him.

"Naomi Collins Chukwumerije..." He stopped and grinned, clearly pleased with his pronunciation of her surname. "Would you do me the honor of marrying me?"

Her heart stopped for an instant then did a happy dance all its own.

"Oh, Finn... I... Of *course* I'll marry you!"

He leapt to his feet, pulled her into his arms and would've kissed her until the sun went down if some of the other doctors hadn't started wolf-whistling.

"She said yes!"

A huge roar of cheers and applause rose up around them as he pulled Naomi close to him. "You said yes."

"You're the love of my life," Naomi whispered as he

slipped the ring onto her finger. "I can't wait to let the whole rest of the world know."

Together, smiles lighting up their faces, they entered the hospital with their eyes solidly on the future, knowing they had each other to help them in whatever came their way.

* * * * *

LET'S TALK
Romance

For exclusive extracts, competitions
and special offers, find us online:

f facebook.com/millsandboon

🐦 @MillsandBoon

📷 @MillsandBoonUK

Get in touch on 01413 063232

For all the latest titles coming soon, visit
millsandboon.co.uk/nextmonth

MILLS & BOON
A ROMANCE FOR EVERY READER

FREE delivery direct to your door

EXCLUSIVE offers every month

SAVE up to 25% on pre-paid subscriptions

SUBSCRIBE AND SAVE

millsandboon.co.uk/Subscribe

MILLS & BOON

THE HEART OF ROMANCE

A ROMANCE FOR EVERY READER

MODERN

Prepare to be swept off your feet by sophisticated, sexy and seductive heroes, in some of the world's most glamourous and romantic locations, where power and passion collide.

HISTORICAL

Escape with historical heroes from time gone by. Whether your passion is for wicked Regency Rakes, muscled Vikings or rugged Highlanders, av the romance of the past.

MEDICAL

Set your pulse racing with dedicated, delectable doctors in the high-pressure world of medicine, where emotions run high and passion, comfort love are the best medicine.

True Love

Celebrate true love with tender stories of heartfelt romance, from the rush of falling in love to the joy a new baby can bring, and a focus on emotional heart of a relationship.

Desire

Indulge in secrets and scandal, intense drama and plenty of sizzling ho action with powerful and passionate heroes who have it all: wealth, sta good looks...everything but the right woman.

HEROES

Experience all the excitement of a gripping thriller, with an intense romance at its heart. Resourceful, true-to-life women and strong, fearless face danger and desire - a killer combination!

To see which titles are coming soon, please visit

millsandboon.co.uk/nextmonth

JOIN US ON SOCIAL MEDIA!

Stay up to date with our latest releases, author news and gossip, special offers and discounts, and all the behind-the-scenes action from Mills & Boon...

 @millsandboon

 @millsandboonuk

 facebook.com/millsandboon

 @millsandboonuk

It might just be true love...

GET YOUR ROMANCE FIX!

Get the latest romance news, exclusive author interviews, story extracts and much more!

blog.millsandboon.co.uk

MILLS & BOON
True Love

Romance from the Heart

Celebrate true love with tender stories of heartfelt romance, from the rush of falling in love to the joy a new baby can bring, and a focus on the emotional heart of a relationship.

MILLS & BOON
MEDICAL
Pulse-Racing Passion

Set your pulse racing with dedicated, delectable doctors in the high-pressure world of medicine, where emotions run high and passion, comfort and love are the best medicine.

MILLS & BOON

Desire

Indulge in secrets and scandal, intense drama and plenty of sizzling hot action with powerful and passionate heroes who have it all: wealth, status, good looks…everything but the right woman.